DON'T
SCREAM

An absolutely gripping killer thriller with a huge twist

MARGARET MURPHY

Detective Jeff Rickman Book 3

JOFFE
BOOKS

First published in Great Britain 2020
Joffe Books, London
www.joffebooks.com

ISBN: 978-1-78931-627-8

For Murf

ACKNOWLEDGEMENTS

As always, my thanks go to Chief Inspector Dave Griffin (retd.), for his inexhaustible patience in answering my most bizarre and obscure questions, and more than this, for suggesting procedural details that solve plot problems and enhance the storyline. Also, to Vicki Van-Holsbecke and her team in the pathology department at Warrington Hospital, who gave me valuable insights into their work during a whirlwind tour of their laboratories. I'm very grateful to John Sayle, martial arts, knife fighting and weapons expert, who cast a gimlet eye over the fight scenes. Any mistakes in procedure or interpretation are mine and mine alone.

Thanks again to Daniel Sellers for reading this novel in draft, for his apposite comments and observations — including spotting a few anachronisms — and for cheering me on! Heartfelt thanks to Jasper Joffe and his amazing team at Joffe Books: Emma Grundy Haigh, Laura Coulman, Jill Burkinshaw and Nina Kicul, as well as the copy editors and proofreaders who have read my work with such care, rigour and attention to the finer details. I LOVE you guys!

Finally, love, thanks and deepest gratitude to my husband, Murf, for his support, love, unstinting encouragement and interruptions for cups of tea. (But I really *will* get a 'Do Not Disturb' sign for my office door one of these days.)

CHAPTER 1

Tuesday

The exchange is almost complete. Four sports bags — three red, one black — in the centre of a ring of cars. Mark Davis focuses on the black one: on the heroin. His longing for it is like love, like obsession. His body trembles for it, *aches* for it.

The night is dark, no moon. The only sound is the wind moaning through the empty warehouse behind them. Beyond the hulking brick structures lie the black waters of the River Mersey. On the landward edge, a thirty-foot-high wall of sandstone blocks three feet thick. This is Maitland's fortress — one way in, one way out. His men control the steel gates at the entrance. Two lookouts watch the dock road from the top of the wall. At this time of night, only dockland rats and taxi drivers come this way, and neither linger.

A sudden clatter of chopper blades, then a light so bright that everyone ducks. Maitland's bodyguards shove him behind one of the cars, guns in their hands before the police warning is complete.

Mark is slow, still high from the hit he took earlier to steady his nerves. He stands in the wash of light thinking of *The X-Files* and alien abduction. Then someone shouts, 'The bags!' and he grabs the black, hesitates, goes back for one of the reds. Running at a crouch, he zigs left as gunshots crack to his right, his boss's heavies and the Dutch guys firing at the beam of light. The helicopter engine screams as the pilot pulls back, hard, gaining height and distance. A second chopper appears, trapping those on the ground in a cross-beam as bright as the floodlights at Anfield stadium.

Mark dives for shelter. He crouches behind a huddle of rusting oil drums, hugs the bags to him and closes his eyes against the fierce light, wishing he could close his ears too as the gun battle rages.

Maitland yells, 'You two, cover me . . .' The rest is lost in the *blat-blat-blat* of the helicopters' rotor blades.

One of the Dutch yells, '*We zijn erin geluisd!*' Then, '*Godverdomme!*'

Beyond the gates, lights flicker, blue and red. More police. Gunfire sounds from the wall, then one of the lookouts falls.

A dull *thunk*. Mark flinches. A bullet hits the container to his left. Another shot punches a hole the size of his fist through a drum inches away.

'Fuck!' *They're shooting at me — those mad bastards are shooting at me!*

A voice, strong and authoritative, carries over the helicopter buzz. 'Maitland? You tell your boy to bring my fuckin' drugs back.'

No. Mark is sweating now. They think he's *stealing* the drugs. He peers around the side of one of the oil drums. 'You've got it wrong,' he yells. 'I'm just—' A block of wood on top of the drum explodes, tearing holes in his jacket.

'Jesus!' he screams. 'Stop! Stop it!'

'I'll fuckin' stop it when you're *dead*, English!' The Dutch boss's accent is American, a drawl he must have picked up from the movies. 'Hey, Maitland! Hey, *klootzak!*' Maitland doesn't answer. 'I'm gonna kill you and every one of your *verklikkers* . . .' The police tannoy drowns him out for a second or two, then Mark screams again as more shots are loosed at him.

They whistle, twang, ricochet, over and into and off the drums — burst after burst of bullets. 'Shit, shit, shit!' He screws his eyes shut, crouches lower, waits for death. 'Stop,' he sobs. 'Please, God, make them stop!'

A shot thuds into a pile of sacking to his right. He hears a squeak, then two, three, *four* rats stream out, spilling from the stinking pile like water from a barrel. A fifth follows. They run over and around him, weighty and sleek, as big as cats. Mark shudders and swears, unable to take his eyes off them as they scurry into the dark and disappear.

He blinks. *That's not possible. They can't just disappear.* But they did. They ran across open ground, then vanished.

A pale glimmer of hope ignites in him. They didn't *disappear*, they went to ground. Liverpool folklore has it that a network of tunnels spans out beneath the docks — smugglers' runs that lead from the old pubs in the city centre out to the water's edge.

Mark's eyes focus on the dark patch of ground ten metres away. *If you can get to it — big if, Mark — if the Dutch don't shoot you full of holes, you'll probably get your skinny arse stuck down a manhole and the police'll get you. You're dead either way. You fucking idiot! Why couldn't you just keep your head down and wait for the shooting to stop?*

Sparks fly from another near miss. He whimpers. Then, above the clatter of the police helicopters and rattle of gunfire, he hears a dull roar. Someone has got to Maitland's speedboat.

A volley of shots follows, then gunfire at the gate. Someone is trying to break out through the police cordon. They aren't firing at him anymore. He peers around the edge of the oil drums. The second lookout is gone from the wall: shot or surrendered. The gunfire is centred on the river and the gateway. He's in the clear.

Move.

He wants to. He wills his legs to carry him, but instead he lies shivering, crouched in a corner, surrounded by stinking sacking and rusting oil drums. A shot tears through the sacking, changes direction and slices past his face close enough for him to feel the heat.

He's up and running. Pumping his arms like a sprinter, despite the weight of the two sports bags, rage and fear carrying him forward. It doesn't occur to him to drop them — if he's a dead man, he'd rather be a rich dead man. He trips and falls, sprawling, but still he maintains his grip.

The shooting subsides, and despite the constant clatter of the choppers it seems still and quiet.

He crawls a few more feet. And finds it. A broken metal grille. He yanks and pulls as the police issue orders over the helicopter tannoy, telling the two sides to lay down their weapons. The grille is stuck. He gives it another tug and hears the whine of the electric motor that opens the dock gates.

The police'll be here any second, Mark. You'll get arrested. Get arrested, and you're dead. So get a grip of your wimpy self. He gets to his knees and closes his fingers around the grille, pulls on it, feeling every muscle in his neck and shoulders strain.

It moves. Not much, a little. Enough for Mark to renew his efforts, tugging and sweating, feeling the wind pluck at his jacket like a premonition of his arrest. Suddenly he's flying backwards, the grille in his hands. He lands on his tailbone, winding himself.

Lights bounce over the rough concrete road near the gate. *The police!*

He tries to move, but he can't catch his breath. A police van cuts left, its headlights missing him by inches.

Get off your arse and do something right, for once. He hears his stepfather's voice in his head. Hatred drives him. *Fuck off,* he mutters. *Fuck off and die.* This strikes him as funny, and as he crawls to the opening, dragging the grille with him, he even giggles. *If anyone's gonna die, it's you, Mark.*

He snatches up the first bag and stuffs it down the hole, listening for the hiss of canvas against brickwork. It brushes the sides only a couple of times on the way down, so the shaft is wide enough for him. But the thud as it hits the bottom comes a long time after he drops it. It's a bastard of a fall. He throws the second bag after it, scrambles to a sitting position and eases feet first into the shaft, feeling for toeholds as he goes.

More vans and police cars arrive, blue lights flashing. A headlight grazes the top of his head and he hears them coming straight for him. He slides the grille back in place as they skid to a halt, yards from the shaft. He hears doors slide open, booted feet landing hard on the concrete.

'I saw something.' A young male voice, excited, hyped by the gunfire and the revving engines, the lights and the constant chop of the helicopter blades. 'I *did*, Sarge.'

'You're sure?' An older man, less inclined to excitability. 'Fetch us a torch, then.'

Shit. Mark is balanced a couple of feet down from the opening, his right foot on the rusted remains of an iron rung, his left braced against the brickwork. He looks down into a blackness so profound it might be death itself. Sweat has gathered on his upper lip. *Fuck it.* He lets go of the rail and crosses his hands over his chest like a deep sea diver, plumbing the depths.

CHAPTER 2

Wednesday

Detective Sergeant Daniel Cass sauntered into the CID Room like it was something he practised in the mirror. One hand insouciantly in his trouser pocket, index finger of the other hooked in the loop of his jacket draped over his shoulder. A casual observer might have assumed that he had come in from the autumn sunshine, but he had in fact walked only a few steps across the corridor. A practical person might have thought that a jacket wouldn't be required for such a short journey indoors, but considerations of practicality were less important to Cass than appearance and style.

Half a dozen officers were at work in the room, engaged in different enquiries, following up leads, confirming details by phone, typing up reports. The room was a featureless oblong, the cream walls scuffed and grimy from years of use. Wanted posters, mug shots of local troublemakers, a calendar, rota sheets and newspaper clippings spilled from the pinboard to the wall next to the room's only window. The carpet was worn grey industrial cord, and not much of it visible: fifteen desks, wastepaper bins, a photocopier, filing cabinets and a water cooler filled most of the available space.

Detective Constable Naomi Hart finished a call to the city council ASBO Unit and opened a new document on her computer. Her workstation was in the middle of the room, facing the door. Recently returned from a holiday in Italy, her light tan emphasised the pale gold of her hair, and the sleeveless blouse she wore flattered her slim figure.

Cass finished up at her desk as if by chance. He waited a few moments as if expecting an ovation and, receiving none, leaned over Hart's shoulder and peered at the screen.

'"Kids hanging about on street corners,"' he read from the screen. '"Vandalism, loutish behaviour. CCTV surveillance recommended." Ooh, Naomi, how *do* you stand the excitement?'

She stopped typing. 'Did you want something, Sergeant Cass?'

'Just back from holiday?' His eyes went to her neck, her arms, her breasts. 'You look well.'

Hart turned her cool blue gaze on him. First she looked at the hand, still firmly wedged in his left trouser pocket, then she tracked upwards, lingering a moment on his mouth. The sheen on his lower lip was Vaseline — he kept a small pot of it in his jacket pocket and applied it almost compulsively, four or sometimes five times an hour. She looked him in the eye, then turned back to her computer monitor and resumed typing.

'You know, I could get you off this social work crap and onto a proper investigation.' Cass took his hand out of his pocket and rested his buttocks against her desk. 'A major investigation,' he said, with the emphasis on 'major'.

'The drug thing?' She focused on the computer screen. It wouldn't do to seem too interested.

'Operation Snowplough,' he corrected her, as if — shambles though it was — giving the investigation its title elevated its importance.

'I heard there was a fatality.'

'Bakker, the Dutch boss.' Cass raised one shoulder. 'One less scumbag to clog up the prison system.'

Hart flipped him a look that said she didn't share his enthusiasm for summary justice. 'I thought Larry Dwight was running the investigation.'

'DI Dwight is a busy man — committees, partnership meetings, Independent Assessment Groups.' Cass made no attempt to hide his contempt.

Hart had heard that Dwight was more an administrative type than a hands-on cop. She preferred the latter, except for the likes of DS Cass — she preferred his type to keep their hands strictly to themselves.

'Yup,' Cass said. 'Larry delegates the day-to-day stuff to me. Hiring, firing . . . Of course, you'd have to ask me nice.'

'I thought Snowplough was over, bar the arrest of the main player.' Hart would rather work school crossing patrols than talk 'nice' to a man like Sergeant Cass.

Cass leaned back so she could see his smile, a row of off-white teeth so small and neat they might have been filed down. 'We'll have Maitland in the bag in no time,' he said. 'No time at all.'

'Talking of bags,' Hart said, 'is it true you lost a couple during the arrests?'

Cass stiffened, and for one hopeful a moment, she thought he might leave. Then he settled his backside more comfortably on her desk and rested the elbow of his free arm on her computer monitor. It creaked under the strain. 'Have you been gossiping with the girls, Naomi?'

She tried not to notice his tongue flick out onto his lower lip. Any moment now, he would swing the jacket off his shoulder and go fishing for his little pot of lip balm.

His flat grey eyes went again to her breasts. 'A girl with your obvious . . . assets should be put to better use.'

'Sarge?' Hart lowered her voice and Cass leaned in to listen. She smelled coffee on his breath. And breath mints. *Oh, Sergeant Cass*, she thought. *For me?* She smiled and could almost see the responding haze of pheromones coming off him. 'You're crumpling my ASBO reports,' she said sweetly.

Someone gave a snort of laughter and Cass shot him a furious look. Without the smile, his true nature could be read in the lines etched on his face: the natural downturn of his mouth, the petulant furrow of his brow, the chilly humourlessness of his eyes.

'I thought you had ambition.'

'I do,' Hart confided. 'Just not in the direction you think.'

He shrugged, managing a smile that treated Hart to another flash of his small, coffee-stained teeth. 'Your loss.' He left the room at the same slow saunter, but something in the way he held himself betrayed his humiliation at being turned down.

A female officer drifted past her desk and smiled, closing her right fist in a covert gesture of solidarity. Hart smiled and nodded but didn't feel the sense of triumph was justified. Cass might be a sleaze, but he had influence, at least among the ground troops, and a woman on the force needed all the friends she could get.

CHAPTER 3

Mark Davis checks both ways before stepping out of the hotel. He'd chosen it carefully: away from the main drag, where a chance sighting might happen, avoiding the copping zones and crack spots he knew of, where dealers and users alike knew his face.

By the time he'd found his way out of the tunnel, his clothes were rank with sewer slime. He'd chucked his jacket into a dumpster and washed the worst of the crap off his trousers and sweatshirt in the fountain at the back of Fenwick Street. He stank of chlorine from the fountain, and the night porter wasn't keen — until Mark made his apologies for the late hour with a backhander of fifty quid. He knew how he must look. Tall and skinny, hair a shade of black that could only come out of a bottle, addict-pale skin — he looked like trouble.

He'd grinned, hoping it made him look less like a ghoul. 'Stag night prank,' he said. 'She'll kill me if I turn up at the registry office looking like this.' He didn't need to name the vengeful 'she' — any decent Scouser feared his woman as much as he respected her.

The night porter mellowed, even smiled a bit as he showed Mark to his room. He paid another hundred in cash up front, knowing it would never go through the books. He had an alias ready, but the guy never even asked him to sign in.

He slept well, quelling the shakes by dipping lightly into the contents of the black bag, taking care, because this stuff was pure uncut heaven. Straight into town at nine a.m., back before ten, showered, shaved, wearing a dab of cologne and feeling damn near irresistible in his new slim-fit shirt from River Island and proper trousers instead of his usual trackie bottoms.

Only the night porter would remember him. The chambermaid would find a shirt wrapper in the bin, a price label from the trousers, toiletries and a razor by the sink — nothing else, not even a fingerprint.

Now he's on his way to see Jasmine, pain in his arse, light of his life, mother of his darling child. The 'she' he fears as much as he respects, and he intends to make a proposal, of sorts.

A thin layer of cloud turns the sky milk-white, and Mark shivers as the wind sweeps up from the Mersey. He turns his back on the city centre and walks up the hill towards the university. He has parked two miles away. If he's followed, he'll notice — plenty of time to spot a shadow during a thirty-minute walk.

Mark doesn't know the meaning of the word symbolism but, brought up in the Catholic tradition, he has a residual faith in the power of belief. Belief can make things happen. He believes he can get clean of the drug addiction, he believes he can make Jasmine happy, and he believes he can be a good father. He believes as fervently as he believes in the trinity of God and Family and Football they will get away, start a new life.

He looks for a sign from God. He has always confused faith with the magic of omens — as a child, he believed in fairies and Father Christmas long after other children rejected them as babyish nonsense. The intrusion into his life of a flesh-and-blood ogre in the shape of his stepfather coincided with his loss of innocence, but Mark prefers to avoid thinking of his childhood.

When he grew out of fairy tales and churchgoing required more discipline of him than he possessed, he simply shifted his beliefs to his house parents, Ed and Hilary, building elaborate fantasies around adoption. Those fantasies sustained him through the years in care, and his mother's rejection.

Technically, the care system continued supporting him until he was eighteen, but he was effectively dumped on the streets at sixteen, ill-equipped for life. Ed and Hilary continued to help him — even got him the job at the garage, though Ed would never admit it, kidding him that Mark had got the job on merit. Yeah, right, with six failed GCSEs and a borderline NVQ in Motor Mechanics. Though Mark believed in magic, miracles were harder to accept.

When the garage business failed, Mark believed he had jinxed it.

He lost faith for a while after that, which was when he found cocaine and heroin, and for a few short weeks, it was beautiful. Of course, it didn't last and, strung out and desperate, he sought out a new talisman. This time, it was Jasmine. She demanded that he get himself straight, and he believed that he could. In fact, every time he got himself straight for a few weeks he truly believed with the faith of a convert.

Then a new consignment of heroin would arrive, packed in cling film like sweet brown sugar. He'd start to salivate. Embarrassing, to be weighing out batches drooling like a dog. At first he could handle it. They had taught him about psychological withdrawal in rehab. If you ignored the symptoms, did something to distract yourself, they would ease off.

The drugs counsellors were right — you could put off the cravings, but they didn't stop. Every day, he'd be sitting at the kitchen scales, cutting the mix, fighting the cravings. Coke was the worst. He cut it with sodium bicarb or icing sugar. *God*, he loved the brief cold fizz of icing sugar in his nasal passages. No — 'loved' was too weak a word — it was like an orgasm. But that was wrong, too. It was better than sex, better almost than the hit of cocaine that came after.

Mark stayed off the stuff through all of this, but eventually the drooling stopped, his mouth dried and his stomach cramped. When the cold sweats started, he would have to take a small thumbnail of something just to take the edge off.

And it would work. He didn't get high. Not much, anyway — he'd only take enough to stop the pain. But slowly, with a sneaky insistence, the psychological withdrawal would melt away and the physical symptoms would reassert themselves. He would have to score a bit more and a bit more, his impulsive nature denying him the insight that it wasn't one single moment, but a series of small increments that turned want into need.

'You know I'm trying to stay straight,' Jasmine told him. 'But you bring that shit home and shoot up right in front of me. Don't you think *I* need it, too?'

He thought she meant that she needed to score, but when he offered her some of his stash, she snatched it out of his hand it, ran to the bathroom and flushed it. God, he came close to hitting her then. And she knew it, like she always knew everything he was thinking. Threw him out.

He stayed clean for six weeks, so she would let him see the baby. They named her together: Bryony. He stayed clean two weeks more. But he took a snort of coke after a sleepless night. The baby had kept them both awake with her crying, and he needed to be up and working, cutting and weighing, shifting baggies to Mr Maitland's street dealers.

It never occurred to Mark that his addiction was permanent, that it took only a single lapse to begin the slide from craving to skin-crawling, shivering, snot-nosed dependence. Nor did he realise that he was as much addicted to seeing the dragon's breath of heroin curling from hot foil as he was to the endorphin rush of the drug.

He turns right, cutting though one of the university car parks and keeps pace with a gang of students hurrying to a lecture. One of the girls looks up at him and smiles. It's a good sign. He makes a pact with himself: if the sun breaks through the cloud, if he feels its warmth, if he *believes* enough in its warmth, everything will happen as he wants it, if not as a consequence, then as part of the strange parallel patterns that exist in his world.

He moves on, listening to the rhythm of his footsteps and the push of air from his lungs and as he walks. The heat of exertion becomes an external heat, his imagination transforms it so that to Mark it feels like the sun, warm on his face. The omens are good. Jasmine will see that he means it this time — things will come right for them. This time, she will understand. He'll explain calmly, tell her everything: he's done things, *been* things he isn't proud of, but now he will be different. Baby Bryony is the miracle that changed him. She is fresh and new and perfect.

The sun bursts through the high mist for real, and he nods, smiling to himself — everything will be fine. He is so eager to be there, he's almost running, forgetting to search the shadows for hints of threat, neglecting to listen for the echo of his footfalls. He has taken another small hit, just enough to steady his nerves and stem the cravings, and this too dulls his anxieties and heightens the fantasy that all will be well.

The sun is golden and warm, and the clouds are high and white, like cotton wool. Like sterile swabs. There's a smell in the air. Mark can't separate scents — his nasal lining has been cooked by years of mind-altering inhalation — but this smell is good, wholesome, it fires synapses in a part of his brain that is closed off to him, the happy moments of childhood before his father died. The smell triggers an emotional response he does not understand: excitement, a tickle of glee. He attributes the feeling to the fact that he is alive and rich and he is about to perform a noble act, an act of heroism. A rescue.

By the time he reaches his car, the sun feels warm and soft as cat's fur on his skin. He has willed the warmth into it, just as he'll will the warmth into Jasmine, convince her that he can save her and Bryony. In his heart, he knows that this one unselfish act will lead to more, and he will save himself.

He has enough money to give them all a proper start, to get away from Maitland, buy a nice place, maybe in the countryside. He tells himself that a lot of the lapses were about availability — in the city it's just too easy to get the gear when you have a craving. Might as well be a diabetic and live above a sweet shop. The thought seems profound, as if behind it lies a deeper truth.

The car door feels heavier than usual. He doesn't open it wide enough, ends up barging the steering wheel with his hip as he gets in. He tells himself he hasn't eaten since last night. *Or maybe the small hit he'd taken was more generous than he intended.* He pushes this thought away. He's entitled to take something to steady his nerves. He's doing the right thing, and Jasmine won't make it easy. She'll give him stick, and he needs to keep cool. No point getting into a row with Jasmine — she'll win any argument.

So he practises the moment of his arrival as he drives: Jasmine is nursing Bryony when she opens the front door, cradling the baby in her arms, a shawl hiding the fullness of her breast. She eyes him with resentment. 'I told you, we're finished.' She begins to close the door, but he stops her, opens his jacket and slides a bundle of notes from his inside pocket, just high enough so she can see it's not fake and it's more than a win at the bookies.

Her eyes widen. 'What have you done, Mark?'

'You heard the news today?'

She backs away. 'No,' she says. 'Don't tell me. I don't wanna know.'

He moves a little way into the house. 'It's Maitland's, and if I know Rob Maitland, he's already looking for me.'

'Give him his money back,' she pleads. 'Give it back for my sake.'

'You know Maitland — he'll take it and kill me anyway.' He takes her by the shoulders, makes her look at him.

No. Stop, rewind. If Jasmine's holding the baby, she'll only get pissed with him for waking her up. Better if the baby's upstairs when he gets there. That way, he can take Jasmine in his arms when he finally gets through to her.

He restarts the narrative, but this time, she's alone.

'Go away, Mark. I can't help you.'

This is the good part: he puts his hands on her shoulders, says, 'You need to listen to me, Jaz.' And she looks at him with wary respect, 'cos he's never spoken to her this way, before. 'When Maitland doesn't find me, he'll come after you.'

Her hand flies to her mouth. 'Oh, Mark!'

'I had to warn you.'

Her blue eyes are shining as she stares into his. 'Why didn't you just run? You could've been halfway across the world by now.'

'Because I want to give you a better life — Bryony deserves better than this.' He looks around at the narrow hall, the steep climb of stairs to the two small bedrooms. 'So do you.'

She bites her lower lip, seeing the little house from his viewpoint, noting its deficiencies for the first time.

'I've come to rescue you, Jaz.'

Her forehead crinkles. 'But I was so cruel. The things I said . . .'

'I let you down before' — it's pointless denying that — 'and I hurt you,' he says. 'But I'm going to make it up to you.'

She looks up to him, her eyes filled with uncertainty. 'You mean it? You still want me to go with you?'

'I couldn't leave without you. You and Bryony.' He reaches out a hand and brushes his fingertips against the softness of her cheek. As the tears come, he knows she has been waiting for this moment.

Yeah, Mark thinks. That's how it's gonna be. He won't tell Jaz about the drugs — she'll only flip if he does. When they're back together, he won't need them. He'll sell them, make even more money. It doesn't occur to Mark that selling the heroin will attract attention, that Jasmine, an ex-user herself, will see the signs, will know that he's high. Just as she will know for certain that Maitland won't stop until he finds Mark, the money and the drugs. When Mark practises in his head, everything always comes out right, Jasmine always gives the right answers so he knows what to say next. Mark Davis, master of self-delusion, has a short memory for the many verbal thrashings Jasmine has given him. And anyway, he's got money — who's gonna argue with that?

He parks the car at an angle to the kerb, anxious to see Jasmine again, to sculpt the reality from the clay of his dream. She *will* come with him.

CHAPTER 4

Autumn was gathering pace, hurtling through time and space into winter like a meteor catching its first combustive gasp of air. The trees had smouldered for a couple of weeks, colour singeing only the margins of the leaves, but now they burst into flickering tongues of red, orange and gold. Detective Chief Inspector Jeff Rickman jogged under a stand of beeches in Sefton Park, crunching over beech masts while a steady patter of coppery leaves drifted around him. He felt good, strong emotionally and physically. He was fighting-weight and fit, ready to take on the world again.

In a year he had lost everything and gained so much: his partner — the woman who had given his life meaning — was dead, murdered. But just at the moment it seemed his life was over, his brother Simon had returned after a twenty-five-year absence. With Simon's return, Rickman had learned that he was an uncle to two teenage boys. But Simon had suffered a catastrophic brain injury in a car accident and had almost no memory of the intervening years, and Tanya, his brother's wife, had turned to Rickman for help. And in helping them to face up to Simon's altered personality, Rickman was able to see beyond his own pain. He was healing.

Today, he would see Tanya again, and he was looking forward to it more than he dared admit. Rickman's heart rate picked up, and not from the exercise.

Footsteps pounded behind him and Rickman moved over to make way, but the runner kept pace, his shoes cracking the beech masts underfoot like peanut shells. He glanced right. It was Detective Sergeant Lee Foster.

Rickman kept going.

'What?' Foster said. 'Not even a "good morning"?' Foster spoke with a broad Liverpool accent, running the words together.

'I was hoping that if I ignored you, you might go away.'

'And I thought you knew me.'

'I'm on leave, Lee.'

'Yeah, well, wait till you hear this—'

Foster's explanation for this interruption of Rickman's holiday was delayed by the appearance of a comely brunette at the bend of the path.

'I never really liked the idea of pounding the pavement,' Foster said, with a winning smile for the approaching jogger. 'Had enough of that when I was a plod. But now I'm beginning to see the attraction.' He turned one-eighty and ran backwards a few steps, the better to eye the retreating figure of the woman.

Rickman stood six inches taller than his friend and was powerfully built. He bore a few scars, and his hair, chestnut brown and tending to wayward curls, generally looked like it needed the pass of a comb. Foster's, by contrast, was always as neat as his person, gleaming and carefully styled. Yet it was Rickman who drew appreciative glances as they ran.

He had taken the shorter loop, cutting his normal circuit by a couple of miles, and now he headed up the long slope towards Carnatic Road and home. Foster matched him stride for stride.

Rickman gave him a sideways glance. 'Well, what's the bad news?'

'That fiasco with the drugs thing last night has hoovered up half the manpower in the city,' Foster said. 'And we've got a major incident. The super wants you, pronto.'

Rickman sighed. 'You can tell me all about it on the way in.'

* * *

Jeff Rickman, freshly showered and sober-suited, eased his fleet Hyundai i30 in to the kerb, fifty yards up the road from the crime scene. A white SSU van was double-parked next to a marked police unit and an ambulance. The terrace of narrow redbrick Victorian properties was silent except for the insistent one-note chirrup of a sparrow. It was also unusually empty — murder scenes generally drew a crowd. But the far end of the road ended in a high railway wall, and the first-attenders at the scene had done a good job of blocking access.

'Are you fit, then?' Foster urged him out of the car, eager, as ever, for the off.

They made their way down the street. The murder house was easy to spot: blue-and-white police tape was stretched across the front, out as far as the kerb, clearly marking a common approach path. Designed to reduce the contamination of the scene, the CAP would be monitored by the first officer attending, and everyone entering or leaving the building carefully logged. A 'FOR SALE' sign stood in the tiny front garden, a 'SOLD' strip tacked diagonally across the notice.

Rickman tried not to think of the victim's excitement moving into the house — perhaps her first — of her anticipation of a life filled with promise.

The paramedics were leaving, the younger of the two almost as green as her uniform. They climbed into the ambulance and sat with the windows wound down and the lights flashing, as if there was still someone to save.

'We goin' in or what?' Foster was at his elbow, clamouring for action, but the looks on the faces of the paramedics warned Rickman that this was not a situation to rush into.

'Let Scientific Support do their job,' he said. 'There'll be time enough for us when they've finished.'

Foster knew better than to argue. 'I'll have a chat with the paramedics, then, shall I?' He headed off at a diagonal.

Rickman held up his warrant card for inspection as he approached the young PC guarding the entrance to the house.

The constable's pallor and his inability to maintain eye contact were evidence of the fragile grip he had of himself. His fierce grasp of his clipboard only served to reinforce the impression. Rickman decided that sympathy might tip the lad into losing control. A businesslike approach might be easier for him to handle.

'You're the First Attending Officer?' Rickman's voice was deep and strong, with only a trace of a Liverpool accent. It held authority, but also compassion.

The young officer drew himself to attention. 'Sir.' He was a good half a foot shorter than Rickman.

'You cleared the house?'

'Me and the mobile patrol, sir,' he said, lifting his chin in the direction of the marked car.

'What can you tell me?'

'Female. She's young, sir.' The young officer cleared his throat. Swallowed.

'Do you have a name?'

'Jasmine Elliott — got it from an envelope — there was a few on the kitchen worktop. Sir, she — she's been . . .' He blinked, couldn't go on.

'It's all right,' Rickman said. Bad enough that someone so new to the job had seen the body without him having to describe it. 'The pathologist will deal with that — when he finally shows up.'

There were maybe half a dozen Home Office patholo-gists in the North West who were qualified for this kind of work, and the shootings during the drugs raid the previous night meant they had their hands full.

'What's his ETA?' Rickman asked.

The lad gathered himself, checked the clipboard in his hand, then his watch. 'He'll be down in about hour.'

'Who called it in?'

This time the PC didn't need to check his clipboard. 'Mr Bill Stott.' He pointed to a house opposite. 'Number twenty-three.'

The houses stood barely thirty feet apart. Mr Stott's house was freshly painted in sober black. The narrow strip of garden inside the boundary wall was vibrant with red and bronze chrysanthemums that seemed to glow in the sunlight of this warm autumn afternoon.

Rickman glanced over at Foster. He was leaning in at the open window of the ambulance, chatting to the female paramedic. The sunlight glistened on Foster's carefully groomed hair. It was almost black — softly spiked — and he had a tendency to ruffle it when he was flirting. He was ruffling it now, giving the woman the benefit of his famous smile, though on low output, out of respect for her current distress, and Rickman thought he saw the ghost of an answering smile flit across her face.

A CSI stumbled out of the house in full kit. He dragged the mask from his face and pulled down his hood, then bent forward, taking gasps of air. The young officer turned and stared, reliving, no doubt, the moment he had found the body of Jasmine Elliott.

'Sir, I don't think I can—' the constable said, his voice panicky, cracking as his resolve cracked.

Rickman looked him in the eye. 'What's your name?'

The lad snapped to attention. 'Watson, sir. Two-three-five-oh.'

'Just the name is fine, Watson.' Rickman held his gaze a moment longer, until Watson steadied himself, then glanced at the neatly corralled scene. 'You've done a good job. Keep doing what you're doing, you'll be okay.'

Watson seemed uncertain, but after a moment he nodded. Satisfied, Rickman turned his back on the crime scene and crossed the road towards Mr Stott's house.

* * *

Bill Stott had been watering his houseplants when Rickman arrived. He took a step back from the threshold, the water in the small can he held sloshing with the sudden movement.

'I'm a police officer,' Rickman said, warrant card already in hand. His height gave him a natural authority, but his somewhat battered appearance could give the wrong impression. His face was marked by childhood scars — a legacy of the beatings he had taken from his father — and some found it hard to see beyond the slightly crooked set of his nose to the kindness in his steady brown eyes.

Stott recovered quickly, waving Rickman ahead of him into the little sitting room at the front of the house. He wore a formal shirt, the sleeves rolled to the elbows. The sinewy strength of his forearms hinted at a former power, while the stubborn hunch of his shoulders suggested a resentment of the vulnerability of age.

'Can you tell me how you found the young woman?' Rickman asked, his tone quiet and courteous.

Stott didn't answer immediately. Rickman felt his scrutiny, a quiver of uncertainty in his facial muscles, perhaps wondering whether Rickman's broken nose and the fine, silvery scars on his face signified a good cop or a bad one.

'I heard a noise,' he said, his tone belligerent. 'Car starting up. Revving the engine like a bloody rally driver, he was, trying to turn around. That's what brought me to the window.' He glanced across at the neat bay, and then swiftly away, as if the memory was alarming. 'He practically drove into my front garden.'

'What did he look like?' Rickman asked.

'Mad. He looked raving *bloody* mad. Blood all over him. His shirt, his hands.' He shook his head, as if to shift the image.

'I know this is difficult, Mr Stott.'

'*Difficult?* "Difficult," he says! This day will haunt me till I'm under the sod.' Rickman waited, and the old man took a breath and let it out slowly.

'He was scruffy,' he said, more composed now. 'Long black hair.' His face crinkled in concentration. 'Earrings.

He had them little rings and studs in both ears. One in his eyebrow. Why do they *mutilate* themselves like—' The realisation of what he'd said hit hard. The watering can, still in his hand, seemed suddenly too heavy for him and he swayed on his feet.

Rickman was there in a stride, easing him into a chair, coaxing the can from him. He went through to the tiny kitchen and ran a glass of water, handing it to Stott and faking an interest in his surroundings out of consideration for the old man's pride. When he seemed sufficiently recovered, Rickman said, 'Can you talk now?'

The old man looked up at him. His eyes were a faded grey. Rickman saw fear in them. A fear he had seen before, a fear that never quite went away once you experienced it.

'I'm sorry to have to ask you these questions,' he said. 'But the smallest detail can—'

'I know.' The old man waved Rickman's apologies away, recovering some of his irascibility. 'You've got a job to do. The car was a red Ford Focus. Boy racer type with one of them spoilers on the back. Two thousand and eight reg — heap of rust. Last two letters RJ — didn't get the rest. Sorry.' Even his apology sounded truculent.

'You've been very helpful,' Rickman reassured him.

Stott looked blindly towards the window. 'I've seen it before — parked outside my front door.'

'When?' Rickman asked.

'A few times since she moved in. Always at night. Most folk in the street close their doors and don't stir after nine o' clock. But I've seen him. One time he come with a bloody great teddy bear for the baby.'

'Baby?' Rickman felt a prickle of alarm.

Stott's head came up. 'She's got a baby girl.' He plucked at the open neck of his shirt as if it constricted him. 'Dear God — tell me the baby's all right.'

Rickman was out of the door and across the street before Stott could finish the sentence. Foster leaned off the ambulance door, alert. 'Boss?'

24

Rickman only had to look at him. Foster reached his side at a run. PC Watson held up his hand, batting the air with the clipboard like a marshal on an airport runway. 'Sir, you can't go in there.' He looked ready to tackle Rickman to the ground.

'You told me the house was clear,' Rickman said, only just keeping a lid on his anger.

A look of wild alarm flashed across the constable's face. 'It was — it *is*.'

'Boss. What's goin' on?' Foster demanded.

Rickman kept moving. 'There's a baby in the house, Lee.'

Watson looked stricken. 'Mr Stott never said there was a baby.'

He began to follow them into the house, but Rickman stopped him. 'Make sure the paramedics don't leave,' he said.

* * *

The sitting room was empty, newly painted, dust sheets still covering the carpet. Rickman took the stairs two at a time, past the open door of the murder room without a glance.

The door to the second bedroom stood ajar. Rickman took a breath and uttering a silent prayer to a god he'd long since lost faith in, he opened the door.

Boxes. The room was full of them, neatly stacked, all labelled in black marker pen: BOOKS, DVD's, WINTER GEAR, CD's, JUWLERY. The misspellings and misplaced apostrophes the more poignant because Jasmine had carefully matched the height of each letter. A teenager, striving to be organised, responsible, grown up.

Behind a box labelled TOWLS AND SHEETS, Rickman found a bin bag with a note tacked to it: VARIOUS. Next to it, a plastic box labelled TOYS. The handwriting was different, not so neat, but more confident, more assured, the spelling accurate.

Rickman tore the bin bag open. It was crammed with blankets, duvets and baby clothes. He heard Foster bounding up the stairs and hurried back to the small landing.

'Baby bottles in the fridge,' Foster said. 'Sterilising equipment in the cupboard.'

Tony Mayle, Senior CSI and Crime Scene Coordinator, came to the door of the master bedroom, masked and wearing an all-in-one paper suit. 'What the hell are you doing?' he demanded. 'Where's your zoot-suits?' His favourite term for the disposable suit he wore.

'Jasmine has a baby,' Rickman said.

Mayle looked over his shoulder. 'Oh, God . . .'

Rickman could see little of the room: the end of the bed, a tangle of sheets and duvet, blood blooming on it like a sick rose. A small hump in the bedding. *Please, let it not be the baby.*

Mayle moved aside and Rickman gasped. The girl's body had been posed on the bed, her legs splayed, knees bent. Her face was untouched, almost luminous white, but her torso was filmed with red — a gauze of blood.

Mayle and his colleague began to lift the bed linens, folding it inwards in an attempt to retain fibres, hairs, skin cells. Rickman held his breath, not knowing what to pray for. He couldn't take his eyes off the body. There was so much blood, and yet he couldn't see a major wound. Slowly, the hellish scene began to make an insane kind of sense. A lacing of fine cuts: parallel lines, curls, sunbursts, whorls and geometric patterns had been sliced through Jasmine's skin, as though someone had taken a razor blade to her — not dozens, not scores, but hundreds of times. Her upper-left arm, tattooed with a twist of thorns, was free of cuts, for her killer had devised another exquisite torture: at the tip of each thorn was a bead of blood, as though he had pierced her flesh with a sharp point over and over and held her still until the blood congealed, stark against the white of her skin.

Rickman tasted bitter pennies, smelled the sharp coppery reek of blood. 'Jesus,' he murmured. 'Jesus.' For a second he was elsewhere: another small terraced house, another death scene — one that had shattered his life forever.

'Boss.' Foster gripped his shoulder. '*Jeff.*'

The use of his given name roused Rickman. He was seated on the stairs, not knowing how he got there. 'The baby?' he asked. 'Is the baby all right?'

CHAPTER 5

Mark Davis screams away from the kerb, his car fishtailing down the road, burning rubber. He cuts the corner, coming head-on with a Fiesta. Braking hard, he swerves around it, just registering the shock on the driver's face as they pass offside to offside. Then he is on the main road, weaving through traffic.

The lights change to red, and a pedestrian steps onto a pelican crossing.

'Shit!' Mark stands on the brake pedal, bracing himself for impact. She turns, and in that fraction of a second he sees the silver cross at her throat and her eyes, impossibly wide. Then someone grabs her from behind and yanks her so hard that she falls backwards. His car judders to a halt two feet beyond where she was standing.

For a second or two, Mark is frozen in shock, his breathing harsh, his heart knocking painfully at his ribs. The stench of burning rubber fills the car. Then the baby sets up a wail and he turns, horrified. She has slid forward, despite the seat belt and the layers of padding provided by the blankets he has wrapped around her.

A sharp rap at his window. The man who rescued the pedestrian.

'Get out.' He's forty-ish, his face red with blood pressure or booze. He pounds on the window. 'Get out the bloody car, you lunatic!' He reaches for the door handle, but Mark hits the lock just in time.

'Stay away from me!'

The man kicks the door and something inside Mark snaps. He beats the window with his fists. 'Stay the *fuck* away from me! Stay away from my car! I'll break your *fucking* legs, you touch my car again!'

The man takes a step back, and Mark crunches the gears, trying to find first. The baby's screams become more urgent. He hears somebody say, 'He's got a baby in the car.' And he takes the gear stick in both hands.

'Do something for me, *just once*, will you?' he says, addressing his god as he would an unreliable friend.

More people converge on the car, and he forces the gear stick left and forward, grinding metal on metal. Someone slams their palm on the car roof, and the car jolts, as if in response. Then the engine engages and he shoots off, driving fast, putting distance between him and the horror he has just fled.

Left, down Wellington Road, past Wavertree Playground, blasting his horn, funnelling a whirlwind of fallen leaves in his wake. He wipes his nose on his shirtsleeve, swerving, braking, accelerating. Traffic defers to him, though horns blare and lights flash. He has the unreasoning notion that if he drives fast enough, the sounds of his baby's screams will somehow be left behind.

A few miles up the road, he turns off the main drag and takes it more slowly, trying to think. Bryony's constant cries are deafening, drowning out thought.

'*Shush*,' he soothes, stretching out a hand to comfort her. 'It's okay . . . It's okay, baby doll.' The screams seem to rise in pitch and volume. 'Shut up,' he pleads. 'Please, shut up.' His voice rises. '*Pleeease*, let me think.' He breathes heavily through his nose, trying to stay in control, but the noise — that *fucking* noise — like a road drill in his head. 'Just let me fucking *think*!' He slams his hand on the seat next to her, and Bryony's body jerks in shock. For a second or two she is silent. Then she lets out a bellow of fear and rage, screaming louder than ever.

'Oh, Jesus,' Mark sobs. 'I didn't mean it . . .' The words are far more than an apology to his infant child. His whole life seems to stretch back in a litany of errors, omissions, bad choices, bad deeds. He tries to make shushing sounds, but something in his chest stops him breathing right.

A woman walks past the car and stops a few yards away. As she looks right, she stares towards the car way too long for it to be vigilance crossing the road. Spooked, Mark puts the car in gear and drives off again, keeping it slow, trying to stay in control, trying not to attract attention, trying to think past the awful picture that keeps flashing into his head.

'Stop it,' he says, whispering this time, so it doesn't make the baby kick off worse. The image flashes again. Bright. Red. 'Fucking stop it!' He slaps himself in the middle of his forehead.

The baby's cries have eased a little. Lulled by the throaty thrum of the engine, she continues to grizzle, but with less urgency, and he drives, just to quiet her. He pays no attention to direction or time, driving to stop himself thinking, to stop the noise of the baby's cries. When, at last, he turns to check her at a set of traffic lights, her cheeks are red and glistening with tears, but her eyes are closed. For a second, he forgets everything, captivated by his daughter's perfection. Her lips purse and make little sucking movements.

She needs a feed. The thought triggers the image again. This time he can't will it away. He sees Jasmine. Jasmine, as he left her. It fills his mind like a blown-up snapshot — except snapshots don't have a smell. His stomach does a flip and he takes a few breaths, which only makes things worse. He can smell it on him, the stench of blood, the reek of death. His mouth floods with saliva. *Fuck.* He pulls over to the kerb and yanks at the door handle. It's jammed. Panicking, he slams his shoulder against it. Then he remembers — *You locked it, dickhead.* He lifts the snip, yanking frantically at the lever and the door swings wide, into the path of a following car.

The driver brakes and swerves, blaring his horn. Mark staggers to the front of the car and throws up in the gutter.

Trembling and weak, he leans on the bonnet, his T-shirt drenched with cold sweat and his shoes spattered with vomit. He doubles over again, dry-heaves, then spits, easing himself into an upright position. His hands are stained with blood. He wipes them on his chinos, and sees they're already smeared with it. *Jeez, it's everywhere.*

Through the windscreen, he sees the baby squirm under the blankets on the back seat. She makes a few, tentative noises, more like little coughs than cries. For the first time, the full impact of the events of the last hour hit him, and his legs give way. He collapses onto the bonnet, staring in horror at his child.

God forgive me, what have I done?

Suddenly, the light seems too bright, the cars too fast. There is too much to take in. He needs to think. He wipes his face with his shirtsleeve, blinking back tears of self-pity. Things were going to be so great. But now his life is broken and can never be fixed.

For a long while he sits in the car, hugging himself, but the baby is restless. He'll have to move or she'll start crying again, and he's afraid of what he might do. He has to get somewhere safe. Black Wood is the only place he has ever felt safe. But he can't just show up on the doorstep with blood all over him. *I'll call. They'll understand — they always do.*

CHAPTER 6

Rickman's window didn't afford much of a view: the high wall surrounding the station car park, a corner of playground at the preschool opposite. The day continued warm, and the conflicting autumn scents of richness and decay wafted in, carrying with them the downy seeds of willow-herb from the railway depots on the eastern side of Tunnel Road.

DC Hart tapped on the door and entered. She looked rested and alert after her holiday. Hart shook his hand. Hers was cool, her grip firm. She took the empty seat and Rickman perched on the edge of the desk. Close up, she appeared slight, even delicate, and her fine bone structure reinforced the impression, but Rickman knew her better.

'You've heard about the murder?'

She nodded. Hart had many good qualities, one of which was the ability to wait, rather than trying to second-guess a situation.

'Jasmine Elliott,' Rickman said. 'Seventeen years old. Her baby's missing.'

Hart made a small sound at the back of her throat, then covered with a cough. 'How long?'

'An hour.'

He saw Hart's blue eyes flicker as she calculated the infant's chances of survival: an hour was enough time for a kidnapper to go to ground — but it was still early, and the likelihood of him being spotted between the murder scene and his hideout were good.

'I'm leading the inquiry,' Rickman said. 'I'd like you on the team.'

For a moment she stared at him, then roused herself. 'That's the second offer I've had today.'

There was only one other investigation that might be scooping up officers. 'Operation Snowplough.' Rickman tilted his head. 'A high-profile drugs inquiry is an excellent opportunity. I won't hold it against you if—'

'I already turned DS Cass down,' she interrupted.

Rickman knew she wouldn't answer a direct question, but he also knew Cass's reputation among the female officers and staff, and the curtness of her reply said more than a direct answer. 'It could be good for your career,' he said.

'Terrible for my self-esteem, though.'

'You're a good officer, Naomi,' he said. 'And not all of us are like Daniel Cass.'

'No, but there's just enough of his type in management to make the job *that* much more difficult.' Her tone was savage, and she seemed to check herself, colouring slightly beneath her tan. 'Sorry, boss. You caught me at a bad moment.'

Rickman nodded. The force had come a long way on equality, but it still had a hell of a distance to go. 'You've been shunted around a lot the last few months,' he said. He saw surprise and gratification that he'd checked. 'Take it as an opportunity — you need the experience of different divisions, to build contacts . . . You'll get there, Naomi — but not by avoiding the likes of Cass.'

She lifted her chin, her gaze clear and confident. *Of course I'll get there*, that look said. 'I'd really like a crack at this one, sir. And it's not about Cass . . .' She faltered, seeming unsure of how blunt she could be without overstepping the mark.

'Spit it out,' Rickman said.

'I think I could achieve more on this case than I could as a drone footling on the sidelines of a big-budget production like DI Dwight's investigation — anyway, I heard they've had a few problems.'

He should have realised that Hart would never allow her outraged sensibilities to stand in the way of her career. She had weighed up the advantages of a high-profile operation against the lingering stench of partial failure and, even worse, the taint left by the missing drugs and money.

'So,' she said, evidently unsettled by his steady appraisal of her. 'Am I in, boss?'

Rickman smiled. 'You're in.'

Foster poked his head round the door. 'So, it's you, me and her, then.'

'Eavesdropping is a nasty habit, Sergeant Foster,' Rickman said.

'Only way you get to know anything in this place,' Foster shot back, entirely unembarrassed. Rickman beckoned him inside and he shut the door after him.

'I've drafted in a team of six uniforms for the house-to-house,' Rickman said. 'But the way things are going, we're not likely to get a full team till tomorrow.'

Rickman had spoken to the superintendent by phone. He hadn't been encouraging. The drugs operation had been months in the planning, and it was a serious screw-up: in addition to the missing money and the suspects who got away, an officer had been shot.

'So, what you're saying is, it's really just the three of us?' Foster said.

'We'll manage.' Rickman's tone made it clear this was not an argument Foster could win. 'I'll keep working on manpower,' he said, 'but I don't need to tell you the first few hours are crucial. Local press and media are a good bet — I'll talk to the press office as soon as we're finished here. And Chris Tunstall will be here within the hour.'

Foster groaned.

'Chris pulls his weight,' Hart said.

'He should do,' Foster said. 'He's built like a cart-horse.'

Rickman covered a smile. Tunstall had become something of a pet to Hart, and a large part of Foster's resentment stemmed from his bewilderment at Hart's affection for the big Widnesian.

Hart glanced at Rickman, her eyes dancing with laughter. There was something in the look that Rickman could not quite identify: an unexpected warmth perhaps, and he held her gaze for longer than was warranted.

Foster misinterpreted the look as disapproval. 'What d'you want me to say? He's a Widnes woollyback.' The 'k' sounded like a bronchial obstruction.

'Have you ever even been to Widnes?' Hart asked.

Foster gave her the smile at quarter strength. 'I was a Royal Marine — I've been around the world, Naomi.'

She arched an eyebrow. 'And they say travel broadens the mind . . .'

Foster turned to Rickman. 'Are you gonna help me or what?'

Rickman raised his hands. 'You dug yourself in, you can dig yourself out.'

Foster looked doubtfully at Hart. 'Nah, I know when I'm beaten.' He rubbed his hands. 'So, how're we gonna do this?'

'I've already circulated a description and the last two letters of the car's licence plate to Traffic. House-to-house will need it as well, in case anyone other than Mr Stott noticed this character hanging around. He's been watching the house for a few weeks.'

'Ex-boyfriend?' Foster said.

'Let's find out. Suggestions?'

Hart was ready. 'Jasmine was what — seventeen?'

Rickman nodded.

'So — family first, then school friends and teachers.'

'Have family been informed?' Foster asked.

'Just a mother, according to the registry office. She's not answering her doorbell or phone — uniform officers have tried both.' Rickman handed Foster a slip of paper. 'I'll talk to the education department, see if I can find her last school.'

* * *

Rickman sorted out a press release and set up an evening briefing for the media before leaving instructions for Tunstall. Less than an hour later, he was seated in the office of the Head of Sixth Form at West Derby High School for Girls. Mrs Staines was tall, elegantly dressed in black. A red silk blouse softened the austere cut of her suit. She wore her brown hair long, and when she crossed her legs, Rickman caught a flash of ankle bracelet below her trouser cuff.

She listened intently, her gaze never leaving his face, as she listened to the reason for his visit. 'Jasmine was a poor attender,' she said when he had finished. 'A troubled child — chaotic home life — an intelligent girl in a—' She hesitated, then tilted her head as if acknowledging the fact. 'Yes — a doomed situation.' Her eyes strayed to the window onto the sunny playing fields at the back of the school. 'Jasmine looked for approval in inappropriate friendships.'

'You knew her well?' Rickman saw no files or folders on the neat desk to indicate that Mrs Staines had read up on her ex-pupil.

'Before I was promoted, I was head of upper school discipline.' She smiled. 'Jasmine spent more time in my office than the majority of her peers.'

'These "inappropriate friendships"?'

'Older men, wild boys.' She seemed to catch something in his look. 'I'm no prude, Chief Inspector — I know better than most the pressures teenage girls are under. But Jasmine wasted her intellect — she didn't even turn up for her final year exams.'

'It looked like she was getting her life together,' Rickman said, feeling compelled to defend the child-woman he had seen tortured and broken. 'She'd recently moved into a new house.'

Again, he was struck by Mrs Staines's steady gaze, surprised to see in it the hard, incredulous stare of police and prison officers. *Teens and villains*, he thought. *Accomplished liars all* — and like cops, teachers in her line of work must need a cool head and a hard heart.

But he had misjudged her, at least in one respect. 'I'm glad.' She nodded to herself, as if this had solved some small conundrum. 'And I'm sorry.' She looked towards the window again and this time Rickman saw a tear shimmer on the rim of her eye.

She glanced at her watch and stood abruptly, as if impatient at her show of emotion. 'Almost lunchtime,' she said. 'The girls will be converging on the sixth form common room soon. Shall we?'

'I can arrange for child protection officers to come in and interview the girls,' Rickman said, thinking miserably of the delay that would cause, but feeling obliged to make the offer.

'They are young women,' she said firmly, '*not* children.' She led the way out onto the grey stretch of concrete between the main building and the sixth-form block. On the field, a group of younger girls were playing hockey, the clack of wooden sticks and occasional shouts of encouragement rising and falling on the sweet autumn breeze.

The school was enclosed by high sandstone walls, fringed by mature trees. The maples flamed red, and the sycamores and birches were buttery yellow in the afternoon sun. The sixth-form block was a featureless rectangle in cream-coloured stone, blackened in places by pollution from the ring road a hundred yards away. Many of the windows stood open and Mrs Staines glanced up at a sudden burst of laughter, as if trying to establish which classroom was the source of merriment — though Rickman couldn't tell from her expression if she felt it was a good or a bad thing.

In the common room, two girls huddled either side of a third — a sober-faced girl holding a magazine — while a radio played softly on the window ledge. They started at the sight of Mrs Staines, horror and guilt on their faces.

'Odd,' Mrs Staines said. 'I haven't heard the bell. Perhaps your General Studies teacher sent you to research popular culture?'

The girls laughed nervously, and the one who held the magazine dropped it to the table, as if trying to dissociate herself from it. 'Sorry, Mrs Staines.' She was blushing. 'We were just on our way to the library and—'

'Never mind.' Mrs Staines fixed them with her impenetrable stare. 'Since you are here, you can make yourselves useful. When lunch break *does* begin' — the slight emphasis on 'does' was not lost on the girls — 'I'd like you to round up any of the girls who were in Eleven G with you, the year before last. Bring them to the art room.'

* * *

Over the next five minutes, fifteen girls filed into the art room. It seemed the sixth form were allowed some leeway with dress: they wore a variety of styles, the unifying principle being that the tops were sleeveless and the colour code shades of green. Rickman guessed that the sleeveless rule was imposed by the girls themselves. Some carried cans of soft drinks, several had bottles of water, very few brought packed lunches. None of them looked directly at Mrs Staines, but it was clear they were all acutely aware of her presence, and Rickman sensed a respectful restraint in their demeanour. They perched on tables, chatting idly, curious, but far too sophisticated to openly acknowledge Rickman.

When they were assembled, Mrs Staines said, 'Thank you,' and the girls fell silent. 'This is Detective Chief Inspector Rickman,' she explained. 'He would like to ask you about Jasmine Elliott.'

'Who?' someone said, and a few of the girls laughed.

Mrs Staines cast a gimlet eye on the girl who had spoken and she looked away, taking a large sip of her soft drink.

'Was anyone here Jasmine's particular friend?' Rickman asked. A snort of derision was followed by sniggers. 'So she was the sort of girl who had no friends?'

An olive-skinned girl spoke: 'She's a *weirdo*.'

Mrs Staines was about to admonish the girl, but Rickman said, 'Weird in what way?'

The girl caught a hank of glossy hair in one hand, smoothing it before administering a practised flick, so that it fell in a cascade over her shoulder. 'The usual way. Weird make-up, weird way of dressing. *Seriously* weird taste in music.'

'What d'you expect? She's a smackhead.' The speaker was a pretty girl with a snub nose and a broad Scouse accent.

'A heroin addict?' Rickman asked — always best to be sure, where teenagers were concerned.

'Smack, crack, whatever,' the girl said. 'If you can smoke it, chew it or grind it into powder and inject it, Jasmine'll do it.' A ripple of delighted laughter, then the girls watched for Mrs Staines's reaction. She seemed willing to let them run with it, and for this Rickman was grateful — now was not the time to reinforce school discipline.

The olive-skinned girl spoke again. 'She always had to try to be *different*.'

'She *was* different.' The sombre-looking girl from the common room sat cross-legged on one of the tables, straight-backed and confident, sure of gaining a hearing in this most competitive of environments. Her hair — brown and unhighlighted — was tied back in a simple ponytail and her eyes, pale and luminous, brimmed with intelligence. 'Jasmine's mum is a waste of space. Jasmine's looked after herself since she was about twelve.'

'Were you her friend?' Rickman asked.

All eyes turned to the brown-haired girl. 'None of us were.' Someone gave a shocked giggle, but the girl continued. 'She was hardly ever here — even if you wanted to get to know her.' She stopped, apparently hearing the defensiveness in her tone. 'Has something happened to her?'

Now Rickman was the focus of attention, but of all of them, he felt most acutely the gaze of the solemn girl.

'Yes,' he said. 'I'm afraid it has. Mrs Staines will explain.' Better such news should come from their pastoral tutor. 'If any of you remember anything that might help us — the name of a friend — a boyfriend, maybe . . .'

The girls remained silent until Mrs Staines spoke. 'Jenni?'

The solemn-faced girl glanced at Mrs Staines, then looked Rickman in the eye. 'Is she dead?'

Rickman sensed a collective holding of breath. 'Yes,' he said.

Jenni sighed, and a rustle of whispered exclamations followed. 'From Year Ten on, she was here maybe three days a week,' Jenni said.

Someone muttered, 'If that.'

Mrs Staines frowned, the information not tallying with school records.

'Sorry, Mrs Staines,' the girl went on. 'She'd come in for registration, then hide in the toilets till the coast was clear and sneak out of the side gate.'

'What about that woman, used to pick her up, after school, take her *cruising*?' the olive-skinned girl asked.

Jenni spoke up again, and they fell into guilty silence. 'Kim,' she said. 'I think her name was Kim.'

'Yeah, Kim — Kimberley — something like that. She was gonna be an artist, or something,' the snub-nosed girl added.

'*Piss* artist, more like,' somebody chipped in from the back.

The others gave way to snuffled laughter, a touch guilty perhaps, some hidden behind hands, but all of them enjoying the baiting of a dead girl. In a seventeen-year-old's world, it seemed sympathy and grief were short-lived and shallow.

As they crossed the playground back to the main building, Rickman said, 'I'm surprised that staff didn't report Jasmine's absences.'

'Jasmine could be difficult,' Mrs Staines said. 'Some staff breathe a sigh of relief when certain girls are absent.' She led the way to the school entrance and the car park.

Rickman thanked her for her time and she frowned slightly. 'I'm so sorry, Chief Inspector,' she said with sincerity. 'I wish we could have been more help.'

CHAPTER 7

Jasmine's mother lived off the Lodge Lane end of Smithdown Road, in one of several clusters of studio flats masquerading as houses. Built in the 1980s when Thatcherite principles dictated that everyone was entitled to house ownership, they leaked in the rain, howled up a storm in a light breeze, froze in winter and tore themselves apart with subsidence and upheave in the summer.

Foster pounded on the front door a second time. In the adjoining house a dog was barking itself hoarse, hurling itself with foaming rage at the cracked glass panel of the front door. Mrs Elliott's house was in no better condition: the paintwork had long since lost its gloss, fading from red to scabby pink. The garden was a patch of scruffy turf, blackened in the centre by an oil leak — almost certainly not from a lawnmower.

Foster raised his fist and pounded again, rattling the door in its frame. The windows were shut tight, despite the warmth of the day, and nothing stirred in the house.

'This is hopeless,' he said. 'Let's jack it in, do something useful.'

Hart took a step back to scan the one upper window. DS Foster had a low boredom threshold, but a couple more minutes of perseverance might save them a return journey later. 'Just a minute,' she said. 'I think the curtain moved.'

Seconds later the door flung open and Mrs Elliott thrust her face into Foster's. 'Will you shut that bloody racket?'

Hart wrinkled her nose against the forty-percent-proof air expelled from the woman's lungs.

'That bleeding dog!' Mrs Elliott leaned across the narrow strip of brickwork separating the two houses and slapped the neighbouring front door, which only enraged the animal more.

'Felicity Elliott?' Foster asked, over the row.

She folded her arms. 'Who's asking?'

Foster held up his warrant card. 'Can we talk inside?'

Mrs Elliott gave a brief tut and turned her back on them, shuffling down the hallway in shapeless slippers that slurped and slapped with each step.

Foster cocked an eyebrow at Hart and she shrugged, stepping inside. Mrs Elliott disappeared into a room on the right, and they followed, finding themselves in a small sitting room. The curtains were drawn and pale pink light filtered through them, adding an extra wash to the woman's already florid colouring. The room was crammed with ill-matched chairs, each of which had a slick of black slime along the arms.

Mrs Elliott dropped into one of the armchairs with a grunt and a creak of upholstery springs. She was overweight, but not morbidly so. All the same, her body seemed to lack definition, and it filled the armchair, pressing unyieldingly against its sides. She immediately lit a cigarette, adding to the tobacco reek which overlaid the sweet odour of fermented liquor permeating the room. She didn't invite them to sit, for which Hart was grateful. Hart noticed a few lager cans and cider bottles among the debris of old magazines and full ashtrays, but the alcoholic miasma seemed to ooze from Mrs Elliott's pores. Hart recognised it from the binge drinkers and steady, seven-days-a-week alcoholics she had arrested, cautioned or even worked with in her time on the force.

'We've been trying to reach you all morning, Mrs Elliott,' Hart said.

'That was you, was it? You've woke me up I don't know how many times.'

'Didn't it occur to you to answer the door?' Foster demanded.

'Didn't it occur to youse lot I might need me sleep?'

Foster caught his breath and held it, looking to Hart to take over.

'Mrs Elliott,' she said. 'We're here with good reason.'

They waited for the inevitable questions: *What's happened? Is something wrong?* Always, at such moments, people think about their loved ones. As far as they knew, there was just Felicity Elliott and her daughter. But Mrs Elliott looked at them without curiosity or anxiety.

'I'm afraid we have bad news,' Hart said.

Mrs Elliott glanced around the room before turning bloodshot eyes on Hart. *What could be worse than this?* she seemed to imply.

'It's your daughter, Jasmine,' Hart said.

'I know what she's called.' Mrs Elliott took a drag on her cigarette and squinted at them through the smoke. 'And I'm not interested.' Her voice was coarsened by drink and cigarette smoke, and her features marred by years of alcohol abuse.

'This isn't just a spot of trouble,' Hart said, hoping that Mrs Elliott would make the connection if she gave her a little more time.

'She's dead,' Foster said, more bluntly than Hart would have liked. Mrs Elliott's gaze swivelled to him, but she showed no emotion. 'She was murdered.'

Hart shot Foster a sharp look. 'We're sorry to bring you such distressing news.'

Mrs Elliott tapped her ash deliberately into the heaped ashtray balanced on the arm of the chair.

Foster shifted from one foot to the other. 'Can you tell us anything about Jasmine: her friends, boyfriends, habits?'

Mrs Elliott snorted. 'Habits, yeah. She had a *habit*, all right.'

'Jasmine was an addict?' Hart asked.

'You been doing this job long, love?'

Hart tried again. 'Did Jasmine seem worried or upset recently?'

'I wouldn't know.' Mrs Elliott heaved herself out of her chair, dropping ash onto the carpet.

Hart told herself that the restlessness was a sign of the woman's shock. 'What about boyfriends?' she asked.

Mrs Elliott picked up an empty can and gave it a shake. 'I wouldn't know.'

'Maybe she mentioned a name?'

'*I . . . wouldn't . . . know.*' The repetition and the deliberate spacing of the words conveyed her irritation.

'She never spoke to you about her friends?'

Mrs Elliott lost patience. 'Jesus, are you thick, or wha'? I kicked her out.'

'When?' Hart asked.

'I dunno.'

'Recently?' Foster asked, sounding dangerously pleasant.

Mrs Elliott picked up another can. Shake, listen, replace. 'Depends what you call recent.' Hart doubted if Mrs Elliott paid much attention to seasons, months, days or weeks: her timekeeping was more likely to run in line with the opening and closing times of the local Bargain Booze.

The woman found a cider bottle with a couple of swallows remaining and Hart saw something like happiness in her face. As she seated herself again, Foster's hand snapped out and snatched the bottle from her fingers.

'Hey!' she protested.

Foster held the bottle just out of reach. 'When did you kick her out?'

She wiped her mouth with the back of her hand. 'Coupla years ago. And before you say anything' — she pointed at Foster with the burnt stub of her cigarette — 'I caught her with her hand in me purse.'

'Two years ago, she'd be what age?' Foster asked.

'Underage,' Hart said.

Mrs Elliott stubbed out her cigarette and rummaged in her dressing gown pocket for the packet. 'I done my duty — reported her to the social.'

'You know she had a baby?' Hart asked.

'Oh, aye.' The sneer on her face made Hart want to slap her. 'She come round with it just after it was born.'

It. 'The baby's missing,' Hart said.

'Well, *I* haven't got it.'

Hart bit her lip. 'She'd recently moved into a new house,' she said, unknowingly echoing Rickman's words. 'Maybe she was getting herself straight.'

'People like her *never* get themselves straight,' Mrs Elliott said. She might have been talking about herself.

'You know the name of the baby's father?' Foster asked.

'*He* done it, did he?'

'The name,' Foster said, and she looked from the bottle to his face, as if she was afraid he might swallow the contents himself, to spite her.

'I dunno,' she said. 'Mark?'

'Mark what?' Foster said.

'I dunno!' she exclaimed. 'Mark — she only ever called him Mark.' She reached for the bottle and Foster gave it to her.

'Do you have any letters, photographs or documents?' Hart asked. 'Anything that might help us?'

Mrs Elliott took a dainty sip of cider from the bottle. 'She left some pictures.' She indicated the dusty mantelshelf with a lift of her chin. A clutter of empty cans, junk mail and cigarette packets partly obscured a bright yellow wallet.

Foster caught it up greedily. The seal was unbroken, and he looked at Mrs Elliott, seeking approval. She stared blankly at him. 'I told you,' she said. 'I'm not interested.'

He glanced at Hart as he broke the seal, a mixture of puzzlement and wonder creasing his brow. 'Jasmine and the baby,' he said, shuffling through them. Hart tried not

46

to think of Jasmine, seventeen years old, laying gifts at her mother's feet, seeking approval from a woman who was incapable of feeling anything but resentment towards her.

Mrs Elliott showed no interest. Instead, she tucked the bottle into a corner of the chair to free her hands to light a fresh cigarette.

Hart saw something register in Foster's face. 'Sarge?'

He took the last photo and held it up for Mrs Elliott to see. In the photograph, Jasmine seemed to be showing off a new tattoo, her left sleeve rolled up to reveal a black twist of thorns encircling her upper arm. The boyfriend stood next to her, his arm slung around her shoulders. His hair, like Jasmine's, was dyed black. Jasmine stared straight into the camera, a defiant look in her blue eyes, her head on a tilt, but there was something pathetically vulnerable about her. Perhaps it was the fact that the lad was a foot taller than her, or perhaps it was the slight downturn of her mouth that made her look close to tears.

Looking from Mrs Elliott's ravaged face to the photograph, Hart struggled to see any likeness between this woman and the slight, willowy girl. Perhaps that was it — perhaps it was her daughter's dissimilarity she hated.

'Is this the boyfriend?' Foster asked. 'Is this Mark?'

Mrs Elliott wafted the smoke away from her face with her free hand. 'That's him — long streak of piss.'

Foster's jaw clamped tight, as if he was biting back a retort. 'Does the name Mark Davis mean anything?'

Hart looked from Foster to the woman, but she knew better than to interrupt.

Mrs Elliott raised one shoulder, let it fall. 'Could be. I never really—'

'Gave a shit,' Foster finished for her.

'Look,' she said, 'she was off her bloody head on crack, heroin — anything she could lay her thieving hands on. What was I supposed to do?'

'She was just a kid — you were *supposed* to take care of her.'

Hart expected another outburst, but Mrs Elliott surprised them both. She took a long pull on her cigarette, burning it down almost to the filter, her small eyes watching them through the smoke. 'All her life it was, "I want this," "Can I have that?" She took and took and took. Thieving when I wouldn't give her what she wanted.'

'Let me guess,' Foster said. 'You changed the locks after you kicked her out — called us lot out when she came asking for more.'

Mrs Elliott stubbed her cigarette out, angrily, lighting another before the last wisp of smoke vanished. 'You wanna try it yourself before you start criticising people,' she said, at last a quiver of emotion in her voice, but this was self-pity, not sorrow for her daughter. 'Well, if they're expecting me to pay for the funeral, they've got no chance. I'm flat broke.'

It wasn't clear who 'they' were — presumably the nebulous people in authority that Mrs Elliott had blamed for her difficulties throughout her life.

It fell to Hart to ask Mrs Elliott to formally identify her daughter. She was reluctant to ask the question — it seemed like the final insult to Jasmine that she should be claimed by the woman who had so emphatically disowned her. So it was almost a relief when Mrs Elliott said, 'What d'you need me for? You've got her fingerprints, haven't you? God knows she got herself arrested enough times.'

Hart could see that Foster was close to meltdown. 'Don't you wanna know how she died?' he asked.

'You just said, didn't you?'

Hart saw two stripes of hot colour on Foster's cheekbones. 'She was cut,' Foster said.

'Sarge—' Hart warned, but he went on.

'Not stabbed,' he said. 'Cut — again and again, till she bled to death.'

Hart stared at him in wide-eyed horror, but Mrs Elliott merely shrugged. 'Like I said — I'm not interested.' Nevertheless, Hart saw her eyes dart right and left.

'Don't bother getting up,' Foster said. 'We'll see ourselves out.' He slid the photo wallet into the inside pocket of his jacket. 'You won't mind if we take these.'

'Do what you like,' she said. 'It's what you bastards always do.'

* * *

'You know this Mark Davis?' Hart asked at the car.

'I know him.'

Foster slid behind the wheel, and Hart fastened her seat belt. 'Are you going to tell me?'

Foster turned the ignition key and gunned the engine, winding the window wide before he drove off. 'Let me drive a bit, get the stench of that rathole out of me lungs.'

The drive from Smithdown Road to Edge Hill took less than five minutes. They were almost four minutes into the journey before Foster had calmed down enough to speak.

'You know I was in a children's home as a kid?'

'Black Wood,' Hart said. This surprising little nugget had emerged during an investigation they had worked on the previous spring.

'Mark Davis spent some time there.'

She nodded, not fully understanding. 'The lad in the picture looks no more than twenty,' she said. 'You must have ten years on him.' He didn't try to haggle her down on the age difference. Another surprise.

'Black Wood runs a mentoring project,' he said. 'I was Mark's mentor for a year before he left care.'

'That would be what — four years ago?' He pulled up at the traffic lights at Durning Road and Hart stared at his profile. A muscle jumped in his jaw and she realised, not for the first time, that there was more to Lee Foster than his fondness for booze and women.

'Fat lot of good I did him.'

'You can't blame yourself for this,' she said.

He turned the corner. 'Can't absolve myself, neither.'

Absolve? You can take the altar boy out of the church, but you can't take the church out of the altar boy, she thought. If Foster knew that his blighted childhood and his conscience and his voluntary work were far more attractive than his famous fifty-megawatt smile, would he exploit them? She doubted it.

He sensed her scrutiny. 'What?'

She wouldn't for the world have mocked him about this, and she was relieved to see a diversion ahead in the form of a snarl of traffic. 'Looks like the press have arrived.'

A small crowd of reporters with TV and still cameras were clustered around the main entrance to Edge Hill Police Station and an assortment of media vans and private cars were parked either side of the road, their wheels half on the kerb, narrowing the roadway sufficiently to cause a bottleneck. Added to which, through-traffic was slowing to clock the reason for the gathering.

'Think they're here for us or DI Dwight's mob?' she asked.

'Like shooting fish in a barrel,' Foster said. 'Two major investigations and they don't even have to move their fat arses to chase the story.'

A tea and burger van was parked on the pavement across the street and a queue had formed. Many of the reporters were in lightweight jackets or shirtsleeves, and there was a relaxed carnival atmosphere.

'Makes you wanna pray for rain, doesn't it?' Foster said. He nosed the car forward through the bottleneck, seeking out the left turn into the rear of the station. A few yards on, they passed a uniformed officer, sweating in short sleeves, trying to move the traffic on. 'What's the score?' Foster asked.

'We're expecting royalty, Sarge.' He paused, distracted by sirens in the distance. An unmarked car approached from the opposite direction, lights flashing and siren whooping. 'Looks like they've arrived.' The queue at the van scattered and the less encumbered of the reporters fled like moths to the light.

Foster and Hart got out of the car to watch the spectacle. For a moment, all they could see was the huddle of reporters and photographers around the car, but the crowd parted and they saw DS Cass in his best sports jacket and slacks, his right hand firmly on the elbow of a taller, powerfully built man.

'Is that Rob Maitland?' Hart asked.

Foster nodded. 'Cass is a total wanker. What's wrong with using the back door, like everyone else?'

'And miss a perfectly good photo op?' Hart saw a sheen of Vaseline on Cass's lower lip. 'He must have topped up the lip balm before he got out of the car,' she said. 'And I'll swear he's had a haircut.'

The reporters clamoured for a comment, and Maitland, handcuffed but proudly erect, stopped and turned.

'He's not gonna let him make a speech?' Foster exclaimed.

Cass raised his hand like a statesman. 'Sorry, folks,' he said. 'This man is under arrest. He's not at liberty to comment right now.'

Cass no doubt thought that being on telly was good for his career. Being on telly taking a big-name villain like Rob Maitland into custody was even better. But Hart saw the look in Maitland's eye. She knew Maitland's type: on a slow burn, they had long memories and they never forgave.

CHAPTER 8

Rickman and Tunstall were in the CID Room, watching a video clip of Jasmine with her baby. Rickman nodded to Hart and Foster, and they took up station without speaking. Rickman knew his friend well enough to see that something was bothering him, but for now, he let it pass.

On-screen, Jasmine handled her daughter with a tenderness that verged on reverence.

'I can't believe she's mine,' she whispered. Her ears still bristled with studs and rings, but the fierce defensiveness in the photograph was gone. She smiled into the camera, dimpling prettily.

The baby stirred, her little fists coming up to her face, and Jasmine laughed softly, working one slender finger into her infant's tiny fist. 'Look at them nails,' she said, her voice filled with tremulous awe. '*Beautiful* nails.'

The picture blurred momentarily, then the camera came into focus on the baby's curled fingers.

'*Perfect* little nails . . .' The camera pulled back to Jasmine's face. Her eyes brimmed with tears. 'I'm never gonna let nothing bad happen to her,' she said. 'Never.'

The screen went blank.

'We should send a copy of this to her mother,' Hart said.

'She was unhelpful?' Rickman asked.

'She couldn't wait to get rid of us.' He saw an uncharacteristic anger in her face, carefully suppressed but deeply felt.

'I think we interrupted her happy hour,' Foster said, his outrage undisguised. 'Did you see the way she sucked the dregs out that bottle of cider?'

'She never once used Jasmine's name.'

'Well, somebody cared.' Rickman lifted his chin towards the TV screen. 'This video was on Jasmine's mobile phone.'

'So who shot it?' Foster asked.

'There's a faint reflection on the window. Mebbe tech support can try and enhance it.' Tunstall rewound the clip to the instant a figure ghosted onto the window next to Jasmine, so he missed the surprised expressions on his colleagues' faces: a year ago, he had trouble with basic computer skills — even sending emails was something he would fret over.

'All them rings and tattoos,' he said with a shudder.

'Talismans against the bad men of the world,' Rickman said.

'Her talismans failed her, that day,' Hart said.

'The *system* failed her.' Rickman looked around at the team. 'We can't put that right, but we can help Jasmine make good on her promise to her little girl.'

The four officers glanced one to the other, and it seemed at that moment a silent pact was made: to find Bryony safe, to bring Jasmine's killer to justice. Of all the men and women Rickman had worked with over the years, he felt sure that these three could deliver.

To an outside observer, the group would have made an odd match. Rickman, tall and ascetic-looking in his good suit and polished shoes. Tunstall, as tall as Rickman, but bulky and clumsy, the extra weight he carried stretching the seams of his casual jacket. Foster, by contrast, was just above average height, though well-muscled and with the easy agility of an athlete. And beside them, Hart, slender and elegant. Even lightly tanned, her pale Icelandic features gave the impression of self-possessed aloofness.

'First off, welcome to the team, Chris,' Rickman said, and Tunstall nodded, his neck growing red at the rim of his shirt collar. 'Who wants to go first?'

Foster took the photographs from his inside pocket and handed Rickman the shot of Jasmine and her boyfriend. 'Mark Davis. Boyfriend, the mother said. Druggie. Said Jasmine was into crack and heroin, as well.'

'Her school confirms that,' Rickman said, noticing the thorns tattooed on Jasmine's arms, and flashing involuntarily to Jasmine, dead, with pearls of blood congealed at the tips of each spur. 'We need to show this photo to the witness at the scene — find out if this is the man he saw driving away.'

'I can do that,' Tunstall said.

'Have we got the negs?' Rickman asked.

Foster checked the wallet. 'All here. There's stills of Jasmine and the baby and all.'

'Get them down to technical support. We'll need multiples for press, house-to-house. Could the mother tell us anything about Davis?'

Foster and Hart exchanged a look — Hart's was unusually solicitous, Foster's uncharacteristically awkward.

'Lee?' Rickman said.

'I identified him, boss.' Foster explained his connection with Mark Davis, Black Wood's mentoring scheme. Rickman knew the last part — Foster's involvement in the scheme, though his friend hadn't mentioned individual names. This was for Hart and Tunstall's benefit.

'So this Davis lad was one of the inmates?' Tunstall asked, always slow at processing information.

Foster stared at him. 'Inmates? It wasn't a prison, Tunstall.' Tunstall looked uncertain. 'We weren't offenders,' Foster continued. 'We were kids with nowhere else to go.'

Tunstall frowned, registering the use of 'we'. 'Oh,' he said. '*You* were—'

'An "inmate", yeah.'

The rim of red around Tunstall's collar became a sudden florid flush. Rickman looked at Tunstall, making it plain he expected a response.

The big man shifted uncomfortably in his chair and it cracked alarmingly. 'Sorry, Sarge,' he mumbled. 'I didn't know.'

'Well, now you do.' Foster kept his gaze on Tunstall, who looked ready to bolt for the door.

'You might want to keep that in mind when you talk to any former residents,' Rickman said. Although the irony in his tone was way beyond him, he knew that Chris Tunstall would not forget this lesson in tact.

Tunstall nodded, still blushing, and Rickman saw him write the word 'resident' in his notebook. He underlined it three times.

'Ed and Hilary Shepherd still run the place, so far as I know.' Foster was slow to take his eyes off Tunstall. 'Mark was close to them, as I remember. Might be worth having a word.'

'Okay,' Rickman said. 'Lee, you'll come with me to Black Wood. Naomi, photographs and a few copies of the video, in case local TV can use it. I'll ask about that reflection, too. Chris—'

'The witness at the scene,' Tunstall supplied smartly, in an effort to make up for his gaff with Foster.

'Right,' Rickman said. 'If we get a positive ID, I can use it at the press conference. When that's done, check with house-to-house, see if there's anything needs following up. And remember, at least half of these officers have come in on their off-duty to help.'

He watched Tunstall absorb this piece of information before going on. 'And I have another name: Jasmine's . . . peers' — he couldn't bring himself to call them school friends — 'say she was friendly with an older woman, used to pick her up outside school. Kim or Kimberley. Make sure house-to-house have the name. When they've finished canvassing the neighbourhood, I'll ask them to talk to working girls around the city centre — it's likely Jasmine funded her habit through prostitution. Our job will be to start tackling former residents — anyone who might've kept in touch with Mark Davis.'

'Sir?' A civilian clerk stood at the door. Rickman waved her in and she handed him a slip of paper.

He read it. 'Are police at the scene?'

'Yes, sir.'

'Probable sighting of Davis. Queens Drive,' Rickman explained to the others.

As the clerk disappeared through the door, Rickman turned to a whiteboard to the left of it. He had already noted that Jasmine Elliott's body was discovered at eleven fifty a.m. Rickman drew a line across the board, then added an entry to the timeline. 'Sighting — Queens Drive, Wavertree, one p.m.'

Foster shook his head in disgust. 'He could be heading anywhere.' Queens Drive was Liverpool's outer ring road: six and a half miles, with exits to any one of thousands of major and minor roads, avenues, boulevards and streets — and that was assuming Davis decided to stay in the city.

'I'll check it out, soon as I've sorted technical support,' Hart said.

Rickman handed her the slip. 'Thanks, Naomi. The super has confirmed — no extra support until tomorrow. Make use of whatever goodwill you've built up with the admin staff to help smooth the way, use your time wisely — and prioritise.'

* * *

Rickman almost collided with a DC from the drugs team as he and Foster left the CID Room. 'Where's the fire?' he demanded.

'Sorry, sir. Machete attack at a crack house. It's all hands to the pump.' The officer hurried on, clattering down the back stairs.

'It's paramedics they'll be wanting,' Foster said, 'not police.' They trotted down the stairs, listening to cars reversing and revving out of the car park at the back of the building. 'You'd think that lot would've had enough excitement last night.'

As a marine, Foster had seen excitement of the most dangerous kind, and knew better than most the aftermath of exciting moments. He would flash his Royal Marine credentials at an attractive woman in the same way he would flash his brilliant white smile, but he was no yarn-spinner. Rickman was the only man or woman on the force who had heard about the sweat and the dirt and the fear of battle, the friends Foster had lost to enemy fire and landmines. Foster knew how to handle himself, and he was a good man to have on your side in a fight, but Rickman knew that he didn't feel the need to chase danger.

'DI Dwight's team have a lot to make up for, after last night's op,' Rickman said.

'I heard it was a bit of dog's breakfast.'

'I doubt they'll be able to hold Maitland, and without Maitland, all Snowplough achieved was putting a hole in his profit margins. He'll be dealing again in a matter of days.'

Rickman pushed the release bar on the fire escape door and they were out into bright sunshine. A yellow surveillance van swung into the car park and twelve waiting officers in uniform piled in.

Rickman noticed Foster's expression. 'The chief wants a visible presence on the streets,' he said.

'Seems cockeyed to me.' Foster ducked into the passenger seat of the Vectra as Rickman slid behind the wheel.

'Having a visible presence?'

'Custard-yellow vans doing surveillance. I mean — do they really expect your local scals to do anything with a gang of hairy-arsed woodentops looking on?'

'The reality TV factor,' Rickman said. 'They forget the cameras are rolling. Or maybe they just want their fifteen minutes of fame.'

They followed the convoy out of the rear courtyard, onto the side street, avoiding the camera crews. The others headed into the city, but Rickman turned southwards to the leafy suburb of Woolton. As they drove up Brownlow Hill towards the main university campus, they hit solid traffic.

Rickman cursed mildly, and Foster said, 'That's progress for you.'

Road improvements and building demolitions to make way for university buildings and the new teaching hospital had turned the city centre into a chicane for the past two years. Delays, mismanagement and the collapse of its building contractor, Carillion, had already set the hospital construction back several months. Then the new contractor had discovered potentially catastrophic structural defects. Now it looked like the new hospital would open some five years after its planned completion. Meanwhile, the main arterial roads past the university were in almost total gridlock at peak times, and even short trips were a logistical nightmare. Normally, at this time of day, traffic eased off, but the virtual blocking of Wavertree Road by TV crews and journalists meant drivers were finding alternative routes through the city.

Rickman nosed forward, siphoning into a single lane of traffic, past orange and white barriers. The buzz of road drills in the distance told him they were still some way from the roadworks. Foster shook his head, staring resentfully at the press of traffic. 'New-wave Liverpool,' he muttered. '"Come and visit, you'll never want to leave." We'll never *let you out*, more like.'

'We haven't got time for this.' Rickman drummed his fingers on the steering wheel, working out the quickest way around the jam.

Foster glanced at him. 'You didn't have to be here. Let's face it, you could be filling in questionnaires, or talking to the speaking clock, or whatever it is you do back at the office.'

'When I could be digging into your past?'

'And there was me, thinking you didn't trust me with them two.'

Foster looked straight ahead, but Rickman could feel his friend watching from the corner of his eye. Foster wasn't one to share his feelings, but he was quick to read others'. 'I need to know if you're okay with this,' Rickman said.

'I knew the lad four years ago, Jeff.'

'But it's bound to stir up some ghosts.'

Foster lifted his chin, indicating a sudden movement of the traffic, so Rickman didn't catch his expression. 'I'll handle it,' he said, after a few moments. 'What about you? You're coming up to a bit of a milestone yourself.'

If anyone else had said this, Rickman would have cut them off at the knees, but Foster knew more than most what Rickman had been through the previous autumn, and Foster, more than anyone, had helped him survive it. 'I used to love this season,' he said. 'Now, I just hope to get through it.'

Foster nodded. 'Me mum hated it. She was always worse as the nights drew in.'

Rickman knew that Lee's mother had been a sadness that lingered in his life like a dull ache. But when she died, Foster lost all purpose and direction for a while. Rickman showed up on his doorstep after he'd failed to turn up for work two days running. His friend had handed Rickman his mother's address book and said, 'They need to know she's dead.' *They* being the scant few who had once been a part of her existence.

'Jeff' — Lee Foster's gaze had held such searing pain that Rickman had to force himself to keep eye contact — 'They need to know *how* she died.'

Rickman understood. His friend couldn't bear to hear the short silence, the intake of breath, the tentative question that Rickman heard again and again in the hours that followed. 'Did she . . . ?' They needed to know that it wasn't suicide. So Rickman performed this duty, turning the brittle pages of her address book, dialling the numbers from Appleton to Williams, repeating the same words, until they became almost automatic.

And just as Jeff Rickman had arranged the funeral and flowers, had kept Lee Foster company while he got drunk, covered for him on the days he couldn't get out of bed, so Foster had taken care of Rickman when his partner's murder had torn his world apart. More than this, Foster had seen that justice was served.

Rickman edged the car forward, looking for the first turn-off that would allow him to double back. 'Did you ever wonder what your life would be like, if your mother's depression had been more effectively treated?' he asked.

'Yeah, sometimes. Not much.' Foster slumped back in his seat, resigning himself to the wait. 'I just wish she could've been happier.'

Rickman saw his chance — a side street that wasn't cordoned off. It meant back-tracking, but anything was better than sitting in a queue going nowhere. He cut left, looping back, then scooted south along the grey backstreets of Edge Hill, before turning east towards Woolton's tree-lined avenues.

'So,' Foster said, after a good ten minutes' silence. 'Is that it? We all square?'

Rickman thought about it. 'Yeah. For now, anyway.'

'Thanks for the vote of confidence.' Sarcasm was almost a reflex with Foster. They saw the sign for Black Wood Children's Home a hundred yards up the road. 'Don't embarrass me, right?' Foster added. 'Ed and Hilary, they think I'm a good Catholic lad.'

'D'you ever go to church?' Rickman asked, thinking again of the full requiem mass he had arranged for Foster's mother: incense, altar boys, choir, the works.

'I go there,' Foster said. 'Sometimes. When it's empty.'

Rickman shot him a quizzical look.

'Somewhere quiet to think,' Foster explained. 'What about you?'

Rickman turned into the drive. 'I don't think I've ever been inside a synagogue. My mother had no belief. My father worshipped in the house of Higson's Ale.'

'Do *you* believe in anything?' Foster asked.

Rickman thought a moment. 'Evil. I believe in evil.'

* * *

Four hours. The baby has screamed and bawled and grizzled and whimpered non-stop for four solid hours. Mark Davis hunches over the steering wheel, his hands covering his ears.

'I don't know what to do!'

Bryony hiccups and quietens for a moment. He angles his head to look at her in the rear-view mirror, hardly daring to hope. Then she takes another breath and the screams begin again, pounding his eardrums. He stares at the twitching, screaming bundle of fury and all he can feel is pressure behind his eyes and nothing, nothing, *nothing* in his head.

'Fuck it!' He shoulders the door open and slams it after him, taking a few steps, tempted to keep walking. But the bags are in the car: the money, the drugs, the promise of a good life — a life he was never meant to have and now he *wants* it. The baby's screams follow him and he blames Bryony for slowing him down and Jasmine for getting knocked up in the first place.

He thinks how much easier it will be to disappear without Bryony holding him back.

A woman turns the corner, dragged along by a big dog — all hair and slaver. His heart skips a beat — he's covered in blood! He turns and sidles back to the car, pressing himself against the glass, as though he's making way for her.

She smiles her thanks, passing him at a trot, panting almost as loud as the dog, leaning back at a slant like a water-skier, one hand on the dog's leash. '*Someone* wants a feed,' she says, like he's asked her opinion. She's gone as suddenly as she appeared, and Mark comes to a decision.

He'll go to the chemist, get some baby stuff — a bottle and nappies and that. But not the way he looks now — not with blood all over his trousers. He's parked along a blank stretch of sandstone wall — part of the boundary to Calderstones Park. He checks nobody is looking and locks the car door. *She'll be all right*, he tells himself. *I'll be five minutes — what can happen in five minutes?*

* * *

61

The hot water isn't working in the toilets, and all the plugs have been removed from the sinks after one too many floods. He grabs a few paper towels and stuffs them in the plughole. The shirt isn't too bad, but there's a large browning patch of blood on the left leg of the trousers, and further streaks on both thighs, where he's wiped his hands.

He strips off and plunges the trousers into the freezing water. He works the soap dispenser till it rattles, rubbing an oily gloop of soap into the stain, dunking and scrubbing at the fabric until the water is dark pink, but the stains, though fainter, remain.

Cursing, he pulls the wad of paper towels out of the plug hole and runs fresh water onto the stains. He's weeping and cursing now, muttering to himself, squeezing and wringing and plunging the cloth until his hands are raw.

A movement behind him makes him spin round. A boy in school uniform is staring at him. 'What the fuck're *you* lookin' at?' Mark snarls. He shouldn't even be here, this time of day.

The boy's eyes widen and Mark takes a step, dripping icy water and soap suds onto the concrete floor. The boy turns and flees.

Mark wrings out the last of the suds and leans against the wall to pull on his trousers. His legs are stained with blood: thighs, knees, the tops of his crisp white trainer socks are crusted with it. He feels a wave of nausea, snatches up the sodden paper towels and rubs at the blood. Some has congealed, drying hard and black on the hairs of his legs.

'Fuck.' He scrubs at the mess. '*Fuck.*'

Hear hears footsteps approaching the toilets. The boy must have called someone. The police? Heart pounding, he flings the paper towels away from him, drags his trousers on, crams his feet into his trainers. A man blocks the entrance, but Mark cannons into him, knocks him flat.

He's running. Crossing newly planted beds of chrysanthemums, crushing them underfoot. He leaps a barrow at the edge of the bed, his foot catches the lip and he stumbles, arms flailing. He regains his balance and sets off again. He hears a shout — they're after him. He takes to the path, kicking up fallen leaves, convinced they're within arm's length, certain he can hear the steady thump of boots on tarmac.

Out through the gates. His lungs are screaming but he belts on, until the air burns his throat and chest, his legs give way, and he's forced to stop.

The car is another twenty yards on. He staggers to it as a groundsman skids to a stop at the main gate and looks the wrong way. Mark grabs the door handle, wrenching his shoulder as it refuses to give. He tries again. It won't open. The key!

The groundsman sees him and raises a shout.

Struggling for the key, his knuckles chafed and sore, at first Mark can't force his fingers past the sodden fabric of his chinos, but finally the fob is in his hands and he's behind the wheel.

The groundsman runs towards the car, his face red, his teeth bared. Mark pulls out as the man runs into the road. The groundsman raises his arm and Mark grins in terror and elation.

'Too late, fucker!'

Something hits the windscreen and it cracks, a circular dent of opaque glass appears in Mark's line of vision. Mark swerves. The groundsman leaps back, and Mark sees his rage turn to terror. He laughs wildly, screaming obscenities at the groundsman as he speeds away.

The baby is too quiet. He feels a stab of anxiety. He turns in his seat to get a look at her. She's still, her eyes screwed shut. It's cold in the car — so cold you can see your breath. *Five minutes. I only left her five minutes.* Then she sets up a wail, and he feels the pressure building again inside his skull.

CHAPTER 9

Black Wood Children's Home was accessed by a drive that curved for a quarter of a mile through woodland and rhododendron scrub. The tarmac was pitted and weedy and the air of decay was reinforced by a glimpse of a derelict house just off to the right. Every window was secured with steel plates. Even the front door was clad in sheet metal.

'Looks like the place is in decline,' Rickman said.

'That's the old coach house — it was out of bounds even in my day.' Foster turned to get a better look. 'The big house is in better nick.'

Foster saw Rickman glance in the mirror and turned himself for a better look, but the little house had already been swallowed up by the press of overgrown shrubs.

'The lads loved it,' Foster carried on, in full reminiscence. 'Bottle of cider and a couple of loosies each, we thought we were the biz.'

'By "loosies", I take it you mean cigs and not girls.' Rickman said.

Foster gave him a withering look. 'You've been around me too long, mate. Anyhow, you wouldn't get a girl anywhere near the place. It's supposed to be haunted.' He smiled as they bumped along the last few yards of ruined tarmac. 'Hilary used to call it our Wendy house, just to piss us off.'

Rickman drew to a stop.

Foster was first out. He spoke to Rickman across the roof of the car as he locked up. 'Don't let their cuddly-bear looks fool you,' he said. 'They're sharp.'

* * *

The Hilary Shepherd who opened the door was quite different from the woman Foster had known. She retained the well-padded contours, and the creases around her eyes and mouth confirmed what he already knew: that this was a face more used to smiling than frowning, but Hilary had a harried look, out of sorts in a way he had never seen when he was a resident at Black Wood, nor during the two years that he volunteered for their mentoring scheme.

Flustered, he showed her his warrant card, making the introductions. Then her hand flew to her mouth and she laughed, shedding years. 'For heaven's sake!' she exclaimed, taking his hand and drawing him into the house. 'Ed!' she called over her shoulder, 'Ed, come and see — it's Lee Foster!'

Foster felt a happy thud, of welcome and of anticipation. Ed Shepherd was the closest thing to a father he'd ever had.

Hilary turned back to her guests. 'I'm so sorry. What must you think? As you can see, we're in turmoil at the moment.' She waved her hand to the boxes and bin bags cluttering the parquet flooring and stacked against the oak panelling of the rather grand hallway.

In the years since Foster had last seen her, Hilary's dark brown hair had become streaked with grey, and some of the energy that had been a major factor in her success as a house parent seemed depleted.

'Decluttering, or what?' Foster asked.

'Or what.' Ed himself appeared at the top of the stairs, laden with a couple of boxes. In the shadow, Ed

Shepherd seemed unaltered by the years — athletic, trim, high-shouldered and loose-limbed. But as he came down into the light, Foster saw that he too had aged. He was quite grey, and the quizzical frown that had often furrowed his forehead had become a permanent crease. He dumped his burden on the last riser of the broad sweep of stairs and dusted himself off.

'Lee Foster . . .' He offered his hand, grinning. 'I knew you'd show up, sooner or later.' He looked past Foster to Rickman, politely disguising his curiosity. 'Forgive us,' he said. 'This is a visit we've been waiting on a good while.'

'Detective Chief Inspector Rickman,' Foster said, 'Ed Shepherd.' He paused. 'I'm afraid this isn't a social call, Ed.'

Shepherd's frown deepened. Evidently, he hadn't heard their doorstep introductions.

'Lee is here today as *Detective Sergeant* Foster,' his wife said. Her expression was composed and pleasant, as always, but there was something in her voice that made Foster look at her more closely. Ed Shepherd's grip slackened slightly, then he squeezed a little tighter before breaking the handshake and offering his hand to Rickman. Foster saw Rickman's quick appraisal of Shepherd, and an uncomfortable silence followed.

'Maybe we should . . .' Hilary gestured vaguely along the hallway, and her husband led the way to a door on the left of the hall, into their private quarters. The room had been given a modern makeover: wood floors, plain marble fireplace, spotlights and an expensive-looking hi-fi. DIY and gadgets — Ed's twin passions, Foster recalled.

This room, too, was in unusual disarray, with some of the bookshelves already cleared and several boxes stacked neatly in one corner.

Foster felt an unreasonable pang of alarm. They couldn't be leaving? Hilary, attuned to her children, must have picked up on his bewilderment. 'The diocese is closing us down,' she explained.

'But *why*?'

'"Old facilities in need of costly upgrading," they say.' She sighed. '"Children need to be cared for within a nuclear family."'

'Bollocks,' Foster said. He caught Hilary's disapproving look and, annoyingly, felt a flush rise in his face. 'Diocese in need of money, is it?' he pushed on.

'The developers are moving in as soon as we've packed up and left,' said Ed. They've had surveyors crawling all over the place for weeks already.'

'Ed . . .' Hilary said.

'Well, it's true, isn't it?' he challenged, and Hilary's mouth tightened into a thin line, as though she was afraid that a direct criticism might escape her.

'What's the name of the company?' Rickman asked.

'Mersey Property Development,' Ed said. 'But they won't help you. It's all about the bottom line with that lot.'

Hilary, always the peacemaker, said, 'It's hardly their fault — they're only trying to make a living.' Hilary always was the peacemaker. Ed looked ready to give her an argument, but she changed the subject abruptly. 'How's your mum getting on, Lee?'

Foster glanced at Rickman, who spared him by showing a sudden interest in one of the framed collages of children and families on the wall next to the big bay window.

'She died.' He wanted to say more. It wasn't enough, this bald statement, but the words wouldn't come.

Hilary took his hand and held it. 'I'm so sorry, Lee.'

Foster would have taken his hand away, but Hilary's concern, her sincere regret for his loss prevented him. He met her gaze and felt again, in those green-flecked eyes, the warmth of her affection. He nodded and she released him. Nothing more needed to be said.

'So,' Hilary said, with a slight lift of an eyebrow. 'This is your boss?'

Foster rolled his eyes. 'Yeah, so no getting the photo albums out — there's a few snaps I remember could ruin me air of mystique.'

Hilary gave an easy, mirthful laugh, and Foster was reminded how she laughed often in the old days. 'All right,' she added with a twinkle. 'We'll leave the albums for another time. Now — how can we help?'

'Mark Davis,' Rickman said, leaving out any explanation. Foster knew that this was the best way to get an honest answer, rather than the one that people thought you wanted, but he felt uncomfortable, wanting to explain further. These two were friends — practically family — after all.

'He was the boy you mentored, wasn't he, Lee?' Hilary said. 'Insecure boy. Always taking the blame for mischief others had made.'

'Easy led,' Foster said, almost to himself. 'Has he been in touch?'

'Since he left?' Shepherd asked.

'Recently,' Rickman said.

They looked at each other. 'Not recently.'

Foster frowned. It wasn't unusual for them to be vague about Davis, but he had expected an expression of concern.

'When,' Rickman said, 'exactly?'

'About six months after he left care,' Hilary said promptly. 'Ed set him up with an apprenticeship at a local garage. It went bust. After that . . .' She shrugged.

'Odd,' Rickman said.

'Not really.' Hilary Shepherd smiled, but it lacked warmth. 'We try to make Black Wood a real home, Chief Inspector. But most children can't wait to get away. And they stay away.'

'Not all of them.' Rickman nodded towards the photo-montages on the sitting room wall.

'Not all, no.'

Foster got the strangest notion that she would've liked to tear the montage down to save it from Rickman's scrutiny of her private collection.

Ed Shepherd had been quiet throughout this exchange, but now he spoke. 'What kind of trouble has Mark got himself into?'

'You haven't heard the news?'

Hilary looked around them at the boxes, the signs of upheaval. 'We've been dreadfully preoccupied. If you want the honest truth, the last two years have been hell. "Reorganisation," they said at first. Then, "Closure." For a time we thought we had a reprieve with the possibility of "downsizing" — the coach house was put forward as suitable accommodation. But the developers wouldn't have it. I suspect they thought it would bring down the tone of their "gated community".'

Now that she'd started to express her true feelings, Hilary seemed unable to stop her tirade. Foster glanced at Ed, wanting him to intervene, but he bowed his head, his hands clasped before him, as though he had heard this many times. Rickman, meanwhile, was watching her with quiet interest.

'We've been through meetings, endless discussions, interviews, inspections,' Hilary went on. 'Most of the children have been placed with foster carers, and we've scarcely had time to check if they're settled. We have to be out by the end of the month — we've lived here for thirty years and we've had *two months'* notice to quit.'

She fell silent, and they stared at her for a moment. A strand of hair had come loose from her ponytail, and she pushed it back off her face in a defensive, defiant gesture.

'They've been harassing us for a date, so they can move in and measure up,' Ed said.

'There's someone snooping around the grounds already,' Hilary added bitterly.

Ed leaned forward, holding her gaze. 'We'll be all right, Hilary.'

'Of *course* we will,' she said, impatient. 'But what about the children?'

Her husband shook his head. This was a question he couldn't answer. 'You say Mark was on the news?' he said, bringing the discussion back to the purpose of their visit.

'Mark Davis is wanted for questioning in connection with the murder of Jasmine Elliott,' Rickman said.

Ed's face fell. 'No.'

Foster glanced at his friend. Jeff Rickman was still, his expression unreadable, the blankness of it disconcerting.

Hilary shook her head emphatically. 'No! Not Mark — he's harmless. You know that, Lee.'

'A man can change a lot in four years,' Foster said, with an apologetic dip of his head.

Ed took a breath, as though he was about to say something, but instead, he took an inhaler from his pocket and took a blast from it.

'Not Mark,' Hilary repeated.

'Jasmine's baby daughter is missing,' Rickman said, in the same quiet, insistent tone, and Foster felt another twinge of unease. 'A man answering Mark Davis's description was seen driving away from the scene of the murder.'

Hilary didn't reply, and Ed seemed to be concentrating on his breathing.

'We're deeply concerned for the safety of the baby. If you have *any* information that might help us—'

'We told you, we haven't seen him since shortly after he left care,' Hilary insisted.

Rickman waited a moment or two longer. 'Well, if he should get in touch, you *will* contact me or Sergeant Foster?' He handed her his card.

She took it with stiff formality. 'Of course.'

'And we'll need contact addresses. Anyone who knew Mark, or might have stayed in touch with him. One of my officers will contact you later.'

* * *

'I can't believe they're being kicked out, after all this time,' Foster said as they walked to the car. 'Them two put their hearts and souls into this place.'

'Not our problem, Lee.'

Foster looked at his friend. 'You don't trust them?' he said, voicing the niggling unease he had felt since the start of the interview.

Rickman evaded the question. 'I think Mark has been in touch.'

'No chance,' Foster said, shocked at the notion. 'They wouldn't protect a killer, Jeff.'

'I hope not.'

Foster saw then that Jeff Rickman didn't trust Ed and Hilary Shepherd, didn't like them. As far as he was concerned, they were suspects.

CHAPTER 10

The team assembled for their evening debrief in a conference room at Edge Hill. Rickman had requisitioned it as their Major Incident Room, there being no other suitable place for them at the station, and he was reluctant to move the team further from the murder location. Equipment had arrived ahead of schedule — the sergeant in charge of requisitions at Mather Avenue had red-stickered the request when Rickman explained the situation.

The room was in better condition than most at Edge Hill: carpet tiles in place and tables in oak finish, rather than the standard-issue wood-effect melamine.

Tunstall was first to arrive. In his right hand he carried in a kettle — non-standard issue. Personnel were expected to pay fifty pence a cup for the swill dispensed by the machine in the basement. Hooked on the fingers of his left hand, four Merseyside Police mugs, branded with the authority badge. A supermarket carrier bag hung from his arm.

Rickman watched as the DC set up one of the spare desks as a tea table, plugged in the kettle and switched it on. As Tunstall spooned coffee into the mugs, Rickman realised he hadn't eaten since breakfast, and he guessed the rest of the team wouldn't have thought about food either. The DC emptied the contents of the carrier bag onto the table, item by item, and when Rickman saw a packet of digestive biscuits, his mouth began to water. 'Chris, you've thought of everything,' he said.

Tunstall grinned.

Foster came in next, swooping on the tea table like a city gull. 'Nice one, lad,' he said. 'Me stomach thinks me throat's been cut.'

Hart arrived with a few folders tucked under her arm. She placed these and a couple of thumb drives side by side, before seeking refreshment. As Rickman called the meeting to order, she raised her coffee mug in toast to Tunstall.

Looking around at his team, Rickman read two things in their faces: disappointment and a low-level anxiety that they weren't working fast enough. Bryony Elliott had been missing for a whole day, and her chances of survival diminished with every hour.

Rickman called on the big Widnesian to give his account first.

Tunstall hurriedly swallowed a mouthful of biscuit and brushed the crumbs from the front of his shirt. 'ID confirmed, sir. Mr Stott said it were definitely Mark Davis he saw razzing it from the scene.'

Rickman Blu-tacked a copy of the photograph of Mark and Jasmine to the whiteboard at the front of the room and wrote their names below. The timeline had lengthened, and a couple more sightings of Mark Davis had been added. He made a note on the board that Davis was identified at the scene just before eleven fifty a.m.

'What about the car?'

'The partial VIN Mr Stott gave us matches the red Ford Focus registered in Davis's name,' Tunstall said. 'I've sent it to Traffic.' He passed Rickman a pink slip and Rickman copied the details onto the whiteboard.

'I've distributed photos of Davis to Traffic and House-to-House,' Hart said.

'We need to know what happened in the hours before Jasmine was found,' Rickman said. 'What about this Kim — Jasmine's friend?'

A collective shaking of heads. 'Sod all,' Foster said.

'Okay, let's come back to that.' Focusing on the failures of the day wouldn't help morale. 'What do we know about Jasmine that we didn't know this morning?'

'She was claiming benefits,' Hart said. 'She went into rehab just after she discovered she was pregnant. After that, she was put under a testing order. She's been having regular blood and urine checks since — seems she was clear every time.'

'Have you spoken to her rehab counsellor?' Rickman asked.

'She was registered with the drug dependence unit in Rodney Street,' Hart said. 'Her counsellor said he's never known anyone more determined to kick the habit — said she didn't want her baby born a junkie. She even refused pethidine at the birth.'

'What about support groups?'

They looked at Hart. 'She told her counsellor she had all the support she needed from a friend.'

'The mysterious Kim, no doubt,' Rickman said, with mounting frustration. 'Is that for me?' He indicated the thumb drive on Hart's table.

'Tech Support has cleaned the video up a bit,' she said, handing him a copy of each. 'And I've sent a few clips to the press office for release to the media — the duty manager wants you to approve them before they go out.'

Rickman took it with a nod of thanks. She wouldn't thank him for pointing it out, but for every line of inquiry most officers could get through in a day, Hart could complete half a dozen more, thinking of the off-beat questions, as well as the obvious ones and following them through quickly and thoroughly.

'And they got this from the reflection in the window.' Hart handed him a printout and Rickman held it up for Foster to get a good look.

'That's Davis all right,' Foster said.

'What about neighbours?' he asked Tunstall. 'Mum with a new baby — she's bound to've made some friends.'

'I talked to the bobbies canvassing door-to-door,' Tunstall said. 'Only the old feller across the road seems to know owt about her. She hadn't been in the house above a few weeks.'

Rickman felt a jolt like two-forty volts of electricity. 'The house,' he said.

Foster looked at him like he'd lost touch with reality. 'What about it?'

'You noticed the "SOLD" sign outside?'

'Yeah. So?'

'Jasmine is — or *was* — an ex-addict, living on benefits. Where did she get the money to buy a house?'

'Not from Mark Davis, that's for certain.' Foster finally caught up with Rickman's train of thought.

'New boyfriend?' Tunstall offered.

Rickman snatched up the nearest phone and dialled the Comms Room. 'DCI Rickman,' he said. 'Who's on duty at the Jasmine Elliott scene?' He listened. 'Patch me through.'

The constable on duty gave his name and number.

'Take a look at the "SOLD" sign in the front garden,' Rickman said. 'What's the name of the estate agent?' He pulled a notepad to him as the constable gave him the name. 'Phone number?' He scribbled a note. 'Thanks.'

He disconnected, then redialled, checking the clock. It was nearly five p.m. The phone rang three, four times. On the fifth ring he was ready to hang up when he heard a woman's voice telling him the office was closed. It sounded too irritated to be a recorded message, and Rickman spoke over her advice to call back tomorrow.

'Detective Chief Inspector Jeff Rickman, Merseyside Police,' he said. 'Who's dealing with the sale of fifteen Olive Close?'

'We're just closing,' she said, sounding offended by his persistence.

'So let's do this quickly and then you can go home.'

She huffed. 'What area?'

'Wavertree.'

'That would be Mr Austin. But he's just out the door . . .'

'Call him back,' Rickman said.

'I can't possibly—'

'Call him back, or we'll have to show up at his house and drag him all the way to the office again — and you *know* what traffic is like this time of night.'

The woman seemed to debate the relative inconvenience of the two options for a moment, then a loud clatter signalled that she had put the receiver down on a desk with more force than was strictly necessary. A few moments later, Mr Austin himself was on the line.

'You want to know about Olive Close?' His voice, only slightly accented, was warm and energetic — a good salesman's voice. 'I sold the property six weeks ago.'

'To Jasmine Elliott,' Rickman said. 'I know. But how did she pay for it? A mortgage? A loan?'

'The name isn't familiar . . .' Austin hesitated. 'May I ask what's this in relation to?'

'Miss Elliott was murdered,' Rickman said, wondering how the hell he could have forgotten his client's name so easily. 'Her baby is missing.'

'Oh, God — I didn't make the connection.' Rickman heard a loud exhalation. 'This isn't good.'

'Murder never is. Who set up the loan?' Rickman asked, trying to keep his impatience in check.

'You don't understand,' Austin said, 'I didn't sell the house to a Jasmine Elliott.'

'Then who did you sell it to? A boyfriend? A landlord?'

But Mr Austin was on his own personal tack and seemed not to have heard the question. 'People are superstitious,' he said, as though Rickman had dumped a whole sackful of black cats on the doorstep of his office. 'They'll see our sign and — I don't suppose . . .' He coughed, covering an embarrassed laugh. 'You, um, couldn't ask one of your lads to take it down, could you?'

'Sure,' Rickman said. Austin totally missed the sarcastic tone and began to thank him. 'I'll bring it round to the office myself, shall I?'

'Now, *look*—' Austin said.

'No. *You* look — I've got a dead girl and a missing baby. Answer the damn question: who did you sell the house to?'

'It wasn't a boyfriend. It was a woman.' Austin grumbled, as though the murder victim was the cause of his present trouble.

Rickman took a breath, but before he could say anything, Austin said, '*Okay* — I'm looking it up . . .' An agonizing pause, then, 'Here it is . . . Kim,' he said. 'Kim Lindermann.'

Rickman could have punched the air. 'I'll need an address.' When he hung up, all three members of his team were staring at him with hungry anticipation.

'I think we've found Kim,' he said.

* * *

A cross-check with the electoral register and DVLA confirmed the address was genuine and current, and Rickman despatched Foster and Hart to interview Kim Lindermann.

'What do we know about her?' Foster asked, flicking the windscreen wiper once to clear a spatter of rain.

Hart sifted through a sheaf of printouts. 'Kim Lindermann, née Vince,' she said. 'Former addict. Convictions for shoplifting, soliciting, possession.' There was a sorry arrest mugshot. Kim looked emaciated, her flesh greyish-white, hair bleached blonde and brittle as spun sugar.

'So what happened?'

She glanced at him, frowning.

'Sefton Park address, Naomi. Not exactly social housing, is it?'

She checked the arrest record. 'Her last conviction was . . . five years ago.'

'She cleaned up her act.'

'In a big way.' Hart read from a printout of a webpage Tunstall had found. 'Kimberley Louise Lindermann, age twenty-eight. She enrolled as a mature student at Liverpool John Moores, got a first in architecture and interior design in — *bloody hell* — just under two years. She worked for Urban Splash for a couple of years, then hooked up with Lars Lindermann.' A bolt of recognition. 'Oh, my god — it's *that* Kim Lindermann.'

'You know her?'

'Know *of* her. Lars Lindermann develops properties, then Kim gives them the KL stamp of style.'

Foster pulled up at a red light and turned to look at her. 'How d'you know all this?'

'I based the interior of my flat on one of her designs. You remember my flat, don't you?' Foster had paid a fleeting visit when they had been allocated at short notice to babysit a witness in a murder case. She'd had to go home to pick up toiletries and a change of clothing, and since Foster drove her, it would have seemed churlish to make him wait outside.

Foster closed his eyes briefly, as if visualising the room. 'View of the Anglican Cathedral. Wood floors, a couple of paintings in red and black, muted red sofas, heaps of cushions — what *do* people do with all them cushions?' He didn't wait for an answer. 'Oh, and a state-of-the-art TV.' He slid her a sly look. 'Do I pass?'

Hart tucked a strand of hair behind her ear. She usually played her 'ice maiden' reputation to her best advantage with Foster, but occasionally he caught her on the back foot with his disconcerting insights. 'You pass.' She was galled to see a smile curl at the corner of his mouth.

'You're not gonna gush all over her, are you?'

'I'll try to restrain myself,' she said.

He acknowledged the comment with the merest twinkle. 'Any family?'

'Two kids, aged three and one.'

'So — nice family, nice house, her own business. She really did get her life back on track, didn't she?'

Hart flipped him a look. 'Good for her, I say.'

Foster turned off Ullet Road into the park. On the perimeter road, traffic was thinner, and the sky opened up under a wide expanse of cropped grass and trees in improbable autumn colour.

Moments later, they were drawing up outside a double-fronted, three-storey house. A border sloped to a beech hedge, which topped a low sandstone wall. Foster gave a whistle. 'She *really* got her life back on track.'

A BMW 8-series and a brand-new Chrysler Pacifica stood in the driveway. Foster stared longingly at them as they walked towards the house. 'Did I say—'

'Back on track,' Hart said. 'Yup.'

'Seriously, though — their transport must be worth more than my mortgage.'

Hart chuckled and started up the steps as the door opened.

Kim Lindermann was dressed in cashmere that looked like it had been commissioned from the catwalk. Her pose was nineteen-fifties *haute couture*: one hand on the doorknob, the other clutching a neat leather briefcase that matched the autumn tones of her coat.

'May I help you?' Her voice was deep, cultured, no hint of Liverpool in the vowel sounds.

Hart made the introductions. Mrs Lindermann watched her coldly as she continued up the steps, warrant card in hand.

The woman's hair, a rich, dark brown, was twisted into a knot at the back of her head, in a style that Hart suspected was calculated to recall the fifties gamine look. It seemed that Mrs Lindermann was a perfectionist in matters of style.

'We'd like to talk to you about Jasmine Elliott,' Hart said.

Something flickered in the woman's eyes. They were green, with darker rims to the irises. 'I'm going to meet a client.' The only sign of nervousness was a quick, practised sweep of her free hand over her hair, checking for loose strands.

'This won't take long.' Hart kept moving, confident that Mrs Lindermann would give way. She did. Hart saw two spots of pink bloom on the woman's face as she walked past her. Mrs Lindermann checked her watch. 'I can spare fifteen minutes,' she said.

She led them down a hallway that smelled of beeswax and fresh paint. A wide staircase dominated the centre of the lobby. It led to a gallery that Hart half-expected would be occupied by a forbidding housekeeper in Victorian costume. But the modern sculptures in steel, and the abstract wall decorations in metal and spun glass, grounded the décor firmly in the twenty-first century.

By the time Hart had taken all of this in, Mrs Lindermann was standing by a doorway to the right of the hall, a look of amusement on her face. She disappeared inside, and as Foster brushed past, he touched the side of his mouth with the tip of his finger. 'Bit of drool, there, Naomi.'

She followed him, scowling at his back.

Mrs Lindermann dropped her briefcase and swept her coat from her shoulders, draping it over a cream linen sofa. She wore a copper-red sweater over trousers carefully chosen to match the russets and browns of her overcoat.

'What's so urgent that it can't wait until the morning?' The fastidious diction, the way in which she hardened the 'c' and 't' phonemes suggested elocution lessons — a voice coach, maybe. She stood with one hand on the corner of the sofa, a defensive posture that she contrived to look patrician. She waved them to a seat, but neither Hart nor Foster accepted the invitation — the woman already had an advantage over them.

'You purchased a house recently,' Hart said.

Mrs Lindermann arched one carefully shaped eyebrow. 'I trust the paperwork is in order?'

Hart looked at Foster. *She doesn't know.* 'Have you been letting the property?'

'No.' Hart waited for more, and she sighed impatiently. 'I signed over the deeds of title.'

'To Jasmine Elliott?'

'Yes.'

'Very generous,' Foster said. Normally, an attractive woman like Mrs Lindermann would be treated to the Foster charm, but he didn't even try the famous smile on her.

She seemed to consider the impertinence of his comment, then gave a small shrug. 'Returning a favour.'

'What sort of favour?'

She replied with careful, precise articulation: 'I don't think that's any of your business.'

'I'm afraid it is, Mrs Lindermann,' Hart said.

Kim Lindermann's eyes narrowed in annoyance, then, as realisation dawned, they widened. 'Is Jasmine all right?'

'Perhaps you should sit down,' Hart said.

'Tell me,' she said, 'for pity's sake!' Her hand gripped the sofa, as though she might fall.

Hart glanced at Foster and he gave the slightest nod. 'Jasmine is dead,' she said.

'How?' The woman's voice a horrified whisper.

'She was murdered.'

'Oh, God.' Mrs Lindermann clutched her stomach as though from a physical blow. 'Bryony?' She looked from one to the other. 'What about the baby?'

'The baby is missing.'

She sagged a little more, then with a monumental effort she straightened up, lengthening her body, holding her head erect. She looked past them, as though focusing on something in the near distance. 'Mark Davis,' she said.

Hart avoided Foster's gaze. 'What about him?' she asked.

'That bastard's been trying to drag Jasmine down with him ever since they met.' Mrs Lindermann looked into Hart's face. 'It was him, wasn't it?'

'What makes you think that?' Hart said, keeping her tone neutral.

'A lot of addicts I've known have a drug of choice — booze, coke, heroin, cannabis. Mark isn't choosy, as long as it gets him high. Jasmine thought he was using speed and crystal meth as uppers, when he needed to stay alert.' When she saw that this meant nothing to them, she said, 'I got screwed up on meth a couple of times. If a baby stares at you from its pram — you think it's a government agent, trying to read your mind.'

Foster shifted uncomfortably.

'Jasmine was still seeing Davis?' Hart asked.

'She kicked him out. But he wouldn't let her be.' Mrs Lindermann's eyes glittered hard and cold. 'Bastard . . .' She trembled from head to foot and Hart stepped quickly over, but Kim Lindermann turned on her, flinging her supporting hand away.

'Get the *hell* away from me.' The clipped tones slipped and her voice rose to a scream. 'What use are you now? What use are you to *anyone*?'

Then she was crying, wiping tears from her face and sobbing in great, wrenching gulps. She turned from them and stumbled to the window, while Hart looked helplessly at Foster.

'Mrs Lindermann?' The voice was tentative, young. Hart and Foster turned to the girl at the door. 'I heard shouting. Is everything all right?' She looked anxiously at Hart, warily at Foster.

Kim Lindermann stiffened. 'It's fine, Vicky,' she said, her back to the room. 'Please, go and see to the children.'

The door closed softly as Vicky retreated. Mrs Lindermann remained at the window, hugging herself tightly and taking juddering breaths until the tears subsided.

When she was calm, Hart said, 'I'm so sorry, Mrs Lindermann. We had no idea . . .'

'Jasmine saved my life,' Mrs Lindermann said, her voice muffled with tears. 'Five years ago. Sounds dramatic, doesn't it? But I'm not exaggerating. I'd taken an overdose. It wasn't accidental.' She seemed to think about that for a short while.

'Jasmine wasn't supposed to find me, but when I didn't show up outside her school at the usual time, she came looking. She' — a sigh broke the flow of her words — 'She called an ambulance, performed CPR until they arrived. When I was well enough, she made me go to counselling.' She gave a teary laugh. 'Imagine, a twelve-year-old girl — I was almost twice her age — *I* was supposed to be the responsible one, but she sorted me out.' She looked at them, fondness and bewilderment on her face, asking them to understand the remarkable child who had saved her.

'So, you returned the favour,' Foster said. 'Bought her a house, gave her a chance to make a new start.'

Mrs Lindermann looked around her as if realising for the first time how much more Jasmine had given her than her life. Then she nodded, turning to look out of the window onto the park. 'When I first knew her, Jasmine was wild, but not heavily into drugs. Then she met Mark.' Her voice hardened. 'It was Mark who got Jasmine on crack. She cleaned up when she discovered she was pregnant — swore she wouldn't put her baby through withdrawal. And she did it — she got free of it.' There was pride in her tone. 'But Davis kept coming after her.'

'We know this is painful for you, but we need to find Bryony,' Hart said.

Mrs Lindermann turned, her eyes shimmering, mascara streaked down her face. 'What can I do?' She sounded close to despair.

'Is there anywhere Davis would go? Anyone he would go to?'

'I didn't really know him — didn't *want* to know him.' Mrs Lindermann's eyes darted from Hart to Foster, as if searching for something. '*Oh* . . .'

She took a couple of steps towards them and Hart leaned forward on the balls of her feet, willing Mrs Lindermann to remember.

'The children's home — Jasmine said he was always talking about his house parents. He might have—' She broke off, seeing the disappointment in their faces. 'But you've already spoken to them.'

'They haven't heard from him,' Hart said, sick with regret.

'Then I don't *know*.' Her voice rose in panic. 'I don't know *where* he'd go.'

'It's all right.' Hart laid a calming hand on the woman's shoulder, and this time she didn't resist. 'We have officers out, talking to his former associates,' she explained, wishing they had more: more personnel, more information, more time.

Kim Lindermann took a deep breath, made an effort to regain control. 'Yes,' she said. 'They would know.' She searched Hart's face, looking for an answer Hart didn't have. 'Even a man like Maitland would help, wouldn't he? To protect a baby?'

Hart gave Foster a quick look. 'Maitland?' she said.

'Rob Maitland. Mark works for him.' Mrs Lindermann blinked. 'I thought you knew.'

This was a breakthrough. 'Jasmine told you?' Hart asked. She nodded.

'You know Maitland?' Foster asked.

'What makes you think—' Mrs Lindermann frowned, offended by the question.

'Just the way you said, "Rob Maitland", like you know him.'

She sighed, responding to the accusation in Foster's tone. She went to one of the alcoves and plucked a couple of tissues from a box before answering. 'I was a different person back then.'

'We're not judging you,' Hart said, thankful that Foster maintained a tactful silence.

Mrs Lindermann nodded. 'There is no such thing as dignity in addiction,' she said. 'I funded my habit in ways I'm not proud of.' She wiped the mascara from under her eyes.

'Maitland?' Hart asked.

'Why are you asking me this?' she said. 'It's irrelevant. It's history.' Her voice rose in agitation. 'This isn't about *me* — it's not about what might or might not have happened five years ago. *Please*. Find Bryony — find her safe.'

'We will,' Hart said, then, because there were no absolute certainties — not in this line of work — 'We'll try.'

'It'd help us if we knew something about Jasmine's movements before she was found.' Hart was grateful that Foster had softened his tone.

'I spoke to her at ten o'clock last night. She was—' Mrs Lindermann broke off. 'Stupid . . . I was going to say she was fine.'

'No,' Hart said. 'It's good to have that kind of detail. She didn't seem anxious or distressed?'

'She'd just finished decorating the sitting room — wanted me to help her pick out some cheap prints for the walls.' Tears spilled unchecked down Mrs Lindermann's face. 'She seemed really happy.'

Hart handed her a fresh tissue and she took it with a grateful nod. 'I was wondering . . .' She hesitated, and Mrs Lindermann looked at her in question.

'I'm sorry to have to ask you this,' Hart spread her hands, knowing that this would hurt no matter how she said it. 'We've identified Jasmine by her fingerprints, but it's preferable — I mean we think it's best — if someone formally identifies her. Someone who knew her.' *Someone who cared about her*, she might have added.

Mrs Lindermann blanched. 'Oh, God.' Then she took a breath, steadying herself, and said, 'Of course. Do you want me to come now?' She looked around, as though mentally gathering her coat and her briefcase, preparing herself for the ordeal.

'It's all right,' Hart said, painfully aware that the pathologist would not want a grieving friend at the mortuary spoiling his scientific objectivity prior to post-mortem, and anyway, nobody would be allowed near the body until all possible evidence had been gathered from it. 'We'll let you know when,' she said.

CHAPTER 11

The drugs team was winding down for the night. DS Cass was there, together with a few of the hangers-on who hoped that proximity to him would give them the same air of swaggering insolence. A night shift of three sat at their desks, working their way through paperwork and polystyrene cartons of food. The air was thick with the smells of Chinese takeaways and McDonald's burgers.

Conversation all but stopped as Hart walked in. Amused, she said, 'Did I take a wrong turn — wander into a Sergio Leone Western?'

'Don't know who he is, but you must be lost, love.' Cass was sitting with his back to her, a biscuit in his hand and his feet on his desk. His jacket was carefully draped over the back of his chair.

Did Cass really call me 'love'?

Someone gave an embarrassed cough and came forward. Hart recognised the compact, square-built figure of Detective Inspector Larry Dwight. 'Eight a.m. then, lads.' He tried to make it sound like an instruction, but his tone was too apologetic.

Cass couldn't resist the opportunity to ridicule his senior officer in front of a woman, and he called out, 'Don't be late!'

Dwight laughed weakly, his hand going to his hair. It had a toped appearance — the sandy curls tightly coiled and carefully clipped as though they had been trimmed all over with a pair of shears. He scuttled through the door, avoiding eye contact.

Cass shook his head. 'Our leader.' He smiled, trying to coerce Hart into unpleasant laughter. When she didn't oblige, he said, 'So what're you doing so far from home, Naomi?'

'She's looking for a kettle, Sarge.' More laughter.

'A name has come up,' she said. 'Rob Maitland. I wondered if any of you had any insights.'

'Rob Maitland. Hmm . . .' He fixed her with his flat, grey eyes. Cass evidently hadn't forgotten her rebuff. 'See that computer? You've probably got one just like it on your desk — type in a name, it'll give you the lowdown on any lowlife you're interested in.'

There were a couple of muffled laughs, unpleasant, like kids during a classroom spat, as if they half-expected blood to be spilt. Hart said, 'I thought it might save some time — we're trying to find a missing baby.'

The reminder had a sobering effect on the team. Even Cass was stung, but she wouldn't get their cooperation by alienating them further. She forced a smile, putting enough archness in her tone to make them laugh with her instead of at her. 'And I heard you boys had digestive biscuits going begging.'

Cass laughed along with the rest, even waggled a finger at her as he offered her the packet. Then he placed the remains of his biscuit on the desk in front of him, brushed crumbs from his fingers and actually got to his feet. 'What d'you want to know about Rob Maitland?' he asked.

She nibbled on her biscuit. 'What can you tell me?'

'Major player on the drugs scene. Involved in last night's deal.'

'Was he there?'

Cass smoothed his tie, dislodging a few errant crumbs. 'We believe so.'

'We're getting info about a Mark Davis,' Hart said. 'Informant says he works for Maitland.'

Cass shrugged. 'Pond life. On his way out — even before the raid went down.' He pinched one nostril and sniffed, wiping his nose with the back of his hand in a gesture characteristic of coke addicts. 'Took his work home with him once too often.'

'Is he violent?'

'I never really thought about it — like I said, he's pond life. Bottom feeder.'

'We need to locate him,' Hart said.

Cass spread his hands. 'Wish I could help.'

'Did Mark have any special friends he might go to?'

'I had my sights set much higher, Naomi.' He seemed irritated by her persistence.

'Any chance I could have a word with Maitland?'

'You'd have to speak to his secretary, love. We had to kick him.' It seemed Cass had exhausted his reserves of professional courtesy.

'You let him go?' She had seen Maitland brought in for questioning only a few hours ago. If they had been forced to cut him loose so soon, he must have a rock-solid alibi.

'What can I tell you? Shit happens.'

Hart's head reeled. Maitland looked likely to get away with one of the biggest drugs deals in the history of the city.

'We got the bulk of the drugs and the money, so I reckon we're about even.' Cass picked up his biscuit and began munching again.

Hart stared at him, thinking about the stolen bags and the fact that Maitland, having lost several millions in the debacle, would now only be hungrier and more dangerous.

* * *

The press of bodies in Rickman's newly acquired Major Incident Room was a welcome sight. 'Hello,' Hart said. One of the new faces glanced up and waved. She was wearing a headset and taking notes. Hart's eye lighted on the tea table. There was no sign of the kettle.

Tunstall came in, his tie loosened and a set of document wallets under his arm. 'What's with the sudden influx of personnel?' Hart asked.

'Civilian staff and PCs.' Tunstall grinned. 'The boss must've put a rocket under someone.'

Hart suspected that DCI Rickman's imminent TV news interview was the rocket and the chief superintendent the 'someone' Tunstall referred to. The drugs raid had depleted resources alarmingly: half the force seemed to have been involved in some capacity the previous night, and those who weren't enjoying a well-earned off-duty were answering questions about the way the raid had been botched. She thought it impolitic to comment, however, and quietly finished her half biscuit instead.

A TV had been set up in the corner of the room, and *North West Newsbrief* was showing. 'When's he on?' Hart asked.

'Just missed him,' Tunstall said. 'They showed a bit of the video clip. Already had a few calls in. Got a few names out of the house parents, an' all.' He handed Hart one of the folders and picked up his coffee mug. 'Couple of pals of Mark Davis. Seems he didn't have many friends at Black Wood. I've checked home addresses and printed off everything we've got on them.'

'Arrest records?' Hart asked.

'No. T'other end of system.' Distracted by something, Tunstall's gaze flitted from the tea table to the clutter of desks around the room. 'Where's the—' He did a 360-degree turn. 'What's happened to t'kettle?'

One of the telephonists tilted her headset microphone away from her mouth. 'Health and Safety rep was in,' she told them. 'Something wrong with the wiring, he said.'

'There's nowt wrong with that kettle,' Tunstall said, hotly. 'It's had engineer's clearance not six weeks since. What's this beggar look like?'

She looked at him blankly. 'Sorry, Chris. I was taking a call.'

'Some light-fingered merchant from Cass's crew, I'll bet.' He peeled off his jacket and flung it, one sleeve the wrong side out, onto his chair, then blundered through the door, almost barging into Foster.

'What's up with him?' Foster asked, neatly sidestepping the big man.

'He's gone on a quest for a kettle.' Hart indicated its absence with a lift of her chin.

Foster glanced in the direction of the tea table and rolled his eyes. 'Nice to see him with a goal in life.'

'He's really miffed, Sarge.'

'I'll try not to upset him.' He took in the new staff, making eye contact where possible. A few of the women smiled, and he beamed back. His dark brown hair was artfully ruffled and gelled, and he had the glowing look of a man who had just blown in from a bracing walk — they fell for it every time, despite Foster's reputation as a notorious commitment-phobe. Perhaps that was it — the thrill of a challenge, reforming the womaniser. She wished them luck.

'So,' he said, oblivious of her scrutiny. 'What's new?'

Hart held on to the folder for the moment. 'D'you know anything about Rob Maitland?' she asked.

'I know the history — but if you're asking about Operation Snowplough, that's on a need-to-know basis.'

'The history, then,' she said.

'You're thinking about what Kim Lindermann said?'

She nodded.

'Okay, for what it's worth, when he started out, Maitland's firm was mostly into armed robbery. Then we got ourselves organised, set up Armed Response Units and started shooting back,' he said. 'Which is when Maitland switched to drugs in a big way.'

'How come Snowplough can't pin anything on him?'

'He's careful not to handle the goods. And he's invested a lot in the last five years in legit businesses. He even got an MBA through the Open University—'

'And found Business,' Hart finished for him. 'Like some people find God.' A small frown creased her brow. 'Seems he broke his own rule on handling the goods last night, though — if he really was there, I mean.'

Foster checked that the telephone operators were busy, then drew Hart a little further from them. 'They got nothing on record, but their intelligence said he would be there to check the merchandise personally. And you didn't get that from me.'

She nodded again. Foster's in-house intelligence network, from her understanding of it, brought a whole new meaning to undercover investigation. 'Think we need to talk to Maitland?'

'What d'you think?'

'Cass reckons Mark was on the way out,' she said, reluctant to admit it, but DCI Rickman's advice to prioritise was still ringing in her ears. 'Maitland doesn't trust him anymore.'

'There you are, then. We're tied up enough as it is. But if it makes you feel any better, we'll talk to the boss man when we've cleared up a few other lines of inquiry. How's that?'

In answer, she passed him the folder Tunstall had given her. The Shepherds came up with a couple of names,' she said. 'Pals of Mark Davis.'

'Kate Nolan . . .' he said, skimming the contents. 'Rings a bell. But I don't remember the other one. Worth having a chat, anyway.' He slapped the folder against the side of his leg, impatient to be gone. 'What're we waiting for?'

'Don't you want to see if we get something useful from the hotline?' Hart asked.

'The temptation to stay has got much stronger since certain new arrivals . . .' A few of the female telephonists looked up and he flashed them the smile. A couple of the more susceptible smiled back. 'But if I have to sit here waiting for the phone to ring, I'll start chewing the skirting boards,' Foster said. This time his smile was genuine, more intimate, and Hart realised that revisiting his childhood landscape wasn't proving easy for Lee Foster. A look passed between them, a moment of understanding, and she tried to frame the words that would shape and solidify her thoughts.

'Bold as bloody brass!' Tunstall shattered the moment, bursting through the door, furious but triumphant, kettle in hand. 'Sat right in middle of room it was.'

Hart raised an eyebrow. 'You're sure it's our kettle?'

''Course I'm bloody sure.' He pronounced it shoo-er, and to prove his point, he tipped it upside down, spilling the last drops of water onto the carpet tiles.

'"C. Tunstall" — look.' His name had been inked in indelible marker on the base of the kettle.

'And they just let you take it?'

'Who's gonna stop me?' Gazing up at six foot four of towering indignation, Hart saw his point. 'Thieving bloody sods,' he finished.

That made three 'bloodies' in less than a minute. Tunstall really *was* miffed. Then, as if to prove her wrong, he beamed at them. 'Now, who's for a brew?' he said.

CHAPTER 12

Thirty minutes later, Hart and Foster were seated in the kitchen of a well-kept Edwardian terrace off Aigburth Road.

Kate Nolan greeted them with caution at first. But as she handed back Foster's his warrant card, she seemed to take in every feature, then reappraise, with light dancing in her eyes. She was in her early twenties, a brunette with a good figure and a direct manner. Foster felt her eyes stray to him again and again as she busied herself about her kitchen.

'So,' she said, setting coffee and biscuits in front of them, 'What d'you want to know about Mark Davis?'

'Have you heard from him recently?' Hart asked.

'We stayed in touch for about a year after we left care.'

There was something in her tone that made Foster ask, 'What happened?'

She wrinkled her nose. 'He was mixing with a bad crowd.'

'Bad crowd?'

'Drugs, thieving.'

'Did you know Mark well?' Hart asked.

She laughed. 'Well, *yeah* — we were there for *ever*, me and him.'

A flicker of doubt crossed Foster's mind — why couldn't he place her?

Kate gave him a shrewd look. 'You don't remember me, do you?'

He smiled, low wattage — this was a professional call. 'I don't usually forget a pretty face.'

Kate looked across at Hart, her eyes sparkling with amusement. 'Hasn't changed, has he?'

'I wouldn't know,' Hart said, with admirable diplomacy.

'I had the *biggest* crush on you, Lee Foster,' Kate said.

'I'm sorry, Kate . . .' Foster was completely at a loss.

'I was the one with the dyed black hair and the eyebrow piercings.'

Foster laughed. 'Goth Kate! *You've* certainly changed a bit, haven't you, girl?'

She smiled. 'People do.' She sat with them, sipping thoughtfully at her coffee for a few moments. 'But for Mark to do this . . .'

'We don't know that he did,' Foster said, still feeling an obligation to defend his former charge.

'He's got the baby, hasn't he?' she said, glancing at the empty high chair next to the kitchen table. She looked quickly away, as if thinking about her own child in association with the awful events of the day might jinx her.

'You think Mark's capable of murder?' Foster asked, wondering if he had missed some grotesque deformation of Mark's character.

She grimaced. 'You knew him. He was gormless, soft . . .' She took another sip from her cup, and he felt that she wanted to say more.

'But?' He had thought about this till the twists and turns of 'did he, didn't he?' made him dizzy: Kate was right — the boy Foster had known was inoffensive — even ineffectual. But Mark on drugs was another thing altogether. He had seen what drugs did to people — the way it brought the buried ugliness of their nature to the surface.

'There was a side to him,' Kate said. 'You know what we called him?'

Foster tilted his head in question.

'Dark Mavis.' Foster frowned and she added, 'Mark Davis — Dark Mavis. 'Cos of his black moods.' She nibbled her biscuit. 'Childish stuff.' She gave an apologetic shrug. 'Not much help to you.'

Foster smiled encouragement. 'It all helps to build a clearer picture,' he said.

'He caught a bird once,' she went on, so caught up in her reverie it seemed she didn't hear him. 'Must've fallen out of its nest, just a little chick it was. He prodded and poked it with a stick till it just died of fright.'

Foster felt a chill. How had he missed this?

She shrugged again. 'At the time, I thought he was a nasty little sod who needed a good slap. But I think maybe it was payback, you know?'

Foster thought he did, but he left a silence for her to fill.

'For all the times he'd had to put up with what people did to him,' she explained. 'Mark hated being pushed around — by his stepdad, by the bigger lads, by the system. Back then, he just wasn't strong enough or brave enough to do anything about it.'

* * *

Foster caught Hart's look as they headed back to the car. 'Don't say it.'

'Say what?' Hart flicked the key fob and the car alarm chirruped.

'"I told you so."'

'I wasn't about to.'

'Come off it, Naomi. You think Jasmine's murder was payback because she kicked Mark out.' Foster slid into the passenger seat, beside her.

Hart turned to him, her hand poised to slot the key in the steering lock. 'I'm not trying to score points, Sarge,' she said, a look of mild surprise on her face. 'I just think we should keep an open mind.'

Foster rubbed a hand over his face. 'I know, Naomi, I know.'

But if Mark *was* a killer, he couldn't help feeling responsible for not seeing it in the boy's character when he mentored the lad — and for not staying around to support him after he left care.

Hart frowned. 'It's not your fault,' she said. 'Jasmine's death had nothing to do with what you did or didn't do four years ago.'

She always had been able to see through him — but Foster wasn't about to admit to that. 'You've got a lot of talents, Naomi, but mind reading isn't one of them,' he said. 'I was actually wondering whether you were gonna start the car — we've got people to interview.'

Her frown deepened and she withdrew her gaze, started the engine and pulled away without another word.

He leaned back and closed his eyes. *God, you're a tithead, Foster. She's just trying to be a friend.* But this was too close to home for him. Too *raw*. He had always as fought insecurity with banter, covered emotional frailty with aggression — he didn't know another way.

CHAPTER 13

Mark Davis drives to an out-of-town retail development near John Lennon Airport. He parks next to an empty unit, away from the furniture outlets and clothing stores, beyond the interest of security guards and too far for average shoppers to park and walk.

He can't stop shivering. He turns the car heater to max, but the cold, his wet clothing and blind, gut-churning fear has set his body jerking and his teeth a-chatter. He hugs himself, rubbing at the gooseflesh on his arms till it raises in welts, but the craving has him by the throat and refuses to let go. He succumbs. Just a fingernail of serenity — hardly what you'd call a fix — heated on a square of foil.

Cocooned by the heroin, the baby's cries seem distant, the threat of danger remote. He feels no pain. Every nerve ending feels caressed and soothed and he feels *so warm* . . .

'Okay, let's do it.' His words are slurred by the opiate fumes. It takes fifty minutes more before he rouses himself to attend to his baby's needs.

He changes her, dumping the wipes and the dirty nappy out of sight under the car. Now she's content, cradled in the crook of his arm, sucking on the teat of the bottle he bought from the chemist. With each strong pull on the teat, he feels a tug of response in his chest.

Bryony stares at him with her mother's eyes and makes soft sounds, like a gentle throat-clearing. Sounds of quiet contentment. He realises, not as a blinding revelation, but in the seconds and minutes that pass, in the wordless trust in his baby's eyes, that this is what his whole life has been about. This one perfect moment.

Jasmine had never let him hold Bryony. He'd gone to the hospital to try and reason with her. Had gazed for an hour at the two of them — jealous, almost, of the bond between them. But also in awe of it. Now he understands why Jasmine wouldn't trust something so precious to anyone else. She had sent him away, told him, 'Get yourself straight, then we'll see.'

We'll see, like she was talking to a kid. He had been forced instead to snatch glimpses of them going to or from clinic, to watch through the window of her house, seeing only momentary flashes of Bryony when Jasmine walked past a window with the baby in her arms.

The baby senses his tension and squirms, forcing her tongue against the teat and spitting it out. She makes a few experimental cries, and the moment of crystal perfection is shattered.

CHAPTER 14

To a casual observer, Rob Maitland looked every inch the businessman he aspired to be. Clothes hung well on him, and he went for top of the range: Gucci for day-to-day, Paul Smith if he thought he might run into photographers. Today, he was in a dark grey, three-button Paul Smith.

He gathered the tattered remnants of his army in the conference room of his offices in Old Hall Street. A glass wall looked out over the docks. A passing shower had left a spattering of rain on the window wall, but the sky was now clear, an electric blue that dazzled off the glinting water of the River Mersey.

'What happened?' he asked. The small gathering looked at each other anxiously. Maitland doubted that half of them even ate their meals at a table — his insistence that the meeting take place around the twenty-foot cherrywood boardroom table was calculated to unnerve. It had the desired effect.

A casual observer might be fooled by Maitland's surface gleam of respectability: the suits, the careful — if heavily Liverpudlian-accented — enunciation of his words, his courteous manner, particularly with women. But when you got closer to the man, spent some time in his company, you learned that the air around him crackled with menace.

In childhood, he had watched others, and made the discovery that smiles and charm were the way to make adults do what he wanted them to. He hadn't resented it: they held the power, and Maitland had always respected power. His peers were another matter. Mostly, it was enough just to let his eyes go dead and the kid whose sweets he coveted, or football he wanted, or who occupied the seat he favoured, would give them up like the capitulation was a privilege, like it was something they'd had in mind all along. While other bullies had threatened and blustered, Maitland made an unequivocal statement of intent. While the kids who'd used their fists to beat back their own fear and humiliation flailed and wrestled and gouged, Rob — he was never Robbie — had meted out punishment with a cool head and no mercy. For Maitland, fighting wasn't about fear or anger. It was about power — its acquisition and the exercise of it.

There were no gaps, no empty places around the table, despite the arrests of the previous night, because Maitland always had men in reserve, and the whole gene pool of Liverpool's underworld aspired to work for Big Rob Maitland. He settled his gaze on each of his men and, without speaking a word, let them know that they were replaceable, like the scores of hired thugs who had served, protected, collected, sold, beaten and murdered on his orders.

Graham was the exception. Graham he trusted.

He kept his eyes on the rest until the sweat popped out on their foreheads. 'I'll tell you what happened.' His voice was low and dangerously calm. 'Someone grassed.'

Three of them paled, a couple flushed with anger. Maitland didn't trust anger — anger was a good cover for guilt. But he didn't trust fear either. Fear brought out the survival instinct, even in foot soldiers like this ragbag. It would take more than an accusation to get at the truth. That would come later. For now, what he needed was a show of strength.

He turned to Graham. Graham had been with him since before their first armed robbery — for so long, that even Maitland couldn't remember if Graham was his given name or his surname. He was an inch or two taller than Maitland, built like a bouncer. Solid, in both appearance and personality. He was loyal, not so bright that he might consider himself a contender, but with enough street smarts to find a way around a problem when strength and firepower weren't an option. It was Graham who had got him out of that awful bloody mess the previous night.

'What's the word on the Dutch?' Maitland asked.

'Bakker is dead,' Graham said.

The Dutch boss. 'Takes the sting out of his threat to kill me, doesn't it?' Maitland said.

Graham responded with a smile.

'What about the rest?'

'They're being fast-tracked for extradition.'

'So who's responsible for the machete attack on the crack house in Lytham Street?'

'Birkenhead scals, boss. Must've heard you got arrested, thought they could grab a bit of territory this side of the river.'

'Send them a message,' Maitland said. 'Liverpool is *my* territory.'

Tommy Eames winced. Tommy the Tank liked to think of himself as legit. A businessman in the true sense of the word. He ran Maitland's coffee shops, but they owed far more to coca leaf than coffee beans. Maitland let Tommy live his fantasy, fronting the respectable face of his empire — Maitland understood the lies people told themselves to get through the day. So long as Tommy kept the machinery oiled and his business interests successful, he would have indulged the Tank in a belief in Father Christmas. Today, though, was about Maitland's reality, where scumbags grassed to the police and ran off with his money and stole his drugs, where no-marks from Birkenhead thought they were in with a chance to steal his turf.

'Hit them hard,' he said. 'Break some bones. Make sure they know who gave the order.'

'We'll need to recruit more men,' Graham said.

'Do whatever it takes.'

Graham nodded and Maitland raised a finger in caution. 'No Chinese. No Serbians, no Russians.' Maitland knew better than to put himself in hock to the Chinese: where he ran a family firm, they had entire dynasties. As for the Eastern Europeans — he'd learned from bitter experience that you just can't control the Serbian or Russian mafia.

The phone rang and Maitland answered. Anyone watching would not have discerned a change in his facial expression, even though his voice altered, conveying a warmth he was incapable of feeling.

'Mr Hartley,' he said. 'Good to hear from you.'

Hartley cleared his throat. 'Mr Maitland. I wasn't sure if I'd be able to, um, reach you.'

So, it isn't only the Birkenhead mob who've heard about my arrest.

'Always available to you, Mr Hartley,' Maitland said, smoothly. He wasn't surprised, and he wasn't at all embarrassed by his prospective business partner's knowledge of his criminal background. Hartley must have known about it before he entered into negotiations — he'd be a fool not to.

'I know this is a . . . troubling time for you,' Hartley said. 'But my company will need your audited accounts by Monday at the latest.'

Maitland felt a twinge of something — he found emotions harder to identify in himself than in others. 'No problem.' *Just get off the frigging line so I can get on with what needs to be done.*

Hartley gave another strangulated cough, and Maitland thought, *You're so lucky you aren't in the room.*

'If you could convey our concerns to your accountant . . .'

'He's right here.' Maitland scanned the faces around the table. Bernie Carter stood out by virtue of his very ordinariness. Carter was suited, like the rest, but unlike the rest, he didn't look strangled by his tie, and his face was soft, his expression benign and intelligent behind his rimless spectacles.

'Mr Hartley's worried about the accounts,' Maitland said.

'All in hand, Rob.' Carter was one of a select few allowed to address Maitland by his first name. It was an acknowledgement from Maitland of his respect. Out of earshot, Maitland's men were apt to torment Bernie, and the occasional reinforcement of his position prevented disrespect from sliding into an unproductive contempt for the man who kept Maitland's books straight.

Carter had been sweating over the accounts for a month — bringing them up to date, balancing the numbers, getting creative as only he could. Mark Davis had fucked up his careful calculations, but still Carter was sanguine.

'You go to your business meetings, Rob,' he had said. 'Do the networking, impress the investors — it's what you're good at. Let me take care of the money. I'll massage a few figures, reassess the value of your property assets — I think I can come up with a couple of million more.'

Maitland had laughed. He remembered seeing the hurt on Carter's face, the dark flush of humiliation. There were others present, and they'd exchanged looks, gauging if it was safe to laugh along with the boss. Carter was sensitive to that.

'Don't take it badly, Bernie,' Maitland had said. 'I was just thinking what a bloody miracle-worker you are. If I could make real money as easy as you make the virtual stuff appear and disappear, I'd ditch the criminal lifestyle, become an accountant myself.'

Carter had smiled, gratified, and the men, confused, had settled back. The boss had *apologised* to Bernie the Books. Carter, for reasons they would never fully comprehend, was protected.

Maitland spoke into the phone. 'You'll have your report in plenty of time, Mr Hartley.'

He broke the connection and for a few seconds he concentrated on breathing. 'I want Davis. I want him hurt — and I want him here.'

CHAPTER 15

A soft murmur of voices filled the murder inquiry Incident Room. Civilian staff wearing head mikes fielded calls, took details from possible witnesses and passed on information about possible sightings of Mark Davis.

The only one they'd had confirmed had been within half a mile of Jasmine's house: a red Ford Focus had almost run a woman down at a crossing on Picton Road.

Foster and Hart sat at adjacent desks, sifting through message slips, searching for something that looked better than wishful thinking, over-excitement or plain hysteria.

'Anything?' Hart asked.

'How'm I supposed to tell? Look at this,' Foster said, slapping another pink slip onto a growing pile. 'Everyone wants to be the hero.'

Hart shrugged. 'When a child goes missing, everyone feels it. You must remember one instance as a child when you turned around and found you were all alone.' She realised the tactlessness of her remark and looked quickly into Foster's face. But it seemed he did not make the connection between this and his abandonment as a child.

'Well, I don't see why they have to relive their childhood traumas at our expense,' he muttered.

'They want to bring Bryony home safe,' Hart said, with gentle reproof. This was getting to him more than he cared to admit. She thought about broaching the subject again, but after his earlier rebuff, decided against it.

Foster seemed to sense her hesitation and turned to look at her. 'What?'

'Nothing.'

'If you've got something to say, Naomi, just say it.'

She raised one shoulder and let it drop. 'I just . . .' *This is a really bad idea.* 'I understand why it would bug you,' she said.

He turned to the papers on his desk. 'I never said it was bugging me.'

'You didn't need to.'

Foster didn't reply. She felt his suppressed anger like the silence before a thunderclap.

A Calls and Response operator came over with another bundle of slips, and Foster smiled — an automatic response to an attractive woman. Hart saw him do a double take and turn the wattage up a notch. This one was *very* attractive.

'Thanks . . .' The slight raise of the eyebrows was an invitation, and a question.

'Sally,' she said, with a slow smile.

'Youse lot are doing a hell of a job,' he said, taking the papers from her. 'Do they give you time off for good behaviour?'

'We get time off,' she said. 'How we behave is up to us.'

'Fancy misbehavin' with me?'

And that was it — armour-plate reinstated, Jack-the-lad Foster was back to his usual form.

Hart sighed inwardly and was about to return to work, when Rickman rounded the corner in a hurry, shrugging on his jacket, mobile phone in hand.

Foster switched from flirt to work mode. 'Everything okay, boss?'

'I'm late for the post-mortem.' Rickman's hair was tousled and his left lapel turned inside out. Hart had to quell an impulse to straighten it. 'Anything doing?' he asked.

'Sightings all over,' Foster said. 'Nothing recent.'

'He must have found a bolthole,' Hart said.

'He's run off with a six-week-old baby — he can't have just vanished.' Rickman's finger went to the scar over his right eyebrow. 'Lee — you checked out Jasmine's kitchen when we searched for the baby?'

Foster nodded.

'Was there any blood?'

Foster shook his head. 'It was clean.'

'And there were baby's bottles in the fridge?'

'Yeah.'

Hart forgot Foster's ill-humour and her own frustration with their lack of progress. 'He'll need food for the baby,' she said, her excitement rising. 'Nappies, maybe.'

Rickman nodded.

'I'll put out a message to Foot Patrols.' Her tiredness was gone, washed away by a fresh rush of adrenaline.

'Ask them to check out all-night chemists,' Rickman said. 'And eight-till-late grocers.'

'What about supermarkets?' Foster asked.

'He'd probably avoid anywhere with security staff — but better alert them, just in case.' Rickman checked his watch again, noticed the awkward fit of his jacket and straightened his tangled lapel.

'Go,' Foster said. 'We'll stay in touch.'

'Thanks,' Rickman said. 'I'll be back later.'

'Who's the pathologist?' Foster asked.

'Owen Griffith.'

Foster snorted. 'You'll be lucky to get out by midnight, boss.'

Rickman nodded. 'You're probably right. I'll keep my phone on, so if anything—'

'We'll let you know,' Foster said.

CHAPTER 16

Strains of Mozart's *Concerto for Oboe and Clarinet* drifted from the post-mortem room as Rickman changed into surgical scrubs and hurriedly slipped into standard-issue overshoes.

A forensic photographer hovered in the background, gowned up and quivering like a gundog on point. There were others in the room: a woman CSI Rickman recognised from the crime scene, and two mortuary technicians. One would take contemporaneous notes, while the other handed instruments to the pathologist, bottled specimens for transfer to the path lab, weighed and set aside organs — ready for replacement in the body or for further biopsy. Rickman continued his scan of the room and met the steady gaze of Crime Scene Coordinator Tony Mayle. That Mayle was present at all was a mark of respect for Jasmine against the outrage perpetrated upon her. As CSC, and one of the most senior CSIs on the Liverpool force, Mayle would be coordinating several cases at once, and this post-mortem might take hours.

Rickman nodded, and Mayle glanced briefly at the body and back at Rickman. Mayle had been a cop for sixteen years and had specialised in crime scene investigation for ten more. That look confirmed that even in the world Mayle inhabited, sampling and recording the intimate traces of violence and violations, this one was hard to take.

Jasmine lay on the table. Standing beside her, six foot two and wide as a chapel door, was Dr Owen Griffith.

White light reflected off the stainless steel of the tables, and although the air conditioning was inaudible below the music, Rickman could feel the cool downdraught, designed to push odours and pathogens to ground level before being sucked out into the biological filters of the mortuary's independent air system.

Griffith's eyebrows, black, tufted and curved like question marks over his pale blue eyes, were by no means his most remarkable feature. He had a wide, flat nose and a broad mouth, a long, barrel-shaped body and disproportionately short legs. He acknowledged Rickman with a nod and said, with heavy irony, 'Nice of you to spare the time, Chief Inspector.' His accent retained a faint Welsh lilt, his voice a loud, rich baritone, as likely to be heard singing bawdy rugby songs on the terraces of Swansea United as propping up the bass notes of the Chester Choral Society, of which he was an enthusiastic member.

Without preamble, he began dictating into a mike, suspended at head height above the post-mortem table. 'External examination of female — do we have confirmation of identity?' he asked Rickman.

'The mother refused to make an identification,' Rickman said. 'But we do have a friend who's willing.'

Griffith nodded. 'We've confirmed identity from fingerprints on record, anyway,' he said, speaking clearly for the recorder. 'The victim's name is Jasmine Elliott, aged seventeen.' He paused, then spoke quietly, away from the microphone. 'Now then, Miss Elliott, let's see what we can do for you.' There was an uncharacteristic tenderness in his voice and his demeanour which was gone so quickly that it would be easy to think it had never been there.

'Jasmine Elliott,' the pathologist repeated, projecting his voice, as though he was announcing her in court. 'Seventeen years of age, slightly underweight. Recent caesarean scar.' He leaned closer to the body and lifted one eyelid. 'Blue eyes.'

Rickman forced himself to look at the network of tiny cuts that covered Jasmine's body. The thin gauze of blood that had covered her was beginning to scab and flake on exposure to air. Rickman knew she would already have been photographed and swabbed, her fingernails scraped and her hair combed. Any fibres, flakes or hairs would already have been bagged and tagged by the CSIs and sent for examination. The forensic search of her home would be as painstaking, with fibre lifts, fingerprints and DNA samples taken and fast-tracked for analysis.

'Notice extreme pallor of the skin, particularly the extremities, and signs of cyanosis around the lips and fingernails.' Griffith lifted one slim hand from the table and tilted it for the photographer. Jasmine's fingernails had once been painted a rich aubergine, but much of the nail varnish had chipped and worn off, revealing the tell-tale blue tinge indicating lack of oxygen. Rickman looked at the girl's delicate fingers resting in Griffith's meaty paw and wanted to weep.

The full post-mortem took just over three hours. When Griffith tried to extract blood from the femoral veins, he found that the veins in both legs had collapsed. He discovered a deeper cut, at the back of Jasmine's right knee. It had nicked the anterior tibial artery.

'This would account for the pooling of blood under the body, and on the floor under the bed,' Griffith said.

'Are you saying she died of blood loss?' Rickman asked.

'Would that it were that simple, Chief Inspector. Sudden and extreme loss of blood causes acidosis — high blood acidity, which in turn can damage major organs.' He ticked the items off on the fingers of his left hand. 'Coagulopathy — thickening of the blood, if you will — hypothermia and finally dysrhythmia. The heart forgets its rhythm and eventually fails.'

'Whichever way you look at it, what you're saying is she bled to death.'

'What I'm *saying* is that her body shut down over a long period — maybe hours.'

Griffith hooked his little finger and traced a curve a centimetre above the circle of thorns tattooed around Jasmine's upper arm. 'Notice the beads of blood at the tips of the thorns?' Rickman had been trying not to think about them since he first saw them that morning. 'She would have to remain very still for that precise pattern of beading to occur,' Griffith said.

'Was she drugged?' Rickman asked.

'Or unconscious. I'll know more when the blood screen results come through.' Griffith took a breath, then raised one broad hand to shield the mike. 'This young woman suffered a great deal, and for many hours before she died, Chief Inspector. Whoever did this took his time, and he enjoyed the work.'

* * *

Home for Rickman was a three-storey Victorian property in Mossley Hill. He turned the car through the gateway and had to brake sharply to avoid a car parked outside the front door. 'Bloody hell!' His anger fled when he realised it must be the car Tanya hired at the airport. He was ashamed to admit that he hadn't thought of his sister-in-law since Foster had caught up with him in the park that morning.

A lamp burned in the front sitting room and Rickman felt his spirits lift. The heating was on, creating a welcome he was unused to, and as he dumped his briefcase and keys in the hall, Tanya stepped out of the sitting room. Her hair seemed to shimmer gold and copper under the hall lights.

'Jeff!' Her oval face lit up and she reached out to him, slipping gracefully into his arms for a kiss. Her cheek was warm, after the October chill outside, and she smelled of honeysuckle and darker hints of spice. Rickman held on to her for a second longer than he should and, feeling a quickening of his heart and a stirring of desire he wasn't ready to acknowledge, he took a step back in confusion, holding her at arm's length.

'Sorry for the late hour,' he said. 'New case.'

'I heard it on the radio.'

'I'd hoped to be here to meet you.'

Tanya lifted one shoulder in an expressive European gesture. 'I have a key, it's not like I was waiting in the cold.' She frowned and squeezed his hand. 'It sounds bad.'

Rickman thought about the girl, left without dignity in death, the infant, ripped from her mother, and now in terrible danger. 'It is,' he said with a sigh. 'It's bad.'

Tanya searched his face for a few moments, then gave her head a small shake, as though she had given up on what she was looking for. 'I did some shopping on the drive from the airport.' She walked ahead of him to the kitchen. 'Could you eat?'

He would have said no, but at that moment Tanya opened the door and the combined aromas of oregano, garlic, basil and thick, meaty sauce drifted out.

They shared their meal at the scrubbed oak table, talking about her boys — Rickman's nephews, Fergus and Jeff junior. Jeff had recently enrolled at university, and Tanya was worried about the company he was keeping.

'I'm surprised you came over right now,' Rickman said. 'I'm pleased to see you,' he added, 'don't get me wrong — but I thought you'd want to be nearby.'

She took a sip of wine, and he could see she was struggling with a decision to talk or remain silent.

'Tanya, is something wrong?'

'It'll wait,' she said. 'We can talk tomorrow.'

'I'll be out of the house by seven a.m. — I've no idea when I'll be back,' he said. 'If something's bothering you, I'd rather know now.'

'I didn't want to burden you,' she said. 'Especially with this new case.' She fiddled with the stem of her glass for a few moments longer, then glanced up at him, her brown eyes troubled. 'This is terrible timing.'

Rickman smiled. 'There's never a good time.'

She lifted her napkin from her lap and folded it. 'Simon takes so much of your time as it is . . .'

Simon's amnesia since his car accident, his inability to cope with the world, had reversed their roles, and Rickman had to assume the role of protector and guide to his older brother.

'You're worried about the business,' he said. Simon and Tanya's leatherwear business was the subject of glossy magazine features and their clothing sold to A-list celebrities, but Simon's head injury had wiped all memory of it, and he had no interest in learning about it.

Tanya took a breath. 'I had our lawyers in Milan draw up papers — equivalent to power of attorney here.'

Rickman swilled the wine in his glass. 'Oh.'

'I don't want to cut him out, Jeff,' she said, anxious to explain. 'We lost money this year because the autumn collection wasn't ready in time. Next year, it will affect our market share — I can't risk that. I need to be able to take decisions and implement them without having to waste a month cajoling Simon into signing off on the board's decisions.'

'I know,' he said. 'I know . . .' Nevertheless, it was confirmation, not that it was needed. His brother wasn't getting better. Would never get better. 'Should Simon have legal representation?'

She flushed a little. 'I think he should. The family lawyers are based in Milan, and . . .'

Her voice trailed off. Simon had no intentions of returning to Italy, and she didn't need to say that he no longer saw himself as part of the family. For Simon, there was Jeff and him — nobody else counted. Not his wife, his children, his clients or his employees.

'I wish there was something I could say — something I could do.'

Tanya's fingertips brushed his hand, the merest touch, but he felt it through the whole of his body. 'You're already doing more than any of us could have expected or hoped for.

But Simon isn't coming back to us. We have to accept that.' Tanya softened her words with a smile so sad, he felt it like a pain in his chest.

* * *

Heading for home, Lee Foster tuned the car stereo to Radio Merseyside hoping that the sports broadcast would take his mind off the failures of the day.

Bryony Elliott was still out there, Mark Davis was at best unstable, and every lead had come up with a big fat nothing.

'He's got the ball and he's running,' the commentator said, and Foster snorted in derision. Real sportsmen didn't run with the ball, they kicked it. He pressed the autotune for Radio City. Kaiser Chiefs were playing 'I Predict a Riot' and he was just getting into it when the ads cut in. He muted the speakers in disgust and simultaneously, a text alert flashed up on the digital screen. It was from work, and it was marked 'URGENT'. Foster pulled over.

The message was short. 'Davis cornered at Central Station. Officers need assistance.'

Foster screeched from the kerb and accelerated into the outside lane, executing a U-turn that set car horns blaring.

'Cornered,' the message said, which meant he probably had Bryony with him. If he could talk the stupid bastard down . . .

He swerved around a slow-moving stretch limo, jamming the heel of his hand on the horn to warn the driver. In his rear-view mirror he caught a glimpse of two girls hanging out of the sunroof, waving and laughing. He kept his foot down on the steep incline of Brownlow Hill, screaming past the redbrick facade of the university's Victoria Building, through two more sets of lights as they changed to red. He broke hard at the T-junction, making the sharp jink right, then left, and screeched to a halt on the pelican crossing at the station. Three miles in just under four minutes.

He dialled Calls and Response as he ran for the entrance.

Someone yelled after him, 'Hey, mate! You can't leave that there.'

A taxi horn sounded.

'DS Foster,' he said into his phone. 'I got a text.'

'Mobile patrols are on-way,' the operator said.

'Where is he?'

'Sorry, Sarge, no detail. In the station — that's all we got.'

Foster ran past the small parade of shops at the entrance to the station as he heard the faint whoop of a distant siren. The ticket desk and barriers looked quiet. The place smelled of dust and hot metal. The PA system bing-bonged, and a cancellation of service from the Wirral was announced. Then Foster saw a movement to his left — two youths loped across the dingy tiles of the concourse. There was a pent-up eagerness in the way they moved and he followed them.

Turning a corner, he saw a small crowd gathered around the shuttered doorway of a shop. He could just see the helmets of two police in uniform. Foster fished out his badge and warrant card and edged through the huddle. 'Police,' he said, his voice low and controlled. 'Watch your backs.'

The two officers stood next to a man who lay crumpled against the grey shuttering of the department store. He had Mark Davis's dark hair and long limbs, but Foster couldn't see the face. Both officers had their hands on their batons, though neither had drawn them. The taller of the two emanated fear. The shorter man had the shoulders of a weightlifter and a mad glint in his eye.

'What's the score?' Foster addressed his question to the shorter man.

'They were knocking seven shades out of him when we arrived.' The officer's hackles were up, and he spoke loud enough for all of them to hear.

'Citizens' arrest,' someone called out from the middle of the crowd.

'Resisting, was he?' Foster put enough irony in his voice to raise a laugh.

'You do know who that is?' A man of about thirty stood at the front of the gathering, leaning forward in the balls of his feet. He had the flattened nose and callused knuckles of a boxer.

'Why don't you tell us?' Foster said, tagging him as the ringleader.

'It's that pervert killer — the one who snatched the baby,' the boxer said.

'Well.' Foster rubbed his hands. 'Best get him down the station, eh, lads?'

The short cop looked ready to get moving, but someone shouted out from the back, 'Where's the little girl, then?'

'Give me five minutes with him.' The boxer stepped up, his fists clenched. 'I'll find out.'

'You wouldn't wanna do that, mate.' Foster spoke softly, so as not to antagonise the rest, putting just enough threat in his tone so the guy knew he wasn't intimidated. Then he spread his hands and deliberately relaxed his stance. 'Why don't you give your name to one of the officers, here — you might even get a commendation.'

The boxer sneered. 'Give that shithead a chance to do us for assault? No chance.' He turned away and Foster breathed easier. With the boxer off the scene, there was a good chance the rest would disperse. This would become no more than a good yarn for the lads to spin for their mates and the girls down the clubs later in the evening.

A sudden scuffle at the back of the crowd caused a rumble of protest. The onlookers began to turn as uniformed officers broke through, shoving left and right.

Shit.

The boxer met Foster's eye and there was no going back. He lunged for the man on the ground. Foster moved into his path. The boxer jabbed with his left. Foster parried, but he was too tired. Too slow. The blow grazed his temple, and Foster staggered.

The crowd surged forward, yelling, angry. The police pushed back, forming a ragged line against the mob. Batons were drawn, a few blows struck, and the crowd retaliated with fists and feet.

The boxer aimed a kick at the man on the floor and Foster heard a grunt of pain. Still dazed, he moved forward and grabbed the boxer's left shoulder. The boxer swung round, throwing a punch with his right. Foster blocked with his left and clamped his right hand over the boxer's face, forestalling a headbutt. As the guy's hands came up in panicky defence, Foster stepped in close, brought his right leg behind his opponent's right knee and shoved, *hard*. The leg gave and the boxer fell backwards, crashing into the steel shutters.

'Cuff him,' Foster told the mad-eyed cop. He didn't need to be told twice — seemed almost to enjoy the chaos around him.

'Mark?' Foster crouched next to the figure. He had curled into a ball, his skinny arms covering his head.

'It's all right.' He touched the lad's shoulder. 'It's me. Lee Foster.'

The arms came down cautiously and the long limbs uncurled. The lad eased into a sitting position. There was blood on his shirt and trousers. His hair hung black and greasy, half-obscuring a gaunt face.

It wasn't Mark Davis.

* * *

The baby is quiet at last. Fed and changed a second time, she sleeps heavily, as if exhausted. Mark Davis has been on the move all day, circling and doubling back, resting for short spells in quiet side streets. He snatched an hour's sleep in the multi-storey car park next to the Royal Hospital, after settling his nerves with another small sample from the stolen heroin.

Now he has come home — the nearest to a home that he has known since early childhood. The air is cold, chilling further as the last glimmer of light fades. He pulls a loose fold of blanket over the baby's head to keep her warm.

116

The lamps along the driveway leading to Black Wood Children's Home buzz and flicker, some glowing dull red, others a feeble orange. In the canopy above him, the leaves rustle and fall, spiralling softly to the mulchy ground.

A sharp *crack* to his right.

He spins round. Nothing to see.

He moves left, off the tarmac driveway, into the deepening shadows under the trees, and listens. The faint hum of traffic on the main road. A flutter of wings high above him.

Silence.

Another faint sound, this time directly behind him. The hairs on his neck prickle and his heart begins to pump fast and thick. The lights of the big house are just visible through the trees. He breaks into a run, hearing the crackle of footsteps on leaf litter — multiple steps, chasing, bearing down on him, circling, surrounding. He catches his toe on a tree root, stumbles and falls.

CHAPTER 17

Thursday

Lee Foster stumbled into the CID Room at eight a.m., coffee mug in hand.

DC Hart was setting up a laptop and projector at the other end of the room. On her desk, a pile of phone messages — the lines of inquiry they hadn't managed to finish the previous night, added to a new stack that had been forwarded by the night team. The briefing wasn't due to start until nine, and they had the Incident Room to themselves.

'Morning, Sarge,' Hart said, then did a double take. 'You all right, Sarge?'

Hart looked fresh and bright-eyed, which only made Foster feel worse.

'Fine,' he said.

'I heard about the false alarm.'

Foster shook his head in disgust. 'Some poor sod who happened to have a nosebleed on his way to town for a night on the ale. It's like I said yesterday — everyone wants to be the hero.'

'Is the lad okay?'

'He'll live.'

'Will he press charges?'

'If he doesn't,' Foster said, 'I will.' Foster was barely marked by the scuffle, but the incident had pulled four units off the search for Bryony and wasted a lot of police hours.

He noticed Hart appraising him coolly. 'Did you seek solace with that Calls and Response operator you had your eye on?'

'I don't know what you're on about.' He made his way to the tea table.

'I'm "on about" Sally.'

He saw the amusement in her eyes and took it in good part. 'Is it that obvious?'

Hart tilted her head, still assessing him. 'You look all in.'

'Half the night at a bloody jazz concert.' He picked up a coffee jar and gave it a shake. It was empty.

'You could spend the odd evening at home.'

'Snuggle up with a hot water bottle and a good book? Do me a favour — I'm not dead below the neck just yet.' He could see that stung, and he might have felt bad about it, had she not come straight back at him with an infuriating little smirk.

'A night in doesn't make you celibate,' she said.

His antennae started to twitch. 'What's *that* supposed to mean?'

'Just what I said.'

Naomi was ferocious about keeping her private life out of canteen gossip. Understandable, since there were still a few men — the Daniel Casses on the force — who placed women into three categories: village bike, frigid man-hater or dyke. Foster's interest was more personal: Hart had turned him down three times in the year since they'd met — so if he wasn't her type, who was?

He narrowed his eyes at her. 'Naomi — are you *seeing* someone?'

'I see people all the time,' she said. 'I've got very good eyesight.'

She maintained the Ice Queen coolness, but Foster saw she was regretting the remark, and he wasn't quite ready to let it go. 'I was an altar boy, Naomi. I know what celibate means — and what you just said makes me wonder what you get up to on your cosy nights in.'

'You know, you shouldn't think on the after-effects of a hangover,' she said. 'Not before you've had your coffee.'

It was a good ploy. Hart was good at diversion. He should have been wise to it — hadn't he seen her in action enough times in the interview room? Yet he fell for it anyway. Foster forgot his curiosity for the moment, reminded of his need for a caffeine fix. The second coffee jar he picked up was also empty.

'Didn't you have fun?' Naomi watched him over the top of her coffee mug.

He continued rummaging instead in the desk drawer and found a third jar of coffee. 'Some fat bloke on a saxophone,' he said, spooning out a generous measure. 'I mean, what's that all about?'

Hart took a breath, and for one horrible moment, he thought she might try to explain, but she gave a small shake of her head. 'Never mind,' she said. 'It'd take too long.'

He reached for the kettle. 'After three hours of Mister Sax tootling on his horn, I'd forgotten what *mine* was for—' A rasp of metal on metal, and the kettle jarred to a stop, mid-lift. 'What the f—?' He gave it another tug, and the table jittered, setting crockery and teaspoons jangling. It took him a moment to work out what was causing the problem. A narrow-gauge chain had been wound around the handle and then threaded through the cross bar and leg of the table. He followed the chain back to its lowest point. It was secured with a combination padlock. He turned to Hart. 'Now what?'

She was grinning widely. 'Dwight's crew nicked it again, so Tunstall did the only reasonable thing.'

'Tunstall? Reasonable? Isn't that a whatchamacallit, ending with moron?'

'Oxymoron,' she supplied, in her usual helpful manner. 'And you shouldn't underestimate him.'

At that moment, Tunstall appeared, holding a plastic jug full of water. His hulking frame filled the doorway, and Foster couldn't resist saying, 'It's the genie of the kettle. Do I get three wishes, now?'

Tunstall looked offended. 'No, but you do get a fresh brew, and judging by the way you're hanging onto that kettle, you're in desperate need of one.'

Tunstall's usual response to jibes was 'Cheeky bugger!' — this little speech was virtual repartee, and Foster was so astonished that he let the big man have the last word. He set down the kettle and stepped aside, allowing Tunstall to fill it.

There was enough play in the chain to permit the safe transfer of boiling water to cups, and Foster raised his mug in tribute. 'Got to hand it to you, mate,' he said. 'You're persistent if nothing else.'

'Oh, I'm a lot more besides,' Tunstall said.

Foster saw Hart smiling at him over the rim of her cup. 'Am I losing my edge or what?' he said. 'Trounced by a bloody woollyback!' In the eyes of a Scouser like Foster, anyone born outside Liverpool's city boundaries was only one evolutionary step above a lactating ewe — so this was particularly hard to take. A few more had drifted in during the exchange, which only increased his chagrin.

'Drink your coffee,' Hart said, with mock solicitousness. 'It'll make you feel better.'

'"Genie of the kettle",' Tunstall murmured. 'I think I like that.'

'Well, just don't expect me to rub your spout,' Foster said.

Rickman strode into the room amid a burst of laughter. 'Did I miss something?' He dropped a pile of newspapers onto the nearest desk.

'Only Tunstall, entertaining the troops,' Hart said.

Rickman raised an eyebrow but didn't comment, nor did he remark on the fettered kettle when Tunstall made him a mug of coffee. That was Rickman all over, Foster thought:

a team player, but with no hankering to be regarded as one of the lads.

'What have we got?' he asked.

'You were right about Mark going looking for baby stuff, boss.' Hart clicked the remote and an image filled the projector screen. 'This is a CCTV recording from the twenty-four-hour pharmacy on Parliament Street.'

The camera showed a black-and-white image of ten people in a ragged line. A tall, rangy man stood at the head of the queue. The timer in the bottom right of the frame read '14:27'.

Foster leaned in for a closer look. 'That's Mark all right.'

'He looks stoned,' Hart commented.

'And what's that round his middle?' Tunstall asked.

'Baby's blanket,' Hart said. 'Probably to hide the blood-stains on his trousers. He bought nappies and wipes, a baby's bottle, Ribena and some bottled water.'

'She's barely a month old and he's fed her on *Ribena*?' Tunstall's outrage was another revelation for Foster. He flashed to a mental image of the big man bottle-feeding an infant, the child nestled on one ham-hock forearm.

'Is the timer accurate?' Rickman asked.

Hart nodded. 'They've had to use the recordings for prosecutions a few times, so they're very particular about making sure the time is set correctly.'

A pall fell over the meeting, and Rickman spoke again. 'At least we know that Bryony was alive and well at two thirty yesterday afternoon.'

'Well, that *is* good news,' Foster said.

Rickman looked at him. 'Are you all right, Lee?'

'Sorry, boss,' he said with a guilty dip of his head. Rickman could do without his second-in-command under-mining his efforts to boost morale. Foster glanced at Hart before adding, 'I took a knock on the head during the scrum last night.'

'The "citizens' arrest",' Rickman said. 'Have you been checked out by a paramedic?'

'Yeah.' Foster touched the slight bruise over his right eye. 'I'm fine.'

Hart rolled her eyes.

'There's got to've been a sighting since then?' someone asked.

'Not a thing,' Hart said.

'So either he went to ground, or he moved out of the city centre.' Foster finished the last word on a croak and cleared his throat, wondering if it was the booze or yelling over the racket at the jazz club that made his larynx feel like someone had taken a pipe cleaner to it.

Rickman glanced around the room. 'Okay,' he said, his tone brisk, assertive. 'My turn. These are preliminary PM findings, to be confirmed by chemical analysis.' Foster saw what he was doing — picking up the tempo before they began to despair, getting them thinking about possibilities instead of failures.

'Jasmine died of shock and blood loss. Time of death difficult to establish — the blood loss causes hypothermia, I'm told. But some time between ten p.m. on Tuesday, when she made a call to her friend, Kim Lindermann, and eleven fifty a.m. on Wednesday, when she was discovered.'

Foster glanced at the whiteboard to the left of Rickman. DC Hart had already added the ten-p.m. telephone conversation with Kim Lindermann to the timeline. The blank space between Kim's call and the time of discovery was horribly long.

Rickman seemed to catch the direction of his gaze and paused. When he went on, the brisk, businesslike tone had vanished. 'We're dealing with a sadist who tortured and raped Jasmine over a number of hours.'

'Nobody heard a thing,' Hart said. 'Did anything show on the tox screen?'

'There were hardly any bodily fluids left.'

Rickman swallowed against some unpleasant memory and Foster felt his gorge rise in answer — he'd never got used to post-mortems, and remembering the fine mesh of cuts on Jasmine's body, this one must have been messier than most.

'Toxicology say they'll get the results to us as soon as possible, but they've got to be highly selective and they won't get a second chance at any test they do run.'

They all seemed to hold their breath for a moment, then Tunstall said, 'And now the cracked bastard's got the babby.'

'We don't know that,' Foster insisted. 'We don't know it was Mark.'

'Mark's bloody fingerprints are all over the house,' Hart said.

'That puts him at the scene,' Foster said. 'It doesn't make him guilty. Mark was a tit, always taking the blame for others' pranks — but he was never violent.'

'Kate Nolan said he had another side to him,' Hart reminded him.

Foster had to concede that one.

'And the sixteen-year-old boy you knew could be as different from the twenty-year-old drug addict as a puppy is to a scrapyard dog.' Hart always had a way of ramming a point home.

Foster began to shake his head, but she wasn't finished.

'Think about it, Sarge. He's a junkie. His girlfriend ditches the life, ditches him, gets herself together. He finds out about the baby, tries to make her go back to him, she refuses. He kills, takes Bryony.'

Foster opened his mouth to protest, but Rickman spoke over him. 'We'll know more when the DNA results come through. I asked for premium service on the evidence collected at the scene, but even so, we won't get it before the end of the day — and the killer wore a condom, so there's nothing from the rape.'

Foster furrowed his brow. 'Well, that doesn't make sense, does it? Why wear a condom and leave your fingerprints all over the place?'

Hart tilted her head. 'You said yourself, Mark's a tit. And a junkie.'

That hurt, chucking his words right back at him. He fixed his gaze on her, but she glanced away, taking a sip of coffee.

Rickman stroked the scar that bisected his right eyebrow. 'Kim Lindermann said Mark had been pestering Jasmine.'

'She was convinced he'd done it,' Hart said.

Foster was ready to object, but Rickman held up a hand to stop him. 'Okay,' he said. 'Until we get something better, Mark remains our prime suspect. But our main focus is to find Bryony before she comes to harm. Now, what else needs following up?'

'This lot.' Tunstall waved a handful of pink phone message slips in one hand and completed yellow task reports in the other. 'If you ask me, we're chasing our own tails.'

'We'll have more CID coming in before nine,' Rickman said. 'That'll bring us up to full strength, and we should be able eliminate leads faster.'

'About bloody time.' Tunstall realised he said this aloud and flushed under Rickman's close attention.

'I'm gonna call Ed and Hilary Shepherd,' Foster said. 'See if Mark's been in touch.' He felt sure they would have called if he had, but this was something he felt he had to do.

'I'd like to have a chat with Rob Maitland,' Hart said. 'See if he knows where Mark could have run to.'

Foster glanced at Hart. 'Didn't Cass tell you that Mark had practically been booted out the door?'

'Yeah.' Hart's face hardened. '"Bottom feeder," he said.'

'So why waste time on scum like Maitland?'

Hart hesitated and Rickman silenced Foster with a look. 'What makes you think Maitland's a priority now?' he asked.

'I don't know, boss. Cass *did* say Mark had been side-lined, but—' She shrugged, unwilling, Foster guessed, to say anything that smacked of gut feeling or intuition.

'Is there any proof he was still in Maitland's pay?' Rickman asked.

'Oh!' Tunstall's hand shot up, one of the yellow task slips in his fist. He pulled it down almost as fast, blushing furiously. 'Sorry, sir. I almost forgot — street canvass says the druggies who *would* talk all said Mark still worked for Maitland. They called him "The Weights and Measures Man".'

Rickman was too good a manager to comment, but Foster knew he'd taken note — Cass had fed them bad intel.

'Naomi and Lee, talk to Maitland. Until I can draft in a few more CID personnel, we divvy up the lines of inquiry that came in overnight. And we reinterview the working girls and the addicts, anyone who might be harbouring Mark — anyone who might know where he'd hide.'

He tapped the newspapers on the desk next to him and Foster saw strain in his friend's face. 'The press, the public and our bosses are demanding results,' he said. 'Common *decency* demands it. Bryony's been out there all night. The sooner we find her, the more likely it is we'll find her well.'

CHAPTER 18

Old Hall Street had been transformed since the *Liverpool Daily Post & Echo* offices were given a facelift. The gleaming tower of the Radisson Blu hotel dominated the lower end of the street, and the pavements were startlingly clean. This was business Liverpool, its face scrubbed, and minding its manners so as not to frighten the tourists. DS Foster and DC Hart strode towards Maitland's office premises ahead of a torrent of wind blasting off the Irish Sea.

A row of black cabs was parked on the rank opposite and the cabbie second in line leaned out of his window as they passed. Hart seemed to miss a step and Foster could have sworn a look passed between them, then the driver pulled his head inside the cab and looked straight ahead.

Maitland's apartment and offices were on the twenty-fifth floor of a new glass-fronted tower block. The receptionist announced their presence to Maitland on the phone. 'Mr Maitland will send someone down to meet you,' he said.

'Don't worry,' Foster said. 'We'll find our own way.'

They walked down a tiled lobby that gleamed like polished onyx, past displays backlit with pale green light. Recessed glass shelving held sculptural flower arrangements, and etched glass signs directed them to the residents' café and gift shop. He noticed Hart taking it all in and couldn't resist asking, 'Thinking of putting a deposit down?'

'Living in an aquarium?' Hart dismissed the green, glass-filtered lighting with one encompassing glance. 'Doesn't appeal.'

He smiled, stealing another look at her. She wore a cream linen jacket over her short-sleeved blouse. The cut emphasised her waist and the colour, her tan.

She arched an eyebrow. 'See something you like?'

Always. But he wasn't about to let her know that. 'I'm just not sure what you think you'll get out of talking to Maitland.'

'Maitland is the only real link we've got to Mark.'

'And?' Foster said. 'There was a definite "and" in there.' They stopped at the lifts — a bank of four, set into a wall of waxed beech planking.

'And . . .' She exhaled. 'Here's *my* daft question: what if Davis stole the missing drugs?'

Foster thought about this as the lift door opened and then closed behind them with a self-satisfied sigh as they stepped inside. 'Mark Davis is stupid enough to nick the gear on impulse. But he'd have to've been on hand when the deal went down.' He grimaced. 'Mark's not what you'd call management material, and he's *definitely* not a candidate for hired muscle — when I knew him, he couldn't punch a hole in a wet *Echo*.'

'You knew him four years ago,' Hart said. 'A lot can change in four years.'

'So you keep telling me, but everyone we've spoken to says he's been well into drugs since then — and we're not talking the performance-enhancing kind.'

She acknowledged this with a slight dip of the head. The lift decelerated and the doors swept open with such a flourish that Foster half-expected a fanfare. They stepped out onto a hushed landing. Mint-coloured carpet, curved glass walls.

'Even if he did fall over the stuff and have the nerve to pick it up and run, how did he get away? We had two helicopters and a hundred cops watching the perimeter.

As for Maitland going after Mark — course he would. But Maitland's more a bullet to the back of the head type than someone who'd torture an innocent victim.'

They followed the curve of the wall, past PR and IT businesses, a couple with logos including the word 'inspired'.

Foster was about to comment, when Hart said, 'You're sure Maitland would be there when the deal went down?'

'No question. A deal that big, he'd be there.'

'So maybe Mark escaped the same way Maitland did.'

Foster smiled. 'Maitland's smart and quick — and probably owns a few cops. Mark, on the other hand, is thick and slow and owns a rusty old Ford Focus.'

'You're telling me this is a waste of time,' Hart said.

'I'm just saying there's a lot of ifs attached to that one "What if?" But like Kim said, even scum like Maitland would help to protect a baby, wouldn't they?'

They drew level with Maitland's apartment door.

'Let's hope so,' Hart said. ''Cos the way I remember it, she didn't seem too sure.'

* * *

They were ushered into a boardroom that would put the CEO of an international oil company in the shade. Maitland sat at the end of a conference table that could have doubled as a spare runway for John Lennon Airport. A balsa wood model occupied one third of the table, and adjacent to Maitland, a grey-faced man in a suit.

Lawyer? he wondered. *Architect?*

Maitland waited for them to walk the length of the room before acknowledging their presence. 'Yes?'

Foster made the introductions and Maitland glanced at their warrant cards without interest.

He was dressed smartly, but a Toxteth scal in a designer suit, Foster thought, will always look like a Toxteth scal in a designer suit. The other man, however, looked like he'd been born in his merino two-piece.

He smiled nervously under Foster's scrutiny. 'Do you want me to—' He made a move to stand, but Maitland stopped him.

'No need, Bernie. They won't be here long.'

'I could tidy up some of the figures.' From the gleam of sweat on Bernie's forehead, it was clear he'd rather be anywhere else.

'Bernie . . .' Foster said.

The man obliged by adding, 'Carter.' He bit his lower lip, evidently chagrined that he'd fallen so easily for the ploy.

'Bernie Carter the accountant,' Foster said, committing the name to memory. 'Don't mind us. Personally, I'd be fascinated to hear how you plan to make up for the two million your boss lost on Tuesday night.'

Carter darted a look at Maitland.

'I'm afraid I don't get the joke,' Maitland said.

'You should do,' Foster snapped back. 'It's on you.'

He saw a flash of temper in Maitland's face, and Hart shot him a warning look — they weren't here about the drugs operation, they were here to find out about Mark Davis. But Foster suddenly recognised the balsa model.

'This refurb.' He bent to get an eye-level view of the four-storey brick building, its courtyards and parking bays, the dinky trees and greens for the residents. 'It's the old warehouse, isn't it? Where the drugs bust went down. I got to admire your nerve, Maitland.'

Maitland smiled. 'You should be thanking me,' he said. 'Redeveloping an area reduces the crime rate.'

'Still,' Foster said, 'it must be a choker, losing the money *and* the drugs.' They held each other's gaze for a dangerous moment.

He saw a muscle twitch in Maitland's jaw. 'State your business.'

Foster moved around the conference table and tilted his head to peer at the columns of figures on the accountant's sheets of paper. Carter looked about ready to fling himself bodily onto the paperwork to save it from his impertinent gaze. 'Mark Davis.'

Maitland matched his terseness. 'What about Davis?'

'He's been on every news bulletin since yesterday morning, Mr Maitland,' Foster said. 'Don't come the innocent.'

'I'm aware you're looking for him.' Maitland stared at them without emotion, but Foster could feel the murderous intent coming off the man in waves. 'I just don't see what it has to do with me.'

'Mark works for you.'

'He used to.'

'Give him his cards, did you?' Foster turned to Hart. 'We'll have to check with the Inland Revenue — ask for a copy of his P45.' With a witness present, you could only go so far in accusing a man of being a drug dealer.

'He did odd jobs,' Maitland said. 'For pocket money.'

'We heard different,' Hart said. 'We heard he was your Weights and Measures Man.'

'You heard wrong.' The gleam in Maitland's eye said he meant to find out who had been talking to the police.

'We need to find Davis urgently.' Hart glanced at the accountant. 'He snatched a baby from the murder scene.'

Maitland's gaze followed hers for the briefest moment, and Carter's grey complexion became paper-white.

'The baby,' Maitland said. 'Of course. Anything I can do to help.'

'That little detail slip your mind, did it?' Foster had to admire Hart's reading of the situation — even an animal like Maitland didn't like to look insensitive to the plight of an infant.

Maitland sucked his teeth, then managed a sympathetic smile. 'I'm afraid there's not much I can tell you — Mark was unreliable and volatile. He was unsettling the clients.' He shrugged. 'I had to let him go.'

'Who would he run to?' Hart asked.

Foster wouldn't normally have let it slide that Maitland's 'clients' were junkies and prostitutes, but Hart often got more out of interviews than he did, and he was willing to concede her more diplomatic approach had the edge on his.

Carter shuffled his papers together and cleared his throat. Maitland gave him one look and the accountant spread the papers out again on the table, his hands trembling slightly. The man's anxiety seemed to help Maitland regain a measure of equilibrium. He folded his arms and gazed at DC Hart.

Hart wasn't intimidated. 'Is there a friend he might go to? An associate?'

'You should ask Sergeant Foster.'

'You *what*?'

'It's a tragedy, what happened to that poor girl,' Maitland went on, as if he hadn't noticed Foster's outraged exclamation. 'Mark was always a tragedy waiting to happen.' Maitland looked at Foster through half-closed eyes. 'Isn't that right, Sergeant Foster?'

From the corner of his eye, Foster saw the accountant staring at him. Was he *enjoying* this? He only had to glance in Carter's direction and the man picked up a pen and pretended to scan the lists of numbers in front of him.

'Just answer the question, Maitland,' Foster warned.

Maitland pushed harder. 'Mark was just a big kid, really — liked to hang round with the hard lads — eh, Sergeant?'

'You wanna watch your mouth.' Foster leaned forward on the balls of his feet, ready for a ruck.

But Maitland wasn't a man to back down easily. 'Mark thought you were *magic*. "Foz the joker", "Foz the marine".' His wide-set eyes had a manic gleam in them. 'Funny — he never mentioned "Foz the cop".'

Hart moved in — no more than a fraction — but enough to break the head-to-head. 'We're just trying to find Bryony safe, Mr Maitland.' Foster heard the reproach in her tone, and he turned his temper down a couple of notches. 'Does he have any friends or family who might shelter him?' she asked again.

Maitland made a show of thinking, ended the pantomime with a shake of the head. 'A man gets that low, he doesn't have many friends.' His gaze skimmed Hart's contours, as if seeing her for the first time, liking what he saw.

Hart returned Maitland's stare with cool dignity, and a measure of contempt. 'You need to account for your whereabouts on Tuesday night.'

Maitland was stung — it didn't show in his face, but there seemed to be an increase in the electrical static in the room. 'I've already done that,' he said. 'In an interview with one of your colleagues, yesterday,' he said evenly. 'I was released without charge.'

'You were released on bail,' Hart corrected.

She waited for an answer and Foster again saw anger cross Maitland's face like a passing shadow. *Good on you, Naomi.*

The accountant stared at Naomi with a mixture of horror and fascination, a hungry anticipation just beneath the surface, and Foster had the sick feeling that Carter was the kind of physical coward who liked to see men like Maitland lash out in temper — who even got a thrill, being close to a man capable of sudden violence.

Foster readied himself to intervene, but Maitland seemed to shake the tension out of his shoulders before answering. 'I spent the evening at a dinner party with my solicitor, Mr Yates, of Jarrow, Klipman and Yates,' Maitland said. 'You can check with him.'

'I'm sure he's been fully briefed,' Hart said. 'But we will check anyway. And the hours between midnight on Tuesday and eleven a.m. on Wednesday?'

He stared at her. 'What would I gain from killing the girl?'

'Spoken like a businessman,' Foster said.

Maitland gave him a hard look.

'Mr Maitland?' Hart said.

Maitland exhaled through his nose. 'You're coming after me for the murder because you can't make the drugs charges stick — un-*believable*.'

'You can answer the question here or at the station,' Hart said. Maitland locked eyes with her, but when she refused to back down, he shook his head, smiling a little.

He might be a thug, Foster thought, *But he knows when he can't win.*

133

'Okay. Here's how it went — you might want to make notes. Dinner party ended late, I drank a bit more than I intended. Stayed the night at my solicitor's house, rather than drive home — wouldn't want to break the law.' He flashed Hart an unpleasant smile. 'Wednesday, we got up late — bit of a hangover, to tell you the truth.'

Foster smiled back. 'You wouldn't know the truth if it bit you in the arse.'

* * *

'What now?' Hart asked. Heading down the hill, they were walking into the wind. It snatched Hart's words from her lips and lobbed them halfway up the street.

'Now we're gonna waste another hour checking with his slimy solicitor, knowing full well he's gonna back up anything that lying bastard says.' Foster was still stinging from Maitland's remarks. What stung worse was that he had allowed himself to be rattled.

'*Another* hour?' Hart repeated.

They turned the corner into King Edward Street, headed for the car park. 'Yeah. *Another* hour.'

'Mark's a loner with no family or friends we know of. Up to now, we've been chasing shadows. Maitland is a definite associate — it was a good line of inquiry.'

She was right. Foster knew it, but he'd felt impotent in the face of Maitland's jibes — he'd had no comeback because he couldn't reason himself out of the responsibility he felt for Davis. He should have told Hart what he was thinking, but the comfort Foster sought from women was of a more physical kind.

'Yeah, well . . .' he muttered, and carried on walking.

He wanted to recover his good humour, make some weak joke about Sally the telephonist and late-night sax. But he couldn't bring himself to do it, not right now.

'Maybe if you hadn't antagonised him so much—'

'Sorry, Naomi,' he said, a bit too heavy on the sarcasm. 'Being a mere man, I find it hard to be *nice* to vicious scumbags who deal in drugs and trade on other people's misery.'

She took a couple of steps, turning to block his path. 'That,' she said, 'was uncalled for.'

She was right. Naomi had handled the interview far better than he had. He was too angry to apologise, but she must have seen something like regret in his face, because she took a deep breath, and walked on. When she spoke again, she sounded conciliatory. 'Look, Sarge.' She had to raise her voice above the bluster of the wind. 'I know this is hard for you. Mark—'

'Who said this was about Mark?'

'I didn't say it *was*.' They stopped again at the entrance to the underground car park. 'We all feel for Bryony, we all want her back safe. Maybe you more than most.'

He wasn't a complete prick — he saw she was trying to give him a way out of the row that had been building between them all day, but Maitland's taunts had got right under his skin, needling and burning like an attack of hives. Mark had admired him, looked up to him, and he'd let things slide, allowed them to lose touch. He'd known in his heart that Mark wouldn't survive outside of the care system without a lot of help — help that he should have offered.

'*Don't* think you understand me,' he said, ''Cos that's . . .' He nearly lost it and had to take a moment before finishing. 'That's just not possible. What would *you* know about me, anyway, Naomi? I mean, how could you *begin* to understand?'

'At least I'm trying, instead of wallowing in self-pity—'

If it had been Maitland standing where Hart was at that moment, Foster might have taken a swing at him. But Maitland was safely tucked away in his glass tower, so Hart took the brunt of his anger and self-disgust.

'Let's get this straight. I don't need your sympathy, or your understanding.' He was contradicting himself. He knew it and he hated himself for it, but he couldn't stop. 'What I *need* — Constable — is for you to do your job and stay out of my face.'

He wasn't sure how long they remained there, buffeted by the wind, while a single gull sobbed overhead. It felt like minutes, rather than seconds.

He had no right to pull rank on her when he'd been anything but professional dealing with Maitland. He'd probably be facing an assault charge, if Hart hadn't been there, calming the situation, keeping him on track. A part of him wanted Hart to yell at him. At least then he could have yelled right back, could have used it as an excuse to pour out the impotent rage he really felt — for Mark, for Jasmine and for Bryony — for all the kids who got mashed by the system, bent out of shape before they ever got the chance to grow into the people they could have been.

But she didn't. She just turned and walked away.

CHAPTER 19

Mark stirs, imagining himself underground in the sewers and tunnels of dockland Liverpool. He clutches a bag to his chest. Something squirms and cries within the canvas webbing. He is anxious he will lose it and hugs it closer as he passes a huddle of kids around an oil drum. They suck smoke from a hose-pipe stuck through the side of the drum. The sweet herbal reek of hash triggers a craving in him like a hunger pang.

It begins to rain. At first, it's just a few drops, but soon it's falling fast in hard, straight sheets. He looks up and sees he is now outside, on the street. The raindrops pelt down like missiles, bubbling and boiling on the road, filling the gutters and spinning into drains barred with steel teeth. The current tugs at his ankles, he loses his footing and is carried like flotsam by the undertow, swept along with waste paper, old cans and bottles.

The jaws of the drain creak open with a groan like a subterranean beast, and he bobs and spins, dragged closer and closer to its hungry maw. He turns, swimming against the current, grasping for an anchor, but the kerbstone looms several feet above him and he can't find a grip in its steep sides.

His clothing catches on the steely teeth, then the jaws snap shut. Razor-sharp teeth — *shark's* teeth — sink into his thighs, ripping the fabric of his chinos, tearing flesh and sinew, clamping hard on cartilage and bone, dragging him down, under the water, into the suffocating darkness.

He screams.

Awake now, coughing and spitting dust. Each cough racks him. Pain shocks through his pelvis and lower limbs. He shoves away a piece of splintered wood and pain sledge-hammers through his legs. He screams again. His legs are twisted under him. There's blood on his hands and clothing. Fresh blood — his blood. The cuts on his hands and face and chest have split open again, but they are no worse than paper cuts, compared with the raging torment in his pelvis and legs. His lower limbs feel huge, out of proportion with the rest of him. Planks of wood lie all around him — what is left of the steps. Red and grey dust billows like smoke in the failing beam of the flashlight, lying half-buried under the rubble.

'Bryony?' *Oh, God, the baby!*

It's dark, and the dust . . .

'Help me! Somebody!' He hears a brief flutter of wings, high in the rafters of the old house, then, stillness.

The beam of the flashlight, filtered by the dust, glows orange, lighting faintly, some distance away through the murk, a tiny bundle, wrapped tight in her little blanket.

'Bryony!' He reaches for the baby, but a jolt of pain rips through him, tearing a scream from him, and he looks down again at his mangled legs. He breaks out in a cold sweat, and half groans, half sobs.

He takes a few breaths, psyching himself up. He has to get to the baby. It's cold in here, so cold . . . He uses his hands, gouging the fall of plaster with his fingertips, dragging himself forward inch by screaming inch. He feels something give inside him, bone grinds on shattered bone. He greys out, coming to moments later. There's blood on his lips, he can taste it. He spits to clear his mouth and, supporting himself on his elbows, taking shallow breaths like a weightlifter push-ing himself to the limit, raises himself so that he can see the baby more clearly.

There's dirt on her face, dust on her peach-perfect skin. He begins again, screaming with every tiny movement, but with more determination than he imagined himself capable of. Reach, dig, pull, reach, dig, pull. Screaming and cursing and praying, calling to his infant child, 'I'm coming, baby. I'm coming, Bryony. Don't be scared — I'm coming.'

Agonizing minutes later, his fingers brush against something soft. He sobs, shushing and crooning, as much to soothe himself as his baby.

He pulls gently on the fabric, feels the bundle shift and tugs again, little by little, drawing his child to him.

'See, babe?' He bites down to stop his teeth chattering, to stop the screams that bubble up in his throat. 'Nothing to be scared of.'

There's dust on the baby's lips, in her nose, and Mark blows gently, wipes her little face with the silky binding of the blanket. 'There's my little darlin',' he coos. 'There's my brave girl.'

She is brave, his little one, for she doesn't cry. Not even a whimper. He feels absurdly proud, and hugs her to him, despite the pain that now seems to burn him. His groin, his legs are on fire.

A shudder shakes his body and he screams. Then the shivering begins and he moans, 'Oh, God, not now, *pleeease* . . .' He has staved it off for as long as possible, but now he needs a fix. He needs it or he will die. Another shudder convulses him and the fire in his pelvis leaps and crackles, sending shooting sparks up his spine. He passes out.

When he awakes, the feeble glow of the flashlight is dimmer. If he stays very still and keeps his breathing shallow, the pain isn't so bad. And the light is like a candle, flickering as if in a draught of air, hypnotic and soothing, keeping the night terrors at bay.

Darkness. His heart cramps with fear. Light again. He stares at the flashlight, as if the force of his will can keep it alight. For a moment it flares bright. Then it falters, shivers and dies. Mark gasps, feeling again the damp air wrap around him like a suffocating blanket. On the brink of panic, he pulls back, takes another breath, forces himself to be calm. Tonight, for his little girl, he will be brave — for Bryony, he will be a man.

He begins to croon a nursery rhyme to soothe her, a simple, repetitive ditty they taught him in primary school. He has a light, tuneful voice, and the sound of it, rising tremulously through the house, helps to ward off the darkness. Sometimes the pain surprises a yell from him, but Bryony is quiet and good, and Mark begins to believe that someone will come, that they will save his baby.

He bends to kiss the baby's downy head. There's grit in her hair, and he tries to stroke the dirt from her scalp, taking special care over the soft patch, where the pulse may be felt like a distant echo of an infant's heart. He kisses that delicate spot and feels . . . nothing.

A terror more searing than the fiery jolts of pain tears through him. *'Bryony?'*

The house seems to shudder in answer. It groans and shifts and a powdering of plaster sifts from the ceiling above, falling with a hiss, like sand into his hair, like earth into a grave. The timbers tick and he senses movement, though he can see nothing. A louder *crack* is followed by the squeal of wood on wood. It is as if his screams have disturbed the house, awakening it, arousing its fury. He curls his body to protect the baby. Never mind the pain — though he screams anyway. He can't help himself.

He hears a *flump*, as though a large animal has dropped with a sigh onto the floor above. Then another high squeal, and a chattering, like children playing, like dishes being stacked in Hilary Shepherd's kitchen. Like—

The ceiling bows and bursts. Plaster, ceiling laths, floorboards fall, and after them roof tiles, sliding over each other in a shrill clatter of noise, cascading inwards, and the children's chatter becomes the screams of the tormented in hell.

CHAPTER 20

Jeff Rickman stepped out of his car. He fished his mobile out of his pocket and dialled Foster's number, listened to it ring. A flock of screaming gulls circled and wheeled overhead, tumbling and turning, quarrelling in a sky innocent of clouds. The wind had died, and the air was cold and still.

Foster's voicemail clicked in, and Rickman considered hanging up: this wasn't the sort of news you wanted to hear over the phone. After a pause, he said, 'Lee. Get to Black Wood as soon as you can. I'll be at the old coach house.'

The coach house was partly hidden by rhododendron bushes and accessed by a tarmac driveway curving right off the main drag. Smooth green tufts of moss cobbled the drive, and the way was narrowed in places by an overgrowth of rhododendrons. Here, the light failed and the air became still and fetid.

Rickman stepped over recently snapped branches and a moment later the track opened on to a semicircle of stone sets at the front of the coach house.

Once a pretty portal to the grandeur of the mansion, the coach house was now in ruins. The carved filigrees that ornamented the eaves had long since been softened to a grey pulp by the steady drip of water and the slow creep of algae.

The roof timbers had given way in places. There was a hole in the roof to the left of the doorway, and the rest sagged, spilling red shingle tiles into the guttering and onto the path. An ancient wisteria twined along the length of one wall. Lacking sufficient sunlight for robust growth, a few pallid clusters of lilac flowers hung here and there, like withered grapes on the vine. The front door stood open and an eerie glow spilled from it, but every window was secured by steel shutters, like pennies on the eyes of a corpse.

A white Scientific Support Unit van was parked near the front door. Next to it, another van, this one a red Mercedes bearing the logo of Mersey Property Development. A man sat in the driver's seat with one foot on the sill and the other in the foot well, as though arrested in the act of getting into or out of the vehicle. The company's mission statement was etched under the logo in gold lettering: *Making your dreams a reality*. The expression on his face said this man's nightmares had been made reality.

A young police constable approached, one hand raised. 'Sorry mate,' he said. 'No civilians allowed.'

Despite the suit, Rickman was often mistaken for a scrapper — an ex-boxer, or maybe a bouncer who had risen through the ranks to security manager. 'DCI Rickman.' He flashed his ID and the constable dropped his hand and stepped aside, flustered. Rickman jerked his chin towards the Mercedes van. 'Did he call it in?'

The constable followed Rickman's gaze. The look of horror on the man's face was unchanged. 'He's a surveyor. Been poking around the place for a couple of days, sussing it out for development.'

'Got his details?'

The constable tapped his clipboard. 'All in here, sir.' He lowered his voice. 'Sir, he's been sitting like that for the last half hour.'

Rickman nodded. 'When you've logged me in, see if you can get a medic to have a look at him.' White crime scene suits and hard hats had been laid out by the back door of the

142

Scientific Support van. He grabbed one of each and tore the plastic wrapper off the oversuit as he strode to the front door of the coach house.

He had to duck to avoid the door lintel, but the hallway, though narrow and musty, was high enough to accommodate his six-foot-four frame comfortably. A halogen-white glow from a doorway to the left of the hall pinpointed the scene.

The doorway opened on to a twelve-foot drop. The wooden steps lay splintered and scattered over a five-foot area, half-buried under ceiling plaster, laths and dusty cobwebs.

Rickman heard the steady sound of scraping from one corner of the room, but only one CSI was visible, labelling a plastic crate filled with what looked like rubble. The heat of the lamps carried dust and the smell of ancient decay from the cellar below.

The CSI glanced up, shading his eyes against the glare. 'That you, Jeff?' Rickman recognised Tony Mayle beneath the mask. A senior CSI and Crime Scene Coordinator managing the scene personally — this one *really* must have got to Mayle. 'I see you've snagged yourself a zoot suit,' he went on. 'You can come and have a look if you like — just keep to the stepping plates.'

An aluminium ladder had been secured under the opening and Rickman climbed down, stepping directly from the ladder onto the first creaking section of aluminium plates. With the hood of his suit up and a mask with dust filter in place, Rickman could see only Mayle's eyes and forehead. The air in the cellar was damp and cool, but the CSI was sweating profusely.

'Has the pathologist been already?' Rickman asked, surprised that they had started work.

'On his way.' Mayle pulled the mask from his face and tilted his hard hat back a little. 'Police surgeon declared.'

Life extinct. Rickman felt a cold, hard lump, like a stone in the pit of his stomach. The basement extended the length of the house, approximately thirty-by-thirty square, the main structure of the house supported by brick pillars. The sagging ceiling had been shored up in places with steel props. Algae slimed every flat surface and one wall gleamed white with fungus.

Mayle led the way along the aluminium plates to where two white-suited CSIs worked quietly behind one of the pillars, scraping at a pile of grey dust in the harsh glare of two arc lamps.

Momentarily, Rickman formed an impression of sand sculpture, of bodies petrified in ash at Pompeii. Mark Davis lay on his side. His shirt was in tatters and hung on him like a rag. Something about the way his right leg was angled suggested a fracture. Curled in the crook of his arm, Bryony.

Rickman felt it like a punch to the chest. She looked perfect, untouched, but for the grey dust caking her face. 'How long—' His voice caught and he had to clear his throat. 'How long have they been here?'

'Hard to say. Some of the blood is still wet, so probably a matter of hours.'

'Hours,' Rickman repeated. Bryony had been here hours. If they'd found her earlier — a matter of *hours* earlier — might she have survived?

He looked more closely at the bodies. 'I don't see any blood.'

One of the CSIs kneeling next to the bodies indicated some marks, showing dull red through the thick coating of plaster dust on Davis's skin.

The bodies were surrounded with red tiles, many of them broken into glass-sharp shards. Rickman looked up. The ceiling had collapsed, and the one above that. A square of perfect blue was visible through the hole in the roof. 'Roof tiles,' he said. 'Could they have caused the injuries?'

'Possibly,' Mayle said. 'We're collecting samples for DNA analysis. What's odd is, the male has extensive contusions and lacerations, but the baby seems unmarked.'

Did Mark try to protect his daughter in those final moments? Looking at the child's face, at the destruction of so new a life, it didn't seem to matter. Experience had hardened Rickman to the practical realities of death: the blood, the decay, even the stench. But he had never been able to toughen himself against its futility.

'Murder or accident?'

'Not for me to say, Jeff.' Mayle glanced behind Rickman at the drop from ground floor to basement. 'But judging by the damage to the staircase, he could have been looking for shelter, suffered a fall. We'll have to wait for the PM.'

Rickman heard footsteps above them. Then Foster's voice.

'It's Mark, isn't it?' Lee Foster stared down at them, shielding his eyes against the glare of the arc lamps.

'Looks like it,' Rickman said.

Foster came down the ladder like he was still in the Marines: a foot either side of the main struts and he was down in a second. Rickman was relieved to see that he was fully kitted out — oversuit, gloves, the lot — though he hadn't pulled the hood up, and he held the hard hat in his hand. *Afraid of messing up the hair*, Rickman thought.

'Keep to the stepping plates,' Mayle warned. 'And use the hood and the hat.'

Foster scooped his hood up as he approached. For a long moment he said nothing, merely stood with the hard hat clasped in his hands, his head bowed, in an attitude of prayer.

At last he raised his head and stared at the bodies. Rickman could see that he was struggling with violent emotions.

'Lee?'

Foster exhaled. 'I'd kick his head in if he wasn't already dead.'

Mayle glanced at Rickman, his concern clear — the mood Foster was in, he might just aim a kick at the corpse. Rickman placed a hand on his friend's shoulder and Foster looked into his face, his blue eyes glittering with rage.

'Mark knew this place was dangerous,' he said. 'He *knew* it. Why the hell would he come to this rathole — why would he put his baby in danger?'

'Come on,' Rickman said. 'Let the CSIs do their job, there's nothing we can do here.'

Foster seemed to debate a moment, then he turned and, without a word, climbed the ladder with an agility almost equal to his descent. Rickman followed more slowly. They paused outside the front door.

'Where's Hart?' Rickman asked.

'With Maitland's solicitor. Listening to the same pack of lies Maitland told us.'

'He's using his solicitor as an alibi?' Rickman asked.

'The way he talks, you'd think them two were joined at the hip.'

Rickman judged by Foster's tone of disgust that the interview hadn't gone well. As he stripped off his overshoes and white suit, he noticed the surveyor still hadn't moved. Rickman glanced at the constable.

'On their way, sir.'

Good — he didn't like the grey cast to the surveyor's skin. He'd seen enough people in distress to know that this man was in shock, and a quick evaluation put him in his mid-forties and slightly overweight — the perfect candidate for a heart attack.

'"Merseyside Property Development",' Foster said, glancing at the name on the side of the van. 'Ed and Hilary said the vultures were circling.'

'Not our problem, Lee,' Rickman said. 'But if they've been here a couple of days, he may have seen something useful.'

'None of it's gonna be any use to Bryony,' Foster said. He wrapped his suit into a neat bundle and tucked it under his right arm, curling his left around his hat like it was part of a naval uniform.

Rickman left his crime scene clothing and hard hat next to the door and headed for the surveyor's van. Foster made as if to join him, but Rickman said, 'I'll do this — you need to cool down.'

The surveyor stared through Rickman as though he was invisible, or perhaps no more than a screen upon which he

146

played and replayed the awful scene he had witnessed in the basement.

'Sir?' The man seemed to come to, looked surprised and rather worried to find himself sitting half in and half out of his van. Rickman introduced himself. 'And your name?'

'Cook.' It was as if stating his name re-established his connection with ordinary life, a life untroubled by the shocking discovery he had made. His brow cleared and he made as if to stand.

Rickman placed a hand on his shoulder. 'You can stay seated, Mr Cook,' he said. 'When did you find the bodies?'

Cook passed a hand over his forehead. 'Ten o'clock. I popped into the office, then came straight here. I—' He seemed to realise that he was talking too much and stopped.

'And the door was unlocked?'

Cook nodded. 'I got a call as I was locking up last night. I was distracted. I—'

'You forgot to secure the padlock.'

Another brief nod, then Cook closed his eyes tightly and tears squeezed from under the lids.

'When did you leave?'

'Five.' Cook wiped his eyes with the heel of his hand. 'Around five p.m.'

'Were the steps in that condition when you left?'

Cook shook his head. 'I've been using them for two days — the lads who came to put the steel props in used them. They were rickety, but . . . Why the *hell* would anyone take a baby into a place like this?' he burst out, looking to Rickman for an explanation. It was almost word for word what Foster had said, and Rickman guessed that it would be asked by commentators, presenters and the thousands of others who had invested so much emotion in Bryony's plight. The fact that Mark Davis was on the run from the police might go some way to explaining it, but why didn't Mark go to the house? Why didn't he go to Ed and Hilary Shepherd?

A paramedic unit pulled in alongside the surveyor's van, and Rickman stepped back to let them check out Cook.

Moments later, a man appeared at the end of the drive. Rickman recognised him as Ed Shepherd. His wife followed, brushing dead leaves from her coat.

Rickman caught Foster's eye and jerked his chin towards the couple.

Foster followed his line of sight and uttered an oath. He hurled his protective clothing to the ground and made a move in their direction. Rickman manoeuvred himself in front of his friend. 'Go easy,' he said.

Foster barged past him. 'You know what we found in there?'

Ed Shepherd paled.

'That place has been a death trap for years,' Foster said.

'Which is why there are steel plates on the windows and door,' Hilary said. She looked at them quizzically, as though she had not grasped fully the reason for their being there.

'So how did he get down there with a babe in arms?' Foster asked.

Hilary gasped and her hand flew to her mouth.

'You found Mark?' Ed Shepherd looked past them to the doorway of the coach house.

'And Bryony, yeah.'

Shepherd groped for his wife's hand and she grasped it firmly, as if bracing herself for the next blow.

'Did Davis call you?' Rickman asked. 'Did you know he was coming here?'

Ed Shepherd's lips began to form an answer, but it was his wife who spoke. 'We would have contacted you if he'd called.' Here was a glimpse of the steelier nature of the woman.

'Can you explain, then,' Rickman said, 'how he turned up in the basement of your coach house?'

It hardly seemed possible, but Ed Shepherd paled further, his skin almost luminous white in the gloom under the tree canopy. He tried to speak, but his breath creaked in his chest.

His wife turned to him. 'Ed!'

Shepherd waved her away, fishing in his trouser pocket and bringing out an inhaler. He took two sharp hits, then bent forward, his hands resting on his thighs as he fought to control his breathing. 'Jesus, Hil — he was here,' he gasped, a sick sheen of sweat emphasising his pallor. 'Mark was here.'

He took one great inhalation and seemed to stop. In the awful silence that followed, Rickman said, 'I'll fetch one of the paramedics.'

'No,' Hilary said. 'He'll be fine.'

But the medics had already noticed Shepherd's distress and hurried over. Within half a minute, they had him on oxygen in the ambulance.

Rickman and Foster followed it as it bumped over the tarmac with Ed Shepherd on board.

'Shit,' Foster said. '*Shit* . . . I've never seen him so bad.'

As the ambulance emerged onto the main drive, it had to squeeze past a Fiat Punto on its way to the big house.

The driver, a woman, rolled down her window and leaned out, her face anxious. 'Is everything all right?' she asked. 'Hilary and Ed, are they . . . Has there been an accident?'

'Mr Shepherd had an asthma attack,' Rickman said. 'We're police officers. Are you family?'

Her eyes widened. 'A friend,' she said. At that moment, Hilary Shepherd emerged onto the drive, looking bewildered. 'Hilary!'

'Anna!' Hilary hurried over to the passenger door of the Punto. 'Can you take me to the hospital? It's Ed — they wouldn't let me go with him in the ambulance.'

A child suddenly set up a wail, and Rickman bent to check out the Punto's interior. A two-year-old, fastened in the back seat, plucked ineffectually at its child restraints. The woman blushed, confused, looking in some consternation at the child, then back to Rickman.

'And you are?' he said.

'Oh, for heaven's sake!' She leaned across the passenger seat and popped the lock to allow Hilary Shepherd into the car. 'Shouldn't you be chasing criminals?'

Rickman traced the scar tissue above his right eyebrow as they watched the Fiat Punto back up and then turn in the drive.

'What d'you think?' Foster asked.

Rickman made a careful note of the licence plate.

CHAPTER 21

The boy's death gave him no pleasure. The light was poor and Davis struggled so violently he couldn't take the care he needed to craft the work. Davis was stronger than he looked, but the habit of victimhood, his horror of pain, and concern for the infant child robbed him of the power of action. Davis feared that if he failed, his child would certainly perish, even though logic and the evidence of what had already been done to him and to Jasmine Elliott indicated that she would perish no matter how he tried to appease.

Jasmine . . . breathe it softly. Her skin was the same creamy white, her nature as climbing and ambitious as the flower that was her namesake. When he touched her bare flesh for the first time, it was cold — shock, the drugs, her nakedness. A good sign, tacit acceptance of what he was about to do: she would not bleed too heavily when he cut her.

He had coveted that perfect, unblemished skin since the day he first saw her — three years ago? More? Then, she had been a child with the attitude of a streetwise teenager and the self-reliance of a mature woman. Her boldness, her refusal to be coerced, the arrogant superiority that kept her apart, always a notch above the others, always just beyond his reach, had both maddened and captivated him.

Being no career addict, Jasmine hadn't stayed long within his sphere, and he had thought her lost to him — which added a piquancy to his final possession of her. He had discovered at a young age that both pleasure and revenge are the more satisfying when deferred, and Jasmine's death had elements of both. Jasmine had understood this, and had known her fate as soon as she'd opened the door to him.

Davis, lacking her intelligence, had been childish in his assessment of the threat. Like the abused child he had been, he'd entertained the hope that if he did as he was told, he would be rewarded. Life should have taught him to see the lie in that line of reasoning — but fear, like a circular argument, brought Davis back to the starting place, his death and the death of his child made a certainty by his own unwillingness to act.

CHAPTER 22

Jeff Rickman skim-read his notes while a make-up artist dabbed at his forehead with a sponge and the sound technician made a final adjustment to the radio mike attached to his lapel. An ambitious producer on the evening news programme had seen the potential for national coverage of the deaths and the schedule had been cleared, with local news and travel consigned to the late-night slot in order to free up the necessary airtime. It meant Rickman travelling to Manchester — a one-hour trip each way — returning to Liverpool for the debrief, a press conference and two more post-mortems, but he was more than grateful for the opportunity.

They had three bodies and only Mark Davis as a likely suspect. Maitland's solicitor was unshakeable — he claimed to have spent the entire night with his client, that Maitland had stayed overnight and remained with him the next morning, discussing investment contracts. He had backed up Maitland's story word for fictional word, so unless Scientific Support turned up something new, they were in an investigative cul-de-sac.

The presenter was Quentin Knight. Smaller in the flesh than he appeared on television, he was sharply dressed in a dark grey suit, white shirt and grey silk tie. His dark hair looked freshly trimmed and gleamed under the studio lights. He was in conversation with a woman who wore a head mike and a battery pack clipped to her waist. At the call — 'Forty-five seconds!' — Knight finished his conversation and gathered his facial features into an expression of concern.

The presenter moved to his mark at the front of the studio, while Rickman was directed to a desk, complete with computer monitor and a dummy phone. Cameras pivoted and rolled forward as if by some choreographed arrangement.

Knight pressed the earpiece into his ear, shrugged his shoulders and then tilted his head down and to the side in a gesture that was at once serious and challenging. 'In a change to our advertised programme, *North West Newsbrief* investigates the brutal murder of a teenage mother on Merseyside. The nationwide search for little Bryony Elliott was brought to a tragic end this afternoon, with the discovery of two bodies — an adult and a baby — in an outbuilding of Black Wood Children's Home in Liverpool. The adult has been positively identified as Mark Davis, Bryony's father. The body of the infant has yet to be formally identified, but police have stepped down the search for the missing baby.

'Bryony was snatched from her home after her seventeen-year-old mother, Jasmine Elliott, was raped and brutally murdered.'

The presenter spoke to camera as if he was addressing the one viewer in all the millions watching who could help them. 'We'd like your help in finding out exactly what happened in this tragic series of incidents. Detective Chief Inspector Jeff Rickman is the officer in charge of this investigation.' He turned and Rickman's heart rate picked up a notch. 'Chief Inspector, can you give us an update on this disturbing and shocking chain of events?'

Rickman focused his reply on the presenter, as he had been instructed. 'Don't be tempted to divide your attention between the presenter and the camera,' the research assistant had told him. 'You'll only look shifty.'

'Jasmine Elliott was seventeen years old,' he began. The screen lit up on the computer monitor to Rickman's right. It showed the narrow terrace where Jasmine had lived, a police officer standing guard at the front door, the 'SOLD' sign in the little strip of garden behind the low brick wall that fronted the house.

Rickman talked over the footage, describing the discovery of Jasmine's body the day before, Bryony's abduction and the sightings of Mark all over the city in the hours that followed, finishing with the discovery of the bodies in the basement of the coach house.

On the second clip, an officer stood at the barrier tape near Jasmine's house accepting bouquets and wreaths from a small crowd of people waiting on the other side. The camera zoomed in on a row of bouquets lined up against the redbrick wall.

'"God keep her safe",' Knight said, reading from the close-up of one of the cards. 'The local community really have taken Bryony to their hearts, haven't they?'

'Bryony was just a few weeks old,' Rickman said. The camera cut to a still of Bryony asleep in her cot. 'I think every decent person must feel for her.'

'Mark Davis is a suspect, isn't he?' Knight said.

'Davis and Jasmine were separated,' Rickman said, 'and Davis was believed to have been pestering her.'

'He was seen driving away from Jasmine's house mid-morning on Wednesday.' The presenter wasn't trying to lead him, merely to ask the questions that would be uppermost in the minds of the public.

'Yes.'

'And this was shortly before Bryony's mother was found murdered.'

Neat touch — call it the murder of a mother, you'll always get a better response. 'We're keeping an open mind,' Rickman said. 'But someone out there might have seen or heard something. We'd like to know where Mark Davis was between eleven fifty a.m. on Wednesday and two thirty this afternoon, when the bodies were found.'

Two images appeared on a split screen — Mark's car and a picture of Mark Davis himself, looking gaunt and much older than his twenty years.

'Did you see this car?' Knight asked, addressing his one in a million again. 'Do you recognise Mark Davis? Are you a friend — did he contact you in those crucial missing hours before the discovery of the bodies? Call the emergency line and let us know — in confidence.'

The next shot was of the entrance to Black Wood, and a CSI van leaving the premises. 'Mark Davis and the as-yet-unidentified baby were found in a derelict building in the grounds of this children's home. Did *you* see Davis arrive?'

He addressed Rickman. 'Why is it taking so long to identify the baby?'

'Mr Davis was identified from fingerprint records, we have to wait for DNA results in order to positively identify the infant found at the scene.'

'Do we know how they died?'

'Post-mortems will be carried out later this evening,' Rickman said.

'And you're keen to talk to anyone who might have information about these two deaths,' Knight said. 'And the murder of Jasmine Elliott.'

'Naturally,' Rickman was grateful for the prompt. It was hot as a blast furnace under the lights, and the constant movement of cameras and the shadowy figures beyond them were distracting. 'Any information about Mark and Jasmine, their friends or associates could be crucial. Between ten p.m. on Tuesday and eleven fifty a.m. on Wednesday, Jasmine Elliott was subjected to a violent sexual assault and murdered,' he went on. 'You might have seen someone acting suspiciously outside the house. Perhaps you saw Jasmine's boyfriend arrive or leave. The time he arrived is vital to our investigation.

'Mark's Davis's car was found abandoned in Quarry Street, about half a mile from Black Wood Children's Home. He may have taken a short cut through the grounds of St

Francis Xavier School — perhaps you saw him. He was carrying Bryony, who was wrapped in a lemon-yellow blanket.'

The image of the entrance of Black Wood was replaced with one of Mark Davis's red Ford Focus, and Knight repeated the licence plate number for the viewers.

'Davis might have abandoned the car some distance away to disguise this destination,' Rickman said. 'We'd like to speak to anyone who saw Davis leave the car or walk the half mile to Black Wood Children's Home.'

'Did *you* see anything that might help police?' Knight demanded to know — as a duty — from every viewer. 'Jasmine Elliott had a difficult childhood and adolescence. She found herself in a downward spiral, addicted to heroin and cocaine. But she enrolled in a drugs programme when she realised she was pregnant, and never looked back. Jasmine was a devoted and loving mother to her little girl. Her life was cut short by a horrifying and brutal act.'

He stopped for a moment, giving the listeners time to reflect, then switched his attention to Rickman.

'But Jasmine *was* a former addict, and her ex-boyfriend was possibly dealing in drugs, so it's likely that people with information might be involved in criminal activities. Do they have anything to fear in coming forward?'

'If they weren't directly involved in the murders, they have nothing to fear,' Rickman said. This assurance had to be convincing, and he abandoned the agreed script in the heat of the moment. 'Jasmine was alone in the world, a young woman bravely trying to put right her past mistakes. She was horrifically assaulted and murdered while her baby daughter, Bryony, slept in the house.' He paused. 'We need to know the truth of what happened so that justice can be done.'

The presenter left another silence, which served to underline the imperative. 'There's a reward,' he said after a few seconds.

Rickman nodded. 'The *Liverpool Echo* has put up five thousand pounds and Crimestoppers is matching that amount.'

'So, a ten-thousand-pound reward . . .' Knight looked straight into the camera lens. 'That's a substantial amount for just picking up the phone. Now, if you're watching, and you're wondering whether to come forward with information, just take a look at this.'

Video footage played of Jasmine with Bryony in her arms — Jasmine, her defences down, staring at her baby in wonder and love, eyes brimming with tears as she says, 'I'm never gonna let nothing bad happen to her' — and Rickman knew that the millions watching would be more deeply moved by this intimate moment of tenderness between mother and child than by the descriptions of their deaths.

* * *

Rob Maitland had done his bit in the interests of law enforcement. *His* law, *his* methods of enforcement. But the crew of heavyweights he'd sent over to Birkenhead only seemed to inflame the situation. Attacks on his street-corner touts had escalated — beatings, mostly, but it was only a matter of time before someone ended up dead. Not that he objected to this in principle. His objection lay in the certainty that even one death would bring a heavier police presence onto the streets — and that was bad for business. So he had sent for someone who would have the insider knowledge he needed.

'Have the city's finest been attending to the threat to my business?'

'Oh, yes, Mr Maitland.'

'Is that it?' *Does this prick think his reassurance will be sufficient?*

The man standing on the other side of the desk shifted his weight from one foot to the other and looked at him in confusion.

Maitland prompted with an irritable, 'And?'

He was new — a civilian, average height, soft-looking, lacking the bulk of Maitland's enforcers and bodyguards.

'I — I don't know what you mean.' He sounded like a bewildered child.

'What's your name — Ellis, is it?'

The man nodded.

'Ellis. Pretend you're chatting on one of your online group-wank forums — tell me more than I ever needed to know.'

Ellis flushed and paled in quick succession. 'Kyle Nealy was arrested this morning for the machete attack — he still had blood on his trainers.'

Maitland nodded. This was more like it. 'And his brother?'

'Word's out on Darren — soon as he's in custody, you're in the clear.'

'Am I?' Maitland had wide-set eyes and a steady gaze that could take in a man entirely and always seemed to find him lacking. 'In the clear, that is?'

Ellis straightened, sensing that he had made an assertion too far, but willing to back up his assumptions with data. 'They've got nothing, Mr Maitland. You're not on the video footage of the drugs bust, and the alibi Mr Yates gave you is so rock solid, you could practically build a house on it.'

'You a lawyer, Ellis?'

The man's neck reddened. 'No, sir.'

'Piece of advice — stick to your own area of expertise.'

'I'm just saying what's in the reports, Mr Maitland.'

'You saw the report on my interview?'

'I downloaded it — it's all on here, sir.' He fished in his jacket pocket and produced a thumb drive.

Maitland turned the gadget over in his hand. It was a flat, silver-coloured stick, two centimetres long. 'All on here, huh?'

'The Nealy interviews as well, and a few emails. Anything they've got around to entering on the system.'

In days gone by, Maitland would have bought himself a pocket policeman, maybe several, because one man couldn't know everything Maitland needed to know. But modern technology dispensed with the need for risky relationships with cops. It provided him with virtual spies at every level

— you just needed to find the man with the right technical skills for the job.

'And my money?' Maitland glanced at the papers on his desk: profit and loss accounts for his coffee shops and the office block refurb that now housed his own office quarters and private accommodation. Bernie Carter had worked a miracle getting the accounts in order before the weekend, but the investors would expect more than a neatly packaged audit: Maitland would have to put his share of money into the pot. 'The Dutch consortium's drugs?'

The man winced. 'The drugs were never found. The m-money's already in the works,' he stammered.

In the works and out of his reach. Maitland felt sick with the loss of them, but he would rather kill this man than admit to the blow this news meant to his business. This office, the gleaming wood and glass of this entire building, were visible signs of his wealth, and of the legitimate side of his business. But he had other reserves, and he would recoup his losses — in pain and blood.

His desk phone rang, and he picked up.

It was Graham. 'Something you should see on TV, boss. BBC 1.'

Maitland clicked the remote control and two images appeared on a split screen — Mark's car and a picture of Mark Davis. Maitland felt a sour churning in his guts. Ellis nervously jingled the change in his trouser pockets and Maitland stared at him, wanting to reach across the table and grab him by the throat. The geek shifted his weight again, anxious to be gone, but Maitland wasn't quite ready to release him.

He almost missed the word 'bodies' with the roar of blood in his ears.

'Fuck,' he said, without expression. He still held the handset, but Graham remained silent, awaiting instructions. The air around Maitland always seemed to crackle with static. Now, as he thought through the implications of this new crisis, the electricity built around him like a gathering storm.

'A ten-thousand-pound reward . . .'

Maitland looked into the presenter's steady blue eyes on the TV screen and imagined he saw a hint of mockery in them. Ten thousand pounds' reward in exchange for two million. He kept his eyes cold and dead, and his guest stopped jingling the money in his pockets. As he swallowed, Maitland heard the dry click at the back of his throat.

'That's a substantial amount for just picking up the phone,' the presenter said. He even sounded like he meant it.

Not enough, Maitland thought. *Not nearly enough to compensate for what I'm going to do to anyone who does pick up the phone. I'll rip their fucking tongues out — I'll scoop their eyeballs out of their sockets and feed them to them with a spoon — I'll pour boiling fat into their ears and laugh my fuckin' arse off while they scream—*

He saw Ellis's eyes widen and wondered if he'd said any of this aloud. 'What do you know about this?' he demanded.

'Nothing — it's nothing to do with me,' the man protested, as if Maitland had accused him of the murders.

Maitland waited for the panic on the man's face to turn to cold, comfortless fear. 'Tell me,' he said. 'What am I paying you for, if you don't know what's going on?'

The question was rhetorical, but the man saw the need at least to attempt a reply. 'I looked up the files on the drugs investigation, like you said. I didn't think—'

'You persuaded me that your expertise would get me an all-access backstage pass to any investigation, any time.'

'It can — *I* can,' the man said, 'But I need to know—'

Maitland held up a finger. 'Don't interrupt. *You* said having a computer engineer on the inside would be like having a chief superintendent in the palm of my hand.'

'I can get you any file you want,' the man said, more subdued this time, but recognising that a lucrative sideline — and maybe even his life — depended on making a convincing case for himself. 'But I need to know what to look for.'

'Okay. Here's my shopping list: I want to know who's been interviewed and who's given Rickman information. If they so much as commented on the weather, I want to hear about it.'

Ellis nodded. 'You will, I'll find out.'

He seemed anxious to leave, and Maitland was keen to get on with what he needed to do, but names were no good on their own. 'I haven't finished yet,' he said. 'I want phone numbers, mobile numbers, addresses, family details — the lot.'

Ellis stood blinking at him.

'Go and do your homework,' Maitland said. 'I'll be in touch.'

Ellis headed for the door just short of a run, and Maitland tilted his head right and left, hearing a satisfying click with each movement.

He spoke into the phone. 'You still there?'

'Boss.' Graham, calm, unflappable, always ready to do his bidding.

Maitland gripped the handset so hard he heard the plastic creak from the pressure. 'We've got a situation,' he said.

CHAPTER 23

The TV played at low volume. Bernie Carter was nursing a gin and tonic and waiting for the local bulletin. A key rattled in the front door and he felt a spasm of tension — Meg and the girls, back from some sports event or other. They would scavenge something from the kitchen first, but soon they would tumble into the sitting room and disrupt his one quiet moment of the day. His hand went to the remote control next to him on the sofa.

He heard a laugh — Julia's — high and unpleasant, no doubt tormenting her younger sister. Sally whined in complaint, then Meg's voice, low and warm, gently reprimanding. The kitchen door opened and closed, and the sounds were shut out. He tried to focus on the TV but kept straining to hear the girls. Ten minutes — all he needed was ten minutes to watch *North West Newsbrief*. He thought he heard the scrape of a chair in the kitchen and was on the point of abandoning the sitting room for the sanctuary of his study, when the *Newsbrief* banner flashed on-screen.

'In a change to our advertised programme, *North West Newsbrief* investigates the brutal murder of a teenaged mother on Merseyside . . .'

Carter's heart picked up the rhythm of the introductory drumbeat.

'The nationwide search for little Bryony Elliott was brought to a tragic end—'

A tragic end? His mouth dried. *No . . .* The sound seemed to fade for a few seconds as fearful thoughts intruded.

'—the discovery of two bodies,' the presenter went on, each sentence underlined by another insistent drum roll.

'God, no . . .' *Jesus . . .* His heart hammered in his chest and he took a swallow of his drink, setting it down on the glass coffee table with a clatter.

'. . . an adult and a baby.'

The sitting room door burst open and his girls bounced in.

'Daddy!' As the younger of the two, Sally was still pleased when Daddy came home early from work. She flung herself next to him and leaned against him like an affectionate puppy, happily chomping on an apple.

'Not now, darling.' Carter tried to ease away from her, but she slipped one slightly sticky hand through the crook of his arm and pressed her cheek, still cool from the night air, to his shirtsleeve.

Julia was twelve, and too mature for such childish displays. She plonked herself to his right. 'The *news?*' she said, as though she had caught him watching porn.

He turned up the volume. The presenter said Mark Davis was suspected of murdering Jasmine and snatching the baby.

'Can't you watch this in your study?' Julia demanded. '*Hollyoaks* is on.'

'No!' Sally clung to him. 'I want you to stay *here.*'

'Girls, *please.*'

'Sally, *please,*' Julia mimicked, leaning forward to taunt her sister.

How much more can go wrong?

He recalled Maitland's little barb at the sergeant that afternoon: 'Redevelopment reduces the crime rate,' he'd said. *Or uncovers crimes that would be better left undiscovered.*

'Daddy, Sally stuck her tongue out at me.'

'Be quiet, Julia.'

Sally squeezed his arm tighter, a gesture of solidarity. 'Yes,' she said, 'Be quiet.'

Maitland was bad enough after the shambles on Tuesday. Now nobody will be safe.

His head began to throb, and he put his fingers to his right temple. Julia seized the opportunity to snatch the remote control and switch channels.

'Give me that,' he said.

'No.' Julia gave him that practised insolent look he was sure she had learned from her loud friends. 'Go and watch the boring news on your *own* TV.'

Carter felt a hot flush of blood to his face and the headache began to pulse. 'Julia.' He untangled himself from Sally's grip and stood up. Spots of dark colour bloomed at the edges of his vision: the headache was worsening rapidly. 'Give me the damn control.'

Julia folded her arms, tucking the wand tight against her bony chest.

'Now, Julia.'

'Daddy, you're in the *way*.' Julia angled her body to look around him at the TV screen.

Carter slapped her.

He didn't think. It wasn't premeditated — it just . . . happened.

The girls stared at him with a look of frightened wonder, like they had felt a small earthquake, and weren't sure any more if the ground would support them.

Carter blinked. 'Julia, darling—' He reached out to touch the livid marks of his fingers on her cheek and she leapt to her feet. The control slipped through her fingers and rattled onto the coffee table.

'I hate you!' she screamed, trembling from head to foot.

Meg came into the room, drying her hands on a tea towel, and Sally slipped from the sofa to go and stand by her mother.

Meg looked from her husband to her daughter. 'What on earth?'

Julia burst into tears, sobbing into her hands.

Sally whispered, 'Daddy smacked her.' Her awe and horror at this aberration were reflected in Meg's expression.

'Bernard!'

'I *need* to watch this programme.' He scooped up the control. The sudden rush of blood to his head set it throbbing till he thought his skull would burst. 'I'll talk about it later,' he said. 'But please let me finish' — he had to swallow against a wave of nausea — 'let me finish watching this programme.' He flicked back to the news.

The presenter had asked Rickman a question Carter had missed.

'Post-mortems will be carried out on Mr Davis and the baby girl later this evening,' Rickman replied.

Meg raised her voice. 'For God's *sake*, Bernard.'

'Later.' He tried to sound reasonable, but he heard the tremor of rage, and so must they, because for a blessed moment Julia stopped crying and ran to her mother. He turned to the television. 'Now get out.'

His wife was so startled that it took her a moment to find her voice. 'What on earth has got into you? Why must you watch that vile stuff anyway?'

He wheeled back to her. 'All I *want*' — he was shouting, losing control in a way he found undignified and humiliating, but which he was powerless to rein back, despite the pain that hammered at his temples with every word — 'All I'm *asking* is to watch what *I* choose on my *own* TV in my *own fucking sitting room.*'

Meg gave a little gasp and now both girls started to weep, Sally providing a counterpoint to her sister's wailing.

They were afraid of him at that instant, and Carter felt ashamed, but self-pity overwhelmed any nobler instinct.

You don't know what fear is, he thought.

* * *

166

By seven p.m. Rickman had left the TV studio and was on a long, curving stretch of the M62 heading for Liverpool. A waxy moon, the colour of a cadaver, hung low on the horizon, revealing thin trails of mist on the flat, featureless farmland either side of the motorway. Rickman felt his attention wander and cracked open a window to keep himself awake. The air smelled of marsh water and leaf fall.

He'd borrowed a firm's car in case he needed the sirens and the option of using the hard shoulder to slip through the rush hour traffic. He eyed the radio, willing Foster or Hart to get in touch — even a call from the ponderous Chris Tunstall would be welcome to break the silence. He fiddled with the controls to convince himself the damn thing was still working: if the TV coverage didn't bring forward viable witnesses, they were sunk.

After another ten minutes, he muttered, 'To hell with it.' He fished his mobile from his trouser pocket, pressed the contact number for Foster then switched to hands-free and propped the phone on the dashboard.

'All right, boss.' It wasn't an enquiry after his health, merely Foster's version of a neutral greeting.

'Tell me it's good news,' Rickman said.

'Fifty calls so far.'

'Anything we can use?'

'A lot of new leads to follow.'

Rickman swallowed his impatience. 'We'll have twenty more officers and civilian staff by tomorrow — now tell me what the hell is happening.'

'Sorry, boss — looks like we'll be able to put together a timeline, once we've sorted the sheep from the goats.'

Rickman was surprised by the metaphor, but then he remembered Foster had been educated by Jesuits, and it seemed less remarkable. He slowed at the junction with the M6 to let a couple of HGVs on from the slip road.

'We got a call from someone who claimed she knew why Mark Davis was at Black Wood.'

'Don't we know that already?' Rickman asked. 'I mean his connection with the Shepherds?'

167

'That's what I thought,' Foster said. 'But she hung up before the operator could get a name or contact details out of her, so we haven't been able to check. Knight put out an appeal at the end of the programme, guaranteeing her anonymity and protection.'

'Let's hope she calls back.'

'Um . . .'

'For God's sake, spit it out, Lee,' Rickman exclaimed, way past exasperation at this point.

'Okay. Jasmine Elliott's mother called. She's threatening to sue Merseyside Police for making her look like a bad mother.'

'She did that all by herself,' Rickman said. 'Let me know if anything urgent comes up. I'll go straight to the hospital for the PMs.' The post-mortems of Davis and the baby were timetabled to run consecutively.

'Will you head back here, after?'

'If Dr Griffith finishes before midnight — otherwise, I'll see you in the morning.'

He broke the connection, still thinking of Jasmine Elliott. Neglected and ignored by her mother, she was among those Rickman thought of as the lost souls, the invisible children whose bleak adulthood seem presaged by their childhood. A few, like Foster, made something of their lives, overcoming the impediments of birth and family, but they never got out unscathed, not entirely. He recalled the photograph of Jasmine with Mark Davis. Jasmine staring out at the world, strung out, defiant, vulnerable. Inevitably, the images of Jasmine, murdered and defiled, came unbidden into his mind, and he thought that, despite the beatings and the scars, his own childhood had been a walk in the park.

The motorway ended abruptly, tailing off to a fifty-mile-per-hour speed limit, then forty, fetching up among 1940s semi-detached suburban properties owned by comfortable middle-class families. He continued towards Edge Lane and joined the slow crawl of traffic.

It took thirty minutes to make the two-mile journey to the hospital. He parked across the road in the multi-storey and made his way to the mortuary with a heavy heart.

* * *

The post-mortems took longer than expected, and Rickman left feeling wrung out. The sight of the tiny baby on the table, grey, almost doll-like, seemed a travesty, and even Griffith had been subdued as he worked on the child.

At one thirty a.m., Rickman eased onto the silent streets, desperate to empty his mind of what he had just seen, aching for rest. Sometimes, in the quiet hours when sleep evaded him, Rickman would drive the deserted streets, past silent homes, searching for something — he wasn't sure what — perhaps for peace, a little respite from the guilt that had tormented him since November of the previous year.

At first, he had relied on booze to ease his pain, but he'd gone through too many nights of broken sleep, waking in a sweat, his heart pounding, his mouth dry, the memory of that day searing with colour and sound and emotion so strong, it was like reliving it second by monstrous second. He preferred now to work himself to exhaustion, in the hope that if he did dream, he would be so stupefied that, on waking, he wouldn't remember.

The journey home was soothing, and when he turned into the drive of his house, he was ready for sleep. He dumped his briefcase and overcoat in the hallway, and a movement at the top of the stairs caught his eye: Tanya. She pushed a lock of hair from her face and peered down at him.

'Jeff? Is that you?' She sounded anxious.

'Yes,' Rickman said. 'Are you all right?'

'Simon was here.' She gathered her dressing gown around her and tied the belt.

Rickman felt a jolt of alarm. The energy Simon carried with him in recent months had an unpredictable quality to it. Before, it was fed by a restless enthusiasm and interest in

169

everything, now it seemed nourished by a darker force, and there was an uneasy aggression at the root of his nature that reminded Rickman disconcertingly of their father. 'Did he . . .' Rickman didn't know how to word it. *Did he have one of his episodes? Did he frighten you?*

'He wouldn't come in.' She stepped lightly down the stairs in her bare feet. 'He was calm,' she added, evidently following Rickman's train of thought. 'He asked me why I was here.' She smiled, her mouth twisting in uncharacteristic bitterness. 'Actually, he said, "Why are you even here?" I tried to talk to him, to explain to him about the legal situation.'

Shit. Rickman remembered he had promised to find legal representation for Simon. 'What did he say?'

'"Anything to get you off my back."' Tanya looked more hurt than offended.

Rickman took her hand. It felt cold. 'Come and have a drink with me, we'll talk about it.'

She shook her head. 'There's no point, Jeff.'

'Disinhibition,' he explained. 'It's just another symptom of the brain damage. He doesn't mean it—'

'Yes,' she said, 'he does.' She exhaled slowly, and when she spoke again, her voice wasn't quite steady. 'He just doesn't know how to suppress the urge to say it.'

Rickman wanted to tell her she was mistaken, but his lips wouldn't form the lie. 'God, Tanya, I'm so sorry.' He drew her into his arms and embraced her. She rested her cheek against his shoulder for a moment, then gently disengaged herself.

'The papers are with my British lawyers,' she said. 'I'll pass on copies to you when they've finished the necessary amendments.'

CHAPTER 24

Consciousness came slowly. An awareness of the dark and of something not quite right. A noise? Lars Lindermann reached for his wife, a gesture of protection and reassurance. The sheets were cold. He listened — perhaps one of the children had woken her. Vicky would tend to them, but Kim couldn't bear to think of Oliver and Leonie alone in the dark. She would go to comfort them, often sending the nanny back to bed, while she soothed the children to sleep.

No sound.

Lindermann swung out of bed, his long, bony feet seeking out the leather mules he wore as slippers. It was chilly and he shivered as he slipped on his dressing gown and padded along the landing to listen at the nursery door. All was quiet.

Puzzled, he turned the corner to try Kim's office door. The room was empty, the swatches of fabric she had been experimenting with earlier in the day lay abandoned on the sofa, along with her workbook.

Lindermann leafed through her sketches and notes, marvelling at his wife's imagination and versatility. As much at home with bold colours and flamboyant soft furnishings as she was with pastels and hard architectural lines, Kim had taken three identical apartments and created unique living spaces, each with its own mood and distinctive atmosphere.

At times like this, his love for her took him by surprise, knocking the wind out of him. It was Kim's exuberant creativity that had seduced him at the beginning, and she was still capable of taking him unawares — giving him an emotional dig in the ribs to remind him why he had first fallen for her.

He replaced the sketchbook and tiptoed out of the office, afraid, almost, of disturbing the swirl of creative energy in the room.

He found Kim in the TV room, sitting cross-legged on the floor, one of Leonie's soft toys hugged to her chest. Her hair, almost black in the poor light, tumbled over her shoulders, partly obscuring her face, but he knew she was crying.

Lindermann recognised Jasmine Elliott on the TV screen. '*Perfect* little nails,' Jasmine said. 'I'm never gonna let nothing bad happen to her. Never.'

Kim rewound the recording and played it again. And again. Lars sat next to her and closed his hand gently over hers.

'You're freezing.' He put his arm around her. The skin of her arms was marked with striations — faded pink parallel lines, some straight, as though drawn with a ruler, others in swirls and circles. The scars were almost invisible in this light, but he could feel them under his fingers, and though it pained him, he could never forget that they were there, nor what had been done to her.

Kim turned from the TV screen, her startling green eyes magnified by tears. 'She saved me, Lars,' she said. 'Why couldn't I save her?'

He folded her in his arms, and she buried her face in his neck, her tears burning his skin. 'I should have saved her,' she whispered.

CHAPTER 25

Friday

Mist settled in the colder dips and pockets of Mossley Hill like the first damp breath of winter, as Rickman made his way to work early the next morning. A ground frost glistened on the pavements. Autumn was gathering momentum — the fiery reds and oranges of the maples and beeches in the leafier suburbs augured another iron-grey winter.

The car park was emptying when he arrived at Edge Hill Police Station at seven fifteen. The Targeted Patrol Team were leaving for home and a few hours' sleep. For CID, the day had not yet started.

He skimmed the phone messages that had come in since the TV appeal — close to two hundred at a conservative estimate. He rapidly sorted the low-priority tasks into a separate pile, then checked his emails. CSC Tony Mayle had made a couple of findings that might prove useful. He printed the text and attachments from Mayle, then rummaged in his briefcase for his notebook to cross-check the PM results.

'Well, *you* look like shite.'

Rickman looked up from his work. Foster leaned against the door frame, Rickman suspected, more for support than effect. 'You're looking frayed around the edges yourself.'

'It's all relative, mate — and at least I *enjoyed* getting wrecked.'

'Did you?' He knew Foster too well to be fooled by the bravado and the banter.

True to form, Foster looked ready to make a flippant remark, but then he shrugged. 'Half a bottle of whisky watching crap on the box on your tod doesn't strictly qualify as enjoyment, I'll grant you that,' he said. 'But it got me pissed enough to pass out before the reruns of *Kojak* started, and that's something to be thankful for.'

Rickman was supposed to laugh — that would be the easy way past this difficult moment, but ignoring problems just drove them deeper, burrowing under the skin like a canker. 'You couldn't have prevented these deaths, Lee,' he said.

'Naomi said that, an' all.'

From the rueful look on his face Rickman guessed that Foster hadn't reacted too kindly. He tilted his head. 'Well, Naomi talks a lot of sense.'

Foster sighed, giving up on the bravado. 'Maybe I could've helped Mark adjust once he left care. Maybe I could've kept him away from drugs. Maybe I could even have prevented their deaths. Fact is, Jeff, I'll never know.'

Rickman could find no words of comfort, and after a short silence Foster cleared his throat. 'So, how was the PM?'

Rickman closed his eyes and got a flash, vivid as dreaming, of Bryony on the post-mortem table, the infant's marble-white skin against cold, unforgiving steel. 'Rough,' he said.

The room shifted sideways and he gave his head a shake, which only made him feel worse. 'Let's grab a coffee.' He bundled together the phone slips, papers and his notebook and headed for the door. 'The PM results threw us a few curve balls and I want you to hear them before the additional support staff arrive.' He checked his watch — it was still only seven thirty, and they had worked late the previous night. 'Ideally, I'd like Tunstall and Hart in on this.'

'They're already in, boss,' Foster reassured him. 'I saw Hart pull in to the car park as I got here.'

Rickman noted that Foster hadn't spoken to Hart. Whatever had happened during the course of their interviews the day before, it seemed they hadn't yet resolved their differences.

* * *

Foster walked into the Incident Room ahead of Rickman and nodded a greeting to Tunstall and Hart. During his whisky-soaked broodings the previous night, he had tried to think of a way of making things right with Naomi. He had discounted flowers almost immediately — too patronising, and they might send the wrong message. He considered a straightforward apology — Maitland had got to him, he had lashed out at the nearest person, and he regretted every word he'd said. Of *course* Naomi couldn't understand what life was like in care, but it didn't matter that she couldn't understand, so long as she could sympathise. Perhaps that was the problem: Foster himself was as much a product of the care system as Mark Davis was. He didn't mind if Hart thought him an idiot, a shallow flirt and a womaniser. But he couldn't abide the thought of her seeing him as pathetic.

So he did the only reasonable thing, under the circumstances — he went on as if nothing had happened, greeting Naomi with a neutral, 'All right?'

She responded with a wary, 'Morning, Sarge.'

Tunstall gave them both a bleary-eyed look. 'You two're a bright pair of little sunbeams this morning, aren't you?'

While Rickman set out his notes and the pink message slips, Tunstall moved to the tea table, looking like a large grazing animal in search of fresh pasture. 'A nice cuppa'll set us right.'

'Make it quick — we need to focus,' Rickman said. 'You've seen the stack of phone messages from the TV coverage. There'll be the usual cranks, crackpots and time-wasters, so they'll need sifting, but I had a skim through and there's also a number of potentially useful leads.'

'Well I hope one of them's got a plug on the end,' Tunstall said mournfully, ''Cos I can't get going without a decent brew.' He held up the kettle, still with its chain attached. The electrical lead was missing.

'Don't tell me they've nicked it!' Foster exclaimed.

'What the hell has got into that lot?' Rickman demanded.

'All the excitement must've made them giddy,' Foster said.

Rickman lifted his chin, an invitation to him to explain.

'A couple of kidnappings overnight,' Foster said. 'The victims were dumped at the Royal in the early hours. Had the shit kicked out of them.'

'Whose mob?' Rickman asked.

'Nobody's talking, but the victims have been identified as Maitland's lads.'

'Payback from the Birkenhead crew?'

'That's what I'm thinking,' Foster said. 'It looks like Darren Nealy used his Saveaway tickets to Ferry 'Cross the Mersey and exact a bit of revenge for his brother's arrest.'

A hubbub of conversation drew the team's attention to the open doorway.

'DI Dwight's called an early briefing,' Foster said. 'Trying to make up for all the brownie points he lost on Snowplough.'

Thirty or more officers, some in plain clothes, some in uniform, trooped past their door into the drugs inquiry Major Incident Room, talking, coughing. It was too early for laughter.

Rickman closed the door. 'Lab results first,' he said. 'DNA from the vomit found at the scene of Jasmine's murder belongs to Mark Davis. We already know there's no DNA from vaginal swabs. No blood from Davis at the scene, but his fingerprints were found.'

'I've said it before — why wear a condom and not gloves?' Foster asked of nobody in particular.

'On that subject, Ed Shepherd's prints were found on the padlock on the coach house front door.'

Foster thought for a moment. 'Ed used to do regular checks — they were terrified someone'd get trapped down there.' He realised what he'd said and gave his head a shake.

'We need to ask, anyway,' Rickman said. 'COD on the infant was respiratory failure. Tox screen results have come through as well — they found morphine.'

'In the *baby's* blood?' Foster said.

'Jasmine was back on the drugs?' Hart asked.

'No,' Rickman said. 'Jasmine's blood was clear — except for traces of Rohypnol.'

'The date rape drug?' Tunstall said.

Hart exhaled. 'That's why nobody heard anything — he kept her subdued with roofies.'

'Dr Griffith thinks it was administered in carefully measured amounts, so that she was aware, but unable to put up much of a struggle.'

'Bastard,' Foster muttered.

'What about Jasmine and Mark?' Hart asked.

'Mark was subjected to a prolonged attack.'

'Mark was *attacked*?'

'It looks like it,' Rickman said.

Tunstall chipped in. 'He was buried under a ton of rubble — couldn't that've caused the damage?'

'He had a broken nose, a fracture to his cheekbone, and a shattered pelvis,' Rickman said, trying to block the details of what he'd seen from his mind. 'But Griffith couldn't state with absolute certainty that those injuries were caused by anything other than an accident.'

Rickman handed out photographs from Tony Mayle's message. 'You're looking at blood spatter on the walls and some pooling on the basement floor of the coach house. It was displaced from the final position of Mark's body. There was so much rubble overlaying it, they missed it at first.'

Foster angled the printout of one of the walls, tilting it to the light. The black-and-white image wasn't entirely clear, but the pattern of spatter gave him a sudden jolt. 'Cast-off?' he asked.

Rickman nodded, and Tunstall crowded Foster to get a look at the image. Hart looked across and Foster handed her the photo. She took it with a polite, 'Thank you,' and studied it more closely than the subject matter warranted.

'So far — and they've only been able to do preliminary tests — all the blood is Mark Davis's,' Rickman said, glancing from Hart to Foster, a slight frown on his face. 'However, he did find multiple wounds — slashes and superficial stabbings.'

'That sounds familiar.' Foster's heart thudded with suppressed excitement.

'Not identical to Jasmine's injuries,' Rickman cautioned. He handed out the post-mortem photographs as if to spare himself the need of describing the difference. 'Some of the shallower, parallel cuts bear a striking resemblance to the wounds on Jasmine's body. Dr Griffith says Jasmine was tortured with intense control and precision. Mark—' Again, he seemed at a loss for words. 'Well, Mark wasn't.'

'Less control,' Hart said. 'So whoever killed Mark was in a rage?'

'Could be,' Rickman said. 'Griffith would only say that some of the wounds required "considerable force".'

Tunstall seemed to let all this pass him by, his thought processes several synapses behind the majority. 'I don't want to sound silly,' he said, his face screwed up in concentration, 'but d'you get cast-off from suicide stabbings? I mean, is it possible Mark killed *himself* — out of remorse, like?'

'For blood spatter, the arc of the swing would have to be big enough to get some momentum behind it,' Rickman explained. 'Typically, cuts from self-harm are tentative. The knife is held close to the body, so you wouldn't expect to see cast-off.' Tunstall took a breath as a preliminary to another question, but Rickman forestalled him. 'Just so we're clear,' he said. 'Dr Griffith thinks that Mark was murdered.'

Foster suppressed an eyeroll. He was learning that Tunstall had his strengths — quick thinking just wasn't one of them.

'Did they find any blood from the baby?' he asked.

Rickman shook his head.

Hart spoke up, tapping her notepad to emphasise the point. 'A moment ago, you said, "All the blood is Mark's *so far.*" Does that mean they're expecting to find somebody else's?'

'Scientific Support found blood on a wood splinter from the staircase,' Rickman said, and Foster saw a smile of approval touch the corners of his mouth. 'It's a tiny amount, and it's been contaminated with plaster and brick dust, but the lab's doing what it can. Could take a while.'

'So, either Mark killed Jasmine and someone caught up with him—'

'*Or,*' Foster interrupted, flipping through the blood spatter photos and staring at the slight differences in pattern and angle like they were a cartoon animation, 'Mark found Jasmine dead, rescued Bryony, made a run for it and . . .'

'Someone caught up with him,' Hart finished for him.

'Maitland?' Foster asked.

'He's the most dangerous man Mark or Jasmine knew,' Rickman said. 'He certainly had reason to come after Mark. And for what it's worth, I'm with you on this, Lee — I don't think Mark killed Jasmine.'

CHAPTER 26

He carries a scalpel with him at all times. He'd tried a craft knife in the early days, but the tiny serrations at the edge of the blades tore rather than cut the flesh. Such wounds don't heal so well, and the scars are untidy, ugly. After several exploratory sessions, he'd he settled on the Swann-Morton disposable — he had even tried it on himself once, to feel what it was like. It was like nothing he had ever experienced. The pain was acute, intense, hot. The sight of his blood seeping from the wound had alarmed him: he was fearful it wouldn't stop, that his life, his energy would flow out of him unchecked. Panicked, he'd bound the wound tight and waited, counting the fevered minutes until the wadding came away dry. He didn't care to repeat the experiment.

In contrast, the girls' blood excites him. Each incision gapes infinitesimally, like lips responding to the angel kisses of his scalpel. He knows precisely how deep to cut, how much pressure to apply with clean gauze before administering the next. He creates symmetry — finds the beauty underlying the blandness of unadorned flesh.

A psychologist would no doubt say that his artwork was about control, power. They would be wrong. It's not the girls' powerlessness that excites him, it's their submissiveness. It's true, there is a sexual charge in watching their faces as he hurts them. Their fear is exciting, and their pain sends bolts of energy through him, so that every nerve ending feels juiced with electrical charge. But it is the girls' passivity, their willingness to give themselves to him, that is most seductive. He hasn't the insight to understand that their submission conveys power to him.

CHAPTER 27

A sudden burst of noise from the corridor roused Foster from a study of the hotline messages. It seemed that the drugs team in the Major Incident Room next door were playing a video recording. The hallway reverberated with the sound of revving engines and the scream of brakes, overlaid with a commentary typical of police pursuit.

'Sounds like Dwight's lot are auditioning for *Police, Camera, Action!*' Hart commented.

'*Keystone Kops*, more like,' Foster said, glad of the opportunity to engage her in conversation. 'The Eye in the Sky was in the area when Maitland's lads got dumped. They're watching the video footage.'

'How do you *know* all this?' she asked.

Normally, he would make a flippant remark, such as, 'Nose to the grindstone, ear to the ground.' But his heightened sensitivity that morning made him reinterpret her comment as an indictment.

A cheer went up in the MIR, followed by a loud bang. The audience gave a low '*Ooh!*' and broke into ragged applause.

A rattling of chairs from across the hall signalled the end of the session, and the drugs team emerged from the MIR, laughing, keyed up for the day's work. One wit shouted above the rest, in a nasal-American accent, 'Let's do it to dem before dey do it to us!'

Naomi Hart rolled her eyes. 'With all this testosterone floating around, I think my voice is dropping.'

Foster felt it as a personal jibe, but when he looked at her, Hart was jotting a note down on the pad in front of her.

The phone on the desk next to Hart trilled, and she picked up and gave her name. Foster noticed her tense. 'For DCI Rickman,' she said.

Foster jerked his chin in question.

She covered the mouthpiece with her hand, a fire in her eyes. 'No name, but she says she heard the appeals to call back — I think it's our mystery caller.'

Rickman had just left the room and Foster ran out to call him back. The DCI had been held up by the crush of drugs inquiry team members and returned in a moment, took the receiver from Hart and pressed speakerphone. Hart, Foster and Tunstall all leaned in to listen.

'Are you the feller off the telly?' The caller sounded young, female.

'I'm Detective Chief Inspector Rickman,' he said. 'I'm leading the inquiry.'

An ex-resident? Foster wondered. *Someone who knew Mark from the children's home?*

'There's a reward, right?'

Straight to the point.

'For information resulting in the prosecution of suspects in the murder of Jasmine Elliott,' Rickman clarified.

'So, how do I get the money?'

'The way it works is we take some details, and get back to you if your information helps us to catch the killer.'

'I'm not giving my name!' Her voice became high and panicky.

'You can make one up if you like,' Rickman's voice was warm and reassuring. 'As long as you use the same name each time, to keep things straight — how's that?' They heard her breathing and the sound of traffic close by.

183

'Melanie Townsend,' she said at last. 'I won't talk to no one but you.'

'That's fine,' Rickman said. 'I can give you my mobile number if you like.'

'I haven't got a pen!' Again, the panicky note in her voice.

'Don't worry,' he soothed. 'Just remember for next time — I'll give it to you then.'

Foster knew that his priority was to establish reliable means of contact — after all, she might hang up and never call back — but he wished to God Rickman would ask her what she knew.

'How can I reach you?' Rickman asked.

'You can't,' she said, sounding immediately suspicious.

'Okay, but this is on your bill. Do you want me to call you back?'

She hesitated. 'I'm in a phone box.'

'No problem, just give me the number, I'll call you right back.'

Foster mouthed, 'What're you doing?' Rickman was taking a hell of a risk.

'You send anyone, I'm gone,' she warned.

'I won't send anyone, I promise.'

He jotted down the number and she hung up.

'Are you off your trolley?' Foster demanded. 'What if she isn't there when you call back?'

Rickman handed the slip of paper to Hart as he dialled. 'There aren't many usable phone kiosks left in Liverpool, and most of those are in the city centre,' he said. 'See if there's any CCTV in the vicinity, will you?'

That was DCI Rickman for you — hard to read. Crazy like a fox.

DC Hart zipped out of the office as his mystery caller picked up. 'Miss Townsend,' Rickman said, and she giggled.

'Call me Melanie.'

'Melanie. You said you knew why Mark Davis was at the children's home the night of Jasmine's murder.'

''Cos of the baby.'

'Bryony?' Rickman said. 'Was Mark going to leave Bryony at the home?'

'Sort of. They buy them.'

'I don't understand,' Rickman said, his voice calm, but Foster knew him well enough to hear the agony of anticipation in it — hell, he felt it himself. 'Who buys what?'

'Them two that run the home. Hilary and Ed — they buy babies.'

Jesus . . . The hairs on the back of Foster's neck stood up. *Baby trafficking?*

'How do you know this?' Rickman asked.

'Kel— my mate told me. She got put in the home for a bit.'

Kel? Kelly?

Rickman jotted the name on a slip of paper and added, 'Former Black Wood resident?' Foster scooped up the sheet and turned to one of the computers. His hands trembled as he called up the database of former residents' names.

'She left at sixteen. Got pregnant. They took her baby.'

'*Took* it?'

She tutted impatiently. 'Well, they didn't grab it out of her *arms* or nothing. They did give her cash for it.'

'How much cash?'

'Dunno — a few thousand?'

Hart returned, and Rickman covered the mouthpiece.

'She's on Lime Street Station,' Hart said, keeping her voice down. 'They'll email a couple of screen-caps to my computer.'

Rickman asked the caller, 'When did all this happen?'

While Rickman talked, Hart accessed her email.

'Melanie, are you there?' Rickman asked. 'When did your friend—?'

'I'm thinking, aren't I?' she snapped. She left an angry silence before saying, 'Five years — about that, anyway.'

Hart angled her monitor so that Foster could see it. The CCTV screen capture showed the woman entering the phone box. Mid-twenties, overweight, fair, with a face that already looked battered by life's disappointments. Foster shook his head. She didn't look familiar. Rickman gave Hart the thumbs up.

'Melanie, I have to check this, but—'

'*Fine*,' she said. 'Call me a liar.' The line went dead.

'Shit!' Rickman pressed the receiver to his brow.

Tunstall said, 'Oh, hell . . .'

'She'll call back,' Hart said. 'Greed like that, she's bound to call back.'

Foster exhaled in one long breath. 'We've got her on camera — if all else fails, we can put out an appeal.'

Rickman hung up, looking disgusted with himself. 'Anything from the database?'

Foster stared in dismay at the table of names — thousands of children, going back ten years, some of whom would have stayed at Black Wood for a matter of days, others for years. 'It'll take a while.'

Hart peered over his shoulder. 'You need to interrogate the database,' she said — and when it was plain this meant nothing to him, 'Do an advanced search.'

'You what?'

'Look.' She leaned across him and typed swiftly at the keyboard. He couldn't follow what she did, distracted by the heady scent of her perfume and the closeness of her. Moments later, the printer whirred into life.

'I searched for "kel" or "quel" in the given and surname, from the present to six years ago.' Hart handed Rickman the sheet of paper. 'Which gives us a list of fifty-three girls.'

'And another fifty-three possible witnesses to interview,' Rickman's thumb traced the line of the scar on his chin. 'Looks like we just got thrown another curveball.'

'Have we just added Ed and Hilary Shepherd to the list of suspects?' Tunstall asked.

'Lee.'

Foster focused on Rickman's face.

'Are you okay with this?'

He felt like someone had punched a hole in his chest and dragged his beating heart out through his ribcage, but he wasn't about to admit it. He sensed Tunstall and Hart's scrutiny, but mostly Naomi's, and again the notion struck him that he would rather have her disapproval than her pity.

'Just let me at 'em,' he said.

CHAPTER 28

Within thirty minutes, Rickman's commandeered conference room was packed with civilian Calls and Response operators, CID and uniforms, including some trainees and cadets. DC Hart turned her chair to face Rickman. His tall frame almost filled the area of the whiteboard on the back wall, where he stood, calmly surveying the growing numbers of police and civilian staff, his expression serious, thoughtful. He had to raise his voice to call them to order, but after a flurry of excitement they quickly settled and silence fell.

Rickman gave a brief outline of the investigation so far, including the post-mortem findings. 'The weapon would tell us if Jasmine was murdered by the same person who attacked Mark Davis,' he said. 'So we begin with a search of Black Wood. DC Tunstall will lead the search.' Tunstall positively glowed with pleasure at being given the responsibility. It was one of Rickman's strengths, Hart thought — seeing beneath an unpromising exterior to the potential.

'Trainees and cadets will work with a trained officer,' he explained. 'You'll search the grounds, initially. If we can get a warrant for the main house, you will move on to that later.'

He checked the time — the hotline was due to open in twenty minutes. 'Calls and Response, if a "Melanie" or

188

"Melanie Townsend" calls, she's to be put through to me without delay — clear?' The operators made a note of the name. 'Your role is crucial,' Rickman went on. 'We're relying on you to act fast on anything that might give the investigation a shove in the right direction. Key points . . .' He paused and you could almost hear the rustle of clothing as everyone sat up and listened.

'Where did Davis go after abducting Bryony? Who might have had a grudge against him or Jasmine? And of course, any information on the alleged sale of babies.' He turned to Foster. 'Lee?'

Foster stood up. 'At the end of the briefing, I want the following to report to me.' In normal circumstances, Lee Foster would begin with a joke, but today he was deadly serious. Hart listened while he reeled off a list of seven names, all signs of his earlier hangover pallor gone.

'You'll interview ex-residents of the children's home,' Foster said. 'You're looking for anyone who might've stayed in touch with Mark Davis, names of girls who might have given up babies, names of adoptive parents — the kids might know them as friends of the Shepherds. Did any of the former residents see or hear anything unusual? Look out for anyone who might have seen or heard about the trafficking — earwigged conversations, rumours, anything like that.' He broke off, scanning the team, and Hart saw fury in his eyes. 'We think that Black Wood is the probable hub of "Kiddies R Us". You need to ask about any unusual activity — especially at night. Babies crying, noises or movement at night, visitors turning up at odd hours. *Anything* out of the ordinary.'

His team of interviewers made a note.

Hart recognised the 'Kiddies R Us' crack as part of Foster's defensive shield. Make a joke about it, and people will think you don't care. She had mishandled the earlier briefing. Her intervention over the database must have seemed impatient rather than helpful. Hart was like Foster in one respect: she was bad at apologising. More surprising even than this was the fact that, on both sides, their difficulty in admitting fault was a defence against a hostile world. In Foster's case, it was a carry-over from his days in care. For Hart, it was a natural response to a hierarchical male-dominated workplace in which an apology could be seen as weakness.

Rickman took over. 'The Shepherds will be here at ten o'clock. I want as much evidence as we can bring together between now and then — I need more than an unsubstantiated accusation to take into the interview room. For now, they think they're helping us to narrow down the field of interviewees — they *do not know* they're under suspicion, so if you deal with them, I want them shown courtesy and respect.'

Hart saw a muscle twitch in Foster's jaw.

'Until we have more, we're grateful they've taken time out to talk to us — okay?' He got a murmured acquiescence, though not from Foster.

'DC Hart.'

'Boss?'

'You will interview Mrs Shepherd with DS Foster.'

She nodded, already working on approaches and questions, pleased to have been selected from such a large team.

'In the meantime,' Rickman said, 'see if you can get hold of Davis's mobile phone records for the week prior to his death — then I'd like to see you and DS Foster to talk interview strategy.'

* * *

Rickman wound up a few minutes later, after taking questions, and Foster dialled Kate Nolan's number on his mobile, immediately. 'Mrs Nolan? Kate?'

'Yes,' she said, uncertain. Then, with a laugh, 'Lee Foster!'

'Sorry, Kate,' he said. 'I'm on the clock, here. I need to ask you something.'

'Ask away.' In the background, he heard a babble of baby talk, and a man's voice, sounding grumpy, demanding something.

She must have cupped her hand over the mouthpiece, because her voice became muffled, directed at somebody else. '*Where it always is.*' When she spoke again, she said, with careful emphasis on his title, 'Sorry, Sergeant. What did you want to ask?'

Foster heard a stifled apology.

'Did you ever notice anything . . . odd going on at Black Wood?'

'Odd?' she said. 'In what way?'

'Comings and goings, maybe,' he said, deliberately vague.

'Oh! There were always kids coming in at night — you remember that?'

'Yeah, I remember.' He had been one of the late-night arrivals on more than one occasion. 'But I'm talking about stuff you'd think of as strange.'

She was quiet for a moment, the sound of the child's contented burble the only confirmation that the line was still open. 'You did *hear* things at Black Wood,' she said at last. 'Noises in the woods around the house.'

Foster's stomach tightened. 'Noises?' he echoed.

'Foxes or cats, Ed Shepherd used to say.'

There was a hint of doubt in her voice and Foster said, 'But . . .'

'Sometimes,' she began, 'I thought . . . Well, I thought it sounded more like a baby crying.'

Foster made a note on the pad next to the phone, adrenaline tingling in his blood.

'Ed said it was cats — you know — gone wild, staking their territory.'

'But you thought it was a baby.'

'Yes,' she said, her voice distant, as if listening for the ghost of a cry. 'A few times.'

'You heard it more than once?' Foster asked. 'When?'

'What time of night, you mean?'

'Time of night, time of year — whatever you can remember.'

She thought for a moment. 'Late at night — after we'd all gone to bed. As for time of year, take your pick — it wasn't what you'd call seasonal.'

Foster heard the occasional clink of a spoon against a breakfast bowl and couldn't help thinking that the cosy domestic scene it conjured in his mind seemed far removed from the sullen goth he had known all those years ago. 'You can't be more specific?' he asked.

'Sorry, Lee. Dates and times get muddled in your head when you're a kid.' She paused, and Foster sensed a sudden awkwardness. 'D'you mind me asking,' she said at last, 'what's this got to do with Mark?'

'You've been a great help,' he said, dodging the question. 'If you remember anything else, let me know, okay?'

* * *

It didn't take long to get the necessary clearances on Davis's mobile phone. Hart sat back from her computer monitor and stretched. Now came the hard part — waiting for the printout to be sent to her. Behind her, the civilian phone operators were taking a steady stream of calls, and at the newly arrived desks CID officers worked the phones and sifted the pink message slips, searching for the one that might change everything.

'All right, Naomi?'

She turned to face Chris Tunstall. 'I thought you'd be gone by now.'

'Just finished briefing the lads,' he said, with ill-disguised pride. 'Time for a quick cuppa before I shoot off — fancy one?'

'Fifty pence for scalding dish water from the machine?' Hart said. 'I thought you had a more discerning palate.'

'I'm not talking about the muck in a plastic cup some laughingly call tea,' Tunstall said.

There was something in his tone. Glee — triumph, even. She narrowed her eyes at him, and he grinned, stepping aside. The kettle was in its rightful place on the tea table, with lead attached.

Hart sat back in her chair. 'Well, I've got to hand it to you, Chris — I thought that'd gone for good.'

'It was well-hid, but I tracked it down using my superior detection skills,' he said.

She smiled. 'In that case, let's celebrate while we can. You *do* know they'll nick it again?'

'I'd like to see 'em try.' There was a gleam in Tunstall's eye.

'Chris Tunstall, what *have* you done?'

'Here.' He offered her the kettle. 'Have a go.'

She approached the tea table. 'No chain?' she observed.

'The chain wasn't whatchamacallit — satisfactory. Go on,' he urged. 'Unplug it.'

She took it from him warily. 'Tunstall, if you've got this rigged for electric shock—'

'Do me a favour,' he exclaimed. Hart fixed him with a beady eye and he sighed. 'It's safe, I promise.'

She pulled at the plug at the back of the kettle. It wouldn't budge. She tried again. It was rock solid.

Tunstall grinned. 'Now try the mains socket.'

The same thing, it wouldn't move. 'Chris,' she said. 'What . . .'

'Superglue,' he said, unable to contain himself any longer.

Hart blinked. 'You superglued the plugs?'

He beamed at her. 'Brilliant, i'n't it?'

'If Health and Safety get wind of this, they'll scalp you!'

'I said it were brilliant, I never said it were me,' he said. 'And if they do come after me, I shall invoke my right to silence.'

Hart laughed.

'See,' Tunstall said, puppyishly pleased to have made her laugh. 'There's nothing like a nice cuppa for giving you a proper slant on the day.'

* * *

193

'You ready?' Rickman asked.

Foster was in the process of jamming a set of box files between a cabinet and the wall. He straightened up, slapping the dust from his hands. 'We've had a feng shui consultant in — like the look?' He pronounced it 'feng shoo-wee', and he didn't seem amused. 'We're gonna need more space — we haven't even set up an Evidence Room yet, paperwork's stacking up and the sodding drugs team's bagged every storeroom, office and broom cupboard going.'

Rickman surveyed the room. There weren't enough desks for all the new staff, they were still waiting on the delivery of extra filing cabinets, and he wasn't sure they'd have room to house them, if they ever arrived. 'Have a word with Larry Dwight.'

'I did — when he finally showed his ugly mug. He's been out since the morning briefing, "consulting with the local community". When he come back, he said they couldn't spare the space.' Anger had a detrimental effect on Foster's grammar.

Rickman raised an eyebrow. He knew Dwight to be a careerist and a political animal, which was fine by him, so long as he didn't blow off the men and women in the field who did the practical job of policing. Especially not the men and women on Rickman's team. 'Where is he now?' he asked.

Foster looked around distractedly for space to cram in a few more boxes. 'I dunno. I'm just glad he's not round here — I might not be responsible for me actions.'

* * *

Rickman found Detective Inspector Dwight in his office, on the phone. Dwight was wedged into a chair that was too narrow for him. His sandy hair, as always, was neatly clipped, and his desk, unlike Rickman's, was clear of clutter, the surfaces looked freshly dusted. Rickman thought he could even smell a faint whiff of furniture polish. The rest of the room was just as neat.

Dwight held up one stubby finger, indicating that Rickman should wait, then he swung his chair around and continued his conversation with his back to Rickman. A moment later, Dwight laughed. 'You're kidding?' he said, still chuckling. 'Yeah — put him on — I'd like to hear this for myself.'

Rickman, however, did not. He took the phone out of Dwight's unresisting fingers and spoke into the mouthpiece. 'He'll call you back.'

'What the *hell*?'

Rickman held up one finger while he replaced the receiver carefully in the cradle. 'DS Foster requested storage space for my investigation.'

'Oh,' Dwight said, as though he had only just realised what this was about. 'You know, I'd like to help — I really would — but . . .' He spread his hands.

'That's all right,' Rickman said, with a tight smile. 'I don't need your help. I just need a storeroom.'

Dwight shook his head with an exasperated little laugh. 'Well, if you can suggest somewhere suitable . . .'

'The one opposite the CID Room will do. And I'll need an Evidence Room as well.'

Dwight looked a little queasy — perhaps it was the smell of furniture polish. 'I'm investigating a drugs war,' he said. 'Operation Snowplough was an international inter-agency investigation — I have a truckload of paperwork—'

'On the scale of things,' Rickman interrupted, with a slight tilt of the head, 'two murders and a suspicious death makes mine bigger than yours.'

Dwight huffed and puffed, but Rickman could see he was ready to cave in. The inspector chewed his lower lip for a moment. 'You'll have to talk to DS Cass. But he's not going to like this.'

Rickman smiled: much of police work was about the balance of power — who had authority, who was prepared to use it — and that went as much for police officers as it did for criminals. Rickman knew that DI Dwight's reluctance to help out was more about his reluctance to approach DS Cass than the usual problems of power play between two senior investigating officers.

'Tell you what, Inspector,' Rickman said. '*You* talk to Cass, and if he doesn't like it, I'll shoulder the burden of his disappointment.'

Dwight straightened up, recognising Rickman's use of his rank for what it was — a reminder that Rickman was the senior officer. 'But I was on my way out, sir,' he protested.

'Talk to Cass before you leave,' Rickman said.

'I have a meeting.' Dwight was beginning to sound desperate.

'So, the sooner you sort this out, the sooner you can be there.'

When Rickman met his gaze, Dwight looked away. 'I'll see what I can do,' he murmured.

'Fine. As long as I have two adequate storage facilities by noon.'

CHAPTER 29

Rickman had a tussle with a couple of chancers on the drugs team when he tried to book separate interview rooms for the Shepherds. It seemed that the disrespect for authority among Dwight's crew was a malaise that threatened to spread beyond their own SIO. The station was busy with civilian traffic: a stretch limo filled with twenty-something women out on a hen night had pulled into the Royal Liverpool Hospital A&E at two a.m., just as Maitland's street-corner pushers were being dumped by the opposition. The bride-to-be had broken her ankle in an accident involving eight gin mixers, a pair of five-inch stilettos and an undignified exit from a night club on a cobbled back street. The witnesses, now sober and regretting some part of the night before, were giving their statements.

Rickman agreed to a compromise: one interview room and one consultation room. The consultation rooms were designed to put prisoners at ease while they consulted with their legal representatives and were not set up with recording equipment, but Foster had managed to scrounge a recorder from Allerton station.

Rickman had chosen the unfamiliar and disorientating environment of the station, rather than going to the children's home to interview the couple. An interview at the police station reinforced the seriousness of the situation. It also allowed him to split the house parents up. To get near the truth, Rickman would have to disrupt the almost psychic connection between Ed and Hilary Shepherd.

Rickman and Foster stood in the large foyer, beyond the station reception area. Red lights shone above three of the interview rooms and one of the consulting rooms, warning of interviews in progress. DC Hart kept herself at a distance, waiting outside the consulting room where she and Foster would conduct their interview with Hilary Shepherd.

Ed and Hilary had been fingerprinted — for elimination purposes, they had been told — and were already installed. Ed, being the more susceptible of the two in Rickman's estimation, was in the more hostile setting of the interview room, going through the slow fermentation process that is so helpful in breaking down the resistance of interviewees.

'Ready?' Rickman asked.

'As I'll ever be,' Foster said. 'I talked to Kate Nolan — she heard goings-on year round — and she was there for *years*. If this is what we think it is—'

'It could involve a lot of children,' Rickman finished. 'I know.' He saw anger and turmoil in his friend's face and added, 'If you don't want to do this, Lee . . .'

A muscle jumped in Foster's jaw. 'Oh, I wanna do it all right.'

'Naomi's an experienced interviewer,' Rickman said. 'Let her take the lead.'

Foster looked over at Hart. She didn't exactly avoid his gaze, but Rickman sensed a barrier between the two of them. He'd noticed a coolness earlier, during their management meeting, and Hart had been unusually reticent during their meeting to discuss interview strategy.

He lowered his voice. 'Is everything okay between you two?'

'Why wouldn't it be?'

'That's not an answer,' Rickman said, injecting an edge to his tone.

Foster glanced again at Hart. 'Truth is, she's pissed off with me.' He gave a shrug. 'I don't blame her.'

Foster might be insensitive and laddish, but he was also self-aware.

'You could apologise.'

'There are some things you can never take back.'

'You'll never know, unless you try.'

Foster remained silent.

'Is this a problem?'

After a moment's indecision, Foster said, 'No. And you're right — Naomi should lead.' Rickman heard sick disappointment, as well as determination in Foster's tone. This wouldn't be an easy interview for Lee. He turned to the interview room, where Ed Shepherd was waiting.

'Jeff!'

Rickman scanned the mass of faces beyond the reception desk. Detective Superintendent Cliff Maynard. His voice carried well, and a few heads turned. Maynard was buzzed through on the nod and he took in the three officers with a glance. 'Before you make a start, I'd like a word.'

Rickman glanced at Foster, eyebrows raised in question.

'Fine by me,' Foster said. 'Let them sweat a bit longer.'

Rickman and Maynard ducked into the small room that housed a microwave, a hot drinks machine and a sink. A couple of PCs sat huddled over biscuits and coffee.

'Give us a minute, will you?' Maynard said, in a tone that assumed compliance. Maynard had the deliberate manner of a cop with more than thirty years in the job, mainly in operational posts. He combed his hair in a side-parting, which dated him, but it was as thick and dark as in his Hendon training days.

'You're not thinking of letting Foster interview the children's home couple?' Maynard asked.

'Hart is leading the interview with Mrs Shepherd,' Rickman said. 'But Foster's knowledge of the home and of the two house parents is likely to prove invaluable.'

Maynard drew his eyebrows down in an expression of disapproval. 'You must see how it looks, Jeff.'

'No,' Rickman said, feeling a rumble of resentment. 'I don't.'

'Foster knows the Shepherds,' Maynard said. 'He knew Mark Davis. Now Davis is found dead in the grounds of his old home — and his former house parents are being interviewed about illegal adoptions.'

'You're talking like he's involved in all this.'

'I'm not suggesting he is, but the media will certainly smell a story — ask questions — and I needn't tell you how damaging speculation can be.'

Rickman had personal experience of press 'interest', but he also knew how damaging in-house gossip could be to an officer's reputation. 'As far as Foster is concerned, there is no story.'

'Then the press will create one,' Maynard said.

'I have every confidence in Detective Sergeant Foster's integrity.'

'Noted. But with Bryony dead, it won't take long for the media to start looking for a scapegoat.'

Rickman deliberated. As a senior ranking officer, Maynard was well within his rights to insist that Foster be pulled off the interview team. What galled Rickman most was that the superintendent had a valid point.

'All right,' Rickman said. 'I'll reassign him.'

'You have to see how this looks from a PR angle, Jeff. And I'm sorry to have to do this . . .' Maynard's conciliatory tone was a warning of worse to come. 'But Foster should report immediately to DI Dwight to assist in the drugs inquiry.'

Rickman stared at him. 'Foster is part of my team.'

'Not anymore.' Maynard's manner switched from conciliatory to sharp in an instant.

'Sir, I need every available officer.'

'Foster is *off* the case,' Maynard said. 'It's non-negotiable. He can hear it from me or he can hear it from you. Your choice.'

This was stand-off Rickman couldn't win. He knew it, but it didn't stop him wanting to fight. 'One concession,' he said.

Maynard inclined his head, indicating at least a willingness to listen.

'Foster makes the move voluntarily.'

'I've told you, Jeff—'

'I know,' Rickman interrupted. 'Non-negotiable. I'll persuade him.'

Maynard considered. Finally, he nodded. 'Actually, that would look better all round. Responsible policing, sensitivity to public perceptions.' The consummate politician, Maynard would already be rehearsing his press statement.

* * *

Rickman found Foster in the CID Room, working at one of the free desks. He was on his feet and heading for the door before Rickman could even speak.

'Let's get the show on the road, boss,' he said, with a glance at his watch.

'Not yet,' Rickman said. 'We need to talk.'

Foster gave Rickman a sardonic smile. 'Is that a "This isn't working, we need to cool it for a bit" kind of talk?' Rickman made no comment. 'What, no comeback?' Foster said. 'Bloody hell, it must be bad.'

Rickman fixed him with a look that left Foster in no doubt it was worse than he could imagine. 'My office.'

Ten minutes later, Foster was still arguing. 'What about you, Jeff? D'you think I'm bent?'

'Nobody's saying that, Lee.'

'The super's taking me off the case—'

'He's allowing you to make the move voluntarily — he wouldn't do that if he thought you were in any way implicated.'

'Don't kid yourself.' Foster paced the small floor area of Rickman's office, his fists bunched. 'He just thinks it'll look better in the press.'

Rickman had to agree — Foster might not be subtle, but he understood police politics as well as anyone. 'Well, at least it'll make you look good.'

Foster stopped pacing and stared at him, and Rickman had to smile. Foster had reached the rank of sergeant and would rise no further precisely because he didn't care about looking good — unless it involved his reflection in a mirror.

'Okay,' Rickman said. 'Let me rephrase. If the press latch on to you as a liability, we've less chance of getting the public support we need. I know you want to nail this illegal adoption scam — so, what's it to be?'

Foster stared at his feet, struggling with inner thoughts Rickman could only guess at. He shook his head, took a deep breath, then exhaled slowly. 'I don't like this, Jeff,' he said. 'I don't like it one little bit.'

They walked back to the CID Room together. 'You might want to see what you can find out about Maitland's relationship with Mark Davis, now you've got an in,' Rickman suggested.

'Top of my to-do list,' Foster said, with heavy sarcasm.

Hart met them at the door of the murder Incident Room with a wodge of papers in her hand. 'Mark Davis's mobile phone records,' she said. 'I've marked up the recipients' names next to the relevant numbers.'

Rickman glanced at the list and felt a tickle of excitement.

'Are we doing this or not?' Hart asked, eager for the off.

'*You* are,' Foster said, and she frowned.

'Find an interview partner,' Rickman said.

She looked quickly at Foster. 'I thought *we* were—'

'Me, I'm changing sides,' Foster said.

'What are you talking about?'

'I'm going where careers are built and men walk bow-legged from all the testosterone floating around.'

This wasn't humour, it was rage, but to her credit Hart didn't respond to his crude attempt to needle her. Instead, Rickman read alarm and concern in her face. She had been there when the detective superintendent arrived, she was in the CID Room when Rickman called Foster out, and Hart was more than capable of drawing the obvious conclusions.

'DS Foster has voluntarily withdrawn from this investigation,' Rickman said, 'because of the possibility of misperceptions among the press and media.' He had spoken loud enough for a few heads to come up. Now he had their attention, he looked Foster in the eye. 'I respect that decision.' He glanced at Hart. 'When you're ready, DC Hart.'

He waited for her to go ahead of him. As she crossed the threshold, she glanced over at Foster like she wanted to say something but couldn't find the right words.

He followed her through, but Foster checked him. 'Boss—'

'What?'

'Don't let Shepherd use his asthma to make you back off.'

'Would he do that?' Shepherd hadn't struck Rickman as the manipulative type.

Foster sighed. 'I don't know what he'd do, Jeff — not anymore.'

Hart was waiting for Rickman in the corridor. 'Sir, this is wrong,' she said.

'It's out of my hands, Naomi.'

'Foster is the best link we have with the children's home. He knows Ed and Hilary Shepherd like family.'

A muscle twitched in his jaw. 'Isn't that the point?'

'He's *not* implicated.'

'I know that.'

'I've conducted God knows how many interviews with him,' she insisted. 'DS Foster has played it straight down the line.'

'I know.' Rickman's eyes were hazel, but sometimes when he was angry they would spark amber. She caught a flash of amber now but pushed on.

'Then why don't you back him up?' She raised her voice, and two civilian staff passing them turned to look. 'Don't you trust him?'

'With my life,' Rickman said quietly and emphatically.

Hart felt hot — fevered almost with lack of sleep and frustration and the injustice of it all. In a space of days, Foster had seen Davis — a boy he had tutored and mentored — first accused of murder and then found mutilated, the victim of a sadistic assault. It didn't take a genius to work out that Foster felt some measure of responsibility. And as if this wasn't enough, his faith in the people who had acted as his surrogate parents for the better part of his childhood had been shattered. Now Foster's closest friend and ally was abandoning him — or so it seemed to Hart.

'They're stringing him up like a sacrificial lamb,' she exclaimed.

Rickman took her by the elbow and steered her towards the fire escape. 'We need to reassess interview strategy,' he said, loud enough for the few people remaining in the corridor to hear. 'Let's talk.'

Rickman's height and unshowy physical strength had always been reassuring to her. Although she felt no personal threat, she could see now why the hard men showed Rickman a respect they rarely extended to others. He didn't relax his hold on her until they were through the door and on the staircase.

'First off,' he said, 'there is no "they", DC Hart. That kind of thinking is the way to career suicide. Secondly, *never* question my motivation. I'm here to find Jasmine's and Mark's killer — I want to know who abandoned Bryony to die. I won't give up until I know.'

He held her in his gaze and Hart bowed her head, taking a few breaths before answering.

'I'm sorry, sir.' She was. Exhaustion and concern for Foster had made her push beyond the boundaries of acceptable professional conduct. 'I didn't mean any implication against you.' She meant to stop at that point, but she found herself again staring into his face, the words tumbling out despite herself. 'But the super taking Lee off the case like that — you must see how it looks.'

'It looks like political manoeuvring — which is what it is,' Rickman said. 'And Chief Superintendent Maynard has a point: we can't do our jobs if we're wasting our energies fending off unwarranted criticism.' He studied her for a few moments as if trying to make his mind up. 'Whatever happened between you and Foster, make it up.'

'I'm sorry?' *How could he know that?*

'Foster has his faults, but he's a good man, and he needs his friends right now.'

'He's a colleague,' she said. 'But I wouldn't call him a—'

'You should,' Rickman interrupted. 'He's been a friend to you — whether you know it or not.'

He looked into her eyes, and this time she thought she saw a shimmer of amusement lighting his solemn features. 'Don't waste your energies kicking against an open door, Naomi. And don't fight battles you can't win. If you're in for the long game, you need to be more selective.'

There were moments in her life that in retrospect Hart saw as milestones, nuggets of advice that, with time and use, would acquire the patina of wisdom. Often, she discounted them at the time, and it wasn't until years later that she understood their importance. But this moment — these words — seemed already to gleam with the worth of precious metal. Rickman was offering her the hand of friendship and his protection in the competitive and often hostile world of policing. She tested her feelings. Did she feel patronised? No. Compromised? Certainly not.

'I'll keep that in mind, sir,' she said.

He kept his gaze on her a few seconds longer, until he was sure she was sincere, then he nodded. 'Let's go to work,' he said.

* * *

Foster walked into the drugs team's Major Incident Room and was greeted by DS Cass.

'Come to join the big boys, have you?' Cass said.

'You look like you need all the help you can get,' Foster said.

Cass pointed to a desk in the far corner of the room, with a plastic tubular frame chair, facing the wall. No computer, no phone, just a large stack of A4 sheets placed tidily in the centre of the desk.

'We're running HOLMES 2 on this one,' Cass said.

'And?' HOLMES, the Home Office Large and Major Enquiry System, now in its second iteration, was used routinely in complex enquiries where a large number of leads was likely.

Cass's hand went to his trouser pocket and he withdrew his pot of lip balm. 'I'm handling task allocations.'

'Well, I hope you washed your hands.'

Foster focused carefully on the little pot, enough to make Cass self-conscious. Cass stopped just short of flicking the lid off it, but held it, rotating it in his hand as he spoke. 'There's a few pended items — families away on half-term holiday and so on. You can have a crack at them, see if the contactees have become available.'

'Contactees?' Foster whipped out his notepad and pencil. 'Can you spell that for me?'

Cass glanced sideways. Most of the team were out on inquiries, but a few CID officers were dotted about the room, and Foster and Cass both knew that they would be listening to this particular head-to-head. 'You're not under Rickman's protection now, Foster.'

Foster laughed and a slow, dark blush spread up Cass's neck. 'I can take care of meself, thanks, Dan.' The angry flush spread from Cass's neck into his face. *Result*, Foster thought, smiling pleasantly. 'There's a few *contactees* you could help with, though.' He didn't wait for a reply. 'Rob Maitland, for example.'

Cass looked fractionally away, then back. 'What *about* Maitland?'

Interesting. Foster had half-expected Cass to turn and walk away. 'He's still on the loose,' Foster said. 'Why isn't he banged up with the rest?'

Cass gave him a flat, dead-eyed look. 'He wasn't at the bust.'

'Wasn't he?'

Again, Foster saw a flicker as Cass looked away, then back. 'He's not on the video recordings, he wasn't seen at the docks, and his solicitor has provided him with an alibi.'

Foster nodded. 'Question: why are scientists switching from rats to lawyers for experiments?' He waited until he was sure he had an audience. 'Answer: the lab technicians don't get as attached to the lawyers. And there are some things a rat *just won't do*.'

The joke got a good response from all but Cass.

Laughter, Foster thought, relaxing a little. *The best medicine. I might even like working here.*

This time, Cass did use the balm.

'My point being — Maitland is a known drug baron,' Foster said. 'Youse lot have been working on this, what — a year?'

Cass's mouth tightened and Foster said, '*More?*'

'We tried to link Maitland's assets to drugs money. It's impossible — his accountant makes sure of that.'

'Bernie Carter.' Cass's surprise at his knowing the name gave Foster another thrill of pure pleasure. 'Sounds like old Bernie's due an audit. Now, I know he wasn't banged up as of Thursday, 'cos I met him at Maitland's offices. So has he got a "Get Out of Jail Free" card an' all?'

Anger flared briefly in Cass's eyes. 'I interviewed him the night after the raid.'

'And?'

'He said he'd already made a donation to the Police Benevolent Fund.'

'Funny,' Foster said.

'He wasn't joking.' Cass opened his pot of lip balm, changed his mind and tightened the lid, slipping the pot back into his pocket. 'The night of the bust, he was at a police fundraiser. He gave the after-dinner speech.'

'Good alibi,' Foster admitted. 'But a bit too smart-arsed for his own good. I think I might go back and have a chat with Mr Carter.'

'You can have a go,' Cass said, with a shrug. 'But you'd be wasting your time — if the taxman couldn't trip him up, the likes of you's got no chance.'

Foster blinked. 'The likes of me?'

Cass shifted stance. 'Us,' he said. 'I meant the likes of us.'

CHAPTER 30

A female DC was leaning against the back wall when Rickman entered the interview room. Rickman nodded and she took her seat. Shepherd sat at the other side of the table, hands clasped in front of him, emphasising the high, slightly hunched set of his shoulders, and Rickman had a twinge of worry.

'You've seen the police surgeon?' he asked. 'He's passed you as fit?'

'I've run a children's home for thirty years,' Shepherd said. 'I think I can answer a few questions without incident.'

'And you have your meds?'

In answer, Shepherd took out a blue inhaler and placed it on the table.

Rickman started the recorder.

Shepherd looked uneasily at the machine. 'I thought this was an informal chat.'

'It just saves time on note-taking and ensures accuracy.' Rickman smiled. 'Do you mind?'

Shepherd seemed unsure, but politeness and natural reserve prevented him from making a fuss, and he muttered a reluctant consent.

Rickman introduced the constable, then reminded Mr Shepherd that he was not under arrest, nor was he obliged to answer any of the questions put to him, taking care to speak in a relaxed, conversational tone, as if continuing the reassurances of the informality of the interview. 'Of course, if you would prefer to have a legal representative present, that's your prerogative.'

'Ask away,' Shepherd said. 'I've nothing to hide.'

Rickman placed a fat buff folder in front of him. It was stamped with the Merseyside Police badge and labelled with Shepherd's name, and beneath it 'Black Wood Children's Home'. No case number or dates, for now. If he'd asked for a glimpse at the contents, Mr Shepherd would have found mainly blank sheets of paper, but the advantage of a fat folder was the psychological expectation it set up in a suspect's mind.

'Did you see Mark Davis the night Jasmine Elliott died?' Rickman asked.

'No.' Shepherd answered without hesitation.

'Did you speak to him over the phone?'

'No.' Shepherd seemed less sure of himself this time. His gaze slipped away from Rickman's and found the folder, lying between them. Rickman tapped it with his fingertip, and Shepherd licked his lips. He took a breath and seemed to hold it.

'Are you all right to continue, Mr Shepherd?' Rickman asked.

Shepherd nodded.

'Have you any idea why Mark Davis was in the basement of the coach house?' Rickman asked.

'No.'

'Or why he would be anywhere near Black Wood?'

'No.'

Rickman nodded. Now he had the denials he needed when he hit Shepherd with their latest discoveries, he changed tack. 'Tell me what happened on Wednesday night.'

'I don't understand the question,' Shepherd said. 'Nothing happened. It was a normal night.'

Rickman fixed Shepherd with a look, softened it with a smile. 'Talk me through a normal night.'

Shepherd sighed. '"Normal" is perhaps not the word I was looking for. Since we had news of the closure, we've undergone a period of upheaval.'

'I'm sure,' Rickman sympathised.

'We spent most of the evening packing,' Shepherd said. 'Went to bed early.'

'Did you maybe take a walk around the grounds, first?'

'No.'

Rickman frowned. 'I'm a little confused, Mr Shepherd.' He opened the folder, tilting it away from Shepherd to hide its contents, then slid a photograph from the stack of papers. 'This is a photograph of the padlock used to secure the front door of the coach house.' He riffled through the file contents again, taking his time to find the next image. 'This is the back of the lock.' He placed it side by side with the first. 'See here? A fingerprint.'

A momentary panic flitted across Shepherd's face.

Rickman placed a copy of the fingerprint on top of the two photographs of the lock. The date and location were documented, along with the name of the CSI who had recovered the print.

Shepherd leaned back, as if trying to distance himself from it.

'You remember we asked for your fingerprints — for elimination purposes?'

Shepherd said nothing.

Rickman placed a tenprint form next to the fingerprint from the scene. 'Your fingerprints,' he said. 'See this print here?' He pointed to the box labelled 'Right fore'. 'It's a perfect match to the one found on the padlock.'

Shepherd relaxed a little. Rickman let him.

'I must have checked it the day before,' Shepherd said. 'The surveyor isn't always as conscientious as he should be about security.'

'The day before,' Rickman repeated. 'But definitely not Wednesday night?'

'No.'

'Well, now I'm even more confused,' Rickman confessed. 'The problem is, our forensic specialists say that the padlock had been wiped clean.' He watched Shepherd try to think ahead of him. 'Only *your* fingerprint was present.' Rickman pointed to the photograph again. 'See? Right there.'

'The surveyor must have—'

'He says he's been handling that padlock for days and it's never occurred to him to wipe it clean — I mean, it's just not something you do, is it?'

For a moment, Shepherd seemed at a loss. His colour was hectic, and he stared intently at his hands clasped in front of him, squeezing and releasing, squeezing and releasing, as though massaging a heart back to life.

'Of course,' he said, as though in a sudden flash of clarity. 'I *did* do a quick check. With all the rush of moving out, I get confused over the days.'

Rickman smiled and settled back in his chair. 'Well, that would explain it,' he said. Shepherd smiled back. He thought he was in the clear. 'What did you see?' Rickman asked.

'See?' Shepherd frowned. 'Nothing. I just rattled the lock to make sure it was secure, then went back up to the house.'

'That's impossible, Mr Shepherd.'

Shepherd gave an exasperated laugh. 'I'm telling you—'

Rickman leaned forward again, abruptly decreasing the space between them. 'The lock was open. And since the only prints on it are yours, I'm thinking you opened it.'

'No.' Shepherd glanced at the DC, then beyond her to the door.

Animal instinct — find an escape route when cornered. 'If that was the case, you would have been the last to see Mark Davis alive. D'you know what that makes me think?' Rickman let him sweat for a few seconds. 'Well,' he shrugged. 'What would *you* think?'

'Wait.' Shepherd pressed his hands to his temples. 'I know it looks bad — and I'll admit, I did see that the lock was open, but—'

'Please — don't tell me you didn't go inside,' Rickman warned.

Shepherd took a few breaths, then picked up his inhaler, but seemed to change his mind and set it down on the table again.

Rickman gave the table a sharp rap and Shepherd jerked convulsively. 'Stop wasting my time, Mr Shepherd.'

'I'm trying to remember!' Shepherd's shoulders were up and his breathing was becoming laboured. Time to ease off.

Rickman leaned back in his chair. 'Perhaps you should use that,' he said. He waited while Shepherd took a hit from the inhaler and gave him time to calm down.

'I was on my rounds,' Shepherd said. 'Force of habit, after thirty years.'

'What time was it?'

'Late — after eleven, I think. I saw the padlock was hanging loose on the hasp.' Rickman nodded encouragement. 'I went inside.'

'Wouldn't it be pitch dark in there?' Rickman asked. 'Middle of the night, and all those shutters on the windows.'

'I always carry a torch on my rounds. I saw there'd been another fall.' His voice tightened. 'The place was full of plaster and roof tiles. It looked like a roof collapse.'

'You didn't go downstairs, into the basement?'

Shepherd shook his head. 'The steps were shattered.'

'You didn't think that maybe someone had fallen when the steps disintegrated?'

'I assumed they'd been destroyed by the weight of debris.'

'Well, that's plausible at least.'

Rickman knew his choice of words would not be lost on Shepherd: innocent people made reasonable assumptions. Liars were *plausible*. But the look of offended pride on the man's face angered him — Shepherd had no right to the benefit of the doubt. He hardened his voice just enough to expose the absurdity of Shepherd's assumption. 'I mean, who would have thought that a man would hide in a damp, dark basement with an infant barely a month old?'

Shepherd's Adam's apple bobbed.

'Mr Shepherd?'

'I wish I had thought. I wish I'd been more thorough — if I'd troubled to look more closely, I might have seen them. If I'd had the courage to venture further, I might have saved them. Don't you think I know that?'

Rickman didn't answer, and Shepherd stared at him in anguish. Finally, he looked away. 'I'll live with the guilt for the rest of my life.'

'You weren't to know Davis was even in the grounds,' Rickman said. 'After all, he hadn't contacted you . . .'

'N-no.'

Rickman, the DC — even Shepherd — heard the slight hesitation of speech, and Rickman pushed harder. 'But why would Davis come to Black Wood and not phone you?'

'Mark was a troubled young man,' Shepherd said. 'How could I know what was in his mind?'

'Would you care to speculate?'

Shepherd shot him a bitter look. 'You seem to be doing very well on your own.' It seemed that Shepherd was not going to fall for Rickman's pretence at puzzled ingenuousness a second time.

'Okay,' Rickman said. 'Since I'm doing so well — I'd speculate that Mark Davis did phone you that day.'

Shepherd was not a stupid man: this time he didn't bother to deny it. Instead, he stared resentfully at the folder in Rickman's hands.

Rickman found the printouts he needed and placed them at the top of the stack. 'This is a copy of Mark Davis's mobile phone records. These are calls he made on Wednesday.' He turned the folder so that Shepherd could read the list. 'Highlighted in orange — six calls to your landline.'

Shepherd stared at the sheet of paper.

'This call' — Rickman indicated one of the highlighted rows — 'lasted fifteen minutes.' He looked Shepherd in the eye. 'He must've had a lot to talk about.'

Shepherd swallowed. For half a minute, the only sound in the room was his breathing. 'I tried to persuade him,' he said. 'I told him he should turn himself in, but—'

'He wanted to see you.'

Shepherd nodded, tiredly. 'I was afraid if I pushed too hard, he'd disappear.' His eyes were dark and troubled. 'He kept saying he needed a safe place for Bryony. "They killed Jasmine, and now they're after me," he said.'

'"They"?' Rickman repeated.

'He was raving, Mr Rickman.'

'So he didn't give a name.'

Shepherd shook his head. 'But the people he mixed with . . .' He twisted the wedding ring on his finger.

'You know the people he mixed with?'

'Not personally. But Mark was an addict. His friends were dealers and addicts.'

'So he *did* stay in touch after he left Black Wood.'

Shepherd looked down at his wedding ring. 'Sporadically. Usually when he needed something.'

'What did he need this time?'

'He wanted to leave Bryony with us — *God*, I wish he had.'

'He wanted you to find a family for her?' Rickman asked gently.

Shepherd stiffened. 'I don't know what you mean.'

Rickman let that one bide. 'Did he ask for money?'

'This wasn't *about* money,' Shepherd said. 'Mark just wanted somewhere safe for the baby.'

'I think it was all about money — at least for you.'

'This is preposterous!' Shepherd rose to his feet, leaning on his knuckles.

The DC shifted in her seat, but Rickman lifted one hand, warning her off. He looked down at the folder in front of him and turned the page. 'Yesterday, as you were being taken into the ambulance after your asthma attack,' Rickman said. 'A woman drove into the grounds. Your wife called her Anna — asked her for a lift to the hospital.'

'What of it? Anna's an old friend.' Despite the gruff irritation, Rickman sensed a wariness in the man.

'I was troubled by her reaction when we introduced ourselves,' Rickman said. 'A nice, middle-class woman with a lovely little girl. A well-educated woman, judging by her accent, yet she seemed nervous of us — the police, that is — resentful, even. Now, I'm like a dog with a bone when something like that doesn't sit right, Mr Shepherd.' He gave an apologetic shrug. 'I made a note of the car's licence plate.'

A tremor ran down Shepherd's arm, but he remained standing.

'Fiat Punto,' Rickman said, reading upside down from the DVLA printout. 'Registered to Annabelle Kirkham. Now with that information, it was a short step to find out the rest. Married to Mike Kirkham. Three-year-old daughter, Bella. It's funny — I thought the little girl was younger.' He smiled. 'Small for her age, huh?'

Shepherd's legs seemed to go from under him and he sat down heavily in his chair. His gaze darted wildly around the room, as though he was suddenly aware of its confines. He reached for his inhaler and took a hit from it, closing his eyes.

Rickman recited the official wording of the caution. 'Do you understand?' he asked.

Shepherd nodded, shakily.

If he went straight in with questions about illegal adoptions, Rickman knew that Shepherd would close down. An indirect approach might yield more. 'Tell me about Annabelle Kirkham,' he said.

Shepherd remained silent for a moment, concentrating on his breathing. Rickman waited.

'What do you want to know?' Shepherd said at last.

'What relation is she?'

'To us? No relation.'

'An ex-resident?'

'No.'

'So, give me a clue here, Mr Shepherd.'

'She — we got to know her through the playgroup Hilary helps to run.' Rickman maintained eye contact. 'You can check if you like.' The two angry blotches on his cheekbones were the only colour in Mr Shepherd's face.

'Oh, we will,' Rickman said softly.

Shepherd wiped the sweat from his face. Rickman again noticed the slight tremor.

'D'you think if we request DNA tests on their daughter, we might come up with a couple of surprises?' Rickman asked. 'Little Bella's DNA not matching either Mummy's or Daddy's, for instance?'

Shepherd stared at his hands, frowning hard, the furrow deep as a fault line between his brows, his eyes red with unshed tears.

'We know about the babies, Mr Shepherd.' Rickman waited for Shepherd to deny it. He didn't. 'We have a witness who says you bought babies for adoption.'

Strictly speaking, they didn't have their witness — only an uncorroborated phone call from 'Melanie' and Kate Nolan's belief that she'd heard babies crying in the night. But he hadn't heard a denial from Shepherd — yet — and that encouraged Rickman to push harder.

'I think Mark knew about your illegal adoption agency. He needed money to get away, and he tried to blackmail you.'

Shepherd shook his head. 'No . . .'

'I think you agreed to meet him,' Rickman said.

'No . . .' Shepherd laced his fingers, but still they shook.

'Look at the facts,' Rickman said. 'Mark called you six times on the night he died. He was found on your premises. Your fingerprints are on the padlock. You've lied and lied and—'

'That's not how it was,' Shepherd said.

'He demanded money,' Rickman went on, hearing Shepherd's desperation, knowing that he was at breaking point. 'You argued.'

'No.'

'There was a struggle and Mark fell.'

'*No.*'

'The stairs were dangerous. It was probably an accident—'

'You've got it all wrong!' Shepherd exclaimed, striking the table with his fists. 'I was trying to *help* him.'

Shepherd wiped tears from his face with a trembling hand. Rickman waited, once more allowing the silence to do the work for him, waiting for the pressure to build until the less-experienced man had to break it.

'*He* offered *me* money,' Shepherd said at last.

'How much?'

'A hundred thousand,' he said.

Rickman gave a low whistle. The drugs raid. So, Davis *was* there. 'Did he tell you where he'd got it?'

Shepherd shook his head. 'He never named the people who were after him — said it would be safer if I didn't know. I *can* tell you that he said there was more if we needed it.'

'You believed him — that he had the money?'

Shepherd nodded. 'I really *was* hoping to persuade him to give himself up.' Shepherd took a long, slow breath, and Rickman heard a slight asthmatic crackle in it.

'When he didn't turn up, I went looking for him.' He gave an apologetic shrug. 'I wasn't entirely honest about that. He should have been with us just after dark — around six p.m.'

'So you went looking . . .'

Shepherd gave a jerky nod, staring past Rickman, his face exhausted and empty. 'It was cold. I . . . don't do so well in the cold.' He rolled the inhaler between his thumb and forefinger. He seemed to brace himself. There was more. 'I found the lock, just as I told you. I shone the torch into the basement, but I couldn't see anything.'

Rickman gave no response — not even a flicker of a facial muscle.

'There wasn't anything *to* see,' he said, as if Rickman had questioned his poor observational powers. 'You saw the place — it was a mess. The timbers shifted. I felt the whole *house* move. I thought it was going to collapse.' He glanced at Rickman, then swiftly away again. 'I got the hell out of there.'

Had he known they were in there? Did Shepherd leave Davis and the baby, knowing they had been buried alive? Rickman fought to keep the anger and disgust out of his voice. 'And when Mark still didn't show?'

'We thought he'd found a better prospect, changed his mind, recovered from whatever drug-induced delusion that had him in its grip.'

'We?' Rickman said.

He blinked. 'Sorry?'

'You said "*We* thought".'

Shepherd swallowed. 'You're mistaken.'

Rickman smiled. 'Shall we replay the recording?'

Two spots of high colour appeared again on Shepherd's cheekbones. 'I meant to say *I*. Hilary knew nothing about it.'

Rickman let it pass for the moment. 'You said you wanted to persuade Mark to turn himself in.'

'Yes.'

'A nationwide appeal for help, a missing baby, her mother murdered — you had direct contact with the prime suspect, yet you didn't see the need to report any of this to the police?'

'You've no idea the strain we've been under,' Shepherd exclaimed.

'I think I do, Mr Shepherd,' Rickman said. 'You've watched the place you built up over thirty years being slowly dismantled. You're facing the loss of your jobs and your home — I think you were more than happy to take Mark Davis's money.'

'But Mark didn't show up.' Shepherd stopped, perhaps hearing the accusation in Rickman's tone, and a succession of emotions chased over his features. 'You think I *took* the money from him? That *I harmed* him?'

'Did you?'

'No! God, no!'

Rickman had to admit that the theft of his drugs and money made Maitland a stronger suspect for the murders, but Shepherd was in a tight spot, and Rickman had seen ordinary people turn to violence for smaller prizes than a hundred thousand pounds. He watched Shepherd calmly. 'Look at it from my point of view.'

Shepherd sat back, hollow eyed. His outrage suddenly dissipated, and his hands slid into his lap. 'I know what you think, Mr Rickman, but I'm not a bad man.' He looked up, his face tormented. 'I never harmed anybody — I swear on all that's holy to me, *I did not know* that Mark and Bryony were in that basement. Mark was vulnerable — easy prey for the jackals of this world. I would never exploit that.'

Rickman felt a slow, powerful surge of anger. 'Tell that to Annabelle Kirkham and all the other desperate couples you sold babies to,' he said, sick of Shepherd's self-pity, his whining self-justification. 'Tell it to the young women who gave up their babies for the promise of money or a better life. Mark Davis is dead. His daughter, Bryony, is dead. And the killer could well go free because you wanted to protect your sordid scam.'

'I wouldn't expect you to understand,' Shepherd said.

Still no denial, but that wasn't enough — Rickman needed an admission, and for a man with no police record, Mr Shepherd certainly knew how to manipulate an interview. How many of Shepherd's clients, Rickman wondered, were police or lawyers or barristers — people who knew how the system worked? Was Shepherd just bringing in to play all he had learned from drills and simulations conducted by the experts?

Rickman tried another tack. 'You knew that Davis was on his way to you. You *knew* he was on the run from far more than just the police — and you said nothing.'

'I had others to think of,' Shepherd replied. 'Others to protect.'

'You mean your illegal adopters.' Shepherd stared at him, refusing to confirm or deny. The hurt and resentment on the man's face fuelled Rickman's anger. 'You as good as watched Mark Davis walk to his death.'

Shepherd frowned at his inhaler on the tabletop. 'I was trying to help,' he repeated dogmatically. 'I was only ever trying to help.'

Rickman shook his head in disgust. 'The law draws a line at your kind of "help",' he said.

He saw a flash of anger in Shepherd's gaunt face. 'The law leaves children with parents who are barely able to provide for their own needs, let alone a child's,' he said. 'It returns children to abusive households — to violent fathers and incompetent mothers. The care system is shored up by the goodwill of underpaid and poorly trained staff, in facilities that are crumbling from lack of investment. So don't try to tell me about the law, Mr Rickman. The law is as neglectful and incompetent a guardian as the parents we remove children from — more so, because it damn well ought to know better.' He finished out of breath, his voice a harsh rasp, but this time the asthma was not to blame.

Shepherd's passion, his absolute belief that what he'd done was right, gave Rickman a twinge of uncertainty. He hesitated, inadvertently giving Shepherd the upper hand. But the gleam of triumph in the man's eye reduced all the persuasiveness of his arguments to meaningless cant.

'You treat children like something you'd pick up off the shelf at Tesco,' Rickman said.

'I *protect* them from falling into a cycle of deprivation and failure.'

'How can you be sure of that? Do you know that the men and women you sold children to always had the best intentions?'

Rickman saw a flicker of uncertainty, but Shepherd rallied. 'I'm satisfied that—'

'What gives you the authority to judge the suitability of people to be parents?' Rickman interrupted. 'You sold children for money, for God's sake!'

'It's what the courts do.' This was close, tantalisingly close. 'It's what Social Services do.'

'*Not*,' Rickman said, 'for money.'

Shepherd snorted. 'Don't kid yourself.'

'Social Services are accountable,' Rickman countered. 'The courts are accountable. They have strictures and rules, checks and balances. Who the hell are you accountable to? Your God?' He wasn't shouting — not quite — but his voice was roughened with emotion, and he was breathing hard.

'I've made my peace with God,' Shepherd said, suddenly calm again. 'I won't be afraid to face His judgement.'

Rickman stared at him for some moments. 'People with your kind of certainty terrify me,' he said.

Shepherd gave him a wan smile. 'Then you're afraid of the wrong people.'

CHAPTER 31

Hart met Rickman in his office an hour later.

'Mrs Shepherd has asked for a brief,' Hart said.

Rickman leaned against the wall, his long legs crossed at the ankles, his arms folded. He looked exhausted. 'Did you get anything out of her?'

Hart shook her head. 'The woman's got nerves of steel.' In an interview, Hart would use her good looks, lulling macho male suspects into underestimating her, coaxing the susceptible into her confidence. Mrs Shepherd had not been susceptible.

'When I accused her of being a baby broker, she said, "This isn't *America*, young woman." That was it — I must have asked the question in twenty different ways. Not even a "No comment".'

'I listened to the tape while I was waiting for you,' Rickman said. 'If it's any consolation, I think they've been coached.'

Hart exhaled in a rush. 'If they've got lawyers and police on their client list, we're sunk.' She caught his glance of approval that she had made the connection. It was almost enough to make up for her fruitless questioning of Mrs Shepherd. Almost.

'So,' she said. 'No joy from Ed, either.'

Rickman shifted positions. A finger went to the scar over his right eyebrow as he thought. 'It's debatable. He admitted that Mark telephoned him the day he died. He claims Mark offered him money.'

'*He* offered *them* money? That could only mean—'

'Mark took the cash that went missing from Operation Snowplough.'

She thought about it for a moment. 'But no confession?'

Rickman titled his head. 'A few suggestive responses, but certainly no confession. And he's insisting that Hilary isn't involved.'

Hart shot him an incredulous look.

'I know.' He fell silent. When he spoke again, it was as if in response to some internal debate. 'We need access to the children's home, but all we have right now is an informant's uncorroborated word that these two deal in babies.'

'Which won't get us a warrant.' Hart recalled Mark's mobile phone records, the six calls to the Shepherds' landline. 'We can prove that he lied about speaking to Mark the night he was murdered.'

'That'll help,' Rickman said. 'And if I can persuade the magistrate to listen to the interview tapes, I might be able to swing it for us to get that search warrant.'

'Can't we get it on the basis of obstruction? Perverting the course of justice?' Hart asked, her frustration evident. 'Shepherd took those phone calls from Davis and did nothing.'

'If I have to go with that, I will,' Rickman said. 'But it would limit the scope of the search.' He ran a hand through his hair, leaving it tousled. 'D'you think you could buy us some time? Delay Mrs Shepherd's solicitor?'

'Oh,' Hart said with sly satisfaction, 'I can do inefficient.'

'I very much doubt that,' Rickman said with a smile, and she again felt the motivating warmth of his approbation. 'But if you can manage slow, that will be fine.'

* * *

Rickman took the recordings to the magistrates' court himself. The rest of the team worked on existing leads, interviewing Black Wood's ex-residents, following up calls to the hotline. Hart arranged for Hilary Shepherd to have private access to a phone — the delay, she said, was caused by the huge influx of witnesses in the drugs investigation. Hilary seemed patient and understanding. *North West Newsbrief* agreed to put out another appeal on the evening bulletin for the mystery caller to ring back. Hart spent the next half hour shredding her nails and watching the clock while she pretended to catch up on paperwork.

At twelve thirty p.m., Rickman returned, and the room fell silent as every pair of eyes focused on him. 'We got it,' he said.

A cheer went up, followed by the rustle of twenty CID officers dropping paperwork and reaching for their jackets.

'The warrant takes in any adoption papers, suspected counterfeit documents, photographs of possible adoptees — and the missing money.'

Someone said, 'Bloody hell, boss, you must've caught him in a good mood.'

Rickman recognised the voice and located the speaker. Will Garvey — he'd worked with Will on a couple of cases and knew him to be experienced and reliable. Good — Rickman had a job in mind for DC Garvey. 'Let's just say we established a rapport,' Rickman said.

He read out a list of names. 'You'll come with me to Black Wood. Keep in mind the forensic integrity of the scene,' he warned. 'If you find anything that might yield fingerprints or DNA, bag it and document it, per the handbook. If it's too big to bag, talk to me, and I'll call in Scientific Support.'

He saw disappointment on the faces of those not chosen and said, 'I need three more volunteers to go to the Kirkhams' house.'

'You really *did* hit it off with the magistrate, didn't you, boss?' Garvey said.

Rickman allowed himself a smile. 'He felt the risk to Bella Kirkham outweighed any evidential inadequacies, on this occasion.'

Hands were already up, and Rickman said, 'Garve, I want you to lead this. You choose your team. You will arrest the Kirkhams on suspicion of kidnapping.'

'It'd be a pleasure,' Garvey said.

'Child Protection officers will meet you at the house. Social Services will also send a representative to take the child into safe care.'

They were on their way by twelve forty.

* * *

Ed Shepherd was remarkably calm, given the circumstances. He listened carefully to Rickman's explanations and instructions, acknowledging each with a nod of his head. He read through the warrant quietly, seated in the back of an unmarked car as they made their way through afternoon traffic.

'Where's my wife?' he asked.

'She's consulting with her solicitor,' Rickman said. There was a stillness in Shepherd that Rickman hadn't seen before. Perhaps he really had made his peace with his god. A backlog at the station had conveniently delayed the process further. Thus it was that Mr Innes, Hilary Shepherd's solicitor, only got to meet his client *after* Rickman and a convoy of four cars had left the station.

Most of the TV crews that had clustered at the entrance of the children's home the previous day had now relocated to Edge Hill Police Station, but Scientific Support were still at the scene, and the narrow drive to the coach house was taped off. Shepherd glanced at it as they drove past, and Rickman wondered just how much hurt Catholic guilt could cause a man. He hoped a lot.

Hart used Shepherd's key to open the front door. Shepherd stood between her and Rickman, his hands in his pockets, his mind evidently on other things. Hart stood back to let Rickman through first and he was struck by the smell of furniture polish in the hallway — before, when he and Foster had first visited, it was dusty and even a little stale. He was puzzled, too, that the stacks of boxes he had seen on his previous visit were absent. The hall was empty and glowing, the floors freshly waxed and the wood panelling buffed to a shine.

Rickman had a bad feeling about this.

A middle-aged woman stepped out of one of the rooms to the left. She was dressed in a business suit, and her hair gleamed with almost the same lustre as the woodwork. 'Just about finished, Mr Shepherd.' She beamed at Ed, acknowledging Rickman with a polite nod. 'I supervised the job personally.'

Shepherd avoided his gaze, and Rickman's unease began to take shape. He looked at the woman. 'You are?' he asked.

'Emily Nickson,' she said. 'Top-to-Bottom Cleaning Services. Who are you?'

'Police,' Rickman said. 'Stay here.' He headed for the couple's private quarters. The blinds were closed, and Rickman reached for the light switch. The spotlights gleamed on the newly polished wood, highlighting faint oblongs on the walls, where the great photomontages had hung. He turned full circle, noting four places where picture frames had been removed. More photographs had stood on the shelving, he recalled. There was no trace of them. *Damn. Damnit!*

In the hallway, Shepherd was still in contemplative pose, hands in his pockets, eyes downcast.

'You knew why we asked you to come in today,' Rickman said. This realisation triggered another — both Ed and Hilary had deliberately drawn out the interview process to ensure that the house had been scoured by the time they arrived.

Ms Nickson looked to Ed Shepherd for an explanation. 'What on earth is the matter?'

'Where are the boxes?' Rickman asked.

'Boxes?' she repeated.

'The hall was stacked with them.'

'There were no boxes,' she said. 'We're here to do a thorough clean before the new tenants arrive.'

'Is that what you told them?' Rickman asked, but Shepherd remained silent. 'There are no new tenants, Ms Nickson.'

Hart came down the stairs, ushering three anxious-looking women ahead of her. 'Not one photograph, postcard or letter,' she said, looking shaken. 'Every surface has been recently polished or wiped down.'

Rickman looked again at Shepherd. 'You've been planning this since I came here with Lee Foster two days ago.'

Shepherd roused himself at last. 'I told you,' he said, 'there are others to protect.' For a second, he glanced into Rickman's face, and Rickman saw that the apparent calm took an effort of will. Shepherd's eyes burned with feverish excitement.

'You're only making things worse,' Rickman said.

'For me, yes.' Shepherd was quite calm. 'But not for the families we saved.'

'*Saved?*' The man's arrogance was breathtaking.

'Yes, saved.'

Rickman looked down the hallway. Hilary Shepherd had arrived. She stood in the small porch, looking a little flushed. Strands of her hair had escaped from her ponytail and she reached up and tucked them behind her ear. 'We call them our saved children, Chief Inspector.'

'You admit that you were involved in the buying and selling of babies?'

Hilary ignored the question. 'Annabelle, Mike and Bella are long gone.' Her gaze remained on her husband, love and sadness brimming in her eyes — this information, Rickman thought, was no taunt — it was for Shepherd alone. She waited until her husband looked at her. 'The other families are safe.'

This was the closest Hilary Shepherd had come to a confession.

'You'll go to prison,' Rickman said.

She smiled at him. 'Wouldn't you go to prison to protect your child?' she demanded. 'Do anything it takes to protect your grandchild?'

'Grandchild? You buy and sell these children like goods in a supermarket.'

Neither of them spoke.

'I want everyone off site.' Rickman reached for his mobile, disgust and rage burning his insides like acid. 'That includes Mr and Mrs Shepherd.'

Hart began the evacuation immediately. Rickman scrolled down his contacts list to Tony Mayle. 'I'm at Black Wood,' he said. 'They've had a commercial cleaning firm in.'

He listened a moment, then smiled at Mrs Shepherd. 'You think these guys are good?' He nodded towards the retreating cleaning staff. 'Wait till you see what our CSIs can do. Their equipment will pick up stuff an industrial vac would miss.' He saw a satisfying flicker of uncertainty in Hilary Shepherd's face.

'While they're busy with the house, we'll be checking phone records, credit cards, bank statements — we don't need the originals, we can go to source for those. And that's before we even get started with the adoption agencies.'

Hollow though the victory was, Rickman was pleased to see anxiety in the look that passed between the couple. 'We'll find something,' he said.

* * *

Hilary and Ed Shepherd drove away without a backward glance, bumping along the uneven driveway, and steering around the bigger potholes as, Rickman suspected, they had done throughout their lives. When they disappeared at a curve in the drive, he made a second call.

'Tell me you've got something, Garve,' he said.

'Sorry, boss. According to the neighbours, the Kirkhams left five minutes before we got here.'

229

Rickman exhaled slowly. Would one small break on this case be too much to ask?

'Mike Kirkham took a call on his mobile in the middle of a planning meeting at the council offices. Walked out without a word of explanation,' Garvey went on. 'Neighbour saw Annabelle Kirkham loading up the family Espace with suitcases at about the same time — I've sent a message to mobile patrols to watch out for them.'

'You've checked the house?' Rickman asked.

'Empty.'

'Secure the scene, and get Scientific Support on the job, will you?' Rickman said. 'We need as much evidence as we can get on these bastards.'

'Already done, boss.'

Rickman broke the connection.

'Boss.' It was Naomi Hart. Her Icelandic blue eyes flashed with a rage he had never seen before in her. 'The cleaning staff have agreed to come down to the station to make statements.'

Rickman felt an answering flash of anger and got a hold of it — he needed a clear head. 'They've been thorough,' he said. 'So we'll need to find a paper trail — I doubt they would be foolish enough to accept cheques in payment, but on their salary, large cash deposits or withdrawals would take some explaining. Phone records are more likely to help us find their contacts.' He frowned, trying to remember if he had seen a computer in the house. 'Emails?'

Hart shook her head. 'No sign of a PC or laptop in the place,' she said.

'They must have this stuff stored somewhere. Get someone to check all the storage and removals firms in the area.'

They watched as the first of the white, unmarked CSI vans arrived.

He keyed the number for the emergency hotline and identified himself. 'Anything from Melanie?' he asked.

'Sorry, sir.'

'Okay. Call me immediately if she gets in touch.' He broke the connection. 'We need to find Melanie or her friend.'

'Kelly,' Hart said. 'Last I checked, we'd narrowed the list down to eight.' Hart sighed. 'What kind of person would sell her own baby?'

'The desperate kind,' Rickman said. 'Can you find out who issued the adoption papers? If there's the faintest whiff of irregularity, we'll put pressure on them. Hilary's probably warned them, so we need to act fast.'

'I'll make a start as soon as I get back,' she said.

What else? What else needs to be done? Rickman looked up into a blue sky streaked with mare's tails, the sign of a coming storm.

* * *

Lee Foster pounced on him when he arrived back at the station.

'Go back to the drugs team, Lee,' Rickman said.

'Just one question.' Foster followed him onto the concrete stairs of the fire escape, dogging his footsteps. 'They cleared the house, didn't they?'

Rickman stopped. It was impossible not to admire the information network Foster operated. 'You really do have spies everywhere, don't you?'

'Oh, yeah,' Foster said, bitterness and frustration etched on his face. 'Nothing slips past me — I was working side by side with them two and I didn't have a clue they were running a cottage industry in off-the-shelf babies.'

Rickman continued up the steps. 'I can't talk to you about this, Lee.'

'I know. But they must've cleared out fast — forensics—'

'Teams of CSIs are scouring the children's home and the Kirkham family home as we speak,' Rickman interrupted. 'Tony Mayle is coordinating. You don't get better scientific support than that.' They continued onto the next flight, their footsteps creating a stuttering echo in the bare concrete well.

'Did they do it?' Foster's voice, roughened by emotion, echoed up the stairwell to the top of the building. 'Jeff — did they kill Mark?'

They reached a turn in the staircase and Rickman stopped again. Foster rarely used his given name on the job — he was asking this question as a friend. 'No, I don't think they killed Mark.'

'But they *are* running illegal adoptions?'

Rickman started walking. 'It's an ongoing investigation.'

Foster ran up the remaining steps. 'Come on, Jeff, gimme a break!'

'Lee, you're *off the case*.'

'Jesus, Jeff, I'm just asking for a straight answer. Them two were my childhood bloody heroes.'

The pain in his friend's eyes told Rickman that he was only just holding it together. A sound lower down the stairwell decided him. Rickman opened the door on to his office landing and held it for Foster to pass through. 'Come on,' he said.

Inside his office, Rickman locked the door. 'The money that was missing from the drugs raid?'

Foster nodded.

'Seems Mark took it.'

Foster closed his eyes for a moment. 'The soft *get* . . .'

'He offered a hundred thousand to Ed Shepherd to take Bryony.'

'Have you charged them?'

'With what?' Rickman asked. 'We don't have any solid evidence, Lee. Our suspects are refusing to talk, they've forensically cleaned the scene, and our one possible witness is proving hard to trace.'

Foster grew quieter, his face more grim. 'So Tony doesn't hold out much hope on the forensics?'

'Scientific Support might pick up DNA from the Kirkhams' house, but it could take weeks, and it won't help us find them.'

'Oh, crap.' Foster slumped into a chair.

'I'm sorry, Lee,' Rickman said. 'I know you want to bring them down as much as I do.'

Foster dragged his fingers through his hair, playing havoc with the carefully gelled spikes — a sure sign of his distress. For a while, he seemed to be struggling with some inner turmoil. 'Tell you the truth,' he said at last, 'I don't *know* what I want. They were good to me.' He shifted position in the chair, folding his arms. 'What am I on about? They loved me — and hundreds of others.' Anyone else would be shocked to hear Foster being so honest about such a personal matter, but he and Rickman had seen each other at their darkest moments, and such experiences had only heightened their mutual regard.

'Ed and Hilary weren't about professional distance and behaviour modification,' Foster went on after a lengthy pause. 'They made you feel safe and loved when the world outside seemed cold and ugly and dangerous.'

'They took children away from their mothers and sold them on like commodities, Lee.'

'I know — the cop in me says they should be locked up. But us looked-after kids grow up in a different world from what most kids know — I don't need to tell you that.'

Rickman had no answer. He knew the ugliness and deprivation most looked-after children came from and were destined to perpetuate.

Foster shook his head, staring angrily at the point of his shoe. 'I suppose what I want is for all this not to be true.'

'For your sake, I wish it wasn't,' Rickman said. 'For the sake of the children.' He didn't want to think too much about what had happened to the missing boys and girls. He remembered the photographs of happy families on the wall of Ed Shepherd's private sitting room and wanted to believe the surface image. But Rickman knew a smile could hide a lot of pain.

CHAPTER 32

Late afternoon. The musical clink of wine glasses and the buzz of animated conversation rose above the constant hum of traffic. The sun burned through a milky haze of high cloud, bathing the city in autumn sunshine. The wind had picked up, plucking at the skirts of the women and ruffling the hair of the men who, unable to find room in the sequestered courtyard at the back of the building, spilled out onto the paved area at the front.

Recently arrived, Rob Maitland sipped champagne and conversed politely with an earnest young man, nodding and murmuring encouragement while he scanned the crowd for more engaging company. Maitland stood out in the suited business crowd. Though not conventionally handsome, his physical charisma meant that the eyes of the other guests would frequently stray to him, and he enjoyed the attention.

A scream from across the street caused a sudden lull in the conversation. Heads turned. A woman and two men appeared from behind the corrugated iron fencing that encircled an old warehouse — one of the few remaining in the city centre that had yet to be renovated. The woman, stoned and uncoordinated, swung wildly at a bearded man in a tattered suit jacket and jeans. He caught her arm, twisted it, and she fell, swearing loudly. The second man laughed and slipped his arms around her waist, groping at her breasts while he helped her to her feet. The screaming continued.

Though the scene played out across maybe twenty yards of waste ground and a busy road, the business types were becoming jittery, and the photographer and reporter circulating the crowd started showing an interest.

Maitland touched his earnest companion's arm, excusing himself. The restaurant was corralled off from the street by a low wall with iron palings, and one of his men was stationed at the gate, doubling as bouncer and bodyguard. Maitland moved at a lazy saunter, but energy fizzed off him.

'Sort that, will you?' he said quietly. 'It's spoiling the vibe.' Then he turned his back on the spectacle as if it meant no more to him than sparrows squabbling over a crust of bread.

Maitland's man crossed the road onto the wasteland, his shoes kicking up small puffs of brick dust from the bulldozed ground. The woman, by far the most vigilant of the group, stopped mid-scream, instantly wary. She detached herself from the other two and stood twirling a lock of her hair anxiously between her fingers as Maitland's man spoke.

Across the street, those of the business party who watched saw initial bravado in the two men. Then Maitland's bodyguard made a half-turn and nodded towards his boss. The ragged threesome stared into the crowd on the restaurant courtyard. Maitland was laughing at some joke with one of the businessmen. He patted the man on the shoulder, then moved on, into a space. With a clear line of sight over the roadway, he stared in silence at the trio who had disturbed the party.

The woman took flight, and the two men followed after, scrambling across the waste ground like mice disturbed by footfall. He watched until they disappeared behind the corrugated steel fence.

The restaurant owner came over, smiling. 'Got any more where he came from?' she asked, lifting her fine-boned chin in the direction of Maitland's bodyguard. She was tall and long-limbed, her hair copper gold and tightly curled, her skin warmed by Jamaican blood a couple of generations down the line. 'A quiet word from the right quarter and trouble just disappears.'

'Protection isn't really my bag,' Maitland said.

She blushed, suffusing the golden brown of her face with a coral glow. 'God — I didn't mean—'

'I'm just messing with you.' He flashed her an ortho-dontically enhanced smile. 'You all know me — and I'm not proud of my past — but I'm not ashamed of who I am, either.' He'd practised his Business Scouse — people didn't seem to mind if your accent was strong, as long as you enun-ciated clearly, ensured the beginnings and endings of words were distinct.

The restaurant owner laughed, nervous, still a little embarrassed. 'Well, I'm glad you could make it.'

'So am I.' He leaned closer to her and caught a whiff of perfume that made him positively giddy with desire. 'Between you and me, I'm supposed to be sitting in my office, working on a planning application — they want to know how one of my development projects will benefit the local community. Then I saw this on the Chamber of Commerce website.' He smiled down at her. 'No contest.'

'My guess is you did the local community a lot more good just being here today,' the woman said, with another glance across the street. 'It doesn't encourage inward invest-ment, having that kind of thing disrupting a business net-working opportunity.'

'Drug addicts?' he asked, his tone sympathetic.

She nodded. 'Homeless, most of them. They hang out in the old warehouse.' Her face darkened for a moment. 'The police are worse than useless, and it's costing me customers.'

'Well, we can't have that, can we?' He looked into her eyes and she blushed again, looking away. Her skin glowed like sun-warmed honey and he wondered how it would taste — sweet or salty?

'Tell you what,' he said. 'I'm always looking for property to redevelop. I'll make some enquiries, see if we can't get them shifted for good.'

She gave a little gasp of amused astonishment.

Maitland dipped into his pocket. 'In the meantime, if they give you any trouble, give me a call.' He held out a business card.

She didn't take it immediately. 'I don't know what to say . . .'

'Go 'ead,' he said. 'This *is* a networking opportunity, isn't it? We *are* supposed to be making contacts, seeing how we can help each other out . . .'

'Well, yes.' She took the card. 'But . . .'

'You're wondering what you've got to offer?' He went on, before she made the obvious assumption. 'You can tell me how you got this place up to standard.' He eyed the building's exterior appreciatively. 'Georgian, isn't it?'

Her eyes lit up. 'We've kept as many original features as possible. Would you like the grand tour?'

'I thought you'd never ask.'

He offered her his arm and, after the briefest hesitation, she took it, asking with a sideways glance, 'At the risk of repeating myself — got any more where you came from?'

Maitland tilted his head back and laughed.

* * *

Tommy Eames was sweating. He was a big man, he owed his size to his job. Being in control of thirty coffee bars was not the way to keep a youthful figure. Tommy — more recently 'the Tank' — didn't know if he was more angry or afraid. This wasn't supposed to happen. Not to him.

To make matters worse, he'd had a lapse in concentration and left his jacket in the boot of the car with the shooter in the pocket. The boy's fault, prattling on about profit and loss differentials, trying to impress, desperate for the job to pay off his university debts. If the kid really was any good,

Tommy thought bitterly, he wouldn't *have* any debts to clear. But Mr Maitland wanted clean frontmen for the shiny new businesses he was setting up, and you didn't get much cleaner than Michael Aldiss.

Tommy had seen the Beamer several times during their tour of Maitland's outlets: two men, one bearded, one shaved smooth as a billiard ball. He had seen them and dismissed them as he turned off the M53 towards Chester. They'd vanished somewhere around Handbridge. He had worried about a similar car that had stayed two cars back all the way between Royal Birkdale golf course and Southport. *Paranoid*, he told himself, when he thought he'd caught a glimpse of a bald man in the passenger seat of a BMW that overtook them on Strand Street, as they headed back into Liverpool.

He checked his rear windscreen as he turned into a multi-storey by the firm's offices. All clear. One last check as he took the second ramp.

The BMW loomed suddenly behind him, filling the rear-view mirror. Tommy felt his heart contract painfully: the two men were unmistakable. They tailgated him, almost forcing him up the slope. Heart racing, mouth dry, Tommy called up the phone icon on his smart screen and hit speed-dial.

'Billy?' he said. 'Trouble. Two apes in a Beamer, getting cheeky.'

Alarmed, the boy glanced at him, then started to turn, but Tommy put a hand on his arm. 'Sit still.'

'Where are you?' Billy asked.

'I'm in the multi-storey, round the corner. Have we got any lads handy?'

'How many d'you want?'

'Send whatever you've got, pronto, and make sure they're well equipped.'

'Just keep moving,' Billy said.

'Don't worry, I'll be circling like a friggin' shark.' He glanced again at the two men in the car behind him. 'And when I'm done, I'm gonna pick these fuckers' bones clean.'

He kept the line open as they spiralled upward, the car tyres squeaking on new concrete, the reek of fresh paint, car exhaust and the dizzying motion of the car making him slightly queasy.

He pressed a button and the doors locked down simultaneously. Aldiss turned to him, his eyes wide with fear. 'Who are they?' the lad said. 'What do they want?'

'You don't need to know. You *do* need to listen.' The boy glanced wildly over his shoulder. 'You wanna work for me, you've got to do what I say — now face the front and fucking *listen*.'

The boy's head snapped forward. His chest rose and fell as he took rapid, gasping breaths, and Tommy felt perversely calmed by his anxiety. 'You listening?'

A nod.

'Stay in the car. Doesn't matter what happens, we just stay in the car and wait for backup, all right?'

Two short nods.

Sunlight dazzled suddenly through the windscreen. They had reached the top level.

'What now?' The note of panic in the boy's voice caused a momentary spasm of answering fear to cramp Tommy's gut, then he had it under control.

'We head back down, and when my lads arrive, these clowns are gonna be very, very sorry.' Another nod, stoical this time, and Tommy began the turn onto the down ramp.

'Fuck!' A Toyota SUV shot up the ramp and he braked hard, finishing up nose to nose with it. He slammed the gears into reverse. There was nowhere to go — the Beamer was hard up against his rear bumper.

'Bill!' he yelled into the phone. 'Get in here, *now*!' No reply.

He revved his engine, backing up against the BMW in a cloud of screaming, burning rubber. The Beamer gave way a little, then came back at him, matching him rev for rev.

'What's happening?' Aldiss yelled. 'Mr Eames — what's happening?'

'Shut the *fuck* up!' Tommy screamed, revving the car into the red zone. The instrument panel lit up with red and amber warning signs, electronic alarms jangled, and now he smelled burning metal along with burning rubber.

'Bill. Where the *fuck* are you?'

The BMW lost grip, sliding a few yards back onto the flat. The boy reached for the door handle.

'Don't touch that!'

The handle flipped, the door remained locked. *The fail-safe*, Tommy thought. *If he gives it one more tug, it'll open.*

'Don't you *fuckin'* touch it!' He punched Aldiss in the head, losing control of the wheel for a second. The car lurched left and the boy fell with it, made another dazed grab at the door handle. It gave, tumbling him out onto the concrete.

Aldiss scrambled to his feet as the passengers of the two cars leapt out. The Beamer's passenger — the bald guy — stood in the gap between the wall and the car, spreading his arms wide, like a goalkeeper. The boy lunged, but the man got him by the neck and swung him round, slamming him into the car, then he switched grip, clamping the boy in a headlock.

The door swung wide and, horrified, Tommy threw himself at it, reaching for the grab-handle. His car lurched and stalled, and the sudden release of pressure surprised the BMW driver. The pursuing car surged forward and fishtailed left, nearly sideswiping his own man. The rear impact cannoned Tommy into the dashboard. He felt a sharp pain in his side as the airbag deployed, then the door was snatched away from him as the second man twisted it back so hard the hinges groaned.

The man ducked his head and said one word: 'Out.'

Tommy made a move and gave a gasp of pain. He felt cold metal against the flesh of his cheek. 'Now,' the man said.

Tommy crawled forward, grunting with the pain in his rib. The man gave him a tug as he tried to position himself to step out of the car and he fell, bruising his hands and knees.

They shut off the engines and the silence hissed in his ears.

'On your feet.'

All four were on the concrete now, the bald man still with a tight grip of the boy.

'Give us a second—' Tommy gasped between thuds of pain. 'Busted a rib.'

One of the men grabbed him by his shirt collar and lifted him. Tommy grunted as another stab of pain shocked through him. This guy was strong, and even without his injury, Tommy was way out of condition. He stood as straight as he could, sweating and hurting and thinking how much he was going to hurt these bastards.

The bald guy released Aldiss, and the boy swayed a moment, pale and terrified, almost sagging at the knees.

'You are *so* fired,' Tommy said, though he could see from the look on his face the boy was too terrified to hear anything but the screaming in his own head.

Tommy scanned the faces of the four men and singled out the one he guessed was the leader, a stocky bastard with a gleam in his eye.

'My men' — he gave a grunt as he breathed too deeply and sent splintered bone into the soft tissue under his ribcage — 'My men are on the way.' He took a shallow sip of air. 'And you'd better be gone when they get here.'

The men looked at each other and the stocky guy smiled. Tommy was going to enjoy carving that smug look off his face.

'I don't see them, Tank,' the man said. Nobody called Tommy Eames 'Tank' to his face. 'I don't hear them.'

'Do youse know who I work for?' Tommy demanded. These four must be part of the Nealy boys' crew. If so, the Paddies were better organised than Mr Maitland had given them credit for. He spoke with a bravado he didn't feel: 'My boss eats gobshites like you for breakfast.'

'Funny you should say that,' the stocky guy said.

The rear door of the SUV clicked open, and a fifth man walked up the ramp to join them on the roof. This man Tommy did recognise, and the recognition gave him a moment of bowel-churning fear. He understood now why Bill had been so slow to send reinforcements, why the phone had remained stubbornly silent as he'd screamed for help.

The fifth man was Graham. This was no revenge attack by a few Birkenhead yobs out to gain a bit of territory — Graham acted under nobody's orders but Rob Maitland's. He stood square and implacable, watching Tommy's reaction without expression. Graham matched him in weight, but where Tommy had gained his extra pounds on a high-carb, low-exercise regime, sweating over accounts books, Graham's were solid muscle built by working out two hours a day in the gym, every day of the week, by eating well and never giving up. He was as immutable as the rock on which the city was built.

Tommy licked his lips. 'Look,' he said, 'I don't know what this is about—'

'Where's Carter?' Graham interrupted.

Tommy stared at him. *Carter? Oh, Jesus . . .*

He tried a laugh, but it came out high-pitched and panicked. 'The boss having trouble with the taxman, is he?'

Graham's hand shot forward, fingers straight, stabbing at Tommy's injured ribs. He doubled up with a yell of pain. 'Fuck!' He raised one hand to ward off another blow, but Graham, always controlled, waited patiently while he got his breath again.

'He's an accountant, he's probably at home doing things accountants do.'

Graham shook his head as if sorely disappointed in him. 'Where is Carter?'

'Honest, Graham, I don't know,' he said. 'Look, what's this about anyw—'

On a signal from Graham, two of the men grabbed Aldiss and hauled him to the edge of the roof, lifting him.

'Woah!' Tommy yelled. 'Wait!'

The kid swung his feet, trying to find purchase, but the tips of his shiny new shoes barely scraped the ground. He gasped, 'Nuh! Nuh! Nuh!' a few times, then started to mewl weakly, tears coursing down his face.

'Last chance,' Graham said. 'Where is Carter?'

The boy struggled, his eyes fixed on Tommy, pleading and lost, wondering how he had ever blundered into this nightmare. Tommy took a step forward, but the stocky guy gave him a dig in the side and he crumpled, fighting for breath, dots of bright light swimming in front of his eyes.

'I don't know!' he wheezed. 'If I knew — honest to *God*, I'd tell you. Look, let the lad go — I'll find out. I'll find the fucker and bring him to you.'

Graham tilted his head, considering. 'Okay.' He glanced at the two men. 'You heard the man — let the lad go.'

Tommy's eyes widened in horror as he saw what they were about to do. He lunged, but they held him back as the two men heaved the boy over the wall.

And let go.

For one terrifying moment, he seemed suspended. Then he was falling.

A scream.

A thud. Then silence. Only the hum of traffic seven storeys below and the hiss like tinnitus in Tommy's ears.

Graham put his hand on Tommy's shoulder and he flinched. A smile flickered over Graham's face. 'You've got forty-eight hours,' he said. 'After that—' He glanced over his shoulder at the sound of dismayed shouts from the street below. 'Well,' he said. 'Just bear that in mind.'

* * *

In the air-conditioned cool of the restaurant's office, tucked under the eaves of the house, Rob Maitland admired the simplicity and elegance of the refurbishment.

'Makes me almost eager to sit down and work on my planning application,' he said. The woman — he had learned her name was Leoni — smiled at him, her face flushed with pride.

'You've taken a wall down, here?' He pointed to a beam that stretched from wall to wall across the width of the room.

'And here,' she said, moving towards the back wall. 'I wanted open plan — these rooms were horribly poky and dark before we opened them up.'

He nodded. 'Quite radical, though.'

She let her gaze track through the length of the room. 'And you wouldn't *believe* the structural work they had to do to make it safe.' She shrugged. 'But as my granny always said, you can't make an omelette without cracking eggs.'

At the exact moment Michael Aldiss's body hit the pavement, Maitland turned south-west, tilting his head as if he heard something.

'Is something wrong?' she asked, vague alarm showing in her face.

Perhaps she thinks the addicts came back.

'Not a thing.' He took her arm, strolling with her through the sunny office. 'Just cracking a few eggs.'

CHAPTER 33

Merseyside Police Headquarters stood edge-on to the docks in Canning Place. A large, nondescript building, its mud-coloured bricks seemed contrived to echo the unlovely architecture of the City Law Courts a few hundred yards across Chavasse Park. Rickman had been called to a meeting to discuss the progress of the case with the brass. Both DS Maynard and DI Dwight had also been required to attend. Meeting over, Rickman turned on his mobile phone as he hurried from the headquarters towards his car, anxious to get back to his investigation.

The rumble of traffic on Strand Street was a constant, day and night, since the radical overhaul the waterfront had received a few years ago. What was once the soot-blackened heart of the commercial district was now a tourist destination.

DC Hart had rung. Crossing the car park, Rickman called her back and she picked up immediately.

'Sir — did you get my message?'

He heard controlled excitement in her tone and felt a responding thrill. 'I haven't checked my voicemail yet. What's happened?'

'I got someone to check hospital records on the Black Wood residents — unexplained dropouts from antenatal clinics. They found a Kelly Rayder.'

'You think this could be Jasmine's best mate from the children's home?'

'It's the right time frame — she dropped out of sight two and a half years ago, five months into a pregnancy. I'm on my way to her family home with Chris Tunstall now.'

Rickman felt a fizz of excitement. 'Give me the address, I'll meet you there.'

* * *

Kelly Rayder lived in a 1990s social housing development in Vauxhall. Each property on the estate had some feature that made it subtly different from the rest: a porch with a pitched roof, a bay window instead of a flat front, railings topping a low wall. The street looked cared for, and several of the houses were festooned with hanging baskets, stuffed with winter pansies and ivy.

Hart and Tunstall arrived moments after him and Rickman bent over the passenger window. 'Naomi, you're with me. Chris, you'll have to sit this one out, I'm afraid.'

Tunstall nodded, a look of stoic acceptance on his broad features.

A woman of about forty answered the door. She was small and had the weathered look of a woman to whom life had not been kind, but her make-up looked carefully applied, and she was dressed neatly in jeans and a sweater. When Rickman presented his warrant card, she seemed surprised and concerned, rather than wary.

'We'd like to talk to your daughter.'

'Sorry, love,' the woman said. 'She just went down the shops. She isn't in any trouble, is she?'

'No,' Rickman said, with a smile of reassurance. 'But she might be a witness.'

The woman nodded, absorbing this. 'She shouldn't be long.' She peeped around the door, past Rickman and Hart, evidently worried about what the neighbours might think. 'Why don't yiz come in and have a cuppa?'

She showed them through to a small sitting room, crammed with ornaments and photographs. In the corner sat a box, piled with children's toys.

'I'll give you a hand.' Hart followed Mrs Rayder through the narrow hallway to the kitchen. Rickman approved — a lot could be discovered during idle chat — and it gave Hart the chance to check another area of the house.

He perused the photographs and found one of a younger Mrs Rayder with two white-haired girls, one aged about five, the other nearer ten years old, both pretty. In a silver frame on the TV stand, another picture. The younger girl looked about sixteen or seventeen, and her older sister in her twenties. Odd that Mrs Rayder hadn't asked which daughter they wanted to speak to. He supposed the older girl had moved out of the family home — she seemed familiar, but he couldn't place her.

He turned as Hart and Mrs Rayder came into the room, Hart carrying a tray of tea things. 'Which is Kelly?' he asked, smiling.

Mrs Rayder stiffened. 'What's Kelly got to do with this?'

'It's Kelly we need to speak to, Mrs Rayder,' Hart said, placing the tray on the coffee table in front of the TV set.

Mrs Rayder put her hand to her mouth, and Rickman looked in consternation to Hart. The DC reached out, but Mrs Rayder waved her away. 'I'm all right. It's just — it's a shock, that's all.' She eased into one of the armchairs and Hart handed her a mug of tea. Mrs Rayder took a sip or two, composing herself. 'Kelly's dead,' she said.

'I'm so sorry,' Rickman said. *The pregnancy? Did something go wrong?* He glanced at Hart. She looked horrified that she hadn't thought to check with the registry office. 'When did . . .' He let his words trail off, giving Kelly's mother the chance to explain.

'She was in a car accident with her boyfriend, eighteen months ago.'

'And the baby?'

'She'd already give him up by then.'

247

'Given him up?' Rickman said.

'To the adoption agency.'

'Are you in touch with the adoptive parents?' Rickman asked.

Mrs Rayder shook her head slowly, but not in answer to his question: her forehead crinkled and she seemed almost to be struggling against a physical pain. After a short while she gave a juddering sigh.

'Do you have any way to contact them? A business card, maybe, or some documentation?'

'Oh, no.' She wiped her eyes with a crumpled tissue. 'Kelly was only fifteen when she got pregnant, she wasn't really ready to be a mother — she never met the people who adopted him. They said it was best she didn't have any contact. Too unsettling — for her and the baby.' Rickman and Hart exchanged a look — this wasn't standard operational practice for legitimate adoption services.

'But *you* would want to know what happened to your grandson?' Rickman said.

She became abashed. 'Kelly wasn't living at home then — there wasn't nothing I could do.' Her voice raised in her anxiety for them to understand. 'She run off with that boyfriend of hers and I didn't know where she was.'

'But you knew she'd put her baby up for adoption.'

'*He* rang me.'

'The boyfriend made the arrangements?' Rickman asked.

'Craig Ely,' she said. 'Wouldn't let me talk to my own daughter. I'd've helped her — looked after the baby. She didn't have to—'

'Is Craig the boyfriend who was killed in the car crash?' Rickman interrupted, and she nodded.

Both the potential witnesses were dead. Did the mother know what was going on? Had Kelly confided in her?

Rickman hesitated. How did you ask a mother if her daughter sold her baby? He decided there was no easy way. 'Was Kelly given any money?'

'They don't give you money, do they?' Mrs Rayder said. But he saw something cross her face — guilt? Or the memory perhaps of something she should have questioned but didn't.

'Do you remember if Kelly seemed flush for cash around then?' Naomi asked. 'Maybe she bought new clothes — or paid for a nice holiday in advance.'

Rickman saw Mrs Rayder's eyes widen, just for a second, then she seemed to shut down.

'Sorry, love,' she said, without looking at Hart. 'I don't know what you're getting at.'

Rickman left his card, and they walked back to their cars.

'She didn't know,' Hart said.

'She suspected,' Rickman said. 'There's no record of Kelly's baby at the General Register Office?'

'Nothing under Rayder,' Hart said. 'I'll check using the boyfriend's surname, but . . .' She shrugged.

'I know,' Rickman said. 'If Kelly isn't named in the records, it isn't likely her boyfriend will be.' He was still troubled by the photograph in the little sitting room. He felt sure he's seen the older girl in the picture somewhere, but he couldn't quite—

A woman turned the corner into the close. She carried a plastic carrier bag in each hand and chided a reluctant boy of about four years old, who dragged a few yards behind her. She froze, and Rickman felt his heart begin to thud in his chest. In her mid-twenties, she was overweight, fair-haired — and she was the very image of the CCTV screencap they'd got from Lime Street Station's phone kiosks. He was looking into the face of the informant who had exposed Ed and Hilary Shepherd. A few years older than in the photo in the silver frame, a few stones heavier, maybe, but there was no doubt: this was 'Melanie Townsend', their mystery caller. She was Kelly's older sister.

Rickman slipped his car keys back into his pocket and took a cautious step forward. 'Melanie?' he said.

She dropped the bags of shopping and bolted. Rickman ran after her. The child, shocked by his mother's sudden action, stood still a moment, then began to bawl. Rickman heard Hart shout to Tunstall to take care of the boy, then her footsteps, following.

Melanie tired easily, almost collapsing at a lamppost fifty yards along the main road. She held onto it for support as she gasped and retched. Rickman stopped a few yards away and raised his arm to waist height, signalling Hart to stay back. The pavement was free of pedestrians, and although cars slowed and drivers ducked to check out the action through their side windows, nobody stopped.

'I just want to talk, Melanie,' Rickman called.

She wheezed a laugh. 'Do I look soft?'

'It doesn't matter to us that Kelly was your sister. If the information you gave is good—'

'It *is*,' she took a whooping breath. 'You arrested them two people, didn't you?'

'We haven't charged anyone in connection with Jasmine Elliott's death,' he began. 'That's why we need you to speak out.'

'Forget it.' She took a few more seconds to catch her breath. 'Youse lot won't never sort this one out.'

'You'd be turning your back on the reward money, Melanie.'

'Not what you'd call cash in hand, is it?' she said. 'I could be old as me granny before I ever see a penny of it.'

'Your evidence could—'

'I said forget it.'

'New trainers, Melanie?' Hart asked. 'Nice jacket, too — Canada Goose, isn't it? I had my eye on it myself, last time I went shopping.'

Melanie looked warily from Hart to Rickman, and he began to understand.

'Found someone else to put up the ten thousand pounds did you, Melanie?' he asked.

She hawked and spat, still trembling from the exertion.

'Tell us who approached you,' Rickman said. 'You could still do the right thing.'

'I *done* the right thing. I *kept* my baby.'

Rickman heard the resentment in her voice, against her sister, the state, the boy who had knocked her up.

'It must be tough,' he said.

'A room at my mum's house, and seventy-four quid a week including child benefit — it's a doddle, mate.' The unfairness of her situation suddenly seemed too much for her, '*She* got a flat and a car,' she blurted out. '*Nice* things, a boyfriend — everything.'

'Your sister's dead, Melanie.'

She gave a shrug, her expression sulky. 'That's not my fault.'

'Her baby was adopted illegally,' Rickman said. 'Whoever offered you money is breaking the law.'

She curled her lip at him. 'It's always illegal when the likes of me gets to make a bit of cash.'

'Take her in,' Rickman said.

'What? I haven't done nothing!'

'Caution her.'

Hart looked uncertain. 'What am I arresting her for, boss?'

'Blackmail, obstruction, perverting the course of justice — I don't care, just get her out of my sight.'

'I never blackmailed nobody,' Melanie protested as Hart guided her back along the main road.

'You got a better deal,' Rickman said.

'No.' She twisted to look at him, but Hart had a tight grip on her arm. '*You* said that. I never.'

To collect the Crimestoppers reward Melanie would have to go to court. She'd probably persuaded herself that by taking money from the Shepherds she was sparing her mother, protecting the memory of her dead sister.

They turned into the quiet cul-de-sac. Mrs Rayder stood on her doorstep, the sobbing child in her arms. She stared at her daughter as though she barely recognised her.

'Mum!' Melanie shouted. 'They've made a mistake!'

Mrs Rayder went inside and shut the front door.

Hart put the woman in the back seat of the car and turned to face Rickman. 'She won't talk, boss.'

Rickman didn't doubt it. Any money the Shepherds — or one of their rich clients — had offered Melanie would depend on her keeping her mouth shut.

CHAPTER 34

Just before four p.m., DS Cass rapped a drum roll on the door frame of the commandeered conference room. 'How's it going at the call centre?' he asked. 'I hope you're logging yourself out for them toilet breaks.'

Hart had a crick in her neck and cramps in her fingers from gripping the phone. Melanie — or Joanne Rayder, as they discovered was her real name — had been closeted with her solicitor for an hour. Hart was due to meet Kim Lindermann at the Royal Hospital mortuary at four thirty to formally identify Jasmine, and she had a gently throbbing headache.

'Have you nothing better to do?' she asked.

'Ooh,' he said. '*Someone's* not taking their evening primrose oil.'

'You're pathetic, Cass.' Hart didn't even bother looking at him.

Cass looked to Tunstall for male support, but all he got was a stony look. He shrugged. 'You're wanted in the MIR in five.'

'I assume you mean *your* MIR,' Hart said.

'Where else?'

'Who's calling the meeting?' Hart asked. If this was one of Cass's attempts to put his greasy mitts all over their investigation, she wasn't about to encourage him.

'Area Superintendent,' he said.

There was no arguing with that. So, five minutes later, Hart walked into the drugs inquiry Major Incident Room. It was practically seething with bodies — seated, standing, leaning against the walls, perched on tables or draped over filing cabinets — there must have been fifty plainclothes and uniformed officers crammed into the space. Despite the blustering wind outside, the narrow letterbox windows provided insufficient through-put of air to clear the fug of fast-food smells and bad digestion.

DS Cass sat at the centre, feet apart, tie loosened, top button popped. 'Well, I hope the boss shows his face for this one,' he said. 'Seeing as he hasn't even put his head round the door all day.'

'Where is he, anyway?' somebody asked.

'Hard to say.' Cass paused in the act of applying fresh balm to his lips. 'Between consultative panels and minority support groups, our leader's hardly got time to keep the likes of you and me informed of his busy schedule.' A few looks were exchanged, guilty enjoyment, sly amusement. After all, it was Cass doing the DI-bashing, not them.

Cass spotted Hart.

'Naomi!' He spread his arms wide. 'Room for one over here.' He had actually reserved a seat next to him. She made a diversion to the water cooler to give herself time to think. When she turned around, Cass's gaze was still on her, sliding over her body like a slug trail.

Cass patted the seat next to him and Hart became aware that the others were watching for her response. There was a space in the far corner near the window, but she would have to walk past Cass, and in the crush, that meant stepping over his sprawled legs. Acceptance offered the unenticing prospect of DS Cass's undivided attention, but refusal would look like weakness.

Sod it! She walked towards him and heard a twitter of excitement. Cass left his hand on the chair for longer than was decent, taking it away at the last moment. 'I kept it warm for you.'

Hart's stomach lurched, but she saw the challenge in his eyes and refused to back down. As she took her seat someone yelled, 'You lose, Sarge!'

Hart guessed that they had laid bets on whether she would accept. She couldn't decide if it made him more or less of a creep that he'd deliberately played up the sleaziness of his invitation.

He joined in with the laughter, showing his grey, strangely even teeth. 'I'd pay youse lot twice over,' he said. 'I can't help meself — I think I'm in *lurrve*.' For one nauseating moment, she thought he was reaching to give his groin a tug, but his hand went into his jacket pocket instead, and he retrieved his little pot of lip balm. Hart looked away to spare herself the queasy spectacle of Cass reapplying the salve to his lips.

'All right, Naomi?' Foster had come into the room.

'Fine, Sarge,' Hart said. It was bad enough that she'd screwed up the previous day, and worse that she hadn't been able to find a moment, or the right words, to apologise. The last thing she wanted was to look ineffectual in front of Lee Foster. She'd been on the force long enough and seen enough wind-ups to recognise this as a no-win situation. The best she could do was smile and ride it out.

* * *

Rickman arrived as Detective Superintendent Cliff Maynard and Detective Inspector Larry Dwight turned into the corridor.

'Jeff,' Maynard said. 'A word, if I may?'

Rickman felt his stomach clench. 'My Incident Room is free,' he said, leading the way. Even the telephonists and civilian staff had been ordered to attend the joint briefing, and the room was empty. It was warm and stuffy, and the evidence of recent activity could be seen in abandoned paper-work — half-finished reports and jotted notes.

'Sir,' Rickman said, dreading what he would hear.

'Joanne Rayder's solicitor is threatening to bring Crimestoppers into disrepute,' Maynard said.

'We found Joanne — alias Melanie Townsend — by chance,' Rickman said. 'It had nothing to do with—'

'I know, Jeff. But he'll make a stink, and scores of other prosecutions could be brought into question. Worse, witnesses will be afraid to come forward in case they're identified and arrested.'

'That's *not* how it happened.'

'It doesn't matter. All he has to say is his client was arrested after making a call to Crimestoppers, and I guarantee we'd lose a few dozen witnesses on current investigations.' Maynard frowned. 'You can't win this one, Jeff.'

Rickman pushed his fingers through his hair. Wasn't that why he had arrested her in the first place? Because this was one he couldn't win — because he felt so maddeningly impotent?

He gave a reluctant nod. 'I'll arrange for her release after the briefing.'

'I'm sorry, Jeff,' Maynard said. 'I'm as sick about it as you are.'

Rickman very much doubted it.

Maynard led the way into the Incident Room. A couple of tables had been set out under the whiteboard, and Rickman, Dwight and Maynard took their places, facing the mass of bodies.

Maynard's eyes swept the room. The super might be more politician than practician in recent years, but Rickman had to respect his quiet authority. It affected even the most battle-hardened of the assembly, and the faint buzz of conversation was silenced.

'You will all have heard about the murder of Michael Aldiss.' His voice was sonorous and bore only the slightest hint of a local accent. 'The Calls and Response department has been inundated ever since. Local and national media are baying for blood.' The detective superintendent let his gaze flit from one to another.

Rickman took a breath and let it out slowly, trying to focus his mind on the briefing.

'The victim isn't some scallywag.' Maynard didn't say 'scal', as most would, but used the whole word. 'Michael Aldiss is a recent graduate with a degree in Business Studies.

'The only person remaining at the scene was Thomas Eames, an employee of Rob Maitland. He was injured and distressed — claimed he and young Aldiss had been set upon by "unknown attackers". We've got the cars on the car park security video tapes — no clear image of the occupants — and the cars were found dumped and burnt out in Huyton an hour ago.'

'Who interviewed Eames?' Rickman asked.

'That'd be me,' Cass said.

It seemed odd to Rickman that Naomi Hart should sit next to Cass. The sergeant seemed pleased with himself, and with men like Cass, that usually involved getting one over on somebody else.

'Did Eames know the attackers?' Rickman asked.

Cass shrugged. 'He says not.'

'That's not what I asked.' Rickman hardened his voice. 'Do I need to simplify the question, Sergeant?'

'No,' Cass said. Then, with an embarrassed glance at Hart, 'No, sir.'

Rickman knew that cost the sergeant dearly. He waited, allowing the tension in the room to build.

'He's in shock,' Cass said. 'It might be worth having another word.'

He's covering his back, Rickman thought. *In case somebody else gets more out of Eames than he did.*

'Make sure you do,' Maynard said, leaving a few seconds to emphasise the point before changing direction. 'So, what was a nice middle-class boy like Aldiss doing with the likes of Thomas "the Tank" Eames?'

Dwight belatedly realised that this was his cue to come in. Flustered, he began sifting through the document wallets and folders on the desk in front of him. 'I've been pretty tied up . . .'

Cass watched, prolonging the agony a moment longer. 'The blue folder, guv,' he said, at last, risking a sly glance at a few of his cronies. 'You were at your three o'clock.' He managed to make it sound like it was in quotation marks. 'I put together the key points, so you know what we've been doing.' The emphasis on 'we' was so slight that, if it hadn't been for the tension in the room, you would have missed it.

Dwight fumbled the folder open and skimmed its contents. He kept running his hands through his hair. It was trimmed so close, the curls so tight, that he still looked neat, but Rickman was close enough to see the sweat on Dwight's pale skin and felt impotent rage coming off him in waves.

'Eames is known to be a key member of Maitland's gang,' Dwight said. He cleared his throat, recalling that this information was already common knowledge, at least to his own team, and added, 'For the benefit of DCI Rickman's crew.'

The savage smile on Cass's face confirmed his contempt of his superior, and Dwight's unwillingness to meet the sergeant's gaze confirmed that the balance of power, never much in Dwight's favour, was swinging even more towards Cass.

Reading from Cass's notes, Dwight continued, 'The victim — Mr, um—'

'Aldiss.' Cass drew out the sibilant.

'Aldiss, yes.' Dwight made a foolish attempt to disguise the fact that he was reading from Cass's notes. 'Michael Aldiss was on a job interview for a manager's post supervising a number of coffee bars across Liverpool and Lancs. He and Eames were on a tour of the outlets he would manage. He was just in the wrong place at the wrong time.' This last sentence was inflected as a question, and Rickman was dismayed that the only brief eye contact he made was with Cass, apparently seeking his confirmation — or worse, his approval.

'A young man with dreams and ambitions,' Superintendent Maynard reminded them. 'Practically a saint, in the eyes of the press. So, DI Dwight will be talking to the media after this briefing. He'll tell them that we will maintain a strong police presence in the city centre and in Toxteth, where most of the gang-related attacks have taken place.'

By 'them', Rickman took Maynard to mean the media, rather than the public. Rickman knew Toxteth well, and a heightened police presence, far from giving pause to the crooks and the dealers, was likely to arouse their indignation. Unless the situation was handled sensitively, it could increase the threat to the law-abiding in the community. But Maynard cared most about public opinion, as represented by the press and TV news. Foster's reassignment to the drugs case was concrete proof of that.

'You'll be wondering why I've called a joint briefing,' Maynard went on. 'An unexpected link has emerged between the arrests made on Monday during Operation Snowplough, and the murder of Mark Davis. DCI Rickman will explain.'

Rickman outlined their findings so far, then fixed his gaze on DS Cass. 'Intelligence passed on from the drugs team to my officers indicated that Mark Davis was not at the drugs raid. It now seems very likely that he *was* there during Operation Snowplough, and that he stole the missing money and drugs.'

There was a ripple of concern among Dwight's crew.

Good — their investigation so far had been a dog's breakfast — but Rickman's intention was to give them a timely boot up the backside, not to alienate them entirely. 'Water under the bridge.' He sought out three or four faces to focus on briefly as a token that he was including them all. 'But with this new information, you might want to rethink the events of the last few days.' He saw a few nods. 'If you have any information about Mark Davis, or his relationship with Maitland, now's the time to say.'

He turned his attention again to Cass — it troubled him that the sergeant had given Naomi bad information. It troubled him far more that Maitland had backed up Cass's evaluation of Mark Davis's place in the firm, when every indication on the street was that Mark had played a central role up until the night of the drugs raid. He did wonder if Cass had been protecting Davis as a source, but a check on the register of informants failed to bring up Davis's name. Cass stared blankly back at him.

'If you prefer to come to me or DI Dwight in private, that's okay. If you've taken an unorthodox approach, bent the rules a bit, it's best you tell us now, rather than us discovering it later.' He maintained eye contact with Cass for one more second, then nodded — to let Cass know that he had the measure of him, and to signal that the matter was far from closed.

Maynard opened the floor. 'Ideas, observations, suggestions?'

'Daft question, sir?'

Chris Tunstall. Rickman might have known that he would be the first to put his head above the parapet.

'Ask it,' Maynard said.

'I were just wondering, like — chucking a lad off a roof, it's a bit . . .' He struggled for the right word. 'Extreme.'

'Agreed,' Maynard said. 'And your question?'

Tunstall shrugged his huge shoulders. 'I was wondering — what did they want?'

'To see if he'd bounce?'

The comment was muttered, and Maynard evidently missed it, but Rickman narrowed it down to either a DC whose name he didn't know or DS Cass. Since the DC looked horrified to be under scrutiny, Rickman's money was on the sergeant.

Tunstall reddened and seemed flustered, and Hart intervened.

'They threw the victim off a roof, but they didn't touch Eames,' she said. 'Why? If this was a rival gang — let's say the Nealy brothers, for the sake of argument — why would they kill a bystander? From what we've just been told, Eames must be near the top of Maitland's management. You want to strike at the heart of the organisation, it'd make more sense to kill Eames, wouldn't it?' She looked straight ahead, but there was no doubt the heat in her reply was directed at Cass. 'But they murdered a kid who wasn't even on the payroll. Seems perverse, doesn't it?' The question was rhetorical.

Maynard nodded. 'Well, Chris, we could do with a few more "daft" questions like that one.' Tunstall had recovered his composure and was trying not to look smug. 'And you, Constable . . .'

'Naomi Hart, sir,' she answered, smartly.

'It's nice to know we've got people thinking instead of just reacting.'

'All the attacks so far have been at street level,' Dwight said, trying to regain some ground for his team. 'Maybe this was the first time they'd got so close to the management, bottled out at the last minute.'

'They dropped Michael Aldiss sixty feet to his death,' Rickman said. 'I'd need convincing they "bottled out".'

'Kyle Nealy's locked up, and he's got three of the four brain cells God gifted the Nealy boys. I just don't see little bruv Darren switching from baseball bats and machetes to *this*,' Cass said, evidently torn between chagrin at finding himself in agreement with Rickman and spiteful glee at wrong-footing Dwight once again. '*And* they got clean away.'

'You have a theory?' Maynard asked.

'Yes.' Cass glanced at his team leader, and Dwight flushed, leafing a little too eagerly through his notes in an effort to find this little nugget of information.

Cass looked away from him with a sardonic smile. 'New player, new tactics.'

'Uh-huh,' Dwight said, clearly wishing he'd said it himself. 'That's it. New player. Well done, Dan.' If he saw the sneer on Cass's face, he didn't acknowledge it.

Rickman was less impressed. This was the first positive contribution DS Cass had made to the briefing, and he viewed it with suspicion. 'Is Maitland's empire really so vulnerable?' He addressed his question to Cass's boss.

'Um,' Dwight said. 'I'm not sure I understand.'

'Challenges from *two* rival firms in a matter of days?' Rickman said. 'I got the feeling Maitland had tight control of his turf.'

Dwight looked to Cass for an answer, but his sergeant shrugged, making it clear he didn't care either way.

Dwight coughed, looking down at his notepad, then muttered, 'We'll look into it.'

'If we have another firm to worry about, I want to know. And soon,' Maynard said. 'This is a public safety issue — I want full cooperation between the two inquiries, and I want a clampdown on drug-related crime. These people need to know we will *not* tolerate a drugs war being waged on the streets of Liverpool.'

The briefing was concluded after allocation of tasks and responsibilities, and Rickman saw Cass lean over to Hart and say something. She stiffened, then stood slowly, speaking in a clear, deliberate tone.

'You know, you're like a little boy who torments the girls because he's desperate for them to notice him. And terrified he won't know how to act if they do.'

Anger flared in Cass's face. Then, unexpectedly, he smiled. 'Don't be like that, gorgeous.' Despite the smile, his flat grey eyes held no humour.

Foster stepped up, his face devoid of all emotion. Rickman had seen that look on Foster's face before, and it meant trouble. He nodded at something Dwight said, side-stepping him, already skirting the table.

Foster squared his shoulders.

'Lee.'

Foster didn't reply to Rickman, but he didn't launch into Cass, either.

'We need to talk about liaison,' Rickman said.

'Be right with you,' Foster said, still with his back to Rickman.

'Now.' Rickman put an edge into his voice.

'Better run along then,' Cass said.

Rickman could hear the venom in Cass's voice. But it was Cass who backed away — backed and turned and left the forum, creating extra noise in the corridor to make up for the loss of face in the stand-off with Foster.

As Hart walked past him, Rickman said, 'What was that about?'

'Nothing, sir,' she said, making a move to carry on.

'Naomi.'

Hart glanced at her watch. 'I should be at the mortuary, boss,' she said. 'Mrs Lindermann's identification of Jasmine — I'm already late . . .'

Rickman let her go, and finally, it was just him and Foster.

'Lee?'

Foster shrugged. 'Just Dank Ass looking for a slap.'

Rickman looked into his friend's face. 'Naomi can sort out an idiot like Cass,' he said.

Foster smiled. 'I know — she's been sorting *me* out for the past year, hasn't she?' He shook his head. 'I know I'm a pain in the arse, but the difference between me and Cass is I *like* women. And for what it's worth, Naomi shouldn't have to sort out knobheads like Cass.'

He's right, Rickman thought, watching his friend walk out of the room. Hart shouldn't have to put up with it or sort it out. Men like Cass sought power over women to bolster their fragile egos. They shouldn't be allowed that kind of power. He wondered how far a man like Cass would have to be pushed to go over the edge. To escalate from mere brutishness to the terrible excesses perpetrated by the monster who had murdered Jasmine Elliott.

CHAPTER 35

His early childhood was glorious. He was the sun, moon and stars of his mother's universe, the centre of her world and core of creation. His father demanded little of him, beyond good behaviour and pleasant manners in adult company. He'd conformed willingly, for his father was strong and tall — a sportsman — a man whom other men sought out for wise counsel. They would listen and nod their heads as if to say, 'Yes, that's how it is — we were sure you would know what to do.' As a boy, he'd wanted to grow up to be a man like his father.

His mother determined that he would not suffer the privations that had proscribed her young life: what the boy wanted, he was given. When he spoke over his mother's conversation, he wasn't 'demanding', he was 'lively'. Wayward behaviour was the outward sign of an uncon-ventional — a unique — personality. Spiteful and destructive acts were redefined as high spirits or experiments resulting from an inquisitive, exceptionally bright mind. His mother protected him from his father's disapproval and nurtured his individuality.

When once a close friend tentatively asked if his behaviour was quite normal, his mother had scoffed. 'Normal? What's normal? "Normal" is the boring lives we lead.' Normal was ordinary, and her son was beyond the limitations of the ordinary. He was extra-ordinary.

Since his mother's love was, in the absolute sense, unconditional and wholly uncritical, why should he care about public opinion? Certain

— not merely of his mother's love, but of her adoration — and freed from the restrictions of societal norms, he had learned to act without compunction or conscience.

The first major blow to his ego came with the installation of an infant into his home. He was seven years old and had returned from school with a special treat for his mother: a painting of him holding her hand, standing next to the house. His father was there, too, though some way off, and much taller than either he or his mother. It was a beautiful painting. Miss Dent said so — and she had given him a gold star.

It was cold, he remembered, but the house was super warm, so it felt like being wrapped up in a big fluffy blanket when he stepped through the door. A neighbour had walked him from school with her children because his mother had been unwell. His present to her had been carefully painted, dried in front of the classroom radiator and carried home unfolded to keep it nice, to cheer her up.

He'd run full pelt into the kitchen, shouting her name, clutching the picture. 'Look what I did for you!'

'Put it on the table, love. I'll look at it later,' she'd said. 'Come and say hello to your new baby brother.' Like his painting was unimportant — something that could wait. But more chilling was the way she looked at the infant on her lap — because it was the way she used to look at him. All her attention from that moment seemed absorbed by the wailing child.

It was never silent, never satisfied. It woke them up in the night to be fed, it stank, it screamed. In later life, rational and mature, he still resented the way it messed up the neat orderliness of his house, the pattern of his life, the status quo in which his mother's affections and his father's approval were his alone.

He had refused to look at the baby, refused to use its name. He'd sung loudly the carols they were learning for the nativity play at school, but his mother hushed him and shooed him away, afraid he would wake the baby.

The house, so warm on the day the baby arrived, was kept suffocatingly hot for the squalling brat. He flung open doors so that she would have to get up and close them again. He crashed in on the cooing circle when his aunts came to visit, climbing onto their knees and demanding hugs. He blew raspberries when they asked about his little brother and

265

pinched the infant when he was offered the chance to hold it. His mother bore it all, seeing how he suffered, but his father would eventually lose patience and send him out of the room.

Hurt and bewildered, he withdrew, becoming silent and sad. He regressed, wetting the bed and screaming himself awake from nightmares. He wanted his mother, but his father came instead. Where his mother would soothe and reassure, his father would 'deal with it', his nose wrinkled in disgust, pulling the boy's pyjama bottoms down unceremoniously, and rummaging through the dresser for a pair of underpants he could wear till morning. Then his father would drag the wet sheets off the mattress and replace them with fresh without even looking at his son.

The boy who had been a supernova in his parents' lives was now little more than a dark star — neutral, shrunk, dull. He wasn't allowed in his parents' bed because of the baby, so he would have to climb back into his own cold bed and stare at the light in the hall to keep the monsters at bay.

His depression didn't last long — he had been used to attention and he would not give it up so easily. Fists curled tightly around a red crayon, he crawled under the dining table and wrote his name again and again. But nobody saw it, so he searched through his father's tool box and found a sharp knife, one with a small hook at the end that was good for gouging the wood of his bedroom door, the banister, the table legs. They noticed him then.

It was a relief when the baby died. It seemed that justice had been done, the creature that had diminished him in his mother's eyes had been punished.

His mother was withdrawn and quiet for a long time, but eventually, with tentative, shamefaced looks, she began to pay him attention again, wanted to take him on her lap, like he was a baby. But he'd kicked against that — literally kicked — he wasn't going to act as replacement for his replacement. For a time, he rebuffed every advance, pushed away every affectionate caress, wiped her kisses from his cheek, refused the presents and special treats, angry beyond rage that she should think him so easily bought. Her attentions became more lavish and desperate, and when his father added his voice to the cajoling, he yielded, begrudgingly at first, somewhat persuaded that he once more fully occupied their hearts and souls and minds.

But from that time, he would constantly monitor his parents' emotions and their reactions. He'd learned to manipulate as well as demand. It became a habit that persisted into adulthood, sharply attentive to any possible slight, not always acting on them, but not forgetting either. And he never lost the compulsion to mark.

His school referred him to a psychologist who suggested that his artistic talent should be given an outlet, so he was taught to carve figures from wood, using tools with arcane names like skews and vee-tools, spoonbits and gouges. He would take his little disappointments out on the wood, paying back the humiliations of life, the hurt and the anger, finding release in cutting, chipping, scraping and gouging.

Later, he would bring the force of his displeasure to bear on the girls he hurt and scarred. The excoriation that he had felt, they would feel under his blade. He never forgot a single insult, and neither would they.

CHAPTER 36

A drugs dive in Tuebrook didn't seem to Foster like the kind of place they'd find the power behind the challenge to Maitland's regime. But apparently DI Dwight was keen to show the area superintendent that he could play the hard man as well as the community negotiator, so he'd ordered a few shakedowns as a show of force on the street. Foster was willing to concede they might get some useful information, and anyway, it kept his mind off the investigation into Ed and Hilary Shepherd.

At six p.m. they crashed through the front door of the target house. Eight officers piled into the house, yelling. Four upstairs, four below. In the sitting room, Foster counted five addicts, all too stoned to react.

One of the officers covered his mouth and nose with his hand. 'Jesus, the stink!' The vinegary smell of cooking heroin was overlaid with the reek of shit and vomit. The place buzzed with flies and hummed with the stench of unwashed bodies and something that smelled ominously like death.

The addicts in here didn't look capable of lifting their heads, let alone resisting arrest, so Foster left two men to watch them until the medics arrived to check them over. He took a female officer and a green-looking kid who looked too young to be in uniform through to the kitchen at the back of the house.

If anything, the mess in here was worse. The bin had overflowed long ago, and takeaway wrappers had been dumped next to it. The sink was crammed with mouldy crockery, the worktops had multiple burn marks and the doors of some of the cupboards had been ripped off.

'Take it easy in here,' he warned. 'The floor's slippery.' He didn't like to look too closely at the cause of the hazard.

Footsteps pounded overhead, officers shouted warnings and orders. Then a crash — a body going down hard. Foster checked the back door was secure then made his way back to the stairwell. Two officers were carrying a man down the stairs. Handcuffed and screaming, he put up a fierce struggle as they manhandled him out into the waiting van.

Glass smashed in one of the bedrooms, followed by a scream. Foster flicked open his Casco baton and took the stairs two at a time, the carpet tacky under his feet, the smell of shit stronger up here. He heard whimpering from the second room down the landing. The first door stood wide. He spread his hand and pushed the door as far as it would travel before stepping inside. A mattress, soiled bedding, surgical swabs and blood-spotted clothing. A door in the centre of the wall to the right was closed. He tried it, but it wouldn't budge.

He moved on to the next room, heart thudding, mouth dry. A man knelt on the floor, his hands clamped to a head wound, blood trickling between his fingers. Cass stood over him. A DC named Smith kept a little apart. His eyes darted to Foster as he entered. Foster thought he saw relief in them. He checked the area: window, second door in the wall to the left — *connecting door to the other room?* Stained mattress, a pillow with a greasy pillow slip, no bedding.

'Smithie, check that door,' Foster said. Then, looking again at the man on the floor. 'He needs medical attention.'

Cass didn't move. 'Well, *I'm* not touching him — he could have hepatitis — AIDS, even.'

'You did the damage.' When he was angry, Foster's accent came on stronger, so the *d*s were slurred.

'He did that himself,' protested Cass. 'With his own fat head.'

'Sarge.' It was Smith.

'What?' Both Foster and Cass answered. Smith sounded shaken. The connecting door stood open. Foster caught a glimpse of tiling, the edge of a bath. Smith looked over his shoulder, the rest of him very still, as though he was fearful of startling something or someone.

'You take care of your detainee,' Foster told Cass. He went into the bathroom. The toilet was slimed with filth, the bath stained brown. Cowering in the corner, a woman. Elderly, small, her hair wild, her eyes wide with terror.

Foster telescoped his Casco baton and slipped it into his belt, then crouched in front of the woman. 'It's all right, love,' he said. 'We're police.'

She looked first at Foster, then at Smith. 'Police?' she said.

'Detective Sergeant Foster and Detective Constable Smith,' Foster said. 'Lee and Smithie. What can I call you?'

'Betty,' she said. 'You've come for my John.'

'Who?'

She angled her body to peer timidly around Foster, into the bedroom beyond. 'My son.' She raised her hand, seeking out Foster's, and he winced at a circle of bruises around her wrist. He took her hand gently in his, covering it with his left.

'He used to be a good boy, Sergeant,' she said.

The 'boy' in the next room must have been forty years old, at least.

'Honest to God — he never give me a minute's worry when he was a lad.'

'This is your place?' Foster asked.

At first, she seemed confused by the question, then her brow cleared. 'It was.' Her voice quavered. 'It used to be. You won't believe it — not looking at it now — but I kept it nice.'

'Oh, I believe you, Betty,' Foster said. 'Look, you must be gasping for a cuppa. Why don't you go with Smithie, here, he'll see you get a hot meal and a nice brew.'

The woman looked like she hardly dared to hope for such kindness. 'Would you?' she said. 'I can't get into the kitchen no more, what with the mess and that.'

He helped her to her feet, and Smith took over, handling Betty with special care. She balked as he led her to the door, and Foster realised she was afraid of passing her own son in the next room. 'Here y'are, Betty.' He slipped the bolt on the door connecting to the first bedroom. 'Save your legs — come out this way.'

Smith gave him a troubled look on the way out. Foster watched her down the stairs, sick at the thought of a frail seventy-year-old trapped in a house full of addicts. He went back into the second bedroom, where Cass was still waiting for the man with the head wound — Betty's son — to get to his feet.

'Are you John?' Foster asked.

The man replied with a groan. 'Bastard's gashed me 'ead.'

Foster dragged the pillowcase from the rancid pillow and flung it at the man. 'You're under arrest — for false imprisonment and assault.'

'You wha'?' John looked up at him. His face was ravaged by drugs: acne scars, rosacea, broken veins, but his eyes held a dangerous intensity.

'Betty — your mum,' Foster said. 'I saw the bruises on her arms.'

John dabbed at the cut on his scalp with the pillowcase. 'Mothers,' he said, with a smile that was more like a snarl. 'Can't live with 'em, can't kill 'em neither.'

'You wanna show some respect,' Foster said, putting enough threat into his words to make the guy think again.

'She's confused,' John said. 'Sometimes I have to restrain her.'

'She's dehydrated and half-starved,' Foster said. 'We'll see how confused she is when she's had a decent meal inside her.'

He was on his way to the door, couldn't say what made him turn back — maybe a sound, maybe a deep-seated will to survive. Seeing only the blur of movement, he acted on instinct. Continuing the turn to his right, he blocked John's lunge with his forearm, throwing him off balance. Then he saw a knife: a Stanley blade, razor sharp.

John recovered and made a second attempt, slashing left to right in a wide arc. Foster leapt back, adrenaline racing through his blood. He cannoned off the door frame and his shoulder screamed.

John's eyes sparked cold flame as he saw his chance, lunged again, driving the blade upwards towards Foster's face.

Foster ducked and shoulder-charged, hearing a satisfying *oof* as his attacker went down. He allowed his momentum to carry him forward into a roll and was up and bouncing on the balls of his feet before John could properly get his bearings.

They'd changed positions: Foster was now in the centre of the room while John was by the door, whooping for breath. The impact had sent his diaphragm into spasm. He still had the knife.

Foster was aware of shouts downstairs, but he kept his mind and his senses focused on the knife.

John moved his free hand back and drew his feet under him.

If he gets upright—

Foster stepped in and booted him hard in the knee. John screamed and grabbed his injured leg, falling back again and dropping the blade. Foster kicked it away and the blade skittered to a halt at Cass's feet. Cass seemed to think this might be an appropriate moment to act and lifted one foot to trap the knife.

Two officers piled into the room and cuffed the addict, dragging him downstairs, while a third — the green-looking kid — hovered anxiously at the door.

Foster straight-armed Cass in the chest and he bounced off the wall. 'Where the fuck were you?' he demanded.

Cass managed a half-smile. 'All those kung fu moves — you looked like you had it under control.'

Foster brought his forearm across Cass's chest, jamming him against the wall, and he lost the smile. 'You failed to clear the area,' Foster said. He shoved hard to emphasise each point. 'Failed to evacuate a vulnerable person at the scene. Failed to search a suspect. Failed to restrain him when he turned violent.' He could have added *Failed to assist a fellow officer under threat* — but even in the heat of this exchange, it was a charge any police officer would be wary of making.

CHAPTER 37

The wind battered against Rickman's office window like a
Liverpool supporter barred from the cup final. He was catching up on paperwork, updating his Policy Book — a legally
required record of management decisions and choices. With
that complete, he picked up his mobile and made a call he'd
been putting off too long.

'David Farmer.' The voice was brusque, the accent
clipped, the agricultural significance of the family name having been consigned to history two centuries before, as the
descendants of the Cheshire Farmers discovered the more
lucrative practices of law and medicine.

'David? Jeff Rickman.'

'Jeff! Not still working, are you?' By the sound of it,
Farmer was not — Rickman heard the cheery background
chatter of a bar. Farmer's favourite venue for an early evening
snifter was, appropriately, Trials Hotel. Convenient to the
Crown Court and his offices, it also had the advantage of
being a good place to network, and David Farmer believed
in the power of good connections.

'Murder investigation,' Rickman said.

'Oh . . . you're on the Elliott case, aren't you?' Farmer
said. 'Terrible news about the baby.'

'Yeah.' Rickman was loath to discuss the case, even in general terms, with half the solicitors, barristers and opportunistic journalists in Liverpool within earshot of Farmer's booming voice. 'But that's not why I called. I need some legal advice — official and on the record.'

'That kind of advice is far beyond the reach of a chief inspector's salary, I fear,' Farmer said, with theatrical regret.

'I wouldn't be paying.'

'I don't do *pro bono* work.' He seemed amused by the very suggestion.

'My brother will pay.'

'Oh . . .'

Rickman heard a sudden drop in the noise level and guessed that Farmer had stepped outside. 'That would be your millionaire brother?'

Rickman smiled despite himself. 'I have no other.' Talking to Farmer, it was difficult not to slip into his elliptical way of talking.

'Not divorce, I hope?' he said, although his tone suggested that the possibility of a nice juicy millionaire's divorce might be *just* the thing he was hoping for.

'Some kind of power of attorney,' Rickman said. 'It would involve the Italian judiciary as well as British — Simon intends to stay here, but the business is based in Milan.'

'The Italian legal system is notoriously slow and complex.' To give him his due, Farmer managed to contain his glee.

'His wife wants an initial meeting in the next few days,' Rickman said. He heard the rustle of paper and could visualise Farmer licking his pencil in readiness.

'How about Tuesday afternoon?'

'Text me a time and I'll let you know.' Rickman hung up with mixed feelings — relief that he'd taken the first steps in giving Tanya back some control over her life, and sadness that the brother he'd so looked up to could no longer be trusted to manage his own affairs.

His next task was to read over his team's reports, check on tasks completed and find out if anything useful had come in during the day. He even put his head around the door of the drugs inquiry MIR. He'd heard about Foster's near miss. There was no sign of him.

He pressed the contact number for Foster on his mobile. 'You okay?' he asked.

'Bruised shoulder. Bruised ego.'

'The way I heard it,' Rickman said, 'You've nothing to blame yourself for.'

'Basic training,' Foster said. 'Never turn your back on a potential threat.'

'The addict or Cass?' Rickman asked.

Foster huffed a laugh.

'Fancy a pint?'

'Is the Pope Catholic? Wait up, though — isn't Tanya staying at yours?' He didn't wait for an answer. 'Better let her know this might be a long session.'

Rickman returned to his own office and rang home. 'Jeff!' The warmth of Tanya's greeting made him smile.

'Good day?' he asked.

'Mm. I think I've clinched a deal with one of the big department stores. Liverpool is definitely on board, and there's a good chance I'll get a nationwide franchise.'

'Wow. And I was thinking you might be at a loose end.'

'I felt the need to set up a few meetings, so that either way my visit wouldn't be a complete waste of time.'

'I have some news on that score,' Rickman said, pushing aside his regret that she would consider contact with Simon a waste of time. He related the details of the Tuesday meeting. 'Farmer is good — he'll see that Simon's interests are protected, but he'll play fair.'

Tanya was silent for a moment.

'Is Tuesday difficult?' Rickman asked.

'Tuesday's fine.'

He sensed a hesitation. 'But?'

'I was—' Tanya broke off. 'I wondered if—' She stopped again with an impatient sigh. 'I don't know what's the matter with me,' she said. 'It's too much to ask. You have this investigation, and—'

'Tanya,' he interrupted. 'If I can help, I will.'

She took a breath and finished at a rush. 'Could you be there? I mean, if you're free?'

'I kind of assumed I would be,' Rickman said, embarrassed by his own presumption, and Tanya laughed a little shakily.

'You don't know how much of a relief that is. It's just, I can't rely on Simon to show up. And if he does show up, that he'll be reasonable.'

'He'll be there,' Rickman said. 'I'll make sure of it. Reasonable is harder to manage.'

She laughed again, and it seemed to him that she was glad of the opportunity to talk to somebody about it. The boys were having a hard enough time. He knew that Tanya was doing her best to put a brave face on things, and that her business colleagues would be the last people she would want to confide in.

'He doesn't mean to make things tough for you,' Rickman said. He remembered his brother telling him how hard it was to be constantly reminded of what he had lost.

'I know,' she said. 'Of course, I do know that. I know he can't help it. But when I look at him, I see *Simon* — my husband, the boys' father. He looks the same and talks the same, has the same voice and mannerisms, but—' She broke off and tried again. 'You have a history with him, Jeff. A life before the accident. He remembers that. But we no longer share any common experience.'

Even for Rickman, the change in his brother was striking, despite the fact that Simon retained an almost perfect memory of their childhood together. Apart from the obvious changes wrought by twenty-five years absence, Rickman had detected other, more subtle differences in his brother: poor attention, a childish egocentricity that prevented him noticing or caring for the needs and feelings of others. The sharp intelligence Rickman had idolised in their boyhood was now largely absent. Simon seemed like the husk of a moon in daylight — pale, transparent, insubstantial.

'Come home soon,' Tanya urged.

Home. Rickman felt an unexpected pang of loss — a recognition of how much he'd missed having someone to go home to — something to go home for. He checked his watch. 'I have to catch up with Lee Foster — should be back in a couple of hours.'

His phone rang almost as he hung up. It was the front desk. 'You're a hard man to track down, Chief Inspector.'

Rickman recognised the voice. 'Moving target, Bill, you know me. I thought you were house-training new intake in Netherley.'

'The damp air down in Belle Vale must've seeped into my bones. Doc prescribed the rarefied air of Edge Hill.'

Bill Williams, or Double Bill, as he was generally known, had been in the force for thirty-five years. He had opted to continue in the job rather than draw his pension, despite arthritis in his left hip and a bad back from years of pounding the beat. He had been Rickman's duty sergeant for three years when Rickman was new and impressionable. Double Bill had taught him the difference between good policing and achieving performance targets, and Rickman still regarded him with affection and respect.

'I've got a caller.' Bill lowered his voice. 'Says he wants protection.'

'Protection from who?'

'He says he's got information about the drugs war, knows why that young lad got murdered.'

'It's not my case, Bill,' Rickman said, with regret. 'Why don't you put him through to Larry Dwight?'

'He'll only talk to you — says he can trust you.'

* * *

Rickman and Foster drove through the Wallasey tunnel and onto the motorway. The wind blasting across the dark expanse of Bidston Moss slammed Rickman's Audi sideways a few times, and he gave the road his full attention until they reached a more sheltered stretch of motorway.

'When you offered me a pint, I was thinking of somewhere local,' Foster said.

Rickman related the details of the phone call. 'Our informant insisted on an out-of-town pub for the rendezvous. I think he's genuine, Lee.'

Foster nodded slowly. 'And was this before or after you suggested a quick bevvy?'

Rickman smiled. 'After. Definitely after.'

'Well, I'm flattered. But what if he turns around and walks out, soon as he sees me?'

Rickman took the off-ramp at junction three and headed for Heswall. 'This drugs inquiry is enough of a shambles without me adding to it,' he said. 'I want you as a witness. If he doesn't like that, I'll arrest him for obstruction.'

Foster grinned. 'Now you're talking.'

Ten minutes later, they were turning left at a roundabout and into the car park of the Glegg Arms. On the A540, at the outermost edge of Heswall, the former inn had been serving travellers for nearly two hundred years. The main entrance opened onto a long, low bar which was part of the original building. The interior walls were painted lemon-yellow and decked out with modern art. Leather sofas, pine tables and waxed wood flooring completed the café-meets-farmhouse feel of the place.

They stopped at the bar for a half-pint of Boddington's, and Rickman sussed out the crowd while they waited. A steady influx of families made their way through to the restaurant on the far side of the bar. It was six thirty — too early for the young crowd, and the main business clientele snatching a swift half on their way home had either been and gone or had settled in for the full session. As yet, the bar was fairly empty.

The slot machines had been relegated to a dark recess at the far end of the bar. One machine was occupied by a man of around forty-five. He was about as wide as he was tall, and he wore a fine grey suit with a black cashmere sweater. Despite the 'no smoking' signs placed in prominent positions throughout the bar, an unlit cigarette was clamped between the index and median fingers of his right fist.

He prodded and poked the buttons on the machine like he was picking a fight with it, all the time glaring furiously at the columns of flashing lights. He'd clocked Rickman and Foster as soon as they'd come in, though, Rickman had no doubt. He caught another swift, evaluative glance as they drew closer. The man played his final spin of the electronic tumblers. They chuckled and burped, then fell silent.

The man gave the machine a sneaky kick, then seemed to flinch. He lifted one shoulder as they drew level with him. 'Kind of luck I'm having right now, you could bottle it up, make a fortune selling it as bad karma.' He grunted. ''Cept I wouldn't wish my luck on me worst enemy.' His accent marked him out as a Liverpool terrier among the Cheshire cats.

'You know who we are?' Rickman asked, wanting to avoid using his ID.

'Rickman.' He jabbed a finger at the DCI. 'I recognise you off the telly.'

'I get that a lot,' Rickman said, deadpan.

'He's famous,' Foster confided, then leaned a little closer and lowered his voice. 'You're not his first real-life stalker, by any chance?'

'Who's the class clown?' the man said without looking at Foster.

'Detective Sergeant Lee Foster,' Rickman said. 'I assume you'd prefer he didn't show you his ID.'

The man showed his teeth in a snarl. 'Proper Laurel and Hardy, aren't yiz?' He took a hit from his cigarette, though it remained unlit, clamping his hand to his face. Then, embarrassed at what he'd done, he held the offending article between thumb and forefinger and squinted at it angrily.

'Can we get on with it?' Rickman said.

Without a word, the man turned and led the way through a door onto a covered smokers' area, lighting up before they had sat down. The glow of a wall-mounted electric heater heightened his already florid complexion. It was dark and intensely cold, and Rickman doubted if anyone else would be foolhardy enough to brave the freezing October air, but the man kept a wary eye on the door.

'What've you got?' Rickman asked.

'First off, I don't want none of Dwight's lot in on this.'

Rickman and Foster exchanged a glance. 'What d'you know about Dwight?' Rickman asked.

'Only that he's boss of the drugs inquiry.'

'And why should we keep him in the dark?'

The man looked at Rickman as if he was a few cards short of the full deck. 'It's a drugs inquiry, isn't it? If they know I'm talking to you, they might think the information's worth selling.'

'But you don't think *we* would?' Rickman couldn't help being amused by the combination of world-weary cynicism and naivety.

The man looked from Foster to Rickman. 'Let's just say I checked youse two out.' That explained his easy capitulation when faced with Foster as Rickman's backup and witness.

Foster jerked his head at the man. 'He's a case, isn't he?'

The man held up his hands, the cigarette still in his right paw. 'This is my *life* we're talking about, Mr Rickman. I been in this business long enough to know some men can be bought and sold like a used car.'

Rickman sucked his teeth. He suspected that this was meant as some kind of compliment — a valediction on his and Foster's incorruptibility. 'You know our names,' he said. 'Why don't you tell us yours?'

'We've got to get a few things straight, first.' He took a pack of Benson & Hedges from his jacket pocket and tipped a cigarette out, lighting it from the stub of the last one. He pocketed the cigarettes, bringing out a small metal box and crushing the fag end into it, flipped the lid closed and slipped it back into his pocket, in what seemed a practised routine.

'I want protection,' he said. 'A new ID, relocation — in Europe.'

'How about a nice chateau in the Rhone valley?' Foster said. 'Nah — you look more like the Costa del Crime type to me. Flash villa with swimming pool and views over Torremolinos would be more your style.'

Rickman silenced Foster with a look. 'Whatever you're selling, it'd have to be good,' he said.

The man took a drag on his cigarette. 'I know why that lad was murdered.'

'What lad?'

'Don't piss me about,' the man warned.

Rickman stared him down.

'Michael Aldiss,' the man said. 'The lad that got chucked off the car park roof — clear enough for you?'

'I'm listening.'

The man took a drag on his cigarette and Rickman could see it cost him in pain. He blew the smoke towards the ceiling, his eyes unfocused, contemplative. 'I want a guarantee, first.'

'There are no guarantees,' Rickman said. 'But if the information's worth it, I'll do what I can.'

The man took another pull on his cigarette, clamping his hand over his mouth as if he was afraid he'd say too much. He exhaled, breathing smoke from his nostrils, and Rickman saw the slight flinch again.

'You wanna look at Rob Maitland,' the man said.

'Why's that?'

'He's after Bernie Carter, isn't he?'

'You're the one with the information.'

The man sighed. 'He is — he's after Carter.'

'So, what did he do to piss the boss off?' Foster asked.

The man shook his head, perplexed, but Rickman noticed he avoided looking at either of them. 'It doesn't make no sense. I mean, Mr Maitland going after Carter — it's like cutting off his own right hand.'

'He must be an important man, this Bernie Carter,' Rickman said.

Foster spoke. 'He's Maitland's accountant.'

'I'm guessing Carter must do more for Maitland than just fix the accounts,' Rickman said.

The man snorted. 'You've got that right. Money, payroll, random checks on packaging and distribution. Bernie does the lot.'

'"Distribution",' Rickman repeated. 'You make it sound like a regular business.'

The man finished his cigarette and went through the routine again of lighting another before cramming the stub into the metal box he kept in his pocket. 'You need a good stock control and reordering system, the size of the operation Maitland runs.'

Foster smiled.

'Listen, mate.' The man leaned across the table, keeping his voice low, but evidently feeling the need to set Foster straight. 'Maitland sells more pharmaceuticals than GlaxoSmithKline.'

Rickman watched him with increasing curiosity. 'And where do you fit in?'

The man took his eyes off Foster grudgingly, took a swig of beer before going on. 'Five years ago, I was running a couple of caffs in the city centre. The business was struggling,' he said. 'Starbucks and Costas opening everywhere — every bookshop bigger than a shoe box was cramming a coffee bar in at the back. There was so many Neros, you'd think the Romans had invaded.'

Rickman felt a spark of recognition. *Coffee bars? Could this be—*

'Let me guess.' Foster cut across his thoughts. 'Maitland turned up with a sack full of cash like a fairy godfather.'

'Not Maitland — Carter. It was his first business enterprise. He offered me cash up front in exchange for a share of the profits.'

'And all his tainted drugs money came out cleaner than me granny's whites on a hot wash,' Foster said.

'Them shops earn a legal profit of one point five mill per annum — net.' The man sounded offended, even hurt, by the slur.

'Legal profits aren't legal if they're paid for with dirty money,' Rickman said. 'You do know that?'

The man looked past him, his eyes narrowing with resentment. 'Makes no odds — Bernie Carter made Maitland a multi-millionaire.'

Rickman took a cold, sharp swallow of beer. 'You'd think Maitland would be grateful.'

'You would.'

'Got any theories on that?'

'Not my job, mate.'

Rickman focused on a trickle of sweat meandering down the man's broad forehead, while he thought through what he had just heard. As an accountant, Carter would work with money in the abstract — statements, expense claims and receipts. But money laundering would require real money siphoned through phoney accounts and businesses — Carter must have handled eyewatering sums.

'Why have you come forward?' he asked.

'I'm attached to me fingers and toes.' The man looked at Rickman, making up his mind about how far he should go. 'Look, I'm just middle management. I'm not into the drugs side of things.'

Now Rickman was certain: the business references, the coffee bars, the thin veneer of machismo — even the flinch of pain every now and then.

The man drew deeply on his cigarette. It flared like a warning light, and as he took his hand away from his face, his fingers trembled.

'How's the rib?' Rickman asked.

The man frowned, but his hand went instinctively to his chest, just under one sagging breast. 'Feels like I got kicked by a donkey,' he said.

Rickman nodded. 'You're Thomas Eames . . .'

'Tommy the Tank,' Foster murmured.

Eames bristled, but didn't comment — Rickman guessed that the hard-man reputation stemmed from the men Eames kept around him. On his own, he looked like any other fat man sweating over a pint. And he looked badly frightened.

'What has Michael Aldiss's death got to do with this Bernie Carter?' Rickman asked.

'Them bastards held that lad over a sixty-foot drop. Kept asking me "Where's Carter?"'

'Why come to you — are you friends?'

'We work together a lot,' Eames said. 'With the coffee bars and that. I see a lot of him. My girls play with his two.'

Rickman noticed he'd fought shy of calling Carter a friend. 'So, where is Carter now?'

'Don't you think I would've told them if I'd known?' The horror on Eames's face said he probably would — if only to save his own skin. 'He's gone. Took his wife, the girls, locked up the house and vanished.'

'You're sure the men who killed Aldiss were sent by Maitland?'

'Had to be.'

More evasion. 'You didn't recognise them? If not, it could have been anyone — a rival firm.'

'No. I got on the blower to my lads — called for backup. They never came.' Eames's eyes reddened at the memory and his breathing became ragged. Reminded of his injury, the man hugged his ribcage with his free hand, frowning against the pain.

'Maybe your lads saw the police arrive, decided to keep a low profile,' Rickman persisted.

Eames opened the metal box and stubbed his cigarette out angrily. 'They never come to help me because Rob Maitland stopped them,' he said.

Rickman held his gaze. 'I'm not convinced.'

Eames paused to light another cigarette and sat thinking a while.

Rickman stood. Eames looked up, startled. 'Where are you going?'

'This has been nice, Tommy,' Rickman said. 'But I've got work to do, and this isn't even my investigation.' He started walking, Foster close behind, and Eames half rose, then fell back into his chair with a grunt of pain.

'All right,' he croaked.

Rickman turned back.

'I was hoping I wouldn't have to tell yiz — he's not a bad lad, really — and he never done nothing to me before yesterday.'

'We'll put a testimonial in your statement if you like,' Foster said, sarcasm vying with impatience. 'How's about you get on with it?'

'There was one face I recognised,' Eames said, sulkily. 'Graham.'

'Graham who?' Rickman asked.

'I dunno, do I? Graham — just . . . Graham. He's been with Maitland forever.'

'Did Graham give the order to heave Michael Aldiss off the roof?' Rickman asked.

Eames seemed torn, but after a few moments gave a tentative nod.

'You need to say it, Tommy.'

'Graham give the order — is that clear enough for you?'

'It'll do,' Rickman said. He took his seat again. 'But you must have some idea why Maitland is after Carter.'

Eames gave a helpless shrug. 'I'm not that close.' This time, he made an effort to maintain eye contact. His attempt at wide-eyed innocence failed to convince. 'You don't get that close to either of them.'

'When did Carter disappear?'

'Yesterday — we had a breakfast meeting scheduled. He didn't show.'

'It's all about the power meetings and the glamour in the drugs world, isn't it?' Foster said.

'I told you — never had nothing to do with the drugs,' Eames insisted.

Rickman smiled. 'Like I said, you don't have to handle the stuff to be guilty. Money laundering carries a penalty of fourteen years — and that's just for starters — I'll bet you're an accessory to at least half a dozen other arrestable offences.'

The skin of Eames's face turned as grey as the ash at the tip of his cigarette. The sheen of sweat and the weight he was carrying gave Rickman a moment's anxiety for the state of his heart. Then Eames took another drag on his cigarette, and he felt reassured.

'I swear to God, man — I didn't know what he was up to, not at first,' Eames said.

'And when you did?' Rickman asked.

Eames scratched the back of his neck, putting a strain on the seams of his jacket.

Foster snorted. 'He was too busy counting his pennies to let a little thing like his conscience trouble him.'

Eames sighed like a man deeply misunderstood. 'Have we got a deal or what?'

'Depends what you can give us on the money laundering,' Rickman said.

Eames sucked his cigarette down to the filter, then flicked it into the dregs of his beer. 'That depends on what you can give me in compensation.'

For a moment they locked gazes, neither giving ground.

'If Maitland knew I was talking to you,' Eames said, 'he'd cut my balls off and make me eat them with fried onions. So whatever *you* come up with better be good.' He stood, hitching his trousers. 'I've got two days. After that, Maitland will come after *me*, instead of Carter. My wife and kids are already gone — somewhere Maitland won't think to look. I'll be out of here by Sat'day night, just to make sure he doesn't shorten the deadline. 'Cos a deadline in Mr Maitland's diary means *exactly* what it says.' Ever the businessman, he dipped in his pocket and slid a card across the table to Rickman. 'You can reach me on my mobile. Don't leave it too late — you might miss your chance.'

Rickman watched him disappear through the door into the bar.

'Tommy the Tank . . .' Foster murmured. 'Think he's genuine?'

'Genuinely scared.' Rickman picked up Eames's card. It was printed on thick black board, a stylised coffee cup over his name in debossed gold print. 'Do I trust him? About as much as I trust DS Cass.'

'Talking of sleazy, lying arseholes, I talked to our friend and colleague about Carter,' Foster said. 'He agrees with Eames — Maitland wouldn't be top turd in his own dung heap if it wasn't for old Bernie the Books.'

'So whatever Carter did to upset the boss, it must've been big,' Rickman said.

'Think he's had his fingers in the till?'

'He's a bent accountant. I'd think it strange if he hadn't. My guess is Eames is mixed up in the whole thing.'

'So, why would Maitland murder a bystander? Why not grab Eames and torture Carter's address out of him?'

Rickman tapped the side of his glass with a fingernail. 'Did you see the look on Eames's face? Like he said, if he'd known it, he'd have given it up. He doesn't know where Carter is, but Maitland must think he can find out.'

'Killing the lad, though . . .'

'I think Maitland used Michael Aldiss to send a message out to the rest of his crew — no second chances, no mercy.'

Foster's jaw tightened. 'So,' he said, 'what's the plan?'

'I'll talk to Dwight.'

Foster was incredulous. 'You're not gonna give him the stuff Eames just told us?'

'We're supposed to be working in full cooperation,' Rickman said.

'I don't wanna get in the way of a group hug or nothing,' Foster said, 'but if Eames gets wind of it, he'll vanish like the froth on one of his cappuccinos.'

'To paraphrase Ed Shepherd, there are others to protect. If someone else gets caught in the line of fire — if another

Michael Aldiss dies because I'm playing political games — it'll be my responsibility.' Rickman got in the next bit before Foster could say it for him: 'I know — if I lose Eames, I could have a lot more deaths on my hands.'

Foster took another sip of beer. 'Catch-22.'

'Who was it said, "Knowledge is power"?'

'Bacon,' Foster said promptly. Rickman couldn't hide his surprise. 'Well, don't look so shocked — I was educated by Jesuits, you know.'

That was Foster for you: a man of many parts. Rickman suppressed a smile. 'Well, you're my man on the inside. I want to know everything you know about Carter, Maitland and Operation Snowplough.'

'Get another bevvie in,' Foster said. 'This could take a while.'

CHAPTER 38

The storm howled and shrieked outside the glass tower, rain sheeting horizontally against the windows. The wind and the angle of the glass sluiced the water sideways, sending frothy spume from the structure like salt spray from the prow of a ship.

Rob Maitland watched it play like a silent movie, the clean-swept streets of the business district below scoured by brine sucked from the city's port by a force-ten storm. A steel hoarding at the edge of some roadworks flapped and shuddered like card, teetered first on one edge of its splayed feet, then the other, building momentum, the oscillations growing larger and larger, like a child on a swing. Suddenly, the barrier fell, crashing onto a car parked next to it. The bonnet crumpled and the windscreen bowed and finally shattered, throwing beaded glass fifteen metres down the road. *Exhilarating*, Maitland thought.

Reflected in the glass, he saw his hired meeters and greeters, clipboards clasped to their chests, hovering by the lift door. A new party had arrived, bringing with it a burst of excited chatter and cold air.

Maitland had quickly realised that the fifty-yard stare unnerved the arty types — they found his stillness intriguing, but they needed the reassurance of an occasional smile. Maitland was prepared to oblige: this was power of a different stamp, and he had always been adaptable. But after an hour and a half, the smiling began to feel like a facial tic. He needed time out, and the storm proved a restful interlude.

He had grown used to creating pockets of repose amid the paranoia and frequent violence of running a major drugs operation, so the clamour of this little gathering posed no problem. It was necessary merely to build a bubble of silence and seal himself within it. He was a still, calm presence amid the frenzy of networking around him.

This 'opportunity' he had set up himself — and before his unfortunate arrest after the Dutch deal went tits up. He'd been tempted to cancel, but his PR consultant, little Billy Peters, had told him to hold his nerve. Press, TV and radio were all represented — in fact, the hike in his notoriety had brought a flurry of last-minute acceptances of his invitation. The chance to observe the suspect on his own turf was too tempting for ambitious local journos and seasoned national press to resist. So, here they all were: social commentators snouting for an inside view, TV producers and directors looking for their big documentary hit, press after the man behind the story.

'Let 'em come,' his agent had said. 'We'll rope them in with a tale of a reformed criminal and turn it into a rags-to-riches story — local lad made good.' Billy Peters was in the business of reinvention. He had carved new life stories for his clients like a Hollywood plastic surgeon sculpted new faces and bodies. It was phoney, all of it, but as long as it looked good, and lasted long enough to fulfil their five-year plan to be famous and filthy rich, who cared?

Maitland's mobile buzzed in his pocket and he answered it with a curt, 'Yeah?'

'Boss? It's me — Eames.'

'Tommy.' The Tank sounded nervous, which was good. 'Got anything for me?'

'A phone number — no address.'

'What good is that to me?'

'I swear to God, boss — it was all I could do to get that.'

'Where d'you get it?'

'Meg Carter.' He heard Eames swallow, as if he wished he could take the name back.

'Maybe I should pay Meg a visit, see if I can get any more out of her,' Maitland said.

'She doesn't know nothing else, boss. You know what Bernie's like — passwords on everything. He only gave her the landline number for life-or-death emergencies.'

Maitland laughed softly, enjoying the irony.

'It's an Ormskirk number,' Eames offered. 'I checked.'

'So you googled the area code. Am I supposed to be impressed, Tommy-lad?' Maitland kept his voice low, but the threat in it was unmistakable.

'Swear to God, boss. I done everything I could.' There was a pause, which Maitland chose not to interrupt. 'Are — are we all square now?' Maitland counted five slow beats of his heart. 'Boss?'

'What do you think, Tommy?' As the Tank started stuttering a response, Maitland broke the connection. He brought up a number in his contacts, connecting with Graham. 'Write this down.' He recited the phone number. 'I want an address.'

Task completed, he turned again with a sigh to face the crowd. He caught a few staring at him. They looked quickly away, and he glanced across at his agent, giving him a sardonic smile. Peters — *"Call me Billy"* — raised his hand and circled his index finger a few times. *Work, work, work,* Maitland thought. He scanned the room for someone he hadn't yet spoken to. The constant new arrivals made the job seem endless.

Maitland snagged a canapé from a passing tray and gave the server a wink. 'No rest for the wicked.' He tossed a minia-ture pizza into his mouth. She smiled, surprised and flattered to have been noticed amid the clamour of people, all eager to be seen.

'Tell me about it,' she said. She was cute — skinny, but well-stacked — and she met his eye with no hint of shyness. The creamy-white perfection of her skin made him want to touch her naked shoulders just to see if they were cool under his fingertips. She tilted the tray towards him. 'Another?'

He selected a pastry. 'Let me guess,' he said. 'Student.'

Her eyebrows twitched. 'Who else would work these hours for these rates?'

He grinned, and for the first time that evening it felt genuine. From the corner of his eye, he saw Billy Peters bearing down on him with another new friend. 'Uh-oh.'

She made a quarter turn, balancing the tray lightly on her hand. 'What?'

'My agent.' The little man at Billy Peters's side wore a brown suit and matching shoes with lifts. He was almost perfectly round. 'And it looks like he's bringing a Malteser in cheap brogues to talk to me.'

She took a moment, following his line of sight, still looking over one shoulder. Her neck had a delicious curve that made him want to lick the length of it, from collarbone to jawbone.

'That's Peter Petronelli,' she said. 'Big TV producer.' She widened her eyes at him. 'I mean *huge*.'

He crinkled his brow in question.

'I'm doing Media Studies,' she said, with the merest hint of a smile.

'Stick around,' he said. 'I'll introduce you.'

She looked tempted, but only for a fraction of a second. 'Another time,' she said. 'Tonight, Mr Maitland, they only have eyes for you.' She clocked his surprise and added, with a smile, 'I do my homework.'

Well, what do you know? Lovely tits, perfect skin — and a brain. He tried to catch her elbow, but she danced away, shimmying through the crowd with the ease and grace of a salsa dancer.

His agent made the introductions and the producer launched into his spiel, making his pitch. It was Billy's job to manage that side of things — the hustle and bustle, the hints and rumours, a dropped name, a significant look. Maitland nodded, tuning him out, while looking over his head to the girl. She gave him a quizzical smile and Maitland fluttered his hand over his heart. She laughed and turned away.

'Rob Maitland?'

Maitland executed a half-turn, the professional smile already in place. This guy was different from the rest: he was taller than most of his guests, for a start, and instead of an awestruck silence or effusive greeting, he appraised Maitland coolly, his eyes dark and unreadable. Maitland could sense aggression like a bad smell. This guy had the physical power for it, but his stance was relaxed, he hadn't come looking for a ruck.

Maitland fell by default into distrust mode. 'Who's asking?'

'Detective Chief Inspector Rickman.' He flashed his warrant card. 'This is Detective Sergeant Foster.'

Foster. 'We've met.'

By the look of him, Foster was holding a grudge about their previous exchange. Maitland filed that snippet away for future use.

Maitland offered Rickman his hand, knowing the photographers were busy, click-whirring — and wouldn't this one make a great front-page splash?

Rickman looked at his hand like he couldn't quite work out what it was for. 'You weren't entirely honest with DS Foster about your relationship with Mark Davis, Mr Maitland,' he said.

'I don't know what you mean, Chief Inspector.'

'Mark was working for you right up to the night of the raid on your dockside warehouse,' Rickman said.

Smart, Maitland thought. *Nothing prejudicial in that — just a plain statement of fact.*

'We also know that he was on the run, and that he was terrified.'

Maitland feigned surprise. 'Of me?' But the pretence was too outrageous, and he laughed. 'I'm messing with you.

A business my size, you have to command respect from the employees.'

'You're confusing respect and fear,' Rickman said.

Around them, conversations had begun to falter.

'Gimme a break, fellas,' he said, spreading his hands, thinking what a good picture it would make, irritated that none of the photographers were quick enough to take the shot.

'The sooner you answer our questions, the sooner we go away,' Rickman said.

Maitland huffed a laugh. Cops like Rickman never really went away. 'Like you said, Mr Rickman — fear and respect get mixed up, sometimes. Why else would Mark latch on to Sergeant Foster here?'

'What's that supposed to mean?' Foster demanded.

Maitland smiled. A front-page shot of Foster throwing a punch at him would be even better than a handshake with the DCI.

'Leave it,' Rickman said, and the sergeant stood down.

Maitland continued smirking at Foster. 'Impressive,' he said. 'Does he go fetch an' all?'

Foster spoke, back in control of himself, refusing to take the bait. 'You're getting careless,' he said, and Maitland felt a thud of apprehension, swiftly quashed. This was just cops playing their games.

'Another of your employees has gone missing.'

They know Carter's missing. How? . . . Tommy Eames. What else had the Tank told them?

Maitland opted for bewilderment. 'I'm sorry,' he said. 'I don't know what you're on about.'

'I think you do,' Rickman said.

Maitland was used to physically powerful men. He set them loose like dogs onto bad payers and wide boys taking the piss. His hirelings showed nothing behind the eyes. Rickman, however, was confident enough to allow a hint of his pain to seep from him like light from under a door, and Maitland found that unsettling.

'Bernie Carter,' Rickman said. 'Your accountant.'

'Why are you looking for him?'

Rickman ignored the question. 'Where is he?' he asked.

'He's been working flat out on an audit for me,' Maitland said. 'Finished it last night. He probably decided to take off for a few days, unwind a bit.'

'Without his wife and children?'

Maitland gave him a comical look. 'You're obviously not married, Chief Inspector.' He got a bit of audience response on that one.

'Where,' Rickman repeated, 'is he?'

'Fishing expedition?' Maitland offered. *Like yourself, Mr Rickman. Very much like yourself.*

'Fishing expedition or fishing bait?' Foster asked. The press vultures circling missed it, but Maitland did not.

He smiled. 'Colourful image, Sergeant, but you've got me wrong. These days, I'm a businessman and patron of the arts.'

'Buying a few dodgy paintings at a student exhibition doesn't make you a Renaissance man,' Foster said. 'You're still a no-mark drug peddler from the arse end of Toxteth.'

Maitland felt a shimmer of anger, then it was gone. 'See the men in suits?' he said. 'They could buy and sell you and half of Liverpool without having to even check their overdraft limit. They know about my past, and you know what? They're falling *over* themselves for the chance to talk to me.'

'You know what I see?' Foster's gaze skimmed the assembly like he was looking for someone to arrest. 'I see sharks circling. You're way out of your depth with this crowd, Maitland.'

'Bernie Carter,' Rickman said.

'What about him?'

'You're not concerned by his disappearance?'

Not anymore, Maitland thought. *Not now I've got his landline number and I'm hours away from having his address and postcode.*

Rickman was waiting for an answer.

In his own good time, Maitland said, 'What've I got to be concerned about?'

'The manager of your coffee chain attacked in broad daylight — an innocent bystander murdered,' Rickman said. 'More than enough cause for concern.'

A hush fell over the gathering. The guests who previously had been more than happy to elbow their way into conversation with Maitland now hovered at a discreet distance, listening. Most of them would not have linked Aldiss's murder with him. Until now.

'You mean the tragic murder of that young boy?' he said, trying to score a point with the media hacks. 'I'm told the police are investigating.'

'Oh, we are.' Rickman's voice was a low growl, but enough people heard it and understood the implication.

There were two or three potential investors in the room. Investors who might be willing to fork out enough to make up for the deficit caused by the dropouts after the drugs arrests. And now Rickman was as good as telling them he was under investigation for the murder of Michael Aldiss.

Maitland saw one of the journalists recording the exchange on his mobile. He visualised ramming the damn thing up the little weasel's arse and felt a little better.

'And now your accountant is missing,' Rickman said.

'I told you, he probably took a break.' Maitland was furious to be forced to speculate in this way. It made him look like an amateur.

'Call him,' Rickman said.

'What?'

'Call him. Tell him the police are concerned for his safety. That he needs to check in — let us know he's all right.' He took a mobile phone from his pocket. 'You can use my phone if you like.'

Maitland stared at the phone in Rickman's hand. 'His number's on my mobile. I left it in my private apartments.'

'I saw you using it earlier, Mr Maitland.' This from the weasel who was recording him. 'It's in your breast pocket.'

'It's only a quick call, Mr Maitland,' somebody else said, and that was followed by a rumble of assent from the rest.

The mood was turning against him. That was the thing with the press: they liked a good party. They'd eat your food and guzzle your champagne like they were chugging down pints of craft ale. They'd even suck up to you — but give them the slightest whiff of a good story and they'd tear you apart to get to the heart of it. This fucker Rickman was turning his party into a feeding frenzy.

'His mobile is switched off,' Maitland said. 'I tried him earlier.' He forced a smile. It didn't feel quite right on his face. 'When Bernie needs a break he just heads for his boat and launches out on the Norfolk Broads. Could be anywhere.'

'That's a shame,' Rickman said. 'Because a call would've put our minds at rest. Ah well, we'll just have to keep looking.'

'It puts *my* mind at rest to know that you take public safety so seriously.' Maitland comforted himself with the thought that he was well ahead of the game. Rickman had no clue where Carter was holed up and could only speculate as to why Maitland wanted him. When he'd finished with old Bernie the Books, he would just have to make sure he disappeared for good.

He tried another smile. This time, it felt more natural. 'Let me walk you out.'

While they waited for the lift, Maitland could feel the eyes of fifty people on his back. 'You'll be hearing from my lawyer,' he said, so that the eavesdroppers couldn't hear. 'Making me look like a thug.'

Foster smirked. 'If the shit sticks . . .'

Easy, Rob. Maitland gritted his teeth. With all the cameras and media types in the room he needed to stay calm. 'If I lose potential investors because of this,' he said, 'I'll sue the police authority.'

'You've been lucky, so far,' Foster said. 'You've dodged assets seizure on your illegal earnings by getting Carter to give them the old oxy-wash treatment.'

'Got any proof to back up that slander, Foster?' Maitland asked.

He saw the first flash of anger in Rickman's eyes, but you wouldn't have known it from his tone. 'He's right — I bet there isn't a single account, property or business in his own name. But your accountant is missing . . .'

Maitland stared at Rickman thinking, *I'll pop Tommy Eames's eyeballs with my own two thumbs when I catch the fat fucker.*

'What's the bet Carter has the cheque books, title deeds, account details, passbooks and passwords — official and unofficial?' Rickman wondered aloud.

There was enough truth in what he'd said to sour the champagne in Maitland's gut. Maitland had accounts in a dozen different names, as well as access to businesses nominally owned by a score more who would pay him eighty percent of their profits. The only other living person who had access to all of it was Bernie Carter.

'You're street-smart, Maitland.' Rickman leaned in. 'But Carter — he's *clever.*'

We'll see, Maitland thought. *We'll see who's clever when Carter is naked and bleeding on the floor, begging me for mercy or death, and unable to tell the difference.*

'You finished?' He was trying not to grind his molars, but the muscle in his jaw was at a jangle, sending out a Morse code of distress, and he thought Rickman was the sort of man who might pick up on it.

'Not by a long way,' Rickman said.

The sexy student waitress stopped to offer him a fresh glass of fizz as the lift appeared. The outrage in her eyes was a gratifying distraction. He forced his muscles to relax, tried to stay cool, even gave her a smile as he reached for a glass.

'Mr Maitland won't be wanting another,' Rickman said, steering her away with the effortless assurance of a man used to being obeyed. 'He's going down.'

Funny, Maitland thought. *Very funny.* For now, he'd let Rickman have the last word. But there wouldn't always be witnesses around, and one way or another, he would make Rickman regret gatecrashing his party.

CHAPTER 39

Larry Dwight was talking on the phone when Rickman knocked at his office door. It was eight thirty p.m., and Dwight wasn't known for putting in long office hours. He eyed Rickman nervously as he continued speaking, and Rickman took a seat in the chair opposite. Dwight's hair was as neatly cropped, his skin as smoothly shaved as before, but his eyes looked shadowed from lack of sleep, and his office looked less polished, more cluttered with paper than the last time. Rickman guessed that Michael Aldiss's death had impinged on the DI's ordered life in ways he could not have anticipated.

From the tone of the conversation, it sounded like he was trying to reassure one of the local interest groups about the police presence in their area.

Dwight seemed to take Rickman's patient silence as a veiled threat. He cut short his call, staring at Rickman with a mixture of resentment and distrust.

'What's this all about?' he demanded, the bluster, as ever, less than convincing.

'Rob Maitland,' Rickman said.

'What about him?'

'That's what I'd like to know.' Rickman watched him closely but saw nothing more sinister than confusion in his face.

Dwight smiled. 'I'm afraid you're going to have to give me some clue.'

'How closely are you watching him?'

'We're tailing him.'

'Twenty-four-seven?' Rickman knew that lack of funding and personnel could mean that suspects were only under surveillance at key moments during the day.

'Twenty-four-seven,' Dwight confirmed. 'And we have a phone tap on him.'

'So you'd know that DS Foster and I spoke to him at his apartment, half an hour ago.'

'*What?*' Dwight half rose out of his seat. 'What the hell for?'

Rickman maintained his comfortable position in his chair. 'I take it, then, that you haven't been informed. You're here, you're available and yet . . .' He left the rest unsaid.

Dwight subsided as he fully understood what Rickman was saying. 'DS Cass is dealing with that side of things.' He winced, realising that he'd just underlined the fundamental weakness of his leadership.

Rickman waited a few seconds to add his own emphasis. 'Maitland has a contract out on his accountant, Bernie Carter.'

Dwight stared at him. 'Why wasn't I—' He stopped himself just in time to avoid another admission of administrative failure and began again with a more guarded question. 'How do you know that?'

'Later,' Rickman said. 'The question you *should* be asking is why I got to know before you did.'

He watched Dwight struggle with that one.

'Trust,' Rickman said. 'Or lack of it. The informant doesn't trust your squad.'

Dwight tried for nonchalance. 'Is that surprising? We've pissed off a lot of lowlifes.'

'Now, why didn't I think of that?' Rickman said. 'It's because you're just too damned effective. But wait — didn't you fail to arrest Maitland at the drugs drop? Please,' he said, forestalling Dwight's protestations, 'don't tell me he wasn't there, because we both know that Maitland wouldn't trust a deal on that scale to menials.

'You have an escalating drugs war. Now, *you* say you came come down hard on that, yet the beatings and machete attacks have actually *in*creased. And now an innocent bystander has been murdered. Got to hand it to you, Larry — you're really cramping their style.'

Faced with the facts, Dwight couldn't brazen it out. 'I'll take Carter into protective custody,' he said meekly. 'Find out what this is about.'

'Too late,' Rickman said.

'What?'

'Seems you let another one slip by you,' Rickman said. 'Carter's disappeared.'

Dwight's eyes widened. Another failure of intelligence within his team. The man was a pompous prick, but Rickman couldn't help feeling sorry for him. 'You *didn't know*? Why didn't you have him under surveillance?'

'Jesus, I didn't think . . .' Dwight ran his hands over his face. 'He's just an accountant.'

'Not according to the informant.' Rickman remembered an earlier conversation with Foster. 'In fact, it's not what your own *team* is saying. DS Cass told Lee Foster that Carter is responsible for building Maitland's legitimate business interests.'

Dwight stared at his hands. 'I didn't know,' he said. 'How could I?'

'You need to stay in touch with your own investigation. For God's sake, Larry — DC Hart practically handed it to you on a plate when she said that Michael Aldiss's murder struck at the heart of Maitland's management.'

Dwight retreated into pomposity. 'Of course, with the benefit of twenty-twenty hindsight—'

'What "hindsight"?' Rickman interrupted. 'Hart was just floating ideas based on the rather sketchy information you put forward at the joint briefing.'

Dwight ran one hand through the tight mass of curls at the side of his head, finishing with his hand clamped to the back of his neck. 'But I didn't *know* he was such a central figure.'

'You damn well should have,' Rickman said. 'Cass is keeping crucial intelligence from you.'

'No.' Dwight's eyes darted right and left, as though trying to replay events in his head. 'That's preposterous!'

'Is it? Did you know that DS Cass interviewed Carter the day after Operation Snowplough went down?' This was another nugget of information Foster had provided over their pint at the Glegg Arms.

'I—' Dwight glanced at the pile of unread reports in his in-tray.

'Don't bother,' Rickman said, 'it's not there. He didn't even log it.'

'It's been hectic,' Dwight said. 'He probably forgot.'

'He lied about Maitland's relationship with Mark Davis.'

'No . . .'

'He said Mark was no more than a gofer — and we both know that's not true.'

Dwight licked his lips like a kicked dog. 'I'm sure he—'

'A lie that was later backed up by Maitland himself.'

'Coincidence,' Dwight said.

'And I believe Cass is working unregistered informants.'

Dwight stared at him, open-mouthed. 'How the hell d'you work that one out?'

'Canteen gossip. And a consultation with the joint investigations liaison officer — you should try it.'

'*Foster*,' Dwight said his name like it left a bitter taste in his mouth. 'Well, he's *way* off the mark. Snowplough was a major inter-agency operation — Dutch and British Customs, two police forces — big bucks. They wouldn't act on the say-so of an unregistered informant.'

'I take it you don't know who the informant is.'

He looked defensive. 'It was strictly need-to-know.'

'Your detective sergeant knows. You should know.'

Dwight rallied. 'Look — is this about Cass's lapse of concentration at the smack house this afternoon? Because I've already spoken to him.'

'That "lapse in concentration" nearly got an officer killed,' Rickman said.

'I'm sorry for that. But this whole scenario with Davis seems a bit — well, far-fetched.' He gave a little laugh. 'I mean, this is Liverpool, not Las Vegas.'

'You really are out of the loop, aren't you?' Rickman kept his tone even, despite his rising anger. 'Cass just feeds you any old line and you trot along behind him, bleating it like you thought of it yourself.'

Dwight flushed angrily, and Rickman wondered if he knew his team called him Larry the Lamb.

'I follow the evidence,' Dwight said, raising his voice. 'Mark Davis was a hopeless junkie — isn't it more likely he just killed his tart and topped himself?'

'Mark Davis didn't "top himself", he was murdered,' Rickman said. 'His "tart" — and trust me on this, the gutter talk does *not* sit well with you — was a young woman who, against all odds, had cleaned up, delivered her baby free from drugs, and was making a home and a new life for the two of them. She was raped and tortured. The torturer cut her, beat her and stabbed her before he finally ended her life. Her name was Jasmine Elliott.'

Dwight's gaze slid away from him. In the seconds that followed, the only sound Rickman could hear was the rush of blood in his ears. Dwight stared at a point midway between himself and Rickman but seemed unable to raise his eyes to Rickman's face, and it was a moment or two longer before Rickman realised that he had begun to speak.

'I didn't mean any disrespect,' he said. 'It's just — I'm working under pressure here.'

The whine in the man's voice sickened Rickman. 'Find Carter,' he said. 'He's the key.' He stood, ready to leave. 'It's your investigation. But I'd get permission for phone taps as well as direct surveillance of Carter's wife. And you should ping his phone — it might just give you his location, if he hasn't switched it off or ditched it.'

'Of course,' Dwight said. 'I was going to—'

Rickman turned away, not in the mood to pander to the man's bruised ego.

'Jeff.'

When Rickman turned back, Dwight was fiddling with the paraphernalia on his desk as though rearranging them would untangle the mess he had got himself into.

Here it comes, Rickman thought.

'How *do* you know that Maitland has a contract out on Carter?'

'Let's just call it a reliable source.'

A look of petulant frustration passed over Dwight's face. 'What happened to working together?' he demanded. 'Sharing intelligence?'

'Sort out the problems on your team — then we'll share,' Rickman said.

Dwight's face darkened. Rickman could see he wasn't about to let this go. 'You're asking me to go to my team with nothing but hearsay.'

Rickman stood over him. 'You have my word. And until you can prove to me that you've brought Cass to heel, that's *all* you get.'

Dwight switched from bombast to wheedling. 'Have a heart, Jeff — I'm trying to be counsellor, politician and police officer here.'

'Maybe you're trying to achieve too much,' Rickman said, relenting a little.

'Meaning?'

'You should spend less time smoothing ruffled feathers in the community and more time managing your team.'

Dwight leaned on his desk and levered himself out of his chair. 'The Crime and Disorder Act requires full consultation with interested groups in the community. We ignore that at our peril.'

Rickman looked at Dwight's broad, stubby fingers splayed on the desk. 'I know the requirements of the act, Larry,' he said. 'But you can't run an investigation like this one if you're constantly looking over your shoulder.'

'What the hell do you mean by that?'

Rickman suspected that most of the heat in Dwight's reply was because he knew exactly what it meant, but he spelled it out anyway. 'You're neglecting the practicalities of leading your team.'

Dwight took a breath, ready to launch an attack.

Rickman raised a finger to stop him. 'Sort it, or I will.'

CHAPTER 40

'Home is the place where, when you have to go there, they have to take you in.' Though Foster's mentor, Father Matthew, had tried hard to persuade him to read the great man's works, Foster had never got around to it, and this was the only quote from Robert Frost that had ever stayed with him.

Home for Foster was Black Wood. But he couldn't go there, not anymore. Foster had a one-bedroom flat in a divided Victorian property. It echoed for lack of the small touches that would have transformed cave into comfortable retreat. He called it his 'place' and occasionally — in self-parody — 'the love shack'. But he never really thought of it as home.

Impatient with himself, he scrolled down the contacts list on his mobile, each one with a photograph next to the number. He called a few, but at eight thirty on a Friday night, everyone was out or just leaving, and he wasn't in the party mood. He caught Sally from Calls and Response as she was on her way out the door.

'Hiya, Lee!'

Promising start — at least she seemed pleased to hear from him.

'Look, hon,' she said. 'I'm just getting in the taxi — late as usual.'

'Where you off to?' he asked.

'Pacific Road.' She said it loud enough for the taxi driver, and he heard the rattle of the hackney cab as it pulled away.

'Pacific Road?' Foster thought he knew every street in Liverpool, just about.

'The arts centre over the water.' No Scouser ever said 'across the Mersey'. When you crossed the strip of water from Liverpool to Birkenhead, you always said you were going 'over the water'.

'What takes you to foreign lands, girl?' Foster asked.

'Tony Kofi. Man can he blow that horn.'

'What is it with you and saxophones?'

'Come with me, I'll give you a demo after the show.' She gave a throaty laugh, dirty and raunchy — an invitation — sex without complications.

He recalled the hangover he'd had after their previous date and felt slightly queasy. 'I had something more like a quiet drink and a chat in mind.'

'A chat?' she said. 'What about?'

'I dunno — the weather, footie.'

'Ar 'ey, Lee,' she said. 'I been talking all day on the phone. I wanna chill out and fill my head with something more than words.' Proper little philosopher, was Sally.

'Enjoy your coffee,' he said.

'*Kofi*,' she corrected, giggling.

'That's what I said. I'll see you tomorrow.'

She hesitated. 'You all right, Lee?'

I'm bruised and sore, and my faith in human nature has taken a battering. 'I'm fine. Have a blast.'

He ended the call and slid the phone into his pocket.

'Get real, Foster,' he said to the empty flat. The only two people he could ever talk to about this kind of stuff were Jeff Rickman and Naomi Hart. Jeff had enough on his plate without Foster piling it with seconds, and Hart — well, Hart wasn't likely to be a sympathetic ear, just now.

So, he went to the kitchen, took down the cheap whisky and filled a tumbler a third full. Placing the bottle back, he caught sight of the faded silver biscuit tin that held all his childhood treasures. He never wondered why he kept the two together — the whisky and the memory box — would never have admitted that perhaps the one gave him permission to indulge in the nostalgia of the other. It just seemed to him that they belonged together. He took a sip of the whisky and opened the lid, breathing in the smells of his childhood. Bubble gum and loose tobacco, and the sad smell of old paper.

Foster had seen enough government climb-downs and strategic planning turnarounds in his years as a Royal Marine to think he had seen every kind of betrayal. He didn't take them personally — political board games were about money and power bases, not people. As an NCO in the Royal Marines he'd had more brushes with death than a road sweeper on the M6, but he had trusted the men under his command with his life, and they had honoured him in turn with their trust.

His mother's betrayals were another matter. She had attempted suicide five times during his childhood, each new attempt resulting in a new care order, and another trip to Black Wood. On every occasion, Ed and Hilary Shepherd had welcomed him like he was coming home. Like they were real family. He was looking at a picture now, taken from his small cache: him with Ed and Hil, looking like proud parents.

Ed had once said, 'Forgive your mother, Lee. It isn't that she doesn't want to live with you — she just doesn't know how to live with herself.'

Now he knew that his mother had had less to be ashamed of than either Ed or Hilary. Theirs was the worst betrayal of all. They had betrayed him and every child they'd ever had in their care.

He buried the photograph at the bottom of the box and his fingers brushed against an envelope his mother had given him when she knew she was dying. 'Don't open it till after I'm gone,' she'd said. It was still unopened, over half a decade after her death. He hadn't yet found it in him to forgive her. He shoved the envelope into the tin and snapped the lid closed, then took an angry swallow of whisky, relishing the punishing burn of it at the back of his throat.

He hadn't done too good on the betrayal front himself. In the year since he'd met her, he'd wound Hart up and pissed her off. She'd laughed at him and teased him, even yelled at him, on occasion. But she'd always respected him as a cop. Seeing her like this — cold and disdainful — tore him up. *Jeff's right,* he thought, for the hundredth time. *I should apologise.*

It took a few more whiskies and a couple more hours to pluck up the courage. Even then, he didn't admit to himself that he was really going to go through with it. Instead, he told himself he was going for a walk to clear his head, and just happened to fetch up on her doorstep at half past midnight and in the middle of a rainstorm. The light was on in her living room, and he took this as encouragement.

The intercom was equipped with a camera, and he looked up, to be sure she knew it was him. The lift up to the fourth floor was a touch too fast, given his delicate state, and he nearly lost the whisky that was warming his belly and messing with his head. She met him at the door of her flat, wearing a silk dressing gown that hung to the knee. He felt giddy just looking at her.

She held out her hand and drew him into the sitting room. 'Jesus, Sarge — you're wet through!'

He was wearing a waterproof jacket, but his hair was dripping wet and his jeans clung to him, chilling him to the bone. He had dim recollections of being jostled by the wind, of forging his way through the storm with his head bowed. At the lower end of Duke Street, something had whipped past his head — a slate, perhaps, or a loose ridge tile from one of the older buildings, but he had barely noticed.

'Are you okay?' she asked, and he realised he had been staring at her stupidly, trying to piece together the last hour.

'Fine,' he said. 'I'm fine.'

'I came looking for you at the station,' she said.

'Didn't feel much like sharing a bit of banter with the lads back at base.' *God*, he thought, *that's a hell of a lot of 'b's.* 'Sorry about that,' he said.

'It's okay, I can take a bit of alliteration.'

'I've had a few drinks,' he confided.

'I guessed.' His spirits lifted a little — if she could take the piss, she mustn't be quiet so mad at him as she was before.

'I was worried.' She touched his arm and he felt a tingle of electricity.

'I didn't come for sympathy,' he said. 'I came to apologise.'

'It was me that messed up, Sarge.'

This take on events didn't compute, and again he stared at her while he tried to make sense of it.

'I'll make coffee,' she said. 'You need a hot drink inside you.'

It wasn't what he'd expected, and he couldn't think how to respond, so he followed her through a door directly off the living room, into the kitchen. A couple of plates were stacked on the drainer, an empty wine bottle stood next to them. Hart liked filter coffee — she had even brought a coffee machine into the station on one case they'd worked together.

She ditched the dregs from the machine and started fresh. 'You should've rung me,' she said. 'We could've gone out for a drink.'

'That's me all over, Naomi — getting things arse-about.' He managed a smile and felt more of an idiot when, instead of returning the smile, she gazed at him, her blue eyes filled with concern.

He took a breath. 'I was wrong about Maitland.'

'Sarge — this isn't necessary.' He had tried and failed, in the months they had worked together, to persuade her to call him by his given name. He suspected she used it as one more weapon in her arsenal, to keep him at arm's length. 'Why don't you dry off in the bathroom — it's the door directly opposite,' she said. 'I'll bring the coffee through.'

The bathroom was neat and uncluttered, though she had dressed it with odd homely touches — candles on the edge of the bath, bubble bath and make-up ranged on a shelf next to the sink. Foster took a look in the mirror and winced. His hair was flattened and dripping and his eyes were bloodshot. He splashed his face with cold water, then towelled his hair dry and returned to the sitting room.

The lighting was subdued, and through the huge plate-glass window he could just make out the hulking shape of the Anglican cathedral, lit up by spotlights and blurred by the wind-lashed rain. Hart still had a hi-def TV, though he thought she'd upgraded to 4K. A Blu-ray disc case lay next to the player. *The Negotiator*. Naomi did like her action flicks. Maybe she was looking for a few tips — he hadn't exactly been easy to get on with the last couple of days.

He didn't think she would appreciate him sitting on her pristine leather sofa soaking wet, so he sank down onto one of the floor cushions, and felt a sharp stab in his buttock. He reached under the cushion, swearing softly to himself, and came out with a set of keys and a wallet. He thought again about the two plates in the kitchen, the empty wine bottle, pieced them together to imagine a romantic evening rudely interrupted. 'Oh, crap . . .'

He should go — of course he should. But drink and bad judgement and, if he was honest, a touch of jealousy made him curious. Naomi didn't date cops and didn't like anyone to know who she was dating. He stole a guilty look at the kitchen door and flipped open the wallet.

The driver's licence was visible through a clear window. Philip Ormerod. Bad picture. A badge clip hung out of the notes section and he gave it a tug. It was a hackney cab licence. Ormerod looked better in this photograph and Foster felt another sting of jealousy.

He heard the clink of crockery near the kitchen door and hastily replaced the wallet and keys where he'd found them. When Naomi came into the sitting room, carrying a tray, he was already on his way out.

'Sarge?' she said.

'I've got to . . .' He couldn't think of a single thing he might be in a hurry to do — except get the hell out of there.

She put the tray down and caught up with him at the flat door. 'Come on,' she said. 'Have your coffee.'

He looked at her, wondering if he should apologise again, decided it couldn't hurt, and steadied himself, monitoring his speech for slurring. 'Naomi—'

'Sarge.'

'I've been a dickhead.' That was it. That was all he wanted to say. He looked into her face, thinking, *If she laughs at me, it'll kill me.* But she didn't. She just nodded, and he turned away.

'I'll see you in the morning, then,' she called after him.

He raised a hand in acknowledgement and headed for the stairwell, feeling that a rapid descent in the lift might finish him off entirely.

'Lee?' she called.

His thought processes were slowed by the drowning effect of half a bottle of whisky on his brain cells, so he didn't get it at first. 'What?'

'I was a dickhead, too.'

His reaction time was shot — he registered the last part of what she'd said first. *Did I just hear Naomi Hart say 'dickhead'?* Then another, more shocking realisation hit him. *Did she call me Lee?* He turned so fast that the alcohol almost spun him off his feet. But she had already closed the door.

CHAPTER 41

In her nightmares, Kim Lindermann heard the whisper of the blade through her flesh. Felt the fearsome burn of it. Sometimes he'd used a knife, but more often he'd favoured a disposable scalpel. Disposable for the sake of hygiene, retractable because 'accidents can happen,' he'd told her once.

When he found a girl whose skin was firm and white and resilient, a girl who healed quickly and was compliant, he would come back again and again, working on her until he was satisfied — slicing and carving and scraping as a sculptor might worry at a piece of wood. Kim had been his favourite, and she'd spent many hours with him in that long summer before her overdose.

The cuts were superficial — he didn't slice deep — but the pain was fierce, and sometimes the thin, hot slashes became infected. He wouldn't touch her then — said he only wanted clean girls. His passion was to mar perfection, to take a smooth, clear patch of skin and mark it for himself. His concentration was intense, and although the pain was now a distant nightmare, she could never forget the way he'd watched her as he cut. That was more terrible even than the searing burn of sharp steel.

He'd worn gloves, always, when he cut, and he never smiled — for him, this was serious work. He'd cut with surgical precision, paying close attention, measuring by eye the length and depth of each parallel slash, each curve, each point of pain, glancing from the wound to her face, weighing the fear and pain in her eyes against the bloody lines in her flesh. At the end of a good session he would sit back, dabbing his brow with the sleeve of his shirt, and she would see a glimpse of satisfaction in his face — that he had done his job well, extracted the maximum torment. Then his eyes would glaze, he would take a shuddering breath and exhale, long and slow. Kim, more than any of them, had recognised it as an addiction as powerful as her own to heroin.

Kim gasped, opening her eyes to the dark. A shadow seemed to pass over her, and she felt a tremor like the warning rumble of tectonic shift in the moments before an earthquake. The earth felt unsteady beneath her feet since she had seen Jasmine's tortured flesh. She crept to the rain-battered windows and lifted a corner of the heavy drapes. The orange glow of the street lamps seemed to flicker wildly as the trees bent and twisted in the storm. Her heart beat fast against her ribcage, but nothing human moved in the street below.

She heard the click of a switch and the room was flooded with light. Her husband was by her, his broad hands on her shoulders, warming them.

'It's only the storm,' he said. 'Come back to bed.'

She allowed him to coax her back, his arm around her, and let him pull the duvet over them both.

'I should have gone with you to the mortuary,' he said.

'No,' she said. 'Jasmine would hate to be seen like that, so exposed — it was bad enough the policewoman being there.'

He leaned on one elbow and stroked her arm with his free hand, gazing with a slight frown at the faded lines that her three-year-old son, in his innocence, sometimes mistook for pen marks. Suddenly ashamed, she slipped her arms under the covers, drawing the duvet up around her neck.

'It's upset you,' he said. 'I understand that. But you don't have to hide the scars — not from me.'

'I know.' She cupped his face in her hands and the duvet slipped so that the lines were visible again. 'I know that, Lars.'

He turned his face to kiss the palm of her hand. 'It's okay,' he said, but he looked anxious and a little frightened. 'I'm here. What happened to Jasmine will never happen to you. I'll make sure of it.'

Lars Lindermann was a powerful man — in business, he could be relentless, and he was physically courageous and strong. But in this, he was naive. She broke down and wept for both his willingness and his inability to protect her, and, dismayed, he reached for her and held her close. 'You have to tell me what's wrong,' he said.

She wiped her eyes and leaned against his chest, content, for a time, to feel the warmth of his skin against her cheek and to listen to the strong, steady thump of his heart.

'How can I help you if you won't tell me?'

She sighed, knowing that she would have to tell him, dreading what must come after. 'The man who did this to me — the man who gave me these scars—'

'You think he's found you?' His heart beat a little faster.

'No,' she said. 'Not that. Worse than that.'

He waited.

'Jasmine.' She gulped back the tears. 'I think he killed Jasmine.'

She heard his heart slow, as it sometimes did when he was under extreme pressure. 'What are you going to do?' he asked.

This was why she loved him — had always loved him: Lars didn't tell her what to do, what her responsibilities were. He asked her. She would decide.

* * *

The house lights were on when Rickman arrived home. He made a dash from the car to the house, using his briefcase as an umbrella. The sound of the key in the lock brought Tanya into the hallway.

'Tanya . . .' he said. 'I'm sorry, something came up.' He dropped his briefcase to the floor and tossed his keys into the bowl on the dresser.

'It's fine,' she said. 'It's just, with the storm . . . I was concerned.' She shook her head, impatient with herself. 'Silly of me.'

'I suppose I'm not used to having someone else around.' He shrugged off his raincoat and shook some of the water from it. 'I really am sorry.'

She gave him a rueful smile. 'Perhaps I'm becoming entrenched in the role of anxious mother — without the boys' timekeeping to worry about, I have to find a substitute.' She turned to the kitchen. 'Come and eat.'

An hour later, they had eaten and were sitting companionably side by side on the sofa in the sitting room, sharing the last two glasses of a bottle of Merlot. The fire crackled, and Rickman was mellower than he deserved to feel, under the circumstances.

'Did you talk to Simon about the Tuesday meeting?' he asked.

Tanya nodded. 'I wish it could be different. I wish — I wish he would come back to Milan with me. The boys would help him, he could relearn the language, the business.'

Rickman remembered a conversation he'd had with his brother.

Sometimes I think it's a good thing my memory's shot, Simon had said. *'Cos I don't remember how easy it all used to be.*

Simon had stared earnestly into his brother's face, willing him to understand. *I can't learn stuff anymore, Jeff. Not hard stuff — not stuff like she wants me to learn.* 'She' meaning Tanya. 'Stuff' meaning the language that had once been his second tongue, the business he had built from scratch, the legal documents and the accounts and all the other intellectual demands that he could no longer cope with.

'He doesn't want us, Jeff,' Tanya said.

Rickman heard his brother's words echoing hers. *I don't want them near me, Jeff.* Simon's eyes had darted right to left in rapid, tiny nystagmic movements — a sure sign of distress. *They keep telling me who I used to be — I can't be that man anymore.*

Tears had started to his brother's eyes and Rickman understood: Simon could function at the lower cognitive level his injury had forced on him — could even achieve a measure of contentment — but to be constantly reminded that he was so much less than he used to be tormented him. In trying to bring Simon back into the circle of his family, Tanya, Jeff junior and Fergus had only made him feel more alienated from them.

Rickman sighed. 'Did he agree to the meeting?'

'He told me to do whatever I want. But he *has* to be there, Jeff — it becomes so much more difficult if we have to do this *in absentia*.'

Rickman heard the pressure building in her voice again. 'He'll *be* there,' he said. 'I'll see to it.'

Her brown eyes were almost black in the subdued light. 'I'm sorry. I shouldn't be burdening you with this when you already have so much to deal with.'

'A young graduate was murdered this afternoon,' Rickman said, half to himself. 'Another team is investigating a drugs operation — it's probably linked with that. But the drugs boss knew Mark Davis, maybe he even knew Jasmine before she straightened herself out. I don't know, Tanya — these kids, do they stand any kind of chance at all? They're ignored or kicked around until the Rob Maitlands of this world find them, then—' He broke off, realising that he had said too much.

Tanya reached across and squeezed his arm. 'It's all right,' she said. 'You can tell me.'

'It's not enough.' He felt hot. Feverish, almost. 'Whatever I do, it isn't enough. I can't help thinking if I'd been smarter or faster or luckier . . . If we'd had more personnel—'

'Don't,' she said.

'Don't what?'

'Don't punish yourself.'

Her brown eyes brimmed with concern, and suddenly the frustrations of the last few days, the lack of sleep, the flashes he kept getting of Jasmine, tortured and violated, were too much for him.

'What the hell kind of world is it where even an innocent isn't entitled to expect compassion?' he demanded. 'Mark's killer left an eight-week-old baby to die in that filthy cellar.'

'The TV news said you'd arrested the people who ran the children's home.'

'Not for the murders,' Rickman said, his stomach tightening as he thought again of the Shepherds' implacable refusal to talk.

She leaned across and kissed him, and he was comforted. She held him to her and the warmth of her, the clean, fresh scent of her, made him giddy with desire. He kissed her eyes, her cheeks, her lips. Breathing hard, heart pounding, Rickman caressed her arms, her breasts, her body, felt her respond, felt the urgency of her response, felt more alive than he had in an entire year.

'This is wrong,' he murmured.

'I know.' She kissed his neck. 'But he doesn't want us, Jeff.' *Hadn't Simon said it himself?* He kissed her again.

'Wait.' She eased gently out of his embrace.

'Where are you going?' Drunk with desire, Rickman felt confused and abandoned by her sudden rejection. Until this moment, he hadn't known how much he had yearned for a woman's touch — *this* woman's touch.

She closed the door and turned the key in the lock. 'Force of habit,' she said, a smile dancing in her eyes. She returned to the centre of the room and the play of firelight on her skin made it shimmer as though burnished. She was shivering, despite the heat. He went to her and lifted one trembling hand and touched her cheek with his fingertips. The fire sparked in her eyes and glowed in the golden highlights of her hair.

'It's all right,' she said. 'It'll be fine.'

And it was.

CHAPTER 42

Saturday

The streets were deserted at six a.m. There were fewer early-morning commuters at the weekend, and the Saturday shoppers were still in bed. Rickman saw a bus idling in a lay-by while the driver snoozed, the occasional taxi driver hoping to scoop up a fare into the city centre, and little else.

The storm had stripped most of the autumn leaves from the trees, heaping them in mounds against the sandstone walls around his home. They lay as a soggy mulch, clogging the drains and banking up in the gutters at the roadside. He headed down Greenbank Road to avoid the inevitable floods around Sefton Park. Even the small lake in Greenbank Park had spilled over, inundating the lawns, and ducks bobbed in shallow water, reflecting an ice-blue sky.

Rickman experienced a confused mixture of elation and guilt at what had passed between him and Tanya the night before. It had been a mistake — their situation was messed up enough without adding the complication of an affair. Rickman felt sick with himself, but perversely, he felt a shiver of excitement recalling the softness of Tanya's skin against his own and the contentment he had felt lying in her arms.

And what about Simon? His brother claimed not to care about Tanya and the boys, but selfishly he was curious about his past and saw them as the gateway to it. They gave him a sense of history, of rootedness, even if it seemed like a story told about somebody else, and he listened, fascinated, if with mild scepticism, about his business, the years spent in Italy, his commissions from pop stars and actors, the magazine articles featuring him and his designs. But Simon had also told his brother about his sense of isolation, of the alienation he felt from his family, with regret. If Rickman tried harder, persevered longer, could Simon come to love Tanya again?

And how did Tanya feel? He went back over the last hour, as they had showered and breakfasted, trying to recall each look, each gesture, and reinterpret it. She'd seemed awkward — but so had he. Was she ashamed of what she'd done? Had they only made love to stave off despair? Rickman probed his feelings once more. He was apprehensive at seeing Tanya again that night, but beneath that and the guilt was a thrill at the thought of seeing her, of holding her in his arms, the warmth of her, the feel of her hair against his skin, the spicy scent of her, the salt taste of her on his tongue — and the simple joy of seeing her smile when she saw him.

A tree branch in the road diverted his attention. He steered around it and made a left turn. Smithdown Road formed the backbone of Wavertree, connecting the poor working-class redbrick terraces at its westernmost point, to the comfortable middle-class villas on the outskirts of the city. At this hour, the shops, pubs and restaurants along its length were closed and shuttered. Litter, roof slates and the odd 'For Sale' sign lay scattered across the pavement and roadway, adding to the desolation of the place.

The road was a steady climb, and as the altitude increased, wealth decreased. Restaurants were replaced by small grocery stores and off-licences whose goods were protected behind reinforced glass and slipped to customers like contraband through serving hatches. Many of the shops that

321

had once teemed along both sides of the street had disappeared altogether, their display windows bricked up, replaced by narrow openings above head height, where unnamed businesses plied their dubious trade.

The Major Incident Room was empty when Rickman arrived. The joint investigation would run on a skeleton crew over the weekend. He went to his office and ran a few checks, then returned to the MIR and sifted through the previous night's phone messages from the hotline. After that, he needed caffeine. He checked out the whiteboard while he waited for the kettle to boil — since Tunstall's superglue brainwave, the kettle had stayed put.

Jasmine stared out at him from one of the photographs. She held her baby close, daring the world to come between them.

Someone had pinned up a recent photograph of Rob Maitland. He was glancing over his shoulder, as if he had heard the click of the camera shutter. Maitland was their best suspect and he had a rock-solid alibi, Bernie Carter had vanished, and Rickman had little faith in Dwight's ability to find Carter and bring him in.

'Boss?' Naomi Hart stood at the door, her pale skin flushed pink by the cold, her fine blonde hair loose, framing her face. 'You okay?'

'Fine, why?'

'You were talking to yourself.' He winced and she added, with a smile, 'The odd word. Nothing indictable.'

Rickman covered his embarrassment by asking a question. 'I thought you were off-duty this weekend?'

She dumped her handbag in her desk drawer. 'Couldn't settle.' She slipped off her coat, the action graceful and fluid. The kettle clicked. 'I could murder a coffee.'

Rickman made them both a hot drink and handed her a mug. 'No milk, I'm afraid. The whole system falls apart when Tunstall's not here to organise it.'

Her mouth twitched. 'You've got to admit, he is more domesticated than your average rugger-bugger.'

They stood side by side at the whiteboard for a few minutes, staring at the snapshots as if they would eventually cave in and talk to them.

'Carter's the man I'd like a chat with,' Rickman said.

She looked up at him, a frown creasing her brow, and he gave her a précis of his conversation with Tommy Eames the previous night.

'Why would Maitland put a contract out on his accountant?' Hart asked. 'And why would he try to get at Carter by scaring the crap out of one of his most trusted men?'

'My guess? Maitland doesn't know *who* to trust any more. Whatever Carter did, I think Eames is in it up to his sweaty armpits — Maitland's only holding off because he thinks Eames will lead him to Carter.'

'No wonder the Birkenhead mob launched a takeover bid,' Hart said. 'It must look like the firm's about to go into liquidation.'

'And Maitland brought in new muscle. Eames said the only man he recognised was this Graham character. I ran a check on him. Neil Graham and Rob Maitland did time together at Thorn Cross Youth Offenders' Institution in their mid-teens — the *only* prison time either one of them has ever served.'

'Impressive,' Hart said, 'given Maitland's history.'

'He's ruthless,' Rickman said. 'Any threat is extinguished without discussion or right to appeal.'

Hart stared at the accumulated photographs and notes on the whiteboard. 'So why did Carter become a threat?'

'I've been asking myself the same question since last night.' They looked again at the photographs while they sipped their coffee.

'D'you think he tried to blackmail Maitland?' Hart asked.

'For what?'

She shrugged. 'A share of the power.'

'It's true Carter would have a hell of a lot he could use as blackmail,' Rickman said. 'But blackmailing a man like

Maitland would be a risky business. Anyway, Maitland is on the brink of respectability, why would Carter choose now to kick off?'

'Transition period,' Hart countered. 'He'd be at his most vulnerable now.'

Rickman took another sip of coffee. This was one of the things he liked about Hart — she would pursue an idea, even if it meant setting herself up in opposition to the boss. 'Okay,' he said, 'let's try that for size. From what we know, Carter is the brains behind the operation.'

'Yes.'

'Maybe he feels he should have had a bigger cut of the profits. He might think blackmail would work. And Maitland might be less willing to act with the press and media focused on him. But men like Maitland have long memories and they bear grudges.

'Maitland said Carter's been working hard on the accounts for an audit — he's trying to find backers for a dockside development.' Rickman felt a prickle of excitement. 'Maybe the audit is the key. Maybe Carter's skimmed more off the profits than even he could hide, and he knows it'll come out in the audit.'

'Then why the rush?' Hart demanded. 'Why not tell Maitland he needed more time?'

Rickman exhaled. 'You're right — it doesn't make sense — but there *had* to be a trigger. One minute, everything's fine and Maitland's on the way up — the next, he's involved in an internecine battle with one of his most trusted men.' Something niggled at him. He picked up a marker pen and went to the wall calendar. 'Carter disappears Thursday or early Friday.' He circled the dates. 'And Michael Aldiss is murdered yesterday — Friday.'

Hart nodded, responding to his pent-up energy.

'Could this be linked to Dwight's investigation?'

'Operation Snowplough?' Hart turned her cool gaze on him, and Rickman saw her weighing up the possibility that he might be on to something. Her eyebrow twitched slightly as though to say, *What the hell* . . . 'They're a close-mouthed bunch, but it's obvious they're going nowhere just as fast as we are.'

'Michael Aldiss was murdered to try and extract the accountant's location from Eames.' Rickman tapped the pen against his teeth. 'And we know that Graham was acting for Maitland.' He focused on the grid of dates on the wall until the lines danced before his eyes.

'Tommy Eames comes to me immediately after the murder, asking for protection. So what happened on Thursday to screw up the status quo?'

She shrugged. 'In his world — who knows?'

'We're part of his world now, Naomi,' Rickman said, and the notion made his skin itch. 'Somewhere between late Thursday and early Friday morning, something soured between Maitland and Carter.'

She nodded. 'We need to find out what.'

CHAPTER 43

Two TV crews were parked in a side street opposite Edge Hill Police Station. A gang of youths, none older than fourteen and all of them boys, hung around on the street corner, waiting for an opportunity to nip in at an open door and find something worth nicking. Two hand mikes and a reporter's handbag had gone that way in the last twenty-four hours, so the technical staff were keeping doors firmly closed and at least one person on watch.

Newspaper and radio reporters who lacked the luxury of a van to retreat to had to face the dual discomforts of inquisitive and abusive youths and the plummeting temperatures: a cold front had followed the storm, with high, cold skies and the promise of freezing fog later. Even now, as the sun began to lower, a thin haze was forming, magnifying the sun like a lens as it dipped towards the brow of Edge Hill.

They scuffed and stamped on the steps of the police station, telling each other risqué jokes and making small talk to stave off the boredom, drinking strong tea, and intermittently grumbling about the lack of progress in the investigation.

When Kim and Lars Lindermann drew into the kerb, crunching a few slates dislodged by the storm under their car tyres, the reporters shifted their weight and peered at their car.

Though alert to a possible story, none wished to be the first to break ranks in case the new arrivals were only there to report a stolen purse or to enquire after a lost cat. When nobody emerged from the BMW, they settled again to their vigil. The gang of boys, however, being well-schooled in the earning potential of a top-of-the-range motor on their patch, paid much closer attention without seeming to notice the car at all.

Lars Lindermann looked across at his wife.

'I'll be fine,' she said, though her hands were cold and she felt weak.

'I can come with you.'

'You should go home, Lars,' she said. 'Take care of the children.'

'Vicky can take care of the children.'

She shifted in her seat to get a better look at him. 'It's Vicky's half-day, and she wanted to do some shopping — it wouldn't be fair.'

Her husband gripped the wheel so tightly that his knuckles whitened. 'You shouldn't have to do this alone.'

She covered his hand with hers, feeling it warm her own.

'I have to,' she said. 'I'm done with being afraid.'

A couple of boys broke away from the main group and sauntered towards them.

'This will be the local protection racket, offering to "mind" your car,' she said, aiming for levity, unable to take another emotionally charged discussion. 'Time I left.'

'I'll wait for you.'

She heard the helplessness and impotent rage in his voice.

'You'll attract attention.' She leaned across and kissed his cheek. 'You already are.' With nothing better to do, the press were showing an interest in the two young gangsters — watching them hassle somebody else would provide light entertainment until something better showed up. 'Go home,' she said. 'I'll take a taxi back.'

She stepped out of the car and crossed the street without looking back, because if she did, she felt her resolve might break. She drew a few stares from the press and media, and a lewd remark from one of the older boys, but she barely registered them. Her scars itched and burned, and she knew they wouldn't let her be until this was over.

* * *

DCI Rickman agreed to see Kim right away. She sensed that by nature he was inclined to be gentle, despite his broken nose and the nicks and scars he bore. He was courteous and kind, a big man, like her husband, though Rickman was broader and carried more weight — all of lean muscle, she surmised, appraising him with a practised eye. Some big men are intimidating, others make you feel safe. Rickman made her feel safe.

He seated her in a chair in his office, then sat behind his desk. He had hazel eyes with a fleck of gold. When she looked into them, Kim saw that he too had suffered — she had always been able to recognise a fellow soul in torment.

She composed herself for what she had to say. 'I identified Jasmine's body yesterday.'

'We're grateful,' he said. 'I know it must have been an ordeal for you.'

'I saw the cuts.' She saw a slight flicker in his eyes, as though recalling the injuries was painful to him.

'I hoped you would be spared that.'

'You don't understand.' Kim folded her hands in her lap and stared at her wedding ring and the hard, cold beauty of her diamond engagement ring to avoid looking into his eyes. 'I know who killed her.'

'How do you know?'

She had expected him to ask for a name, but she supposed the name wouldn't matter if her reasoning seemed irrational.

'I know because . . .' She wanted to tell him that she knew because she had recognised the cuts on Jasmine's body — knew them as well as the scars on her own. But her throat closed, and tears of shame pricked behind her eyes.

'Take your time.' Rickman's voice was warm, and the compassion in it nearly made her crumble. Strange to think that if he had seemed hard and cynical, it would have been easier. She tried again, but her voice cracked.

She shook her head, impatient with herself — angry, too, that the man who had humiliated her could still have such power over her. *To hell with him.* She shook off her jacket and began to unfasten the buttons of her blouse.

'Mrs Lindermann—' Alarmed, Rickman began to stand.

She paused. 'Let me show you,' she said. 'I can't tell you, so let me show you.'

He glanced at the door, then seemed to come to a decision. He nodded, taking his seat again, and she slipped her blouse over her shoulders, exposing her upper arms and back.

Rickman gasped.

The cuts on Jasmine's body had been bloody — the necessity of speedy execution had taken some of the precision from the work — but Kim Lindermann knew that Rickman must see the similarity in the patterns carved into her flesh: the arcs, sunbursts and whorls, the carefully cut parallel lines.

'He prefers to work on a small section at a time,' she said. 'It can take him months to "perfect the art", as he calls it. He's lying to himself — he likes to see the girls' fear grow with each session. That is his "art".'

She buttoned her blouse. 'He supplied us with drugs in return for . . .' She risked a look into his face, expecting to see pity or contempt — most likely both. She saw neither. Rickman's jaw was locked and a pulse throbbed in his temple. She sensed a quiet rage in him.

'We called him the Surgeon. He preyed on the most desperate among us, the girls who would do anything — *anything* — for a fix. He was never short of willing victims. He liked us to be aware, but compliant, so he held back the major part of the operation until after you'd got yourself straight, allowing you just enough of your preferred poison to ease the cravings, but not enough to dull the pain.'

Rickman winced, and she guessed he was recalling some detail of Jasmine's murder that she would rather not know about.

She looked again at the diamond ring on her finger. 'He would wait a bit for the analgesic effects to wear off, then he'd begin. Sometimes he could make it last all night.'

She heard Rickman exhale slowly. 'The injuries to Jasmine's body were all new,' he said. 'She'd never . . .'

'He wanted Jasmine, but she never needed the drugs the way I did.'

'She turned him down.' His voice was restrained, the rage well-controlled.

She nodded. 'He doesn't like to be turned down.'

'And this man's name?' he asked.

* * *

Naomi Hart saw Mrs Lindermann to the rear entrance of the police station, where a taxi was waiting. She looked relaxed and she even smiled her thanks to Hart as she got in. Rickman had asked that Hart return to his office immediately. He stood at the window, breathing deeply as if he needed the air.

'Did she get away all right?' he asked.

'Fine,' Hart said.

'No press?'

'They had a couple of scouts hanging around the back gate, but they didn't show much interest.'

'Good,' Rickman said. 'The longer we can keep the press off their backs, the better.' He turned to face her, his dark eyes sparking amber. 'As of now, Bernie Carter is our prime suspect.'

She frowned. 'The *accountant*?'

'They call him the Surgeon.'

Hart felt a chill ripple under her skin.

'He likes to cut, Naomi.' Rickman looked at her, and then away, as though he could hardly bear to tell her. 'You've seen the PM photographs — the torture marks on Jasmine's body — Mrs Lindermann has identical marks.'

Hart winced, recalling the post-mortem pictures. 'This happened while she was an addict?'

Rickman nodded. 'He uses junkies — cuts them in exchange for drugs.'

'Jasmine was clean,' Hart said. 'The PM toxicology reports—'

'Jasmine passed the time while he waited for Mark to show up.' He smoothed a hand over his eyes as if it would wipe away the stain of the image in his mind. 'Jasmine was for fun.' He dipped his head. 'Maybe payback, too. Apparently, she refused to let him cut her, back when she was an addict.'

Hart felt like she had been punched hard in the stomach. She eased into a chair and thought about it for a few moments. 'Is this . . .' She tried to think of a sensitive way of saying it. 'Was Jasmine the first?'

'Murder victim?' Rickman shook his head. 'I don't know. I'll need you to check the records — any unsolved murders of drug addicts or prostitutes.'

Hart nodded.

Rickman ran his thumb down a scar on his chin. 'But I don't expect you'll find anything,' he added. 'Mrs Lindermann says he liked to use the same girl over and over. She said—' He broke off, took a breath and exhaled slowly, as if trying to quell nausea. 'She said it heightens the victim's fear and sensitivity to pain.'

'Bastard.' For a moment, Hart could find no other words and they stared at each other in silence. Hart went through the facts again in her head — something didn't quite gel. 'You say he went to Jasmine's house looking for Mark?' she said.

Rickman nodded.

'Why Carter, though?' she asked. 'Wouldn't Maitland send his hired muscle to find Mark?'

'I don't think Maitland sent him — I think Carter went for his own reasons.'

The only reasons Hart could think of were evidenced in Jasmine's brutalised body. She shook her head, frowning.

'Snowplough acted on intelligence from one of Cass's informants — what if that informant was Bernie Carter?'

'I don't get it,' Hart said. 'Why would he grass up Maitland?'

'This is highly speculative,' Rickman said. 'But let's say Carter *has* been skimming a percentage of the profits. As Maitland becomes more legit, the anomalies are easier to spot, more difficult to explain away.'

Hart thought back to their earlier discussion. 'The outcome of the big warehouse development audit wouldn't matter so much with Maitland out of the way,' she said. 'The deal might even fall through. So Carter cooperates with Operation Snowplough, informs on Maitland, but the raid is bungled—'

'And Maitland escapes,' Rickman finished for her. 'The audit goes ahead, and Carter is in serious trouble.'

Hart nodded, understanding, but not entirely convinced. 'And you think Carter planned to take over the entire operation?'

'I doubt it. Even banged up in prison, Maitland wouldn't sit still while his empire was stolen from under him. But if Carter played it cleverly, it might take months for Maitland to work out who had betrayed him, buying Carter the time to appropriate enough money from Maitland's businesses to relocate with a new identity, courtesy of Customs.'

'As you say, it's highly speculative,' Hart said.

'Carter is the one player on Maitland's team who wasn't arrested,' Rickman said. 'Customs intervention?'

'He did have a damn good alibi,' Hart countered.

'Fair point. But judging by Maitland's reaction when I asked him about Carter's disappearance, he's certainly worried that Carter has full access to his accounts. And I've been looking at the dates again. Mark and Bryony were found on Thursday. I did the *North West Newsbrief* special on Thursday evening. Carter disappeared shortly after that. By Friday, there was a contract out on him.'

'You think Carter ambushed Mark and took the money and drugs?' Hart was still struggling to square the image of an accountant torturing young girls. 'If you're right, that would make him a triple murderer.'

'The money from the drugs raid is gone,' Rickman said. 'And it would give him some start-up cash, if he needed to disappear fast.'

'But why leave Mark and Bryony where they were sure to be discovered?' Hart asked.

'The coach house looked abandoned,' Rickman said. 'Carter couldn't know the council had surveyors in — he must have thought it was good for a week, at least, giving him time to sort out the mess he found himself in, and arrange for his own disappearance. So, while Mark's body lay undiscovered, Maitland would blame Mark for the theft, think he'd got clean away. But when the bodies were found—'

'And with no sign of the drugs or the cash,' Hart added.

'The spotlight was off Mark Davis and back on the rest of Maitland's crew,' Rickman continued. 'Not that there was much of a field to narrow down — most of Maitland's men are either in police custody or in prison awaiting trial.' He fell silent a moment, and she again had the impression that he found what he was about to say difficult. 'It's my guess Maitland would know all about Bernie Carter's little hobby.'

'You think Maitland protected Carter, *knowing* what he'd done to Jasmine?' Queasy though it made her feel, Hart saw it would make sense in Maitland's world — his priority was to maintain control over his operations, and you didn't do that by going to the police. 'D'you want to call a briefing, boss?' she asked.

Rickman shook his head. 'Carter's gone to ground. I'll talk to surveillance, tell them to prioritise Carter.'

He hesitated.

'Sir?'

He looked past her to the door. Hart took the hint and closed it.

'Look,' he said, lowering his voice. 'I don't know how involved Dwight's team is in all of this, but I want people around me I can trust. I've already called Foster — he's on his way in — but I couldn't reach Tunstall.'

'He mentioned something about a rugby match,' she said, feeling a glow of pleasure at Rickman's trust in her. 'I'll call him.'

Rickman fell into a reverie, raking his fingers through his hair, and his face darkened with thoughts she could only guess at.

'So, what do we do next?' she asked.

The intrusion was deliberate and brusque and, surprised into an immediate response, Rickman's anger finally surfaced. 'We find the sick fuck and put him away.'

'Finding him will be down to the surveillance teams.' He turned a glittering eye on her. 'I mean, won't it, sir?'

'Maybe we can hurry things along a bit,' Rickman said, with grim humour. 'You and I are going to pay Mrs Carter a visit — see if we can rattle her enough to make a mistake.'

Hart began to feel a little better. Any action would be an improvement on sitting around waiting for something to happen.

'Would Customs know where he is?'

'I'll talk to Superintendent Maynard, see if he can pull any strings. Any immunity Carter's negotiated would be on the drugs charges. We're talking murder. In the meantime, I want an alert sent out to ports and airports as well.'

Their eye contact was brief and troubled. Neither one of them wanted to think too deeply about the possibility that Carter had already fled the country.

CHAPTER 44

Mark Davis had stolen the two sports bags thinking he was
stealing two million pounds' worth of redemption. When
he found Jasmine murdered, he'd known he was marked for
pain and death, but he'd thought that by leaving Bryony with
Ed and Hilary Shepherd, he'd found a way at least to keep
her safe — had imagined himself home free when he reached
the magic safety of Black Wood.

But even here the darkness seems to crowd in on him
and every bush seems to quiver with imminent threat. He
falls, sprawling full-length in the soft mulch of a hundred
winters' leaf fall. Startled awake, the baby lets out a scream,
followed by a series of hiccupping cries. Mark scrambles to
his knees, soothing the distressed child. If she's quiet, he'll
find a way through the woods to the big house, flitting from
shadow to shadow unseen. But Bryony won't stop crying.

Another footfall. Still on his knees, Mark gathers Bryony
up, holding her close, and takes cover under a rhododendron bush. He sees leather shoes. Maitland's hard men wear
boots or trainers, but these are expensive loafers, gleaming in
the twilight. A hand reaches down and drags him into the
open. He looks quickly into the man's face, hardly daring
to hope. The face is boyish, despite its forty years, the hard

lines of his jawbone softened by business dinners and a life spent poring over account books and computers. He wears a single-breasted jacket over a polo shirt — Bernie Carter's version of casual wear.

'Carter?'

'That's *Mister* Carter to you.'

Mister? Bernie Carter was lucky if the men called him by his surname — mostly he got Bernie, or 'Bernie the Books'.

Carter stares down at Mark and the baby, an amused expression on his bland face. 'Who did you expect?'

A killer, a hired assassin, a man with a gun and a mission. 'I — I don't know. I—' Mark's relief is so great that he almost laughs out loud. Bernie the Books never harmed no one.

He begins to get up, but Carter stops him with a curt, 'Stay there.'

Mark stares into the creeping shadows, seeing movements, threats in every pocket of darkness. 'You alone?'

Carter smiles, spreading his hands. 'Just you 'n' me, Marky.'

Another wave of relief washes over him. There is hope. *Mr Carter is a reasonable man. Maybe if I give the stuff back . . . Maybe what? A second chance? There is no second chance. Not for me. Not with Mr Maitland. But Bryony* — *she deserves a chance.*

'I'll do whatever you want,' he says. 'I'll go back with you. I just need to see to the baby.'

'You do that,' Carter says, with feeling. 'Its bawling is setting my teeth on edge.'

Mark unwraps the blanket, soothing and crooning while he checks for injuries.

'Shut it up, will you?' There's an edge to Carter's voice now.

'I know we need to talk, Mr Carter.' He's careful to use the accountant's title. 'But see that house?'

Carter glances lazily in the direction of the children's home. The house is a broken silhouette through the trees. Some of the windows are open, despite the chill.

'I'll just take her . . .' *To Ed and Hilary. To safety*, he wants to say, but for the first time in his short life, he sees the likely consequences of his actions and makes the decision not to name the Shepherds.

'I'll just leave her on the doorstep, yeah?'

'D'you think this is a fairy tale, Mark?' Carter walks around him, like he's inspecting a statue. The constant motion makes Mark feel sick. 'You want to leave Little Orphan Annie here on the doorstep of the foundlings' home and one day Daddy Warbucks will come for her and she'll live happily ever after?'

Mark feels a fresh jolt of alarm. 'She never hurt nobody, Mr Carter,' he says. He turns the baby's face in towards his body, covering her head, as if this will make her less visible, less vulnerable. 'I just want her to be safe.' His voice catches on this last word and suddenly he's biting back tears.

'Nobody's ever really safe, Mark. We just fool ourselves that we are, so that we can function in a perilous world. But doors can be broken down, windows can be smashed, and the human body is incredibly fragile.'

The big words confuse Mark, but he understands enough — Bryony is not safe. His daughter, the precious life he swore to protect, is in danger.

Run! Just fucking run! But he is exhausted, sick with hunger and drugs and fear. The weakness in his limbs is beyond the power of his will to command. Carter continues pacing, round and round, till it seems like the whole world is spinning and it's too late to get off — the worst has already happened.

'Like you said, Mr Carter. It's just you and me.' Mark hears the wheedling tone in his voice and hopes that Carter will overlook it. 'I'll tell you where the money is. You can have it — all of it — it's yours. Take it and walk away. Blame me. Say you couldn't find us.'

'Are you trying to *bribe* me, Mark?' Carter clicks his tongue against the side of his cheek. 'Mr Maitland will *not* be pleased.' He stops circling. 'On your feet.'

Bryony's cries are muffled by the blanket, but Mark feels the baby's skin hot through the fabric of his shirt. He struggles to his feet. If he goes with Carter, he's as good as dead. Who will take care of Bryony? Who will care for her?

He shifts Bryony's weight to his left arm and staggers a little, waiting for Carter to come closer. The accountant moves in, ready to shove him forward, but Mark swings back hard with his right elbow, connecting with Carter's paunch, and he goes down with a soft '*Oof*.' Adrenaline and sheer bloody fury carry Mark forward, and he jogs blindly towards the house.

But Carter is faster than he thought. He's on his feet and after him, running, overtaking, turning to face his quarry. Something glints, then Mark feels heat — a searing burn in the flesh of his cheek. He puts a hand to his face and feels blood trickle between his fingers.

'Flesh wound,' Carter says. 'It'll hurt like a bastard, but it won't kill you.' He takes Mark by the arm and leads him back into the woods. 'Not yet.'

* * *

The coach house is darker than he remembers — the shrubs around the building seem to crowd in on it, sucking in the light. Carter takes a torch from his jacket pocket and gestures for Mark to go ahead. The door is shut, a steel plate protecting the old wood, but the padlock swings loose on the hasp, and Mark pushes the door open with his fingertips, his heart hammering in his chest. The hallway stinks of piss, his face is burning from the cut and he's shaking from the incipient cravings of withdrawal and outright terror.

This was their haven as boys, their smoking den, where they would swig cider and talk big, swap dirty stories — Mark always on the edge of the group, there under sufferance. He had always liked dark places, would seek them out as a child. When his stepfather first came into their home,

Mark hid under the bed, climbed into wardrobes, burrowed under bedding in a childish attempt to remain invisible.

Later, he'd discovered the school basement, and was comforted by the dark, the secret rush of water in the heating pipes, the close, dusty warmth. Mark didn't understand that these places represented a return to the dark protective hush of the womb. But he did know that it wasn't the dark that was scary — it was people.

'Down there,' Carter says.

Mark hesitates at the door to the basement. 'Let me leave the baby up here.' He has to raise his voice over her screams. 'We can talk better that way.'

Carter shines the torch beam in his face. 'Move.'

The steps creak dangerously under his weight. He feels something shift and the rafters crack, releasing a puff of plaster dust and a whispering sift of sandy particles. Mark protects the baby's head. He doesn't want to go down there — it doesn't smell right, not like when they were kids. Then it smelled of cigarettes and cider, but now, as he descends into the darkness, it reeks of damp and decay. Another creak and he grabs the rail with his free hand, his heart racing. He can't take Bryony into this terrible place.

'It wasn't planned, Mr Carter, I swear.' *Bonehead, admitting it straight off.* He tries again, modifying the story. 'I was only keeping it till I could get it back to Mr Maitland. It's safe — I haven't spent none.'

'First you say, "It wasn't planned," then, "I didn't steal it."' Carter laughs. 'You're burbling, son.'

He lashes out, rapping Mark's knuckles hard, and the pain and shock makes him he let go of the rail, falling the last two steps onto his back. Bryony's cries ratchet up a notch.

'That *fucking* row is giving me a headache.' Carter's tone is midway between an exclamation and a threat.

Mark tries to shush the child, but she won't be consoled.

'Do something about it or I will.' Carter is standing on the bottom step, the flashlight in one hand, the knife in the other. It's a switchblade, and he holds it comfortably, as though he's used to handling it.

Mark stares wide-eyed into the dark, looking for escape, though there is none. A short distance away an empty cider bottle gleams in the beam of the torch, the neck of the bottle pointing towards him. *Truth or Dare?* Mark kneels, jiggling the baby, feeling desperate and inadequate. *Grab the bottle — use it!* The voice he hears in his head is Jasmine's. *Get Bryony out of here, no matter what it takes.*

'Ah-ah,' Carter admonishes, as though he's read Mark's thoughts. He places the torch on the stair post and steps down onto the basement floor, casually kicking the bottle yards out of reach into a far corner. 'Now, *what* did I just say?'

'She won't stop, Mr Carter — she's frightened.'

Carter darts forward and Mark tightens his grip on the baby, but instead of grabbing Bryony, the accountant rummages through Mark's pockets. 'Hah!' He steps back and opens his fist. One of Mark's foil wraps sits in the palm of his hand. Carter uses the knife to unfold it as he speaks.

'D'you know any history, Mark?'

Mark feels a stab of fear that is as much a throwback to the humiliation of his schooldays as it is to Carter's grossly out-of-character behaviour.

'History?' he echoes.

'Kings and queens, civil war, the Romans — all that,' Carter explains.

'I wasn't much good at school, Mr Carter,' Mark says.

Carter snorts. ''Course you weren't.' He opens the last fold of foil and Mark sees a thin line of white powder. He trembles like a dog straining on a leash, his entire body aching for it.

'In the eighteenth century, opium was called the "poor child's nurse".' Mark can barely hear him, he's so intent on the mound of sweet release in Carter's hand.

Carter steps forward again, and Mark sees the knife glint in the torch beam. 'Hand her over,' Carter says, and Mark feels the sharp point of the knife at his throat. He moves until he can't move any further and feels the bite of the blade in the soft skin of his neck.

'Please, Mr Carter—' But he's already releasing his grip, relinquishing his child to danger.

Carter eases the baby into the crook of his arm in a practised, easy movement, and Mark is reminded that he has two daughters of his own. Carter licks his finger and dips it into the precious powder. 'Of course, the Victorians mixed it with syrup first. Oh, well. Here goes.' He rubs a little on the baby's gums. Bryony squirms and screams, fighting him, but soon she seems calmer, and even begins sucking on Carter's finger. 'There you are!' He beams at Mark like a proud father, gently rocking the baby in his arms. 'They say babies of junkies are born jonesing for a fix.'

'Stop it!' Tears stream down Mark's face, stinging the cut on his cheek. His nose is running and his stomach is beginning to cramp. He struggles to a crouch, but Carter knocks him flat again with a shove from his foot.

'What's up, Daddy? Afraid there'll be none left for you?'

Mark watches in impotent rage and shame, because a part of him does resent the waste of his fix.

Carter dips his finger in the powder again and offers it to the infant, who sucks greedily. He laughs. 'That's got to taste bitter!' He watches as Mark wipes his nose on his sleeve. 'Think Jasmine's been feeding her the stuff on the sly?'

Mark hears Bryony's contented sucking and wants to scream. In minutes, her body begins to go limp. Once, twice, her hands jerk in some kind of reflex, but when Carter places her on the floor of the basement, her head is lolling, her mouth slightly open, her eyes not quite closed.

'Don't worry,' Carter says. 'She's in a good place.'

Mark's hands are shaking and his nose won't stop running. Withdrawal and fear combined sends tremors through his body that rattle his teeth.

'Now,' Carter says. He pockets the foil and turns to Mark. 'You're gonna tell me everything.'

'There's nothing *to* tell.' He eases up to a sitting position. 'Honest, Mr Carter.'

'Sure there is.' Carter sits on the bottom step, holding the knife. The torch, balanced on the post above his head, casts a shadow over his face. 'Mr Maitland wants to know how you got out.'

Mark blinks, remembering the dark places, the secret places of safety he sought out as a child.

'You made a deal, didn't you?'

Mark feels his eyes widen. 'No!'

'Come on, now,' Carter chides him. 'Police helicopters, bullets flying, the Dutch baying for blood . . . The last he saw of you, Mr Maitland says you were standing in the spotlight like you expected them to beam you up.'

'No, Mr Carter. No deal. I mean, who would I make a deal with?'

'That's what Mr Maitland wants to know.'

'But I *didn't*.' His head is burning and his body aches like the worst case of flu. 'I just ran.' The effort of remembering is draining, and he takes a moment to catch his breath. 'There was cops everywhere. I just took the bag and ran.'

'Bag?' Carter says. 'Just one, Mark? 'Cos *I* found two, and unless it split overnight, like a little amoeba—' He sees the look on Mark's face and his brow furrows in fake concern. 'Yes, Mark, I've already got the money. And the drugs.'

Mark stares at Carter. *This is a trick — tell the stupid smack-head you've got the money, he's bound to blurt out where he's stashed it.* But there's no way Carter could have found the bags. No way.

Carter's smile is pained. 'Did you think your NVQ in Motor Mechanics would have me stumped? Poor Mark — your biggest handicap isn't your stupidity, it's your lack of imagination. Door panels, wheel arches, under the spare wheel. First three places even an amateur would look.'

* * *

342

Mark drifts in and out of consciousness, the pain bringing him to and plunging him back into the grey half-light between screaming wakefulness and total oblivion.

He has told Carter everything — the impulse to grab the money, finding the tunnel, the fall. He has told him things he's never told another living soul, yet Carter still does not believe him.

The accountant slips back into focus as the balance tips, and Mark feels again the searing burn of a dozen small cuts to his face and chest. He is lying face down and his hands are tied behind his back with the length of leather cord Mark uses for shooting up. Carter stands over him now with his sleeves rolled up and his face flushed with exertion. There is a guilty excitement in his face — like a businessman playing hooky, knowing he'll have some explaining to do when he returns to work.

'It's my curse,' he says, as though continuing a conversation. 'Always to be underestimated. But it has its advantages.' He picks up his jacket and searches his pockets, grunting with satisfaction as he brings out a pair of leather gloves. 'I mean, *I'm* not under arrest, am I?'

Mark shakes his head — Carter has taught him that to make no response is unacceptably rude and will be punished.

'Why is that, d'you think?'

'I don't know, Mr Carter,' Mark croaks.

'There's no warrant out for *my* arrest,' he goes on, as though Mark hasn't spoken, his eyes glittering in the dim light. 'Do they think old Bernie the Books is too *dull* to be a criminal?'

Mark shakes his head again, whimpering as the movement grinds plaster dust into the cuts on his face and chest. 'N-no Mr Carter.'

Carter gives an *aw-shucks* shrug. 'Oh . . . that's just because you've got to know me better.' He pulls the gloves on tight.

'Yes, M-Mister Carter,' Mark stammers. 'I understand, now. I—'

Carter catches Mark by the hair, dragging him to his knees, tearing afresh the shallow cuts in his skin.

'There are things about me you could barely imagine,' Carter says. 'Let alone understand.' He balls his right hand into a fist.

Mark tries to pull away, but Carter holds him fast.

'Don't, Mr Carter. Please, don't.'

Carter hesitates a moment, staring at Mark as he might a pet dog that had stood up on its hind legs and talked. Then he drives his fist hard into Mark's face. 'Good old Bernie. Dependable — dull — predictable — Bernie!' He punctuates the sentence with a punch, each carefully aimed: the eyes, the cheekbone, the temple, the mouth. 'Betcha didn't predict this, eh, Mark?'

Mark coughs and retches, tears and blood mingling on his face.

'So, Mark. Let's start from the top. What d'you know?'

Mark dry-heaves. 'Oh, God . . .' he groans. His left eye is almost shut, and his lip is split. As it swells, he feels it peel back even more.

'God isn't here, Mark. And I'm still waiting.'

Mark flinches, expecting another blow, but Carter is as good as his word. He waits, a look of quiet interest on his face. 'I don't know nothing, Mr Carter. I didn't think — I just . . . I'm sorry . . .'

He breaks down, sobbing, and Carter ruffles his hair then, unexpectedly, lets him go. Mark sways, his knees creaking with the effort of keeping him upright, afraid to fall because Carter likes to use his feet almost as much as he likes to use a blade.

Carter crouches beside him, a good-humoured look on his round, pleasant face. 'You *say* you know nothing, but I don't accept that, Mark. Now, I've tried to be reasonable about this, but I'm losing patience.' Mark begins to protest, but Carter presses a finger to Mark's cut lip to silence him, and Mark grunts in pain.

'There are many kinds of trauma, Mark. Sharp, blunt — everyone knows those — but there's also drowning, crushing, heat, cold.' He might be discussing flavours of ice cream. 'We've done sharp and blunt — and drowning's out of the question — what d'you say we try hot, next?' A cigarette lighter appears in his hand and he flicks the trigger.

'Nu-nuh!' Mark ducks, but Carter has him.

He realises too late that during the last long hour of torture, Carter hasn't mentioned Maitland. 'You know I didn't grass Mr Maitland up,' he whimpers. 'You *know* that, Mr Carter.'

'Of *course* I know,' Carter says, as though he's been trying to explain for hours and Mark has finally got the point. ''Cos it was me grassed Maitland up.'

Mark understands now — Carter isn't interested in retribution, only in pain. He bucks and lunges, but Carter is stronger and fitter. He twists, sliding his arm around Mark's throat, squeezing his windpipe until the flickering yellow torchlight fades to red. He sees white, bright stars, then, just as the edges of his vision seem to close in, Carter eases off. 'Choking,' Carter says, cheerfully. 'That's one I almost forgot.'

The baby stirs and makes a fretful cry.

Carter drops Mark like an abandoned toy and he falls to the floor, coughing and retching, gasping for air.

'You shouldn't have brought the baby,' Carter says over his shoulder. 'But that's typical of you, isn't it, Mark? You couldn't give a shit about anyone but yourself. Jasmine, the baby — they're just extensions of your sad little ego.' He picks the drugged child up, and Mark gives an involuntary cry.

Carter's hands encircle Bryony's narrow chest. He lifts her, dandling her in front of his face. 'Shall I tell Daddy what I did to your mummy?' He baby-talks in a musical falsetto. 'Shall I? *Hmm?*'

Mark struggles to get up, but he hasn't the strength, and cranes his neck to look up at his tormentor. His face is swollen and bloody, he can't see out of his left eye, and his skinny frame is bruised and battered, but he feels no pain — the fear of what this monster might do to his baby girl is so intense.

Bryony's head lolls, but she's trying to rouse herself — her eyes, though heavy-lidded, are partially open and she's articulating — making soft, meaningless sounds that make Mark's heart swell till he thinks it will burst.

'I screwed your mummy *silly*,' Carter says, still in that vile crooning tone. 'Yes, I did! Then I cut her.' He eyes Mark greedily. 'I scored her flesh like meat. Oh, *baby*, you should have seen it . . .'

Mark sobs in sorrow and guilt and terror, but Carter is without pity.

'I even threatened to cut *you* up into little bits,' he says, giving Bryony a little shake. Unexpectedly, he switches his grip of the baby, cradles her in his left arm. Now his face is serious, his voice cold and hard. 'I threatened to cut the baby and she still didn't give you up. What kind of a mother would put her baby at risk to protect slime like you?'

Mark moans, an almost animal sound, wrenched from deep in his gut. 'She didn't know . . . I never told her where I was staying. She thought I'd left for good.'

Carter stares at him. 'You really *are* a piece of shit — you didn't even give her that much to bargain with. I might have let her live if she'd given you up.'

Mark keens softly. 'You didn't have to kill her. You didn't have to . . .'

Carter looks down at him, a look of disgust on his face. 'Grow up.'

'You've got the money. Do what you like to me, just — *please* — don't hurt my baby,' Mark begs.

'Do you think I'm an animal?' Carter says.

Mark can't see past the terrible picture in his head of Jasmine, bloodied and defiled. Jasmine dead. Jasmine with all the beauty and life torn out of her. Jasmine, his love, the one beautiful thing in his life, made ugly by this man's depraved actions. But still he wheedles.

'No, Mr Carter. I know you did what you had to. I know you don't want to hurt Bryony.' It's a betrayal of Jasmine, feigning an understanding of what Carter has done, but one he thinks she will forgive. 'Take her to the home,' he urges. 'Leave her on the doorstep. They'll find her.'

Carter looks at him in astonishment. 'You really do think this is *Little Orphan Annie*, don't you? Well, guess what, Mark. The sun's not coming out for you tomorrow or any other day.'

CHAPTER 45

DS Daniel Cass was indulging in a little retail therapy. He'd been called in, on his off-day, by DI Dwight, who had administered the required bollocking. Poor record-keeping, using unregistered informants — he had denied that one strenuously — 'misinforming' fellow officers on vital intel. *Misinforming* — he liked that one. Little wanker didn't even have the balls to confront him with the lies he'd told the delectable Naomi Hart. Dwight did say he'd referred the 'incident' with Foster to a 'higher authority', which meant Superintendent Maynard, and a more effective bollocking. Cass had made all the right noises: regret, lapse of concentration, pressure of work, *blah-blah-blah*, and Larry, like the lamb he was, had been mollified.

Since then, his phone had been ringing on and off, almost without let-up. DI Dwight looking for a hand-holder or DCI Rickman out for blood — he didn't care to find out. Either way, he intended to remain invisible until things cooled down a bit. Not that it stopped him staying in touch. His work mobile might be switched off, but he kept a second handy for emergencies such as this.

He'd driven to town to get away from the landline and was now browsing one of the better clothing stores in the city centre. The shop girl was efficient and obliging, had found him the right collar size in the shirt he'd chosen, helped him find a tie to go with it, and was about to take his inside leg measurement for a pair of trousers. An unnecessary pleasure, since Cass knew it, but he felt he'd earned it — it was one of the perks of paying a bit extra, having a pretty girl kneel in front of him, feeling the inside of his thigh.

'I'm sorry, sir. Could you . . .' She blushed, looking up at him. *That's nice*, he thought. *You don't get nice girls like that anymore.* He smiled down at her. 'Sorry, love,' he said. 'I'll stand at ease.'

She returned to the task, looking a little flustered. 'Thirty-four inches.'

'Now you're flattering me.' She looked sharply into his face, her flush deepening, and he grinned. *No, you don't get girls like that anymore.* He sighed happily and dipped in his pocket for his pot of Vaseline, applying the balm to his lower lip as she leaned in, circling his waist with her arms to draw the tape measure around him.

His phone rang and he retrieved it from his jacket pocket with his free hand.

'Sarge. Smith here. Where are you?'

'I'm in the arms of a pretty lady, Smithie, not that it's any of your business.' He looked down at the girl with some satisfaction, and a growing erection.

The girl snapped suddenly upright with a little gasp, and Cass tilted his head in apology. She turned away, under the pretext of writing down his measurements, and Cass said, 'What've you got?'

'I just got word from the office. Carter's missus made a call to her dearly departed.'

Cass closed his eyes. *Stupid cow!*

He took a breath and said, 'Yeah?' aiming for laid-back curiosity.

'I've got an address.' *Fuck! Didn't he tell them no communication?* 'Where?'

'A farmhouse near Ormskirk.'

Cass cupped his hand over the mouthpiece and said, 'Sorry, love. Have to finish this another time.'

The girl turned around, her eyes wide with disappointment. 'But—' She'd done all her figures, neatly noted them in columns, written his name in her best handwriting. He almost felt sorry for her.

'Police business,' he said. 'Look—' He bent to peer at her name tag. 'Shona. Nice name. Tell you what, Shona, why don't you keep a note — I'll come looking for you next time I'm in.' He slipped his lip salve back in his jacket and patted the pocket, then turned his back on her and walked away.

'Are we good to go?' he asked Smith.

'That's why I rang, Sarge. The boss is at an IAG meeting, in Toxteth, and his phone's switched off.'

Cass felt a passing annoyance — calling Larry Dwight 'the boss' was like calling Man City a football team. 'You know what IAG stands for, Smithie?'

'Independent Assessment Group,' Smith replied, the confusion apparent in his tone.

'That's the official line. Anyone who's actually been to a meeting knows it really stands for Irritating Arseholes with Grievances.'

Smith choked a laugh, but he wasn't so easily sidetracked. 'I could send someone over, pass on the message.'

Cass stopped, his hand on the brass plate of the shop door. Dwight would feel the need to tell Rickman, Rickman would send officers to pick Carter up at the farmhouse, and Carter would not be pleased.

'No need for that,' he said.

He had to contain the situation, inform Carter they were on to him and give him the chance to get away. That was what Carter was paying him for: to keep him informed of developments and the police off his back. The money was good, and it was low risk — at least, it had been until Rickman had muscled in on the case. Dwight, he could manage. Rickman was like bloody yard dog — his bite definitely worse than his bark.

'Larry's going on to a social thing,' Smith persisted. 'He might not switch his phone back on.'

'I'm just around the corner,' Cass lied. 'I can be there in five minutes.' As if to underline the urgency of the situation, he crossed the white expanse of Williamson Square at a trot, his breath steaming in the cold air. 'Get the posse together. We'll meet at the ASDA near Switch Island, save on travelling time.' He checked his watch — two o'clock. 'Tell them they've got an hour.'

Smith cleared his throat.

'Did I forget something, Smithie?' He reached the main bus terminus at Queens Square and pressed the button at the crossing, willing the lights to change.

'DCI Rickman.' Smith sounded apologetic.

'What about him?' He felt the muscles in his neck tense.

'Shouldn't we let him know? I mean, he said tracking down Carter was priority, and the super said he wants full cooperation—'

'We've done the graft, Smithie,' Cass interrupted. 'D'you want Rickman grabbing the glory?' The lights changed and he sprinted across the road, heading for his car.

'No, Sarge. But he is the senior officer on the joint investigations and the super—'

Cass shoved his ticket and a tenner at the security guard in reception. 'Trust me, all Detective Superintendent Maynard wants is to look good in front of the press. Anyway, you wouldn't want Rickman taking credit for a game just 'cos he happened to wander onto the pitch after half-time, would you?'

'No, Sarge.' Smith sounded reluctant.

'I'll expect you there at 15:00 hours.' Cass took his ticket and change. 'You're late, the coach leaves without you.'

He ended the call then dug out Carter's mobile from his contacts. It was pay-as-you-go and effectively untraceable. It was also switched off. 'Shit.' The woman next to him in the queue for the lift gave him a look. Carter needed to be out of his little hidey-hole and twenty miles down the road by the time Cass arrived with his posse.

He hesitated, considering the possibility of driving to the farm to warn Carter, then heading back to meet the posse. *'Fuck it,'* he muttered, and drew another disapproving glance. In all the excitement, he hadn't asked for the address. If he called Smith, demanding it now, he'd cause suspicion — especially if they turned up mob-handed in an hour or so only to find the place empty. He let the woman take the lift and stepped outside onto the rough cobbles opposite the Marriott hotel. He dialled Carter's mobile again. The answer-phone clicked straight in and he disconnected angrily. Give a crook a failsafe protocol and you could be damn sure he'd ignore it. They just didn't know how to play by the rules.

Cass checked his watch — he'd be pushed for time, trying to get across town to meet the lads at this hour. He *had* to hold Rickman off till he got to Carter. If it came down to it, he could bring Carter in himself, inform Customs. They would make sure their prize witness was free and clear before Rickman got near him. He hung up and rang the office.

DC Gormley picked up. *Well thank fuck something's going right today.* Gormley was none too bright, and he was easily influenced — in other words, he was the perfect oppo.

'You still there?' he asked.

'On my way, Sarge,' Gormley said. Cass could picture him putting on his jacket to show willing.

'Let's not make it too easy for Rickman, eh?'

'How'm I gonna do that, Sarge?'

'I'll leave that to your discretion.' Carter would never dream of telling an officer to obstruct an investigation — but he hoped Gormley had the initiative to do just that.

CHAPTER 46

Foster arrived at Edge Hill Police Station by taxi, not trusting himself to drive. He was hungover, squinting in the autumn sunshine, despite the wraparound shades he wore. He paid the driver and made his way towards the front entrance as a black cab drew up and the driver abandoned his vehicle by the kerb.

The sun was low in a milky blue sky, and Foster shielded his eyes against the glare. He quickened his pace — he'd only taken a swift glance at the hackney cab licence hidden in Naomi's flat, but he'd swear that the fair-haired guy running up the station steps was Philip Ormerod.

By the time Foster reached the reception desk, Ormerod was asking for Naomi Hart. 'Phil, isn't it?' He took Ormerod by the elbow and steered him through the security door. 'I'll take him up,' he said to the operator at the desk.

Ormerod shook free of him. 'Do I know you?'

'Lee Foster.' He eased his shades down his nose to look over them and offered his hand.

Ormerod's slight hesitation told Foster that his name had come up in conversation — last night, maybe, after he'd staggered off into the storm. Great.

He led the way up the concrete fire escape to the Major Incident Room. 'So, what's this about?'

'I'd rather tell Naomi,' Ormerod said.

'You tried her mobile?'

'She's not answering.'

'Looks like you'll have to make do with me, then.'

Ormerod eyed him warily. Foster could almost see him weighing up the positives against the negatives Naomi had described in his character. 'It's about Rob Maitland,' he said at last. 'He's on the move.'

Foster didn't trouble to ask how Ormerod knew this — he simply changed course and headed for Jeff Rickman's office.

Rickman and Hart were in deep conversation, Rickman leaning against the filing cabinet and Hart half-sitting on his desk. She started up when she saw Ormerod.

'Phil! Are you all right?'

'I'm fine,' he said, though the strain showed in the set of his jaw and around the eyes. 'I tried to reach you.' His tone was apologetic — he hadn't followed the prescribed arrangements.

Hart's hand went to her jacket pocket. 'I must have left my mobile in the Incident Room. Sorry, Phil.'

'He says Maitland's crew is on the move,' Foster said.

Rickman leaned off the cabinet. 'Since when?'

'One fifteen, thereabouts.'

Rickman checked his watch. 'It's three o' clock. What kept you, a good run of fares?'

'I only just got away.'

'Okay.' Rickman folded his arms, ready to listen. 'Tell me exactly what happened.'

'I was flagged by two guys outside Maitland's offices in Old Hall Street.'

Foster sized Ormerod up while the DCI questioned him. He must be thirty or thirty-five years old, Foster guessed. Muscular build — probably worked out — maybe that was how he and Naomi had met. He glanced at Hart, but she avoided his gaze.

'They told me to drive to Mount Pleasant,' Ormerod said. 'I picked Maitland up in a back alley, dropped him back in Old Hall Street. He had a car waiting.'

'Was he alone?'

Ormerod shook his head. 'Driver and bodyguard with Maitland, two more in the following car.'

'Did you get the licence plates?'

'Yes.'

While Ormerod fished in his pocket, Foster stole another glance at Hart. She must have briefed him thoroughly — witnesses never thought to note the car plates. Judging by the look on Rickman's face, he had come to the same conclusion. But Hart was still focusing resolutely on a point in the middle distance, frowning slightly, as if trying to make out a familiar object.

Ormerod finally found what he was looking for and held out a scrap of paper to Rickman. His hand was shaking. 'I would've phoned, but they left two men with me.'

'Jesus, Phil.' Hart paled, jolted out of her feigned reverie.

He gave a self-deprecating shrug. 'They let me keep the meter running, even tipped me a tenner.' He tried to smile, but it came off as a grimace.

Rickman looked from one to the other. 'And you just happened to be in Old Hall Street, at the precise moment Maitland sent for a taxi,' he said.

Hart stared at a point on to Rickman's right, a faint blush on her delicate cheekbones.

'*Post & Echo* offices,' Ormerod said. 'They don't have staff drivers any more — use cabs instead. You can pick up a half-day fare if you're lucky.'

Her facial expression didn't change, but Foster thought he saw a slight slackening of the tension in Hart's shoulders.

Rickman looked long and hard at Ormerod before turning his attention to Hart. 'You wouldn't be so stupid as to involve a civilian in an unauthorised surveillance op, would you, DC Hart?'

Hart straightened, and Foster got the distinct impression she was about to make the monumental mistake of telling Rickman the truth.

'Come on, Jeff,' Foster said, before she could make the biggest gaff of her career. 'How big is the city centre, anyway?

You wanna decent fare, there's only three or four ranks worth waiting on.'

Rickman turned his attention to Foster, narrowing his eyes. It wouldn't have escaped the DCI's notice that Foster had used his first name, which, in their friendship code, was an appeal to the man rather than the cop. After a few uncomfortable moments, Rickman reached for the phone and dialled the Comms Room.

'DCI Rickman. Patch me through to . . .' He riffled through a stack of pink flimsies in his in-tray, looking for the day's task list, and ran his finger down the roster of names and duties. 'DC Ingham.' He switched to speakerphone as Ingham was put through.

'Sir.' Ingham was lead surveillance on Maitland, and he'd drawn the weekend day shift. He sounded bored and tired. Foster recalled a slouching middle-aged cop, with a waist measurement greater than his trouser length.

'What's Maitland doing?' Rickman asked.

'Schmoozing.'

'Where?'

'Whole Earth Restaurant on Mount Pleasant. He went in with some well-dressed business types, about' — they heard a rustle of clothing as Ingham checked his watch — 'two and a half hours ago.'

'Can you see him?'

'It's up off the street,' Ingham said.

'Can you *see* him?' Rickman repeated, not quite keeping his anger in check this time. Ingham must have heard it in his voice, because there was another rustle, accompanied by the creak of upholstery as the officer shifted in his seat.

'Not *as such*, sir. But we haven't moved from here. Haven't even had a break for a brew and a bacon butty.' He sounded almost wistful.

'Go inside. See if he's there,' Rickman said.

'This is a covert op, sir—'

'Not if he knows you're watching him, it isn't,' Rickman growled. 'See if he's there — and stay on the line.'

They listened as Ingham laboured up the steps into the building. A burst of chatter told them that he was inside the restaurant. They heard Ingham's shoes clumping across wood floors, a barely audible exchange with what Foster guessed was one of the waitresses, then a muttered curse.

'He's not in the bar or the main restaurant,' Ingham said. 'I'm sorry, sir—' He broke off, calling to someone. 'Are you the manager?' The reply was indistinct, swamped by the noise of diners' conversation and the clatter of cutlery.

'Rob Maitland was here,' Ingham said. They heard a muffled denial. ''Course you know him.' Another brief exchange, then Ingham raised his voice. 'Look, love, this is a police investigation, so don't piss me about. You let him out the back way, didn't you?' The reply was distorted by the babble of background noise.

Foster heard 'favour' and 'paparazzi'. It seemed the manager had let a violent criminal sneak out the back way because she didn't like the thought of him being hounded by the press.

'She says—'

'I heard enough,' Rickman interrupted. 'More than enough. Get yourselves back to base.' He hung up.

'Naomi,' Rickman said, 'take your friend to one of the consultation rooms till we sort this out.' He handed her the slip of paper. 'Make sure this VIN is circulated to Traffic and Foot Patrols. I'll bring DS Foster up to speed.'

Hart opened the office door but Ormerod hung back.

'Are you still here?' Rickman said.

'Um, I left my cab out front.'

'Park it in the car park at the back.' Rickman turned to Hart. 'Get him settled, then I want you here — and focused.' He waited until she had closed the door after her. 'Bloody idiot.'

Foster rubbed his temples. 'Unconventional but effective, you've got to admit. Everyone knows taxis are the best surveillance network in the city — I mean, they're always on the job, and what could be more anonymous than a black cab?'

'She put a civilian at risk, Lee.'

'If I know Naomi, she told him to keep an eye out — if Ormerod decided to turn amateur sleuth, it's not her fault. And assuming Maitland's gone after Carter, if we find Maitland, Carter's as good as in the bag.'

'That's a lot of "ifs",' Rickman said. 'Added to which, surveillance have lost Maitland, and we've no line on Carter.'

'Yeah, but we wouldn't've known Maitland had gone walkabout if it wasn't for Naomi,' Foster said.

Rickman couldn't argue with that. He picked up the receiver again and asked for DI Dwight's mobile number. He keyed it in but hung up after a few moments. 'Switched off,' he said.

'So, d'you want to bring me up to speed?' Foster asked.

'You know most of it. Kim Lindermann is willing to testify against Carter, but we have to find him first. I took Hart with me to talk to his wife.'

'Shake the tree, see what falls out?'

'That's the theory. She's playing the injured innocent, but I'm hoping our chat will panic her into making an unguarded move.'

Foster saw a tightly wound energy in his friend. Nothing, so far, had gone their way — that wasn't Jeff Rickman's fault, but he knew that Rickman would be blaming himself.

The DCI headed for the door. 'Gormley's on telephone surveillance,' he said. 'Give him a ring, will you? See if he's heard anything. I'll be in Dwight's MIR.'

* * *

The drugs inquiry Major Incident Room had the slightly cheesy smell of a schoolboys' changing room: aftershave overtones, with base notes of sweat and foot odour. One plump DC sat in the midst of littered desks and discarded coffee cups.

'Where's DI Dwight?' Rickman demanded.

'Some community bash?'

'Any sign of DS Cass?'

He grimaced. 'Day off?'

'So, this it?' Rickman asked. '*You're* the drugs inquiry team?'

The DC nodded. He had the disconsolate look of a schoolboy landed with detention on the last day of term. 'Apart from DS Foster,' he added.

Rickman turned and saw that Foster had caught up with him.

'Gormley's not on phone surveillance,' he said. 'The lad on duty hasn't heard anything.'

'Where did Gormley go?' Rickman demanded.

The DC's look of consternation was pitiful. Rickman tried again, hoping for one small item of information that might help. 'Who's on the duty rota?'

The DC perked up a bit. This was a question he could answer. 'Smithie was in, and Williams. They pissed off — I mean, they left,' he corrected himself, eyeing Rickman, a pink flush on his plump cheeks.

'When?' Rickman asked.

'About an hour ago?' His apologetic tone was beginning to grate.

'Did they say where they were going?'

'Smithie got a call at his desk. Him and Williams went out the room for a few minutes. When they came back, they grabbed their coats and legged it.'

Rickman exchanged a look with Foster. 'What's your name?'

The DC gave him a look of alarm. 'Kirkbride, sir.'

'Got a mobile number for Cass?'

Kirkbride nodded.

'Use it,' Rickman said. 'Call Smith and Williams as well. Find out what they're up to.'

'They're not gonna tell the likes of me, boss.'

Rickman ignored the self-pity in his voice. 'Tell them surveillance has lost Maitland. Tell them he might have gone after Carter — they'll listen.'

'Oh, man . . .'

'What?' Rickman asked.

'Smithie said something about Carter.'

'What — exactly?'

'I didn't hear it, just the name.'

'Who was the call from?'

Kirkland was sweating. 'I—'

'An informant? Police? Come on, man, give us some bloody clue!'

Kirkland shook his head. 'I was working on my reports, boss. I didn't really—'

'Forget it,' Rickman said. 'Keep trying those numbers. If you get through — find me.'

He glanced at Hart, who had returned and was hovering by the door.

'Have you contacted Tunstall yet?' he asked.

'He's over in Burscough,' she said. 'Playing rugby. I left an urgent message at the club house for him to call me.' She followed them out of the room. 'D'you think Smith and Williams have gone after Carter?'

Rickman gave a brief nod. 'And with Maitland off the radar, they might just create a few casualties on their road to glory.'

'So what's the plan?' Foster asked.

Rickman thought for a moment. 'Hart — you're with me. Lee — I want the full team in, Dwight's lot and ours. If this goes into meltdown, we'll need as many bodies as we can muster.'

Rickman strode to the end of the corridor with Hart close behind him, and onto the concrete stairs of the fire escape. Since the smoking ban, this staircase had the permanent reek of cigarette smoke. As they trotted up to the top floor, Rickman took out a bunch of keys. Along the main corridor, then through a locked door into a cul-de-sac, housing three offices. This area smelled unused and slightly damp.

'The phone tap on Carter's home phone,' Rickman said, in answer to Hart's unspoken question. He unlocked one of the inner doors and went in.

The room was about twelve feet by ten, the ceiling plaster was bubbled and discoloured by damp, and there was a large, rusty stain on the grey carpet tiles. A detective constable sat at a desk on the far side of the room, under the open window. Headphones on, notebook at his right hand, a flask of coffee close by, he was slumped sideways on his chair at an awkward angle. As they walked across the room, the man's pen slipped across the page and his head nodded.

Rickman placed a hand on his shoulder and the DC yelled.

'Jesus! Don't you fucking knock?' He ripped off the headphones and turned, his eyes widening with horror as he realised who he'd just sworn at. 'Sorry, boss — I thought it was—'

'Never mind,' Rickman said. 'Have you picked up anything of interest — or did you sleep right through your shift?' The man looked, panicked, at the monitor on his desk. 'There's nothing happening, boss. I told DS Foster I would've—'

'Woken up if you heard a voice on the line?' Rickman stared at him until he flushed brick-red. 'Did you make a call to DC Smith, about an hour ago?'

'*I* was the one got the call, boss. Gormless — that's DC Gormley—' He stopped, realising that he was about to land a colleague in trouble.

'Gormley was on duty,' Rickman said. 'I know that. What I don't know is why either of you saw fit to change the duty rota without permission.'

'He said he'd been called away by DS Cass, boss. Said it was an emergency.'

'I'll bet it was.' He might have known Cass was behind this — payback for his reprimand over his sloppy work or taking a gamble on playing the hero, bringing Carter in. But Rickman had seen Jasmine's body, had watched Dr Griffith perform the post-mortem on Mark Davies, had listened to Kim Lindermann describe what Carter had done to her. Carter was every bit as dangerous as Maitland. More dangerous because he seemed so harmless.

Rickman glanced at the monitor. 'I'll need a copy of everything from for the last three hours. Stick it on a thumb drive.'

The constable stared at him blankly.

'Now would be good,' Rickman said.

The man fumbled for a memory stick and began high-lighting and copying files. Moments later, Rickman passed the thumb drive to Hart and she was out of the door and running. The officer shrugged his shoulders apologetically.

'Put your headphones back on,' Rickman said. 'And drink the damn coffee.'

When he got back to the Incident Room, Kirkbride was on his mobile. 'Anything?' Rickman asked.

Kirkbride looked at him, round-eyed and fearful. 'They're not answering, boss.'

'Call DS Cass.'

Kirkbride's distress increased. 'DI Dwight was trying to reach him all morning, sir. He—'

'Call him,' Rickman said. Moments later, Hart appeared at the door, her face pale and grim.

'I've had a listen, and something weird's going on here, boss.' She placed a printout of the list of audio files on the desk in front of him and pointed to the first file name. 'This set of files logs calls from 07:00 hours to 13:00 hours. And this one runs from 14:30 hours. There's no audio in between.'

An hour and a half of telephone surveillance was unac-counted for. 'It looks like our visit to Mrs Carter had the desired effect,' Rickman said.

'Yeah,' Hart agreed. 'What's the bet she called hubby before we'd even pulled out of the driveway?'

He glanced at Kirkbride. 'Have you heard from Cass yet?'

'He's still not answering, sir.' Kirkbride's voice was tremulous, his round face as red as a match head.

Rickman snatched up a phone handset from the near-est desk and keyed the extension for the surveillance room. 'When did Gormley call you in?' he asked.

'Um, two o' clock, boss.' He sounded wide awake now.

Rickman muttered a curse and hung up.

'Gormley, Williams and Smith left just after two p.m.,' he said. 'Maitland has a forty-five-minute start on them. They're walking into a bloodbath, Naomi.'

'D'you want me to trawl right through the recordings?'

He thought for a moment. 'Give them to Kirkbride — Gormley probably took anything of interest, but it's worth checking. I want you to call Mrs Carter. Tell her if she ever wants to see her husband alive again, she needs to tell us where he is.'

He took out his mobile, dialling the number for the Armed Response Unit as he spoke: there wasn't much he could tell them right now, but he could at least put them on alert. His next call was to DS Maynard. 'I need to know if Carter was the informant on Operation Snowplough.'

'Jeff,' Maynard said in a tone of weary admonishment, 'we went through this less than an hour ago. I told you that I would inform Customs of your concerns, and I have done.'

'Sir, Carter is now our prime suspect in the murders of Jasmine Elliott and Mark Davis and the manslaughter of Bryony Elliott.'

'You made all of this clear in our earlier discussion, and I put all of the facts to them,' Maynard said. 'But the evidence is circumstantial.'

'If Customs knows where he is, they need to tell us now,' Rickman insisted, raising his voice over Maynard's continued protestations. 'Maitland left Liverpool with half an army. He's had nearly two hours start on us. DS Cass is unreachable, and my guess is he's leading three other officers into a gun battle.'

Maynard muttered a curse. When he spoke again, he sounded not only weary but old. 'All right,' he said. 'Carter *was* the informant. He fell off the radar just after seven p.m. on Thursday.'

Just after the North West Newsbrief *special,* Rickman thought. *Just after Maitland found out that Mark hadn't escaped with his money, because by then, Mark was dead.*

'I'll get onto Customs now,' Maynard continued. 'Tell them they need to let us know immediately if he gets in touch.'

Rickman broke the connection and scrolled down his mobile contacts list as he walked down to his own MIR. A couple of civilian staff were working the hotline at the far end of the room, but the only CID present were Foster, seated at one desk, and Hart at another. She looked up as he came in, her ice-blue eyes darkened by worry. 'No answer from the Carter home, sir.'

'Where's she based?'

'Grassendale.'

This was an exclusive, eighteenth-century, gated riverside development at the south end of the city.

'Get on to the area inspector — ask him to send a couple of uniforms to wait at the house.' A muscle twitched in his jaw. 'Tell them to bring her in if she won't cooperate.'

'No luck with Customs?' Foster asked, covering the mouthpiece as he spoke.

'They lost Carter on Thursday night,' Rickman said.

Foster cursed. 'So that's it. All we can do now is wait.'

But Rickman was sick of waiting. 'There's one more avenue I can try.'

Foster spoke into the phone. 'Get here as soon as.' He hung up. 'You're not thinking about calling Eames?' he demanded. 'Jeff, think about it — if Maitland knows where Carter is, he probably got it from Tommy Eames. Tommy could've told us, but he didn't. I don't think he ever intended to — he'd rather take his chances with Maitland. I'll bet he only came to us in case he couldn't get Carter's address and needed a safe place for a bit. And if he *is* in touch with Maitland, you'd be warning him our lads are on the way.'

Rickman's finger hovered over the dial key. 'With any luck, Maitland will clear out, rather than risk a confrontation with the police.'

'Since when did we have any luck on this case?' Foster said.

'We've no location and no means of contacting Cass or the officers with him,' Rickman said. 'Eames is our only link to Carter. What choice do I have, Lee?'

Foster stared at him for several long seconds. 'Shit,' he said. 'Do what you have to do.'

Rickman hit the key. 'Tommy Eames?' There was no response, but Rickman thought he heard traffic noise. 'Tommy, this is DCI Jeff Rickman.'

'I know who it is,' Eames's voice rasped back. 'You're on my contacts list. Every time you ring, a little picture of a pig flashes up to remind me what you look like.'

Arrogance or bravado? Had Tommy made his peace with Maitland, or did he feel he was far enough away to be out of danger? Either way, he evidently felt that Rickman no longer had anything to offer.

'I thought we had an understanding,' Rickman said.

'I don't know what you're on about.'

'Don't worry,' Rickman said. 'I'm not taping our conversation. I need your help.'

Eames made a short sound — a cough or a laugh. 'Forget it, Rickman. I'm off the hook, now. All debts settled.'

'So why are you running, Tommy?' There was a silence, except for the steady hum in the background. *Traffic*, Rickman thought. *Definitely traffic.*

'What d'you want anyway?' Eames asked.

'Carter's address.'

'How would I know that?'

'Maitland thought you'd know it. Now Maitland is missing — I think he's gone after Carter.' Eames said nothing. 'You said it yourself, Tommy. All debts settled.'

'Let's say, for the sake of argument, you're right. Why would I wanna piss off Mr Maitland all over again by feeding you information?'

'You think he's really forgiven you, Tommy? Because that's wishful thinking. Maitland is the type who never forgives, never forgets,' Rickman said. 'He expects loyalty, and what you did was anything but.'

'I never done nothing.'

Rickman had expected a denial, but Eames sounded defensive enough to convince him he was on the right track. 'You did *nothing*? You expect me to believe that? Maitland killed Michael Aldiss just so *you* would know how disappointed he was in you.'

'No,' Eames said. 'No — I told you — Graham never *accused* me of nothing. He just asked where Carter was.'

'And why would he think that you, of all people, would know where Carter would hide out?'

'I told you, we worked together on Rob's legit business interests.'

'Carter is on the run from *Rob Maitland*, Tommy. Why would Maitland think he'd trust you enough to tell you where he was holed up?' Rickman saw Lee Foster and Naomi Hart watching him avidly. Even hearing only one side of the conversation, they clearly felt that he was on to something. Rickman felt a spurt of excitement.

'You and Carter made a deal.' *It had to be*, he thought. *Maitland's assets are tied up in business and stock — legitimate and illegitimate — Carter would need someone to facilitate the realisation of those assets.*

Eames remained stubbornly silent.

'You made a deal, and Maitland found out about it.'

'You're pissing in the wind, Rickman.'

'I don't think so, Tommy. If Carter had got Maitland out of the way, you'd take a bigger cut from the coffee houses.'

'Now why would Bernie the Books do that for me?'

'Same reason he came to you five years ago, when you were running a failing coffee chain — only this time, instead of laundering drugs money, he'd be siphoning cash through your books to off-shore accounts in his own name. Fake refurbs, new shops that existed only on paper. He'd have his retirement fund set up in no time.'

Foster grinned, appreciating the simple logic in his reasoning, and Hart nodded her agreement.

'You're in the wrong business, Mr Rickman,' Eames said. 'You've got a bent mind.'

'Think on this, Tommy,' Rickman said. 'Carter is bound to have his own protection. If Maitland *has* gone after him, it's anyone's guess who'll come out of it alive.' Eames stayed silent, and Rickman hammered the point home. 'Like I said, Maitland isn't a man to forgive and forget — if he survives, he'll come looking for you. On the other hand, if *Carter's* the one who walks away, it won't take him long to work out that it was you who turned him over to Maitland. Either way, you're screwed.'

The silence continued a moment. Eames's breathing was heavy and had an odd catch in it. *His cracked ribs, giving him hell*, Rickman thought. 'Look,' he said. 'I'm just trying to straighten out a mess here.' Honesty might work where threats hadn't. 'Help me, I'll see you get protection.'

Eames answered with a snort.

'Police are on their way out to wherever it is Carter's holed up,' Rickman went on. 'Only they're going in half-arsed — you see, they don't know Maitland like you do.'

'Maybe you should tell them.'

'I wish I could.'

Another silence. 'You lost your own surveillance team?'

Rickman ignored the question. 'You do know where he is, don't you?'

Eames didn't answer.

'Help me,' Rickman said.

'You know what your lot come up with?' Eames said — meaning Crimestoppers, witness relocation. 'A shitty flat on a sink estate in Leeds.'

Oh, hell. That explained everything — Tommy had decided to take his chances with Maitland, rather than die a slow death in a grey inner-city slum. Rickman couldn't say he blamed him. 'Tommy—'

But Eames wasn't in the mood to listen. He raised his voice, almost shouting down the line. 'Have you seen my house?

It's a five-bed Edwardian villa on the edge of Calderstones. So, you tell me — are your lads having a laugh or what?'

'I'll talk to them,' Rickman said. 'I'll get you a European relocation.'

'I thought there wasn't no guarantees.' Eames was no fool, he knew the system.

'This is different,' Rickman lied. 'You'd be saving cops' lives — I could make it happen.'

'On my side of the fence,' Eames said, '"saving cops' lives" is a sure way to getting kneecapped.'

So much for appealing to his better instincts. 'Okay, Tommy, here's what will happen,' Rickman said. 'A police officer — maybe more than one — will get themselves killed. And when they do, it won't be Maitland or Carter you'll have to look out for, it'll be me. Because I *will* find you, and I'll charge you with obstruction and conspiracy to murder — and that's before I even get started on your money laundering activities.'

'You can't do that! I'm the victim here!' Eames's voice, coarsened by chain smoking, was made even harsher by fear.

'You're withholding material information, which makes you one of the bad guys, Tommy.'

'What you gonna do?' he demanded. 'Put me in prison?' His voice was a bronchitic rasp. 'You can't frighten me, Mr Rickman. I'm dealing with a psychopath who threw a kid off the roof of a car park like he was chucking away an empty sweet wrapper.' Rickman heard the quiver in Eames's voice and tried persuasion one last time.

'Michael Aldiss didn't deserve to die. I know you'd have stopped that if you could.'

'Yeah, well I couldn't. And that was when I was still on the payroll.'

'Tommy,' he said. 'We can work this out — talk to me.'

'Maitland would carve my tongue out and make me eat it.'

'Okay then, listen—'

'You had your chance, Rickman,' Eames interrupted. 'You blew it. I'm dumping this phone, so don't waste your time tracing it.'

Rickman heard a sudden blast of noise: the crack of a seventy-mile-per-hour wind against the mobile phone's mike, the roar of traffic, then nothing.

CHAPTER 47

Nobody was late. They mustered at three p.m. in the super-market car park, Cass's most trusted colleagues, fizzing with adrenaline and primed for action. This was the edge of Merseyside, the outskirts of the suburbs, bordering flat fields, empty at this time of year. Beyond that, nothing but meres, marshes and dunes all the way to the coast. Wright and Gormley were smoking cigarettes, as they always did when-ever they escaped the smoke-free environment of the station. Williams leaned against the boot of his car, the constant drumbeat of his hands the only indication of nerves. Cass had half-expected Smith would be a no-show. But there he was, standing a little apart from the others, his arms crossed, his long, serious face pale and worried-looking. Smithie was a follower — although he whinged a bit at the sidelines, when it came down to it, he usually did as he was told.

Cass hitched his trousers and sauntered over to the group, gathering them round, secretly revelling in the curi-ous glances of the shoppers, the mums anxiously pulling their children out of reach as they passed the group of tough-look-ing men.

'Here's how it'll go down,' Cass began.

'Sarge?'

'What, Smithie? You forget to turn off the gas at home or something?' The others laughed. 'He looks like a bus driver with piles, doesn't he?' More laughter, but Smith's anxiety apparently overrode his embarrassment.

'DI Dwight.' Smith's gaze swept the group, as though he might find their team leader skulking in the background. 'You said you'd fetch him.'

Cass looked at Williams, who shifted his weight from one foot to the other and gave a little sigh.

'The DI had already left when I got to the meeting,' Cass lied. 'He's not answering his phone, so it must be switched off.' He glanced around the group. 'How *will* we cope?' He camped it up a bit and Gormley chuckled. The looks of quiet disdain on the others' faces reassured him he'd have no argument from them.

Smith frowned, avoiding eye contact. 'We could ring the venue — pass on a message. I think we should tell him, Sarge.'

'So he can call the local focus group to evaluate the disruption to the Saturday badger watch?' Gormley snorted, and encouraged, Cass continued. 'Or maybe we need a risk assessment on the possible damage by police cars to night-flying insects.' The rest of the posse were grinning. 'We could be there and back with Carter in tow while Larry the Lamb's still dithering. You know my motto, lads: JFDI.'

'Just fucking do it!' the other three chimed together, laughing.

But Smith wasn't quite ready to admit defeat. 'There's a contract out on Bernie Carter. What if he's armed?'

The rest of the men shuffled a bit and exchanged glances. They had all considered the possibility — Cass knew his lads — but hearing someone say it was like bringing a hex down on them.

'He's an *accountant*, Smithie.'

'Rob Maitland is after his blood,' Smith said. 'If I was him, I'd hire some serious protection. And let's face it, he's been in the game long enough to know where to look.'

Cass saw an opportunity to ditch the lads and warn Carter the cops were onto him before the cavalry rode in. 'I'll go on my own if you're that bothered.'

'No way.' Gormley folded his arms, and Williams shook his head vehemently.

'We're a team, Sarge,' Wright said.

Cass shrugged. It was worth a try. 'Okay. It's not like we have to go in all *Die Hard*. We evaluate the situation, sit tight and call for armed backup, if it's needed. I mean . . .' He forced a laugh. 'We're not stupid, right?'

Smith flushed, guessing correctly that the 'stupid' crack was aimed at him. Point successfully made, Cass turned slightly away from Smithie, excluding him and addressing the rest.

'Carter's not stupid, neither,' Cass said. 'He'll know we're monitoring his home phone, and after his missus called the landline, he'll assume we're on our way. The worst you'll need to brace yourselves for is the chance that he's already packed up and left by the time we get there.' He prayed to God that Carter had the sense to get out.

'Just so's we're straight . . .' He waited, drawing the silence out. 'Carter is a possible witness, *not* a suspect. We're not gonna arrest him, we just want to ask him a few questions — and if he'll turn against Maitland, we take him into protective custody and earn ourselves about a million brownie points.'

He kept his voice flat, his tone neutral as he went on. 'He's lying low in a farmhouse near Ormskirk. Smithie?' He remained with his back half-turned to Smith and waited.

Smith sighed, reached inside his car, and came out with a tablet. They gathered around as Smith called up an OS map and pinched and expanded it to show the details of the target property.

'The farmhouse is here,' he said. 'Access is via this road.' He traced the yellow line back to the arterial red of the A59. 'This is Grimes Hill Road. This track runs west off Grimes Hill Road about fifty yards from the road to the farm. It's the *only* road.' He looked up at the faces. 'Now, don't be fooled by the name, lads. It may be called Grimes Hill, but this is

Ormskirk — flatlands — a speed bump qualifies as a hill. You can see five miles all round, so they'll see us coming.'

'What d'you mean, "*They'll* see us coming"?' Williams demanded, frowning.

'Like I said, he's not going to be alone.' Smith's expression said, *Finally you're getting the point.*

'Do me a *favour*, Smithie,' Cass said. 'He's an *accountant*, not Mr Big. And it's a good thing he'll see us from a distance, 'cos he'll see we've got nothing to hide.' An idea struck him, and he put it to the men as if he'd planned it all along. 'And of course we're only taking two cars. That way, we won't look like a lynch mob.'

Gormley and Wright nodded. They liked it.

He grinned. 'You know what — he'll probably welcome us with open arms.' He spread his own hands to emphasise the simplicity of their mission. A subtle shift of stance and the posse realigned themselves physically and mentally with him. *Good*, he thought. *Bloody brilliant.*

'What's this at the back of the farm?' Williams tilted the tablet in Smith's hand and pointed to a green, dotted area on the map.

'A wood,' Smith said. 'There's nothing but farmland the other side of that.'

'Everyone clear?' Cass said, eager to get going before anyone else expressed doubts.

Gormley dropped his cigarette and stepped on it.

Wright pitched his own cigarette butt. 'Let's just fucking do it.' He had that glint in his eye that said he was terrified and loving it.

'Smithie, you're with me.' Smith had done a good enough job of spooking the others after he'd got them keyed up and ready — Cass wasn't about to let him finish the job. 'Gormley, Wright and Williams, you can follow in Gormley's car.'

Gormley raised his eyebrows. His BMW was his pride and joy.

'It's the biggest we've got — and the fastest,' Cass said, knowing that flattery would be the best way around him. 'If

Carter tries to break for it, we'll need something with a bit of poke.'

Gormley smirked. 'You heard what he said, lads — mine's the biggest we've got.' He should have left it there, but he couldn't resist adding, 'Just make sure you wipe the crud off your shoes before you get in.'

Williams walked around to the passenger door, grumbling that there was nothing wrong with his shoes, but Gormley made both him and Wright check the soles of one, then the other, before unlocking the doors.

Smith avoided his eye, but his expression gave Cass the faintest hint of foreboding. 'Hey,' he said. 'Is everybody wearing a Met Vest?'

The glint faded from Wright's eye, and Gormley and Williams stopped bickering.

'I thought you said there's no risk?' Smith sounded almost spitefully pleased.

'I *said* we're not stupid.'

The men exchanged glances, understanding the need to take precautions, then Gormley shrugged. 'I'm wearing.'

'Yeah,' Wright said.

Williams looked at him like Cass had asked if everyone had been to the toilet before they left. 'Duh,' he said.

'Smithie?'

Smith met his gaze, and Cass saw resentment and fear. 'Yeah,' he said.

'Good.' Cass turned and walked to his own car before any of the posse had the chance to read him. *So, it's just me then.* He had driven straight from the city centre and was dressed in Saturday civvies — which didn't include a Kevlar undershirt. So what? He didn't need to be a hero. He just wanted to be first on the scene, tell Carter to get the hell out and stay one step ahead of Rickman.

He had tried both Carter's mobile and the farmhouse landline by the time Smith had folded up the map and slid in beside him. Carter still wasn't answering.

CHAPTER 48

Bernie Carter looked out through the French windows of his rented farmhouse. In the short time he had been in this landscape, he had discovered an affinity with its broad skies and flat plains. It was mid-afternoon, but the sun was already beginning to lower, casting sharp shadows through the trees. Carter had been raised in the city. His experience of the countryside was limited to a single skiing trip in the Alps as a schoolboy. His parents had no interest in seaside or country walks — that sort of thing was all very well for *other* people, they'd said, but not for their boy, not for Bernard, who was bright and perceptive, a sensitive child. A prodigy. So they'd holidayed in European cities, seeking culture, punting on the canals of Venice and Amsterdam, visiting galleries and muse-ums in Vienna and Rome, trying to make amends for the few short months of childhood neglect when the new baby had snatched their time and energy and attention from him.

At university, he had experienced again the shock of being ignored. In school, he was head boy, top of his academic classes, but in the maelstrom of university life he was one in fourteen thousand, insignificant, struggling to be noticed. For though Carter was able, he was unremarkable, and his parents had failed, in their efforts to enrich his cultural life, to provide him with the language of contemporary music or TV and computer games. Set against the exotic shimmer of the antipodes and the Far East, his travels in Europe seemed colourless and insipid. He resented his parents for not having initiated him to this more colourful world, even though the thought of Bali or Australia, sweaty and unconfined, secretly appalled him.

He was polite, clean, orderly, yet girls his own age shunned him as small-minded, immature, obsessive. He could talk about books, architecture and art, yet they shrugged their shoulders and turned away.

So he watched them in the students' union bars and the night clubs, a half-embarrassed, half-vicious smile on his face, fascinated by their naked flesh, excited to catch a glimpse of the occasional tattoo — a rose just visible on an exposed shoulder, a butterfly kissing the base of a neck — low key, tasteful, for this was the early nineties, and female body art was not yet entirely acceptable in educated circles. It was during these sessions in bars and at concerts that he first began to fantasise about marking girls' skin.

University, marriage and the birth of his children had tutored him in the harsh reality that he was not the centre of everything. His daughters caused a terrible conflict within him — didn't he create them? Weren't they reflections of him? He loved them with all the passion that he loved himself, and yet they would not always bend to his will. They were noisy and demanded more than he was capable of giving, refused to behave as objects to be placed thus and thus. Exasperated, he left them in the care of his wife, and worked hard in Maitland's employ, craving the compliance of numbers, the predictability of spreadsheets, the comfort of equations. Through the manipulation of numbers, he found a certain equilibrium.

Maitland was a man who thrived on excitement and danger, so although initially he had scrutinised the accounts, asking Carter to explain this or that calculation, he soon became bored. Carter had earned the respect of his employer, because while Maitland did not understand the symmetry of numbers, he understood the power of money, and he knew that Bernard Carter made his money work hard. What Maitland didn't know was that his cash worked harder than the books ever showed.

The men closest to Maitland treated Carter with respect, because they saw that Maitland treated him with respect. The others — those further from the source of power — mistook him for someone they might disrespect and mock. They called him 'Bernie the Books', commented on the way he dressed, disparaged the careful checks he made on Maitland's stock, ridiculing his meticulous attention to detail. At such times, Carter turned to the passive creatures who would do his bidding for drugs or money and they suffered his pain for him.

Yet pain was only one variable of a complex equation. His purpose was not merely to inflict suffering. This, unlike the mathematical formulae of his working life, was an imbalanced equation, a Gestalt, one in which the emotional and intellectual outcomes exceeded the basic input of pain plus scarring. He created art as well as provoking fear, and he changed the girls not only psychologically but physically, irrevocably, so that when they saw themselves they would think of Bernard Carter, and not smile or laugh or sneer. They might hide their scars under long sleeves and full-length skirts, but it was Carter who had indirectly imposed their choice of clothing on them, who maintained control of them long after he had forgotten their names, and thus became godlike in his influence and omnipresence.

The simple truth that lay beneath all of his rationalisation was more mundane, though he never would admit it: he wanted — literally — to leave his mark, like the seven-year-old boy, writing his name again and again on the under-surface of a dining table.

Not that he was without feeling. He loved his family as adjuncts to himself. He even regretted that in the first fevered moments of realisation, the first terrible hours of knowing that his life was forfeit, he had screamed at his wife, frightened his daughters, thinking only that he must get away — must consolidate his capital and then leave. He was tormented by that now. The fury, the cruel things he had said. His wife's call, only hours earlier, had been an opportunity to take back some of those harsh words. And now, watching the sun changing tint as it dropped towards the horizon, seeing its peachy light warm the frosted oaks, he wished he had.

He sighed. This cheap philosophising was the reason he found himself in this predicament. In the wide expanse of fields, in the sweep of land and sky, walkers, a farmer, even the postman labouring along the lanes on his bicycle seemed small and insignificant. The physical perspective was reassuring, and he had fancied himself invisible, forgetting that in an empty canvas, the eye is always drawn to the human form.

Maitland spoke again. 'I asked you a question.'

Carter found it hard to listen. His ears rang — from the gunfire or the wound to his head — he wasn't sure. His head wound seeped steadily onto his collar, slowly congealing, his nose was almost certainly broken and yet he felt serene.

Maitland held a gun in his right hand. There was blood on the grip — Carter's. Carter disliked guns, preferring the subtle finesse of a knife. He relished the hiss of steel slicing through flesh, like a pre-echo of the victim's gasp of pain.

He looked across the room at his two bodyguards, both bound and bruised. Lowe was panting and pale, bleeding from a bullet wound to his shoulder but sullenly defiant. Quinn, wild-eyed, struggled against his bonds.

Carter wanted to tell him to be still, that his troubles were over. He felt a species of pity for Quinn and Lowe. This wasn't their fight — not really — but they would suffer nevertheless.

Maitland followed Carter's gaze to Quinn, who fought the rope till it bit into his flesh.

'Is he distracting you?' Maitland took three steps across the room and shot Quinn in the head. His body jerked, then relaxed, subsiding at last.

Maitland returned to the chair, where Carter was tied, hand and foot. 'Now, do I have your undivided attention?'

Carter heard laughter behind him. Maitland's men, four of them. Graham was there, and three others he didn't recognise — a bald guy and two younger men, pumped up on steroids and their faith in their own invulnerability. Their job was done for the moment, they were playing cards at the dining table while they awaited further instructions. This task Maitland had reserved for himself.

Maitland rested the barrel of the gun against Carter's cheek. It burned and he pulled away, sending a bolt of pain through his head. His ankles were strapped to the chair legs, his wrists to the wooden arms. Maitland placed one foot on the seat, tilting it a few inches backwards.

'This isn't necessary,' Carter said.

Maitland thought for a moment. 'You steal my money, walk off with six million pounds' worth of heroin . . .'

Carter shook his head and Maitland tapped him hard on the nose with the barrel of the gun. A starburst of light exploded behind Carter's eyes and he yelped in pain.

'Don't lie to me,' Maitland said. 'And don't interrupt.'

'I made you millions,' Carter said, avoiding a direct denial. 'I developed a portfolio of legitimate land and property ownership which is the envy of developers across the north of England.'

Maitland leaned forward, and the chair tilted dangerously. 'You *stole* my property.' He took his foot from the chair. It teetered a moment, and Carter braced himself for the crack of his skull on the parquet floor, then, miraculously, the chair fell forward onto all four feet again. Maitland paced to the window, barely glancing at Quinn's body.

'Why?' he asked. Meaning why did he keep the drugs, why didn't he tell Maitland that he'd found Mark and killed him. He sounded reasonable — disappointed and hurt — but reasonable.

'I did as you asked,' Carter said. 'I found him.'

'The Elliott girl told you?' There was no judgement in Maitland's tone, he simply wanted to get the facts straight.

Carter shook his head. 'She wouldn't give him up.'

Maitland turned to face him. 'Maybe she didn't know where he was.'

Carter shrugged. Wasn't that just what Mark had said? In truth he had known ten minutes after he first confronted her that Jasmine was entirely ignorant of what Mark had done. 'You told us you wanted Mark hurt.'

Maitland moved closer, rested his hands on his knees, and stooped to look into Carter's face, as if he was trying to peer through a dark window. Until now, Carter had found it impossible to return that steady gaze. Perhaps it was the anaesthetising effects of shock, but he was no longer afraid. He lifted his chin and stared back into Maitland's wide-set eyes.

'I'm seeing a whole new side to you, Bernie,' Maitland said. 'So. You waited at the Elliott house for Mark.'

Carter nodded.

'Why didn't you finish it then? Why follow him out to the children's home?'

'I thought he might lead me to the money.'

'And?'

Carter looked past Maitland to the windows, where the sun was sinking slowly into an early evening mist. 'He lied, like he always lied. He said he didn't have it — that it was all a big mistake. He told me he'd never even touched the bags. Said the Dutch were mad bastards — that they'd double-crossed you.'

Maitland's eyes flickered a moment, considering the possibility. 'Since the head honcho's dead,' he said, the hint of a smile on his face, 'that'd be hard to prove one way or the other.' He straightened up. 'And why would he double-cross me?'

'The police were already onto the Dutch consortium, but you were the bigger prize.' Flattery usually worked with Maitland. 'They did a deal.'

'And what was that?' Maitland asked. 'Escape a life sentence by getting their heads blown off?' There was a snort of laughter from the card players, and Maitland shifted his gaze briefly from Carter to his bodyguards.

Carter licked his lips. He had to do better than this, but his head was still bleeding, it throbbed like a sledgehammer, and his body ached from sitting immobile in the chair. Images of the real events kept interfering as he tried to piece together a story: Mark, bloodied and babbling, telling him everything in the hope that something might prove of interest. He could have crippled the lad, returned the booty to Maitland, earned himself a pat on the head. He might have found a way to explain the discrepancies in the audit, bought himself more time — but the money was too much temptation. Somehow, dealing with Maitland's accounts seemed abstract. The huge sums of money he shifted from bank account to bank account, or filtered through the espresso machines of Tommy Eames's coffee bars were merely figures in an equation. But when he'd held the money in his hands, it was too much to give away.

After Mark found Jasmine's body, he had followed the addict's erratic course through Liverpool. When Mark's battered old banger had sputtered to a halt, Carter was watching, following the boy's progress as he'd shuffled along the street, the baby in his arms. When Mark turned in to the school gates of St Francis Xavier, Carter had found a tyre iron to force the boot open. No need to force the doors. Mark had left the passenger door unlocked.

Carter toted the bags to his Audi and slid into the passenger seat. He'd balanced a stack of twenty-pound notes in one hand and a block of uncut heroin in the other, seeing a gleaming Merc in his left palm, and his daughters' education — bought and paid for — in his right. The choice was simple: Mark was systematically destroying himself anyway — all Carter did was hasten the end.

'You see what I'm saying, Bernie?' Maitland said. 'The Dutch turning on me — it just isn't plausible.'

'Of course it isn't, but it's what he said. Mark was lying — like he always lied. He tried to blame the Dutch, but he was the one who grassed you up.'

Maitland stared at him. 'Mark didn't have the balls.'

'He was paranoid, said you were planning to kill him. So he went to the police, did a deal.'

Maitland pulled up a chair and sat opposite Carter. 'I'm listening.'

Carter looked back at Maitland. What to tell him? What was he most likely to believe — or least likely to *dis*believe?

'He was high on something,' Carter said. 'Came at me like a wild thing. Completely off his head.' The reality was that Mark had crawled towards him, his fingers digging into the damp sludge of plaster dust and accumulated filth. His pelvis was shattered: Carter had felt it crack under the heel of his shoe, yet Mark had found the strength from somewhere. It was fascinating how the life imperative seemed to survive long past the point at which rationality would demand release from pain and suffering — from life itself.

Mark begged him. *Take the baby. Take Bryony with you.*

An unreasoning instinct had made Carter fearful of this almost-corpse. He'd backed away, feeling the steps creak and sag under his weight. He'd gripped the rail with both hands for support, raised his foot and brought it crashing down onto the first step. It exploded in a cloud of splinters and dust. He'd slipped, overestimating the force that would be needed, had gouged his leg on a shard of wood. He took greater care with the next, keeping one foot on the next riser for balance, backing out of the basement as he broke each step, and with it, any chance of escape.

By the time Carter reached the top step, Mark had passed out. The torch had fallen from the stair post and shone orange-gold through the dust, like a dying sun. The child was still, the silence unnerving.

Suddenly, the timbers shifted and the building moaned, a sound almost of anguish, as if the earth was waiting to swallow them up. Carter pulled the door closed and ran.

'The little shit wouldn't talk,' he told Maitland. 'When he came at me, I had no choice.'

Maitland eyed him. 'Mark couldn't keep his mouth shut to chew his food,' he said. 'My guess is he told you everything from his National Insurance number to precisely where the drugs were stashed before you laid a finger on him.'

That was the trouble with Maitland: he was a thug, but an astute thug.

'You took my drugs, pocketed the money, figured I'd write it off as a business loss.'

'No, Rob. He died before I could—'

Carter's head whipped round so fast he felt his neck crack.

'We're not on first-name terms,' Maitland said. 'Not since you robbed me.'

The slap stung like a burn on Carter's cheek.

Maitland began pacing back and forth in front of the windows. Carter tried to follow his progress, but the constant movement made him sick. So instead, he stared into the glare of the dying sun until his eyes watered.

'Mark was an opportunist,' Maitland said. 'And not a very bright one at that. He took the bags because they were there, he was a shit-for-brains, and he thought he could get away with it.'

'He told me — he went to the police.'

'Now you're contradicting yourself. You just said he wouldn't talk.'

Carter concentrated on breathing. *Just breathe*, he told himself, *and don't say anything else that will show you up as a liar.*

Maitland stood squarely in front of the chair and placed a hand on Carter's shoulders, leaning over him. 'Mark didn't have the nous or the nuts to work out a scheme to get me out of the way *and* steal the money.' He straightened up. 'You, on the other hand, are sharp — in that weaselly way accountants are. And you'd sell your granny for a twenty-percent return on an unsecured investment.'

Carter flinched as Maitland raised his hand, but Maitland only patted him on the cheek. 'Did you think you could file me away all neat and tidy under "life sentence"?'

'You've got me wrong, boss.'

Maitland smiled. 'Now he's calling me "boss",' he said to nobody in particular. 'I'm embarrassed to admit it — I trusted you. Believed that line you spun me about Mark getting away.'

'Boss—'

'There he goes again.' This time, he looked over Carter's head, towards his men, playing cards, waiting their turn. Carter realised with increasing dread that their turn had almost come. 'I'm not your boss, Carter. Not anymore.' The way he said it made Carter think about Mark, about the night he died. About the pain and the blood.

'Somebody put the police right where they needed to be,' Maitland theorised. 'Now, we're agreed Mark didn't have the brains, and the Dutch had a vested interest in a smooth handover. That just leaves you, Bernie.'

Carter sensed that a denial might be as dangerous as an admission, so he hung his head, unable once more to meet Maitland's flat, grey stare. He closed his eyes for a moment, trying to steady himself, to think of some way out of this.

A faint draught of air made him flinch, and his eyes flew open, anticipating another blow. But Maitland was gone. He took a couple of breaths. Lowe looked almost healthy in the red wash of light from the setting sun, but he was weakening, the rise and fall of his chest barely discernible.

Maitland crashed about in the kitchen, through the doorway at the end of the hall, turning out drawers and scooping plates and hardware out of cupboards onto the floor.

'Little lies . . . big betrayals — it's all the same to me.' Maitland raised his voice over the crash of crockery. He sounded almost cheerful. He gave a grunt of satisfaction, then Carter heard the unmistakable *zing* of metal on metal.

'If I can't trust a man, he might as well be dead.' Maitland stood in the doorway, his arm relaxed at his side. In his hand, a black-handled knife with a five-inch blade. 'But you know that better than anyone, don't you, Bernie?'

Carter had arranged payments for maybe fifteen such circumstances over the years. Circumstances in which the victim had lost Rob Maitland's trust.

I'm going to die, he thought.

He tried to maintain eye contact, but the knife flashed at Maitland's side, reflecting the vivid red of the sunset like a premonition.

'Blood fluoresces, given the right treatment,' Maitland said. 'I bet that basement lit up like Blackpool Illuminations when the forensics team worked their magic on it.'

'I was trying to get your money back,' Carter said, his eyes straying to the knife again.

Maitland shook his head. 'You killed Mark to silence him and to put yourself in the clear. If his body hadn't turned up, you still would be. Ironic, isn't it? It's entrepreneurs like you and me turned this city around. Crumbling dives like Black Wood Children's Home are suddenly prime redevelopment sites. You shopped yourself, mate, with your reinvestment strategies.

'Now,' he said, suddenly brisk. 'How many slices d'you think I could take before you die of blood loss or shock?'

Two strong hands seized Carter's shoulders. He strained against them, staring wildly at the blade in Maitland's hand.

'Must be worse for you, Bernie,' Maitland said. 'Having been on the other end of it. Knowing how much pain you can inflict without actually killing a person.' He registered Carter's surprise. 'Did you think I didn't know about your arts-and-crafts sideline with the girls?'

Carter concentrated on his breathing.

'I know all about you, Bernie.'

Not all, Carter thought. *Not the bank accounts under false identities, the skimming of profits for the past ten years.*

Maitland again read something in his expression. ''Course, I didn't see this coming. Funny thing, Bernie — Rickman did. He saw it straight off. Said you'd be sitting somewhere counting your cash. Comes with the job, I suppose — lack of trust.'

Bright light shone through the windows at the front of the house, sliding up the wall to Carter's right, then across the ceiling. Carter's heart leapt. He remembered the call from his wife, his furious words when he realised she had used their home number. 'A visit from the police,' she said. 'They think you murdered that girl.'

He was packing a suitcase when Maitland forced his way into the farmhouse with four armed mercenaries. But if the police *had* picked up on the call, maybe — just *maybe* — there was a chance for him. He strained to hear the sound of a chopper, but his ears were still buzzing and booming from the gunfire.

Maitland jerked his chin towards the door and two of his men walked past Carter, weapons in hand. They turned right, towards the kitchen, heading for the rear of the house.

Maitland watched his men leave, then turned back to Carter, as if returning to a business negotiation. 'Tell you what — you give me my money, I'll make it easy for you,' he said.

Carter watched the blade as a rabbit watches a snake.

Maitland stepped forward and Carter spoke fast and low. 'When I joined the firm, you were a low-end drug peddler whose greatest ambition was to make a deal with the Mancunian Mafia.' No point in begging — he'd seen too many men try that. 'I made you a multi-millionaire.'

Maitland stopped, surprise and perhaps a grudging admiration on his face.

The police will be through that door any minute, Carter thought. *All you have to do is keep Maitland talking a little longer. Keep him talking and delay the first cut. That was always the worst.* His heart raced and he felt a tingling in his fingertips and lower limbs. 'I gave you the respect of the movers and shakers in this city.'

'I always had respect,' Maitland spat.

The threat was imminent, but Carter knew he would hear the rest. Maitland's only weakness was his need for respect, his only insecurity that he hadn't quite attained it from the business class he aspired to join.

'Don't kid yourself, Maitland.' He wound himself up to a rage. Close to collapse, Carter knew that a show of strength was his only chance of survival. Succumb to terror, and he was as good as dead.

'You were just another messy, small-time thug with more power than you knew how to handle. You spent money like a lottery winner from the Dingle, flashing it around with little sense and less taste.'

'You grassed me up because you didn't like my *style*?' Maitland seemed more puzzled than angry. 'What you did to Jasmine — was that *stylish*?'

Carter's gaze flickered towards the kitchen door. *Jesus — where are they?* How long had it been since his wife called? An hour? Two? How long could it take for the cops to trace a landline? He licked his lips, tasting blood on them.

'I grassed you up because you were too stupid to stop me.'

He waited for the first hot slice of metal through flesh, but Maitland simply nodded and the last of the four men came around to the front of the chair. It was Graham. He knelt and began to remove Carter's shoes and socks.

'I want my money. And the drugs.' Maitland unplugged a lamp, cut the flex and then carefully stripped the wires. 'When I have them, we'll talk about the cash you've been creaming off my businesses for the past ten years.'

Carter thought he had reached a plateau of fear, but now his heart began to beat so hard that he felt a sharp pain in his chest.

'You'll never find the money, the drugs — any of it.' He could barely get the words out, his breathing was so ragged.

Maitland smiled at him. 'Never say never.'

Where are the police?

Maitland pushed the plug back into the socket and held up the wire.

Jesus! Where the fuck are they?

CHAPTER 49

Cass crunched up the path to the farmhouse. Traffic at Switch Island and a couple of wrong turns had delayed them, and it was nearing nightfall by the time they found the place. He'd told the others to stay put — give him the chance to have a word with Carter, sort out some kind of game plan. Gormley's BMW idled on the rutted track beyond the sandstone wall that divided the farmyard from the house. Frost glittered on the bare stems of the rose bushes and fringed the leaves of a small shrub next to the front door. The mist that lay like poured milk over the fields was beginning to thicken. The air was still and faintly redolent of brassicas and damp clay. The only sound was the distant razz of a motorbike a few miles across the flat farmland of the Lancashire plain.

The spectacular colours of the sunset were already fading, and in the shadow of the farmhouse, dusk was gathering. Beyond the net curtains, the sitting room was visible, though faintly, as though the mist had penetrated the house. The room extended through to the back of the building. The lighting was subdued — perhaps a couple of table lamps, giving an orange glow. Cass stood to the left of the front door and peered in. Playing cards lay face down on a circular dining table near the front window, as though something had interrupted the game and the players intended to return.

Two men stood just inside the archway leading to the back section of the room. The man on the right rested his hands on something — Cass couldn't see what — a chair maybe.

The second man stood slightly side-on, his hands clasped in front of him, respectful and discreet. Carter's bodyguards, no doubt. Someone else flitted back and forth beyond the two men, shielded from view by their bulk.

He hesitated, wondering how to get their attention without creating a confrontation. His instructions were to phone ahead if he needed to come out to the farmhouse, and he wasn't supposed to come anywhere near the place unless it was life or death.

He heard footsteps behind him and spun round. 'Fuck! Smithie — didn't I tell you to wait in the car?'

Smith peered past him, through the window. 'There's three men in there, Sarge,' he whispered. 'Why don't we just call for backup?'

'Because, if we got the wrong house, we're gonna look like a bunch of dickheads and we don't want that, do we, Smithie?' Cass hissed.

Smith frowned, distracted, dipping his head, as if to get a better look inside.

'What?' Cass asked, turning back again.

'A light just went off in the back room.'

The second man knelt down. 'Think we'd better stop them before he gets the guy's kecks down.' Cass grinned, but Smith remained serious. 'For God's sake, lighten up, will you?'

A noise to their right made Smith flinch.

'Bloody hell, you're a bag of nerves, mate,' Cass exclaimed. He raised his hand to the door knocker as the second man took a step back, lifting his hands up, as if in surrender. A chair — he was definitely standing in front of a chair — and there was someone in it.

A scream tore through the quiet and Cass swore. *Maitland. It has to be Maitland. How the fuck did he find this place?*

Gormley poked his head out of the car window. 'What the fuck was that?'

Smith grabbed Cass's arm. 'We need to make that call!'

Cass hesitated. A second scream, and every hair on the back of his neck stood up.

'Police!' he yelled, and shouldered the door. It creaked but didn't give. Two figures emerged from the back of the house and Cass saw Smith reach into his inside pocket for his ID.

The night exploded in light and sound. Cass dived for cover, dragging Smith with him. 'Jesus,' he muttered. 'Jesus, they're firing on us.' All he could think was, *And I'm the only pillock not wearing a vest.*

'Police!' he screamed. 'Unarmed officers!'

Gormley jammed the BMW into reverse, accelerating back up the single-track roadway towards the main road. He misjudged the curve and the car skidded sideways off the track onto the frozen sward and got bogged down in a patch of mud.

'Go! For fuck's sake, move it!' Williams screamed.

Gunfire flashed. Shadowy figures loomed monstrous in the headlamps.

'What are you waiting for?' Wright yelled. The engine screamed but the wheels spun uselessly. One of the figures raised his arm in their direction and they ducked. Simultaneously, the tyres got a grip and the car shot backwards, spitting clods of earth and spraying gravel like lead shot.

A bullet hit the windscreen. Momentarily it held, then shattered as they hit a rut, showering Gormley and Williams with beads of glass.

Gormley revved the engine, cutting a corner off the bend of the track, crossing the grass. The car's tyres slipped and whined on the icy surface, slewing left and right.

'Jesus!' Wright yelled. 'Watch out!'

The car tilted crazily, pinning them to their seats as it thudded into a ditch. The engine revved, stalling as mud and icy water sluiced into the exhaust pipe, and for a moment there was silence. Wright groaned.

Three shots, in rapid succession. 'They're still firing!' Gormley shouted.

They piled out, Williams first. He fell, his knees and hands cracking through a thin film of ice. He gasped at the shock of freezing mud and water, then he was up and running. They stayed in the ditch, using it for cover, slipping and slithering across the ice, occasionally plunging through and cursing the cold.

At the bend, Gormley looked back at his ruined BMW, its headlamps angled skywards like searchlights.

CHAPTER 50

Rickman looked up as Foster burst into his office. 'The Comms Room's had half a dozen calls — shots heard on farmland out near Ormskirk.'

'This could be it,' Rickman said. 'Armed Response?'

'On their way.'

Kirkland came puffing into the room after Foster, his round face red and sweating. 'DC Williams just called in, sir — he's under fire.'

'Do we have a location?' Rickman demanded, already on his feet and reaching for his stab vest.

Kirkland shook his head, leaning on a chair as he tried to catch his breath. 'Got cut off.'

'See if tech support can triangulate a location based on the last signal.' Rickman was moving fast, heading for the stairs. 'Send it through as soon as you have it.'

* * *

A squad of cars barrelled through the night, sirens wailing and lights flashing. Rickman talked on the radio while Naomi Hart manoeuvred the car smoothly through rush hour traffic.

'Williams, Gormley and Wright are accounted for,' he said. 'Cass and Smith aren't.'

Hart nodded, her concentration on the road forbidding comment — they had fifteen miles to cover and traffic was heavy. Her slim figure was bulked up by a stab vest, her face pale and determined.

Foster sat forward in the back seat of the car, gripping the front seats to brace himself. 'Has Eye in the Sky found the building?' A Eurocopter had been deployed within minutes of the first emergency call.

'It's still searching the area,' Rickman said.

They blasted through the narrow streets of Walton, past tightly wedged terraces, shops, sudden flashes of open spaces and new housing, dropping to the railway line — on, jinking left. Aintree racecourse on the right, unexpected in the midst of low-cost housing — a glimpse of crumbling art deco buildings and on, to a wider arterial road and semi-detached suburbia.

Hart slowed. Ahead, a mile of traffic backed up from Switch Island. They forged a way through, weaving in and out of the lines of vehicles, narrowly missing bumpers, squeezing through impossible gaps. Drivers pulled over to make way for the whooping, flashing motorcade, and Rickman caught glances of anxious faces through windscreens.

The A49 was busy, but traffic made way for them as they swept through, trailing a swirl of mist in their wake. At previously agreed points along the main road, marked cars dropped out of the line, effectively blocking the main routes from the tangle of lanes that led to their target. More would be waiting along the A-roads that enclosed the farms and moorland to the west and north. On the map, the target area looked like a rough diamond, contained and containable, but the reality was fifty square miles of open country, and a thousand places to walk or drive out.

'That lot's wasting their time,' Foster said. 'This place is like a rabbit warren.'

'Well, doing nothing is not an option,' Rickman said.

Foster muttered an apology.

Rickman sympathised — his friend had been through some dizzying turnarounds in the past week. 'Let's just focus on getting the lads out safe.'

Foster's reply was cut off as the lead car turned hard left and Hart jammed on her brakes, dragging the steering wheel, forcing the car into a ninety-degree skid. She just made the turn, and after he'd righted himself, Foster exclaimed, 'Eat your heart out, Lewis Hamilton.'

Hart responded with the ghost of a smile.

A glimmer of bloody light remained on the horizon, but the unlit lanes in the centre of the plain seemed to suck darkness into them.

'Over there.' Foster pointed.

The twin beams of Gormley's BMW pierced the night, and above the stranded car, fading in and out through thin layers of mist, the police helicopter. The EC135 Eurocopter was kitted out with a Nightsun searchlight and thermal imaging sensors and was their best chance of locating the shooters if they'd made a break on foot into the surrounding countryside, but if the mist thickened to a fog, they would have to return to base.

Rickman switched channels and spoke directly to the police air observer, who, seated next to the pilot, would maintain communications. 'Echo Charlie four four. DCI Rickman,' he said. 'What've you got?'

'Still scanning the area.' The officer's voice was blurred by radio static and the whine of the chopper's engine. 'No sign of DS Cass or DC Smith. They could still be in the house.'

The notion that two police officers might be in Rob Maitland's hands burned like molten sulphur in the pit of Rickman's stomach.

'DI Hammond, sir,' a second voice cut in. 'ARU — I've got armed officers moving in on woodland to the south of the property.' He spoke with a faint Scottish burr.

'Have you had any response from the house?' Rickman asked.

'Nothing.' The inspector's voice was almost drowned out by the buzz of the chopper. 'I'd like to send officers in.'

'I don't want anyone going in blind.' Rickman radioed the chopper again. 'Echo Charlie four four, can you shout the house?'

Hart nudged the car onto a broad strip of grass at the edge of the road, joining an array of vehicles — marked and unmarked police cars, a marked police SUV, two vans and, well behind the cordon, two ambulances.

'*You — in the house.*' The Eurocopter's Skyshout system had been designed for major evacuations. It was ten times more powerful than an average stereo on full volume, and had no trouble making itself heard over the clatter of the rotor blades. '*Armed police have the building surrounded. Put down your weapons and come out of the house in single file. Keep your hands visible at all times.*'

They waited.

'They're long gone, boss,' Foster said. 'They wouldn't've hung about once they knew they were shooting at cops, would they?'

Rickman wasn't so sure. He switched channels. 'DI Hammond?'

'Sir.'

'Can you get listening devices in place?'

'Will do,' Hammond said.

Rickman stepped out of the car, holding the passenger door open while Hart scrambled after him. The marked cars nearer to the house had turned off their lights to avoid becoming targets, and Rickman and his team shielded behind their own car as the helicopter buzzed and circled overhead.

Rickman thought he saw movement by the house and his pulse quickened.

'*Keep your hands raised!*' the tannoy boomed.

'Someone's coming out.' Hart stared intently at a spot to the right of the farmhouse.

'I don't see anyone,' Foster said.

The downdraught of the chopper blades churned the air, sending frost whirling like flakes of snow. At last, Rickman saw him — a natty figure dressed in chinos and a sports jacket. He had both hands raised. In his right, his police badge. 'Cass,' he breathed.

DS Cass shouted something and pointed towards a low wall to his left. The helicopter rotated slightly, directing the Nightsun at a few scrubby bushes. Nothing moved. Cass walked forward, still yelling, and two armed officers rushed from the shelter of one of the vans. They grasped his wrists and elbows, half-dragging him out of the range of fire. Rickman ducked low, running to the personnel carrier where they had taken Cass. He was sitting in the corner of the bench seat, his hands clasped and his head bowed, while one of the armed officers talked to him in an undertone.

'Where's Smith?' Rickman demanded.

Cass's head jerked up. 'I've been trying to tell them, boss. He's behind the wall — to the right of the house.' The weariness in his tone suggested that he had already repeated this many times. 'He's bleeding.' He looked down at his hands, at the blood on them.

'Sir.'

Rickman turned.

'DI Hammond.' The DI was small and weather-beaten, his flak jacket giving him the illusion of bulk, a pocket-sized commando. 'I'm lead officer of the ARU.'

Rickman shook his hand. 'Can you get Smith out?'

'We've got the listening devices in place. I'd need the chopper to pull back while we check it out.' He handed Rickman a pair of binoculars, and Rickman stepped out of the van to take a look. The small limpet-like devices were clearly visible on the bay window and the glass of the front door. Rickman gave the order and the chopper peeled away, gaining altitude as it did so. Within seconds, the noise became no more than a faint buzz.

Hammond spoke into his radio. A few moments later, he adjusted the earphone in his left ear, as the information was relayed to him. 'There's two, possibly three people inside.'

'The shooters?'

Hammond repeated the question for the tech support officers. After a pause he shook his head. 'They're not moving — could be they're injured.'

Rickman debated. They hadn't located the shooters yet, and while they were still at large the threat to the rest of the officers present was his main concern. He spoke to the helicopter pilot. 'Is there any sign of movement around the house?'

'No, sir. But we're picking up a heat source on thermal imaging. It's on the perimeter, immobile — could be human.'

'Smith,' Rickman said, with a glance at Hammond. 'The front of the house is well covered,' he told the air crew. 'Focus on the woodland.' Turning back to Hammond, he said, 'Let's get Smith out of there — then you can clear the house.'

* * *

Rickman walked alongside the trolley as four armed response officers in body armour trundled it from the driveway to the waiting ambulance. Smith's skin reflected the lights of the emergency vehicles: red and blue, one moment washed with blood, the next, his face took on the blue pallor of a corpse.

'He reached for his warrant card.' Cass was hovering by the ambulance door. 'They thought he was going for a gun.' He passed hand over his eyes. 'Should've been me — fuck's sake, *I'm* the one not wearing protection.' He reached out to touch Smith's arm, strapped inside the trolley, but seemed to recoil at the last moment. 'Jesus.' Self-pitying tears stood in his eyes.

Rickman's radio spat, then the helicopter observer spoke urgently. 'I've got three — correction — four people in the woods behind the farmhouse. Five more, stationary, just east of them. Wait — one of the first group just vanished off the screen.'

Rickman waited.

'Woah! Another's gone.' He paused, then, 'What the . . .' The chopper lost altitude, buzzing like an angry wasp above them. 'We're going in for a closer look.' The Nightsun came on — thirty million candles of light, and a beam that looked solid enough to climb.

Rickman watched the ambulance pull slowly away, lights flashing, no siren. It seemed like a bad omen.

The helicopter had lost more height and now clattered thirty feet above. Rickman spoke into his radio again. 'Talk to me,' he said, raising his voice over the racket.

The air observer spoke to the pilot, 'Yeah, I see 'em.' Then, 'Sorry, boss. The group of four was badgers. The other five look like green-welly types — and they look terrified.'

Cass gave a high-pitched laugh.

Rickman looked at him sharply. 'Did I miss the joke?'

Cass passed a hand across his forehead. 'We should've warned the local badger watch, after all,' he muttered, still with a sick smile on his face. Then he began to weep.

Rickman took him by the elbow. 'Look at me,' he said.

Cass seemed to have difficulty locating Rickman, and when he did, his eyes were unfocused, as if he wasn't sure what he was looking at.

'You're in shock,' Rickman said. 'Go to the van. Await my instructions.'

Cass stared at him, uncomprehending, and Rickman nodded to one of the armed officers. He stepped forward and took Cass by the arm. Cass yielded, unprotesting. 'Don't let him out of your sight,' Rickman said. 'He talks to no one.'

The solid beam of the Nightsun pinpointed the position of the civilians within the wood. Rickman's next priority was to bring them to safety. He spoke to the air observer. 'Tell them to stay put — we'll come and get them.'

Hammond was at his side. 'I'll send our guys in,' he yelled into Rickman's ear, competing with the blare of the helicopter Skyshout.

Rickman nodded. 'The house?'

'I've a team moving in now.'

Rickman returned to his vantage point next to the police van as armed officers moved in on the house. Foster joined him. Foster must have taken part in more than his fair share of armed ops when he was in the Marines, and he watched the action as though he was assessing a military exercise.

Six armed officers approached the building at a low run. Though helmeted and encumbered by flak jackets, they sprinted like athletes. The first two used a police enforcer to smash the door off its hinges. They moved aside and four more ran into the house yelling, 'Police! Armed officers!' They tore through the house, their yells audible even over the constant clatter of the chopper.

A sharp *crack* from the back of the house and twenty officers on the periphery ducked. Rickman and Foster exchanged a look. Gunfire. A second shot. The chopper veered off, its rotors a high-pitched whine. More gunfire. The chopper switched the Nightsun to wide beam, drenching an area the size of a football pitch with white light. Then it swept in a circle, the Nightsun leaving an after-image like a question mark on Rickman's retinas.

A volley of shots followed from within the woods and Hammond clamoured for information from his team. 'Lima Oscar five, come in,' he repeated. Then, abandoning protocol, 'Frank — what's going on?'

The helicopter observer cut in. 'Echo Charlie four four: two shooters down. No police casualties. Repeat, *no* Yankees injured.' The Nightsun narrowed on an area close to the back of the house and four more armed officers swarmed over the low wall, heading for the light.

'Sir!' An armed officer stood at the door of the farmhouse, his MP5 carbine lowered across his body. 'House is clear. We need a paramedic.'

Hammond looked to Rickman.

'We need to clear the area first,' Rickman said.

Hammond sprinted for the house and Rickman followed, running low and fast. The door frame was twisted and splintered. Beyond it, a warm glow gave a welcome incongruous with the crush of uniforms, all carrying weapons.

Rickman caught a coppery taint at the back of his throat: the unmistakable reek of blood.

A door to his right led into a long sitting room. Bernie Carter sat with his back to him, his head slumped forward. Two officers worked on him: bandages improvised from tea-towels had been tied around his ankles and wrists, and blood had pooled around his feet. Lengths of rope lay cut and discarded on the floor. Carter was barely breathing, his skin paper-white.

One of the men straightened up. 'They cut the major arteries,' he said, his voice not quite steady. 'Hardly a nick in the flesh, but . . .' He looked helplessly at the bloody mess at his feet.

Rickman scanned the room. Two bodies lay slumped in the corner, near the French windows, both with gunshot wounds. 'Okay, there's an ambulance waiting. Take Carter out first — but as soon as practical, I want these men checked out.'

* * *

It was a relief to step out into the cold night air. Rickman took a deep breath, listening to the constant rattle of the helicopter as he returned to his vantage point, next to the firm's car Hart had driven. He glanced up as the chopper engine's tone changed and it banked left, training the Nightsun beam on something at the edge of the wood.

A small knot of people stumbled out of the dense tangle of shadows, blinking in the sudden glare of light. They were shepherded by armed officers towards one of the personnel vans. Rickman counted three women and two men. Two of the women held clipboards, all wore weatherproof jackets and hats.

'They look scared out of their wits,' Hart said, her face hard with anger. 'It'd be good, just once, to make the Maitlands of this world as afraid.'

'Maitland bled Carter like a sacrificial lamb,' Rickman said. 'But it doesn't take back what Carter did to Mark and Jasmine.'

Hart looked at him, more puzzled than chastened.

'In principle, I'm with you,' he explained. 'I'd like to see the bastards suffer — but meting out punishment like that doesn't give men like Maitland insight — it only makes them more determined not to be a victim.'

The first of the civilians climbed into the police van, but the next two seemed reluctant. The man had his arm slung around the woman's shoulder. She huddled close to him, as if for protection. The man smiled and pointed towards a battered old Land Rover parked on the grass verge of the lane. They were too far away, and the continuing racket from the chopper was too great to hear the exchange, but the man produced a set of keys, still smiling. His attitude was self-deprecating, almost apologetic, but he continued towards his car, with a wave of thanks. The officer stared after him for a few moments, then shrugged, helping the final passengers into the van.

As the van pulled away, four armed officers emerged from the rear of the farmhouse, half-carrying two men, both handcuffed and bleeding. Rickman studied their faces as they passed, then looked back towards the couple still heading for the Land Rover. It was impossible to make their features out at this distance, but the woman's body language seemed wrong, and the man was holding her too tightly.

'Maitland.' His heart picked up pace.

'You *what*?'

Rickman grabbed Foster's arm before he had the chance to turn and look. 'Get Hammond. Tell him Maitland has a female hostage, and he's making towards the Land Rover on the roadway. Tell him—'

Automatic gunfire ripped a line of orange light through the darkness ten metres from the police cordon. An officer fell. Others returned fire.

Foster dived for cover and Rickman followed, taking shelter behind one of the cars.

Another rasp of gunfire. 'Christ, they're using Uzis,' Foster said. 'We didn't get them all, Jeff.'

The Uzi spoke again, a rude burst of sound, followed by the rapid *thunk-thunk-thunk* of bullets through metal. One of the cars exploded, sending flames twenty feet into the air. Hot fragments of metal rained down.

Rickman clicked the speaker button on his radio. Nothing happened. He tried again. 'Shit!'

Maitland crouched, fifteen feet from the Land Rover. The woman screamed and struggled as more gunfire punched holes in door panels and sheet metal.

'Tell Hammond!' Rickman yelled. 'Warn the road-blocks.' Foster was off and running.

Maitland slapped the woman, and Rickman felt a surge of rage. The woman stopped struggling and allowed herself to be led towards the Land Rover.

His heart thudding, Rickman abandoned the shelter of the car and made for the vehicle at a loping run.

There was barely a tuft of grass between him and Maitland, but if he could make it to the roadside, he could use the ditch beside it for cover. Maitland had almost reached the Land Rover — he looped around the back of it, using the woman as a shield. Gunfire flashed and stuttered to their right, but it was aimed at the police, closer to the farmhouse.

The woman saw Rickman. Her eyes widened, and Maitland sensed something. He spun round as Rickman dived into the ditch. The thin layer of ice cracked, and Rickman gasped at a surge of bitter cold as water filled his shoes and soaked the knees of his trousers. The noise of the gun battle drowned out the harsh sound of his breathing, and he waited a moment, thankful for the cover of mist gathered in creamy swirls in the colder air of the ditch.

Maitland stood by the driver's door, his gun hand splayed across the woman's chest, forcing her against the side of the vehicle. The barrel of the pistol rested just beneath her chin. Rickman crept closer as Maitland fumbled the key, trying to fit it into the lock. It slipped, and he dropped the fob. Cursing, he took his hand from the woman's chest and bent to retrieve it. Rickman scrambled out of the ditch and launched himself at Maitland.

He saw the gun, the glint of firelight on the car bonnet, the keys, the top of Maitland's head. But what he saw most clearly was the terror in the woman's face. Maitland straightened, already raising the pistol, aiming at Rickman's chest.

'*Run!*' Rickman screamed.

She ran. Maitland fired.

Rickman felt a powerful blow, like a sledgehammer to his chest. He fell backwards, gasping for breath.

He must have blacked out for a moment, because when he next became aware, Maitland was standing over him, the gun at his side. 'The smart-arsed gatecrasher,' he said. 'Get up.'

Rickman tried to force air into his complaining lungs. Maitland reached down and hauled him to his feet. Rickman dry-retched. Gradually the pain eased to pressure, but he felt sick and it hurt to breathe. The gun battle seemed far off and the clatter of chopper blades a distant echo.

'You'll do just as well.' Maitland handed Rickman the car keys. 'You're driving.'

Rickman tossed the keys into the darkness. Maitland cracked him across the head with the barrel of the gun, and he fell to his knees, bleeding from a gash over his left eye.

'I'm gonna blow your fucking brains out.'

Rickman was blinded by the blood and the swelling in his left eye. The vision in his right was blurred, but he could see the gun. 'Don't.'

'Give me one good reason.'

A whole slew of reasons came to Rickman in a jumble — a race, his thoughts tumbling over each other, rapid as his heartbeat. *I want to take care of my brother. I want to see my nephews grow up and graduate — I want to see them marry and have families of their own. I want to repair the damage of the past.* And secretly, not daring to allow the full meaning to intrude, *I want to see Tanya again.*

He forced reason and authority into his voice. 'Kill a cop,' he said, forcing himself upright against the pain that felt like a solid mass in his chest. 'You'll stay in prison for the rest of your life.'

'If they catch me, I'm in for life anyway.'

This was the logic of the street fighter — personal honour, the rep of a hard man. Never show fear, never back down, never apologise.

Was Maitland close enough for him to make a grab at the gun? The thudding pain in Rickman's chest said not.

'You know why murder's taboo?' Maitland asked.

'Because life is precious.' The pain in Rickman's chest wasn't entirely due to the impact of the bullet.

Maitland shook his head. 'Once you've tasted that kind of power, you want it again, till you can't stop.'

'Are you talking about Carter or yourself?'

Maitland shrugged. 'Doesn't matter — I'm gonna save you the bother of finding out.' He slipped the safety off the gun, and Rickman thought of Tanya, the warmth of her body next to his, her long fingers curling around his neck to draw him closer, and he ached for her.

'Don't,' Rickman said again.

A movement behind Maitland caught his eye. Lee Foster stood, braced in a triangular stance. Rickman saw the dull gleam of a gun in his right hand, his left supporting the weight.

An adrenaline surge sent electrical shocks of energy into Rickman's scalp and the major muscles of his legs and arms, but neither fight nor flight was possible, though his body screamed for action.

Shoot, he willed Foster. *Shoot the bastard!*

He heard a dull thumping, and at first mistook it for the deafening thrum of his heart in his ears. He felt a draught of air on his blind side. Maitland half-turned, his eyes widening, gun swinging towards the imminent threat. A streak of red and black stripes took Maitland mid-thigh. He crumpled with a yell of pain. The gun discharged harmlessly, skittering a few yards away.

Rickman rested on his heels, taking small sips of air, and trying to make sense of what had happened. The blurring of his vision slowly cleared, and the striped form resolved itself into DC Tunstall.

One broad hand held Maitland in a wrist lock, the other a pair of handcuffs. His right knee was firmly pressed between Maitland's shoulder blades.

'Chris — where the hell did you come from?'

'The match, sir.' The big man's face was a picture of puzzlement. Still dressed in his rugby kit, a smear of mud across his cheekbones, he had the feral look of an ungainly boy plucked from the pages of *Lord of the Flies*.

'I think he meant how did you find us?' Foster helped Rickman to his feet.

'Oh . . . I was only up the road.' Tunstall clicked the cuffs on Maitland. 'I'd've been here sooner, only the bloody idiot who took the message waited till the end of the game to tell me, and they've put roadblocks up. Oh, and — Sod's Law — my warrant card was at the bottom of my sports bag.' He pulled Maitland to his feet and gave the scene a quizzical once-over. 'Anyway, you don't have to be one of the Wise Men to follow this star.' He squinted up at the hovering Eurocopter, its Nightsun beaming down like a beacon.

Rickman laughed, immediately regretting it. His body armour had absorbed much of the bullet's impact, but he would have a bruise the size of a tea plate for weeks after. He rested his hands on both knees and breathed gently, wincing with the pain.

Foster patted his shoulder. 'Get Mr Maitland settled into something small, with an outside lock, will you?' he said to Tunstall.

Maitland didn't resist, but he stared at Rickman as he passed, the light in his eye somewhere between hatred and hunger.

Rickman watched as Foster pocketed his pistol, leaving Maitland's for the CSIs to process as evidence. He waited until Maitland was out of earshot. 'You're not cleared to carry firearms,' he said, easing to an upright position.

'It's like riding a bike,' Foster said, deliberately misunderstanding him. 'You never forget how.'

CHAPTER 51

They buried Mark Davis next to Jasmine and Bryony Elliott. It was a dazzling day. Sunlight twinkled on the frost-thaw of the closely cropped lawns, and the last few leaves drifted in brilliant colour onto the paths as if to hush the sound of footsteps.

Bryony's remains were placed in a small white coffin in the grave with her mother. Rickman attended, performing the role of pallbearer alongside the other members of his team. Tunstall shed a few tears as the tiny coffin was placed in the earth.

The chief mourners were Kim and Lars Lindermann. Jasmine's former teacher, Mrs Staines, stood next to Jenni, the sober-faced sixth-former who had spoken up for Jasmine. Ed and Hilary Shepherd arrived as the coffins were lowered into the ground.

Foster made a move towards them, but Rickman stopped him. 'They have as much right to be here as any of us, Lee,' he said.

'They should be behind bars.' The Shepherds were under investigation by a team of specialists gathered from the Family Crime Investigation and the Child Protection Units, but for the moment, they were out on police bail.

Foster stared hard at the couple, but they avoided his gaze, fixing instead on the coffins. Mrs Shepherd held a rosary in her right hand, fretting at the beads as she recited her prayers, and bowing her head at each repetition of Jesus's name.

'The adoption agencies are cooperating,' Rickman said. 'But it's a huge task. Give them time.'

'We haven't got a snowball's chance in hell of proving a case against them two,' Foster said. 'No DNA to match up, none of the families identified — apart from the Kirkhams — and you'd have to track them down first.'

Rickman would have liked to reassure his friend, but he had the unhappy notion that Foster's pessimism was well founded. 'Melanie' had remained stubbornly silent since their encounter at her mother's house, and there was no official record of her sister having given her baby up for adoption. The CPS were unwilling to proceed on the basis of Ed Shepherd's oblique confession, they had no photographs, and nobody willing to stand up in court. The entire police case hung on proving that the Kirkham adoption was illegal, and investigations had so far failed to turn up the official signatories on the adoption papers.

Kim Lindermann cut a dignified figure. She stepped forward without hesitation when the priest offered her a sprinkler of holy water to add her benediction to his own. Ed and Hilary Shepherd had remained a little apart from the rest of the mourners, but now they approached the grave, each clinging to the other for support. Foster shut them out, staring angrily at the priest as if he were to blame for their intrusion.

Afterwards, Kim Lindermann shook hands with Rickman. 'I'm ready to do whatever is necessary,' she said. She was talking about Carter's barbarity, the evidence of her own scarred body.

Rickman placed his hand over hers and thanked her. Carter had survived the attack, though his bodyguards had not. He denied all knowledge of the murders of Jasmine, Mark and Bryony, but his DNA matched that found on a bloody splinter of wood in the coach house basement.

Maitland's gunmen were recovering in prison hospital. With Eames gone, it seemed unlikely that Graham would stand trial for the murder of Michael Aldiss. The one glimmer of hope was that against all expectations, Maitland was willing to testify against Carter. Carter's counter-allegations of hit lists, hired killers and drug smuggling would keep the Crown Prosecution Service busy for a good while, but Rickman was confident neither man would see the outside of a prison cell for some time.

Rickman shook hands with the priest and joined the rest of his team. They stood awkwardly at an intersection of the tarmac drives that interlaced the cemetery.

'A short while ago, Lee asked me what I believed in.' Rickman looked around the group. 'I said I believed in evil.' Foster looked at him, his expression unreadable. 'Well, if you believe in evil, you also have to believe in good.' In answer to Foster's sceptical look, he said, 'Basic law of physics, isn't it? Like Tunstall with his kettle — a decent brew is the superglue that holds the universe together.'

Tunstall blushed.

'You all did some good here.' Rickman looked at each of them, making sure that they looked back at him, so they could see he meant what he said. 'Not just today, but in the way you conducted this investigation.'

'Doesn't make no difference to Smith though, does it?' Foster said.

DS Cass was under investigation for his part in the events leading to the shooting of DC Smith. The rest would be difficult to prove. Smith had suffered a punctured lung and lost so much blood his heart went into arrest before the paramedics reached Warrington Hospital A&E. He was revived but suffered multiple system failure and died of a second heart attack, two days later.

'Doesn't make no difference to them.' Foster looked past Rickman to the open graves. 'They never stood a chance.'

His words might have stood as an epitaph for all the lost children — the begotten and forgotten.

EPILOGUE

Foster's flat was cold. He went straight to the kitchen and poured himself a whisky. He hesitated a moment, then reached inside the cupboard a second time and took down the biscuit tin, taking a punishing swallow of whisky before smoothing a hand over the surface and lifting the lid. He found the envelope addressed to him in his mother's hand and held it, tracing his finger over his mother's uneven scrawl. One day he would open it, but not yet. He left the kitchen, snatching up his jacket and keys as he hurried to his car.

At Black Wood Children's Home he walked around the grounds, visiting the scene of old triumphs and scrapes, remembering. For a while, he stood outside the coach house. Hard to recall this rotting, damp ruin as their den, their playhouse. It was barred and shuttered, the perimeter of the CSIs' search grid marked by blue-and-white police tape. A length had torn loose from its moorings, and it fluttered and twisted in the breeze, like a tattered banner.

'Thought I'd find you here.'

He spun round. 'Naomi.' He hadn't heard her approach.

The sun was low, its rays glancing through the shrubs and saplings at the edge of the clearing. Hart, still dressed in black, stepped out of the shadows and the sun caught her hair, beatifying her for a second, then she was not-so-plain Naomi again.

They stood side by side, staring at the slumping wreck that used to be the coach house. Soon there would be no trace of it.

'They're moving out tomorrow,' Foster said, meaning Ed and Hilary.

'I thought you weren't religious,' Hart said.

'I'm not.'

'So you won't be setting yourself up as an avenging angel.' There was a challenge in her clear blue eyes, but no hint of mockery.

'I can't let them walk away from this, Naomi. If they'd come to us — if they'd told us Mark had been in touch . . .' He stopped. He had been over this many times in debriefings and in long, drink-fuelled sessions with Jeff Rickman. It didn't matter that Ed and Hilary Shepherd were responsible — directly or indirectly — for the deaths of Mark Davis and Bryony Elliott. Without proof, the law judged them innocent.

'Lee, it's not your case anymore,' she said.

'No.' He still felt a slight tingle when she called him by his Christian name. 'I know that.' But he was thinking that he might be able to achieve what the CPS could not. If he was patient and kept vigil, somebody would call, or Hilary would arrange a meeting with one of their families. Maybe they'd get greedy and take one more commission, and when they did, he would be watching.

'Haven't you got a home to go to?' he demanded, choosing attack as a form of defence.

'Yeah,' she said. 'But it seems a bit empty at the moment.'

'Phil on the late shift, is he?'

'Dunno,' she said. Foster looked at her. 'Big mistake, getting Phil involved in all of this.' She shrugged. 'He couldn't handle it.'

Foster took a breath, ready to say something meaningless and reassuring.

'It's all right,' she said. 'I know when I've screwed up.'

'We all do, some time or other,' Foster said.

There was a silence, and he had the sense that she was building herself up to something. 'Thanks for smoothing things over for me with the boss,' she said, after a struggle.

'Who says I did?'

'DCI Rickman.'

He winced. 'He just can't keep his gob shut, can he?'

She laughed, and he smiled despite himself.

'Fancy a pint?' he asked.

'A pint.' This time there was a hint of mockery in her eyes, and a warning, though unspoken. *And that's all you get.*

Fine, he thought. *I'll settle for a pint of draught in the company of a friend for now.*

* * *

A light was on in Rickman's sitting room when he arrived home. He felt a thrill of excitement, quickly supplanted by disappointment. Tanya had been gone ten days, excusing herself immediately after the power of attorney was settled.

Rickman should have felt relieved: he no longer felt sick with guilt and self-recrimination. But he would rather that than the hollowness he now felt at his centre. His drinking sessions with Foster brought a welcome, if brief, oblivion. But he grew weary of waking in the small hours, his mind racing and his body so restless that it allowed him no peace.

The bruising to his chest disbarred him from running, but he would cover miles at his long, loping pace, unable to settle, much less sleep, unless he was exhausted.

He dropped his keys into the bowl on the hall stand and slung his coat over the newel of the staircase. The old house ticked as the timbers warmed over the heating pipes, and when he exhaled it seemed he heard an echo of his sigh. He paused between the sitting room and the kitchen, undecided

412

if he should cook or get comprehensively and unapologetically hammered. The light creeping from under the kitchen door drew him on — he thought he had turned those lights off as he'd left for the funeral. He pressed the flat of his hand against the door.

Tanya was sitting at the table.

She rose to meet him, and his heart leapt, but seeing the hectic colour of her cheeks, the agitated way she clasped her hands, he was struck by a terrible foreboding.

'Has something happened?' he asked. 'The boys, are they—'

'They're fine.' She refused his embrace. 'Why would you think—'

'I didn't expect to see you,' Rickman said. 'The way you left—' He broke off, he didn't want it to sound like recrimination.

She lowered her gaze. 'I'm sorry for that. I shouldn't have gone without talking to you — explaining why I had to leave.' She frowned. 'It's just that when you're as lonely as we have been, you take comfort where you find it.'

Rickman felt a tightening in his gut.

'I didn't want to make love out of loneliness, Jeff,' she said.

Rickman nodded. Even if he could find the words, he didn't think he would be able to voice them.

'I'm married—'

'I know,' he said, his voice hoarse with emotion. 'You did the right thing.'

She gave an impatient shake of her head. 'Let me finish.' She took a breath and started again. 'I'm married to a man who doesn't know me.' She gave a shaky laugh. 'God, what a horrible cliché!' She blinked and gritted her teeth, and Rickman saw that she was trembling. 'He doesn't want me . . .' She faltered. Lifting her chin, she forced herself to go on. 'He doesn't want me, and I think you do.'

He sighed and she look into his face, a question in her eyes.

He took her hand. 'I do.'

She touched the healing scar over his left eyebrow lightly with her fingertips.

He bent to her, and she reached up to meet his kiss.

THE END

ALSO BY MARGARET MURPHY

CLARA PASCAL SERIES
Book 1: DARKNESS FALLS
Book 2: WEAVING SHADOWS

DETECTIVE JEFF RICKMAN SERIES
Book 1: SEE HER BURN
Book 2: SEE HER DIE
Book 3: DON'T SCREAM

DETECTIVE CASSIE ROWAN SERIES
Book 1: BEFORE HE KILLS AGAIN

STANDALONE NOVELS
DEAR MUM
HER HUSBAND'S KILLER
THE LOST BOY

Please join our mailing list for free Kindle crime thriller, detective, mystery and romance books, and new releases!

www.joffebooks.com

FREE KINDLE BOOKS